Minor Characters

Minor Characters

STORIES

Jaime Clarke*

*and also by Mona Awad, Christopher Boucher, Kenneth Calhoun, Nina de Gramont, Ben Greenman, Annie Hartnett, Owen King, Neil LaBute, J. Robert Lennon, Lauren Mechling, Shelly Oria, Stacey Richter, Joseph Salvatore, Andrea Seigel, and Daniel Torday

Foreword by Jonathan Lethem
Introduction by Laura van den Berg

with an Afterword by the Author

Roundabout Press   2021

Published by
Roundabout Press
PO Box 370310
West Hartford, CT 06137

"We're So Famous" and "Lindy" first appeared in *The Mississippi Review*;
"The Serial Lover" first appeared in *Agni*; and "The Salinger Principle; or,
A Writer You've Never Heard of Calls It Quits" first appeared in
The Literary Hub under a different title.

Boston Globe review of *Vernon Downs* used with permission of
Anthony Domestico. Copyright © 2020.

Kirkus reviews of *World Gone Water* and *Garden Lakes* used
with permission of Kirkus Reviews. Copyright © 2020

ISBN: 978-1-948072-05-2
Library of Congress Cataloguing-in-Publication Data is available on file

FIRST EDITION
10   9   8   7   6   5   4   3   2   1

For a bonus story, send a blank email to frank@baumsbazaar.com
to receive autoreply.

For Mary and Max

Acknowledgments

My thanks to

Josephine Bergin
Hillary Chute
Stephanie Duncan
Pete Hausler
Dan Pope

and to the brilliant contributors to this collection

Minor Characters

Contents

Foreword

Jonathan Lethem

WHERE DID IT START, FOR YOU? MAYBE IT WAS WHEN J. D. SALINGER'S fiction revealed the intertwining of the fates of the siblings of Holden Caulfield, from *A Catcher in the Rye*, and that of the Glass family from *Seymour: An Introduction* and others of his fictions (if I recall correctly, Holden's brother, killed in World War II, was earlier a contestant on the same juvenile game show as Seymour Glass). Maybe it was when Kurt Vonnegut wandered into *Breakfast of Champions*, a book that was a compendium of characters both minor and major from his earlier novels, including Vonnegut's fictional neglected science fiction author Kilgore Trout. Trout was an obvious transposition of the real neglected science fiction author Theodore Sturgeon, whose unlikely name was nevertheless authentic, and who'd been a friendly acquaintance of Vonnegut's several years before. Bizarrely and wonderfully, Kilgore Trout was also credited with authorship of a mysterious satirical science fiction novel that appeared in 1975, two years after *Breakfast of Champions*, a book called *Venus on the Half-Shell*, which turned out to be written by another science fiction writer named Philip José Farmer.

Or maybe this kind of thing reminds you of Borges, who wrote stories featuring characters who'd wandered in from other authors' writings (for instance, Jonathan Swift's Gulliver, from the travels, appears to have narrated "Brodie's Report"). Or perhaps you were a partisan of Balzac's La comédie humaine, a tapestry in which many minor characters recur and intertwine—major in one piece, minor in another. Maybe you think of Cervantes, whose Quixote, in the second volume of that massive novel, has to contend with rival fictions featuring himself, which he judges as bogus—noncanonical fanfic, in the present parlance.

For Jaime Clarke, it may well have begun with Bret Easton Ellis, Clarke's literary idol and confessed "obsession." Ellis revives characters from his first two novels, *Less Than Zero* and *The Rules of Attraction*, continually through his subsequent works, including the Bateman brothers, the elder of whom becomes Ellis's Holden Caulfield (i.e., his most famous character, *American Psycho*'s Patrick Bateman). Later, in *Lunar Park*, Ellis plays the Vonnegut trick, wandering into his own fictional labyrinth, rendering himself a fictional character before anyone else could do it for him. Of course, Clarke was warming up to do this by translating Ellis into Vernon Downs in *Vernon Downs*.

That, I suppose, is where I come in, since before I was an author who might be asked to write a foreword, I was a minor—at best!—character wandering through a scene in *The Rules of Attraction*.

Really, I barely appeared. It's too humiliatingly paltry to go into in any detail, so I won't. At the time of the book's publication I was, like Jaime Clarke, a bookseller, though not, like Jaime Clarke, a bookstore owner. I was a retail clerk, writing fiction at night, dreaming of glory. In fact, I was a lot more like a Jaime Clarke character than a Bret Easton Ellis one; I'd only gotten to go to that rich-kids' college by a weird act of willful imposture (but then again, hey, that's a fairly good idea for a character—and eventually I'd write that character, Dylan Ebdus in *The Fortress of Solitude*).

There's a superb lineage of such intertextual gamesmanship, in other words, yet I think here Jaime, in his characteristically generous manner, which I might be tempted to call self-effacing solipsism, has raised it to a giddy new level. I don't mind saying I identify with the project on every level. There are certain bullying distortions that both consciousness (which places you-you-always-

YOU! as the first-person shooter, the spider crouched in every web), and fiction (which relentlessly delegates characters into the rigid fates of Major and Minor), and authorship (which tends to claim a nonporous boundary: I Alone Made This Book!) impose, and which it has been my wish to see dissolved. Here, Clarke has done more, even, than Vonnegut in setting his characters free: he's flipped foreground and background, and at the same time invited others in (as one might open the doors of a bookstore) to browse, and revise, and interfere with, and extend, his fictional Who's Who. The results strike me as a kind of party, even if I want to quibble with Clarke's insistence that it is a going-away party (some of the best of which, in my experience, have involved people who did not subsequently go away). Here are both strangers and folks I know, from Clarke's books, and as the authors of their own. Some are old friends—hey, Lauren Mechling, it's been way too long!—and some are new acquaintances. Some I don't really want to hang out with, but at a big enough party you can get a kind of thrill from briefly sharing the space with creeps. And, it is worth mentioning, some of Clarke's own most winning fiction is here. I'm a big fan, for instance, of the exchange of memos between Clarke and the film producers at Little Girl Bay Productions and 808 Films concerning their aborted adaptation of Clarke's first novel. A perfect mise en abyme of the Hollywood tendency to put matters of derivativeness, originality, influence, and resemblance into a blender and throw money at it—only, usually not quite enough money. The story reminds me of another one, by my old friend Carter Scholz, called "The Nine Billion Names of God," the title of which is the title of another short story, by Arthur C. Clarke, an appropriation that, within the story, the "author" character Scholz defends to his skeptical editor by citing Borges's use of Cervantes in his story "Pierre Menard, Author of Don Quixote." Another great hall of mirrors. You can look all this up.

So, what am I doing here? In an introduction to one of his collections of short stories, Bruce Jay Friedman explains that the only way he could get started writing the introduction was to imagine that he was writing a short story about an author trying to introduce a collection of short stories. I'm trying to write myself into a fictional character, then: imagine this poor fool, Jaime Clarke's sole friend whom he *didn't* ask to write a story about a minor character in his fiction! Now, that would be a minor character indeed.

I wasn't on the guest list, Jaime, but I crashed the party.

Introduction

Laura van den Berg

JAIME CLARKE HAS BEEN ONE OF OUR FOREMOST CHRONICLERS of obsession since his debut novel, *We're So Famous*, appeared in 2001. The novel is a wild, kinetic ride that involves pop music and murder, notoriety and celebrity (and the line between the two). In a review of the novel *Entertainment Weekly* wrote: "Daisy, Paque, and Stella want. They want to be actresses. They want to be in a band. They want to be models. They want to be famous, damn it. . . . Clarke doesn't hate his antiheroes—he just views them as by-products of the culture: glitter-eyed, vacant, and cruel. The satire works, sliding down as silvery and toxic as liquid mercury." This restless and relentless wanting, and the way we are warped by the wants of the surrounding culture, would go on to become hallmarks of Clarke's work.

In an introduction to a recent reissue of *We're So Famous*, Clarke writes: "It seems naive to claim that back in the late 1990s, celebrity culture was a relatively new phenomenon, but fame for fame's sake seemed new and curious to me." This curiosity has endured for Clarke, but it has also evolved, with the themes of fame and identity brought to new life in Clarke's trilogy of novels starring Charlie Martens: *Vernon Downs*, *World Gone Water*, and *Garden Lakes*. In that same introduction Clarke notes that he was, at the start of his career, compelled by a desire to "emulate my hero F. Scott Fitzgerald, attracted to and influenced as I was by his narratives about sad young men, a thread I'd pick up later for my trilogy about

Charlie Martens." What happens when these sad young men collide with a fame-hungry culture, one that often rewards vapidness and fakery? What are the consequences, for themselves and for others?

We first meet Charlie Martens in *Vernon Downs*. In an attempt to repair his relationship with his girlfriend, Olivia, Charlie, an aspiring writer, sets out on a mission to befriend Olivia's favorite writer, the titular Vernon Downs. Downs bears a striking resemblance to the novelist Bret Easton Ellis, whose work has been a significant touchstone for Clarke. In an interview Clarke once observed that "Ellis captured something timeless, which is the feeling of being displaced. All the characters in his books are living in a world they don't comprehend, or feel uncomfortable in." The layers of Charlie's own displacement, the ways in which he finds the world incomprehensible, are central to all three novels.

Before long Charlie's project to insinuate himself into Downs's life begins to take unexpected turns. First, Charlie turns out to be uniquely gifted at fakery. At one point he poses as a journalist on assignment to profile Downs; later in the novel he begins to pose as Downs himself, answering fans' e-mails and allowing a case of mistaken identity to go uncorrected. Before long he's not posing as a journalist—but meeting an *actual* journalist while posing as Downs. Is Charlie *really* going to these lengths to save his relationship with Olivia, or has he awakened in himself his true gift—not for creating art, but for impersonating creators? And what does it mean to be a person, let alone an artist, in a world so obsessed with surfaces that a fake passes easily for the real?

In this world, celebrity and obsession operate like a contagion. As Charlie's impersonation of Vernon Downs escalates, he ends up in the sights of one Shannon Hamilton, a writer determined to stalk Vernon Downs until he agrees to help her with her career.

About Charlie Martens, Clarke has said that "Charlie's impersonation in *Vernon Downs* begins benignly enough, and he quickly realizes how seductive and freeing it is to become something other than yourself. But the other half of the impersonation is how readily people are willing to accept the fact, or how little attention we pay to the details of our own lives." In time we come to understand that Charlie's fascination with fame is not only shaped by the surrounding celebrity-obsessed culture, but is also rooted in childhood losses that set him on a path of loneliness and isolation. For Charlie, to be famous is, or appears to be, a corrective for his deepest pain. To be famous is to be seen. He, too, wants.

Charlie Martens has proven to be a vital figure in Clarke's work, going on to star in two other novels, *World Gone Water* and *Garden Lakes*.

World Gone Water unfolds seven years before the events of *Vernon Downs*.

Charlie, after being named a person of interest in a sexual assault investigation in Florida, is concluding a stay at the Sonoran Rehabilitation Center. In the opening he tells us, "I am not a good person. I don't need anyone to tell me that I am not a model citizen. People can always improve and I want to be a better person. I want what better people have." Once again Charlie *wants*.

Through an exploration of Charlie's past romantic entanglements—including his formative high school relationship with Jenny, which leads to Charlie joining the Mormon Church as an act of "romantic sacrifice"—readers come to understand the deeper origins of his obsessive and toxic approach to relationships. Journal entries and essays draw us deeper into the more difficult corridors of Charlie's psychology, including the truth about what happened with his accuser in Florida, Karine, or Charlie's version of it at least (most readers are likely to come away from those passages with a different conclusion than the one Charlie himself draws). This version of Charlie Martens is rawer, creepier, and more disturbed; he has not yet acquired the cool veneer of the burgeoning literary con artist we meet in *Vernon Downs*.

The final novel in the trilogy, *Garden Lakes*, explores Charlie's past, namely a summer fellowship program he attends as a student, in the high heat of summer. Despite the promise of the fellowship—

"Historically, Garden Lakes fellows had gone on to good colleges or to celebrated careers"—the place has an uncanny vibe from the get-go: "From above, Garden Lakes looked like a sophisticated crop circle, composed of two paved roads—an outer and inner loop—with a wide river of dirt flowing between the loops, the brick community center bridging the two loops at their southernmost convex. The man-made lake at the center of the development yawned like an open maw that had only its top teeth." The Garden Lakes chapters incorporate both a collective point of view and Charlie's first-person narration, which allows Charlie to be at once hidden and exposed, a choice that seems powerfully suggestive of the life of incognito and deception that awaits him.

Garden Lakes also introduces us to an adult Charlie, now a journalist in Arizona and feeling, at thirty-seven, as though he's "already lived forever" and with a "nervous and guilt-ridden conscience." He finds himself dialing back to the distant past, namely that seminal summer at Garden Lakes. At first Garden Lakes operates like some combination of a construction work-study scholarship and a summer camp, but when tensions and the summer heat (and snakes!) escalate, the structure starts to fray. The menace is conveyed artfully in the landscape itself, through the experience of one boy: "He looked back in the direction of Garden Lakes, the shadowy points of the Grove obscuring his view, isolating him from the development. The carbon-copy houses appeared fake, a front meant to shake off the cops. He scoured the perimeter, feeling like he'd been lured by the javelinas into a sinister trap." When abandoned by their supervisors, the boys attempt to keep order intact: "It was agreed that, in order to argue successfully for full credit for our fellowship, the schedule would remain intact, as would all the rules and regulations—including the reinstatement of curfew." But, inevitably, life at Garden Lakes begins to spiral. Kidnapping, among other events, ensues.

During this summer Charlie has a powerful reckoning about his place in the world, at his high school and beyond: "The price of lying seemed affordable then. All I desired in exchange was friendship, to break free of my transfer-student status, to find acceptance among some faction of my new peers." Throughout the Garden Lakes passages, flash-forwards foretell the fates of the other boys—some of whom go on to live lives marred by violence and corruption—and indeed, by the novel's end it's clear Charlie has been transformed as well: "Or maybe that's just a story I tell myself to ameliorate the regret for my original sin, which has only led to a life of prevarication and an alienating superiority that has haunted me since."

When asked about the chronology of the Charlie Martens books in an interview, Clarke observed: "As a reader, filmgoer, citizen— whatever—I prefer narratives that I have to piece together. Possibly all writers feel that way, though some are inclined to take the jumble of life and present it linearly. Linear narratives are less interesting to me personally. So within each book, the reader has to do some work to piece together what's going on and then each book itself is another piece in the overall picture of Charlie Martens and how he learns to navigate the world." The collection you hold in your hands, *Minor Characters*, will expand upon this overall picture. Now many of the characters in Charlie's orbit will get their turn to stand in the center of the stage, will get their fifteen minutes.

From **Vernon Downs**

Praise for VERNON DOWNS

"*Vernon Downs* is a gripping, hypnotically written and unnerving look at the dark side of literary adulation. Jaime Clarke's tautly suspenseful novel is a cautionary tale for writers and readers alike—after finishing it, you may start to think that J.D. Salinger had the right idea after all."

—TOM PERROTTA, author of *Election*, *Little Children*, and *The Leftovers*

"Moving and edgy in just the right way. Love (or lack of) and Family (or lack of) is at the heart of this wonderfully obsessive novel."

—GARY SHTEYNGART, author of *Super Sad True Love Story*

"All strong literature stems from obsession. *Vernon Downs* belongs to a tradition that includes Nicholson Baker's *U and I*, Geoff Dyer's *Out of Sheer Rage*, and—for that matter—*Pale Fire*. What makes Clarke's excellent novel stand out isn't just its rueful intelligence, or its playful semi-veiling of certain notorious literary figures, but its startling sadness. *Vernon Downs* is first rate."

—MATTHEW SPECKTOR, author of *American Dream Machine*

"An engrossing novel about longing and impersonation, which is to say, a story about the distance between persons, distances within ourselves. Clarke's prose is infused with music and intelligence and deep feeling."

—CHARLES YU, author of *Sorry Please Thank You*

"*Vernon Downs* is a fascinating and sly tribute to a certain fascinating and sly writer, but this novel also perfectly captures the lonely distortions of a true obsession."

—DANA SPIOTTA, author of *Stone Arabia*

A Review of VERNON DOWNS

Boston Globe
By Anthony Domestico

Writing begins in obsession. It might be an obsession with a beloved (think Dante) or with craft (think Bishop), or even with obsession itself (think Nabokov). There seems to be an elective affinity between the writer and the obsessive: Both see the world as more beautiful and terrifying, more dramatic and meaningful, than the rest of us do.

Jaime Clarke, author of "Vernon Downs" and co-owner of Newtonville Books, is fascinated by obsession—specifically, by the modern obsession with celebrity. In his first novel, "We're So Famous," Clarke examines a group of talentless teenage girls who form a band ("we weren't really *musical,* that was the problem"), research celebrity deaths, and move to LA, all in the hope of becoming celebrities. For these girls, the unfamous life is not worth living.

In "Vernon Downs," Clarke shows that it's not just teenagers who are captivated by celebrity.

The novel centers on Charlie Martens, a mediocre young writer who fears that he has been merely "a bit player in an array of people's lives." Charlie falls in love with a girl named Olivia while studying creative writing at Glendale Community College only to see her move back to London.

Broke and floundering, Charlie latches onto an idea: If he can befriend Vernon Downs, Olivia's favorite writer and a lightly fictionalized version of the real-life novelist Bret Easton Ellis, then maybe he can win her back.

There's a deranged logic to Charlie's plan. Downs is the kind of writer—reclusive, sexy, mysterious—whose ability to elicit passionate reactions trumps whatever talent he may possess.

His most recent novel, "The Vegetable King," was the subject of controversy, praised for its cool depiction of the "threatening and truly unnerving" nature of modern life but also criticized for its "facile and gimmicky" style as well as its misogyny and pornographic violence. (This sounds a lot like the critical reaction to Ellis's "American Psycho.")

But with Downs, the work is always secondary to the fame. The gossip magazines document his every move; he blows money on expensive clothing, Gatsby-esque parties, and inordinate amounts of cocaine.

In the world of EW and TMZ, fame has osmotic properties —to surround oneself with the famous and desirable is to become famous and desirable oneself—and so Charlie's plan doesn't seem so crazy after all.

How can Charlie get close to Downs, though? First, he fakes his way into a fiction workshop at Downs's alma mater. There, he reads publicly from "The Vegetable King" and gets hold of Downs's contact information. Then, he approaches Downs, falsely claiming that a magazine has asked him to write a profile. After this first meeting, a relationship of mutual exploitation ensues: Charlie ghostwrites an essay for Downs; Downs invites Charlie to star-filled parties.

Charlie isn't a gifted writer but he's skilled in the art of fakery. While apartment sitting for Downs, Charlie's deceptions accelerate. He starts answering fans' e-mails in the person of Downs. ("You write how you write. Some people will like it, some people will not like it," he advises one correspondent.) A new neighbor mistakes him for the novelist; he doesn't correct her and the two begin a flirtatious relationship.

Where before he met with Downs while pretending to be a journalist, now he meets with a journalist while pretending to be Downs. We begin to realize that Charlie is less interested in winning back Olivia than in becoming Downs.

Early on, we learn that Charlie has had a difficult, unmoored life. His parents died when he was young, and he was shuffled from caregiver to caregiver—he "simply passed through their lives with an inconsequential nod and a polite smile."

To be famous, then, is be the anti-Charlie: to remain in people's lives, even when—especially when—you're not physically present; to be consequential; to be able to dispense with politeness and indulge your appetites at whim.

Though "Vernon Downs" appears to be about deception and celebrity, it's really about the alienation out of which these things grow. Clarke shows that obsession is, at root, about yearning: about the things we don't have but desperately want; about our longing to be anyone but ourselves.

Anthony Domestico is an assistant professor of literature at Purchase College and a book critic for Commonweal.

Minor Characters from
VERNON DOWNS

Olivia Simmons, twenty-two, Charlie's British girlfriend, whom he meets at Glendale Community College in Arizona. Her favorite writer is Vernon Downs, whom he's never heard of, and when she has to return to England over a visa issue, Charlie believes it's a bump in the road. But it's clear she's moving on from him, and in desperation he becomes infatuated with her favorite writer in a bid to win her back.

Peter Kline, fifties, a reporter for the *New York Post*. He falls for Charlie's impersonation of Vernon Downs, but then he uncovers the truth and blackmails Charlie for information about a secret from Downs's past.

Christianna, late twenties, the aspiring actress subletting the apartment next to Vernon's for the summer. She mistakes Charlie for Vernon Downs. Charlie tries to avoid her, but proximity renders that impossible, so he gives in and hones his Downs impersonation by being with her.

Shannon Hamilton, twenties, an aspiring writer who idolizes Vernon Downs. He asks Charlie-as-Vernon to read his novel and recommend him to his agent, then begins to stalk Charlie-as-Vernon to get what he wants.

Derwin MacDonald, sixties, owner and operator of Obelisk Press, a once-prominent small publisher run out of Derwin's Brooklyn brownstone. When he first lands in New York, Charlie takes a part-time job with Derwin in exchange for boarding in his attic apartment.

Jacqueline Turner, eighties, one of Obelisk's oldest authors. Her first novel, *Esque*, written in her youth, made her famous, along with her model looks. She continued to write books over the years, but fell out of fashion and ultimately became irrelevant.

Burton LaFarge, late thirties, a classmate of Vernon Downs's at Camden College, who accuses Downs of stealing his work for what turned out to be Downs's best-selling book.

Shelleyan, late twenties, Olivia's best friend back in Phoenix. Charlie tolerated Shelleyan's antagonism in order to be with Olivia, but when Shelleyan runs into him in New York, where she's moved to attend Parsons, she's eager to reconnect with a familiar face.

Anonymous letter writer, a student at the summer writing program Charlie attends at Camden in an effort to learn more about Vernon Downs. As part of the program, Charlie gives a presentation on Downs, which is followed by a public burning of his lecture handout on Downs's work and the posting of an anonymous letter by the party who burned it.

Kyra, the young girl who lived next door to Charlie growing up in Sacramento. A gas explosion leveled his house and killed his parents, which began his peripatetic life.

His Mother's Mark

J. Robert Lennon

UNTIL THE MAN GRABBED HIS MOTHER BY THE ARM AND LED HER to the room in the back of the store, Burtie didn't even know that what she'd been doing was against the rules—hadn't even realized it wasn't just a normal part of shopping. Mama's routine: two, three items into the basket, then another one—usually something small—into the pocket. Some things went here, other things went there—why would it be wrong?

Even after the man grabbed her, it took a while for Burtie to figure out what specifically she'd done. It was obvious that there was some kind of trouble, though for a moment Burtie feared that they were going to deliver bad news, like maybe they'd finally found his father and he was dead. (At first Burtie thought the man was police, but it turned out he was a fake, just somebody who worked for the store.) The fake policeman said to Mama, "Ma'am, you'll have to come with me," and she struggled a bit, said to him, "Don't touch me, you brute, you pervert," and a couple of ladies rummaging through a pile of stockings on a table turned and raised their eyebrows. "There's no need for that," the man said, and Mama said, "You're hurting me, you'll leave a bruise, any jury would send you straight to prison, you bastard," and then the man pulled her hard enough to nearly knock her off her feet.

The fake policeman led them down the tiled center aisle, past the dresses and cooking pans and pillows and sheets, as people turned to stare at Mama and then down at Burtie, who tried to make it look like this was a normal thing to be doing, what he'd be doing anyway even if he were by himself. They arrived at a carpeted area, and Mama fumbled in her pocket and some lipstick and nail polish fell onto the floor, and Burtie, trying to be helpful, picked them up and said, "Mama, you dropped these," and the fake policeman stopped, meanly smiled, and said, "I'll take those, son." Mama let out a sigh, shook her head, gazed into Burtie's eyes, and said, "Burtie, you dumbass." He was seven years old.

They were heading for a bank of mirrors now. The ones that ladies looked at with blank faces while they held clothes up against their bodies. None stood there now: Burtie had a clear view of the three reflections—his own, Mama's, and the man's—approaching to meet the real them. He expected they would turn again, away from the mirrors, but instead they drew closer and closer, until they stood only inches from their doubles. Burtie looked small, smaller than usual. He was hiding behind his mother's skirt like a baby, he could see the fabric bunched in his baby fist. So he released the material and stepped to the side and crossed his arms over his chest like a man would.

He thought it must be some kind of ritual: they were to stand here and look at themselves, for some inscrutable adult purpose. Instead, the fake policeman reached for a ring of keys attached to his belt by a chain, tugged the ring forward, and inserted a key into a lock that Burtie hadn't noticed there, floating on the mirror panel like a small, round leaf on the surface of a lake. The fake policeman turned the key and the mirror swung open, revealing a white hallway with black scuff marks on the floor and walls.

"Whoa," Burtie said as the fake policeman jerked his mother through the door, and his mother turned to him and said, "Shut it, Burtie."

They were led to a small, windowless room with a metal desk and a couple of plastic chairs. The fake policeman pointed to the chairs and told them to take a seat. Burtie sat, but his mother just said, "*You* take a seat, pig," and the man shrugged and leaned with his back against the closed door. Mama stood there awhile, shifting her weight from one leg to the other, letting out little grunts. Burtie knew she had leg and knee pains, "from years of supporting your deadbeat father," she was fond of complaining, though Burtie was not so young or dumb that he didn't understand that this was just something she said. He grew increasingly worried as his mother wobbled and leaned, and he risked rebuke when he said, "Mama, sit down with me," but she surprised him by letting out a deep sigh and collapsing onto the chair beside him.

A few moments later a knock came at the door, and the fake policeman stepped aside and opened it, admitting a second man, this one shorter and heavier, wearing the kind of clothes Burtie's father had worn to take him out for pizza the one time he took him out for pizza, which was some time ago now, and also the last time he saw his father: a pair of black pants and a button-down shirt and a business jacket not quite the same color as the pants. The new man, surely some kind of manager, sat behind the metal desk and nodded at the fake policeman, and the fake policeman slipped through the door and closed it behind him, sealing them all inside. On the surface of the desk, between the manager and his mother, lay the lipstick and nail polish that Burtie had picked up off the ground.

"That man framed me," Mama said. "He dropped some of your cheap trash on the floor and said it fell out of my pockets."

"We both know that's not what happened, Mrs. LaFarge."

"Before I knew it he had me by the arm and he was parading me around this dump like chattel, like a slave, and then he planted that hideous garbage on me and told me he would snap my arm in two, I'll snap you like a twig, you bitch, he said—"

"There's no need to use that language, Mrs. LaFarge. Our guard has our abso—"

"'—you *fucking* bitch, he said, and he squeezed me harder, and there will be a bruise to prove it. You will be sued by the day's end, let me assure you of that. Your name will be dragged through the mud and both you and that ape you hired as an enforcer will end up in jail and we'll see how you Nazis like a taste of your own medicine."

"This is the third time you've been caught stealing from this store," the manager said, still calmly, but Burtie could tell that he was getting impatient, the words spat out through a stiff jaw, his folded hands clamped together like Burtie's teacher's when Burtie claimed not to have poked Heather M. in the back through the slats of her chair with a sharpened pencil. It was true, he had poked her, but she'd overreacted by screaming, and it wasn't fair that he should be accused of something much worse than what he actually did, so he said he didn't do it, and that's when the teacher looked at him the way this man was looking at Mama.

Burtie was aware that Mama was lying, but as he listened to her talk, she seemed right somehow, more right than the manager dressed like Burtie's father sweating and gripping his two hands together in a wet knot, more right than the fake policeman who had grabbed his mother, had hurt her, and it made him angry. The manager and Mama were bickering now, or rather Mama was shouting over whatever it was the manager was trying to say. "Give me one reason why I shouldn't call the police" was the one sentence the manager succeeded in getting out, and Mama said, "If you want to be arrested, go ahead, go right ahead"—and then, extraordinarily, Mama leaned forward in her chair and tipped herself up out of it until her head was hovering over the manager's desk, and she reared back like a cobra and, screaming, her elbows thrown in the air, smashed her face down onto the desk's surface.

The desk rang like a gong and the manager nearly jumped out of his seat. Mama lifted her head, and her grin was mad, and then from her bent and squashed nose blood began to pour. "How dare you!" came her rebuke, as though from underwater, and blood spattered the desktop and the man's white shirt and pink face. "Police! Police! He hit me! He punched me! He punched a woman in the face!"

After a moment the door flew open and the fake policeman

appeared, then jumped back, as if he'd stumbled into a cage at the zoo. "Jesus," he said, and gripped the doorjamb.

The manager was cowering now—pressing himself into the corner behind the desk, bloody hands splayed, bloody face stunned. He looked like he wanted to take all his clothes and skin off and burn them. The manager was disgusted, not by Mama but by his own self—what she'd just done had made him horrified to be alive. Burtie was in awe of her power.

"Come on, Burtie," she said. "Let's get out of here." She took his hand in her slick and bloody one and tugged him past the fake policeman, who backed away as though from demons.

As they marched down the white hallway, as they pushed open the mirrored door, astounding with their gore a couple of teenage girls making faces behind big pink sunglasses, price tags dangling at their cheeks, Burtie thought of what he'd do the next time the teacher tried to punish him for something he ought to have been assumed not to have done: he would sit before the principal and tell him Teacher tried to grab his wiener. She almost did that once, reaching across his lap to seize the toy cars he had brought to school in his backpack and which he raced, hidden from view, inside his desk while she wrote lessons on the board. She had very nearly touched him there, maybe she'd actually meant to but he managed to block or dodge her hand. The principal would believe it, he was certain—especially if he made himself cry. He was getting upset right now thinking about it—Teacher tried to grab his wiener when all he was doing was quietly racing his cars!

A few people yelped or jumped as Burtie and Mama made their way out of the store, and soon the glass entryway to the mall loomed, and then Mama was holding out her hand and shoving the door violently open. As they crossed the parking lot, Burtie looked back at her smeared and bloody handprint on the glass: his mother's mark. It might never come off, he imagined—wherever she went, if you crossed her, she would make sure you could never forget. He squeezed her bloody hand tighter, and she squeezed back.

Your Friend, Dorothy

Stacey Richter

DEAR HOUSEMATES:

Let's all work together to keep the kitchen clean! I know that we, as powerful, compassionate college womyn, can labor in unity. This is not just student housing. It is a home we have chosen to live in. Even if this is "just" summer session and a writers' conference, it is still important that we uphold our values. Together, we can make our home a shining alternative to the brutal patriarchal society that surrounds us, as exemplified by Party House. Rotting containers of dairy products, old pizza boxes, pans caked with beans, and garbage cans overflowing with used sanitary napkins are not signs of the effortless cooperation that we, a collective of womyn, are capable of. Let's show "the man" what we can do and pay attention to the chore wheel. (If you need instructions on how to use the chore wheel, see me in room 205.) Our sense of ourselves as members of a warm and welcoming group of sisters shall prevail! Together, we can make the world a better place for all womynkind, keep our common spaces tidy, and set an example for our peers. I know I can count on all of you, including Tanya, the newest resident.

Peace,
Dorothy

Dear Housemates:

I was heartened by the brief uptick in cleanliness last week and have hope that we can keep it up, despite the fact that there has been some resentment pertaining to my role. The question has been posed: Who appointed you queen? The answer is no one, but someone has to do it, and yes, I CARE. Tanya, to address your question: yes, leaving your half-full cottage cheese containers rotting on the counter for a week is a problem for *everyone*, not just me. Odor dissipates through the air and affects all the rooms of the house, though it's true that my room has a large gap beneath it that allows the penetration of odors. But this isn't about me, it is about air quality and the usefulness of our kitchen, and those of you who call me the Dyke Cheerleader are both inaccurate and petty. I'm not sure if I'm a lesbian anyway, because I have never had a girlfriend, and I have not been a cheerleader since my junior year of high school. Yes, I *was* a cheerleader, but we all change and grow and have our consciousnesses raised, as mine was raised when I realized that some of our activities, as cheerleaders, were wrong. Perhaps in the future I will elaborate on this change of heart, as it is very interesting. But for now let's just try to keep the kitchen chaos to a minimum, okay?

Also, whoever is shoving their trash (i.e., empty potato chip bags, bread wrappers, etc.) under my door, please stop it. It's not funny.

Thank you,

Dorothy

Dear Housemates:

Tanya, I realize that you did not "choose" Womynist House and that the housing department assigned you to your "airless room." No one likes the Cave, and we're sorry you have to live there without a window, air vent, or even a proper right angle, as it is an awkwardly shaped room. It's unfortunate that Karen, the previous tenant, painted the walls and ceiling black, so that it is "a lightless hellhole," as you put it, as you have a way with words that befits a writing student. Nevertheless, you still have to abide by the rules of the house: no male overnight guests without prior approval by the entire household! And if you have a male visitor during the day, you MUST post the MALE WITHIN sign on the door of the house, and you MUST strike the Man Gong every fifteen minutes while said male friend is visiting during approved daylight hours (7 a.m. to 7 p.m.). I understand that this seems "idiotic" to you, but there are womyn in the house who have been assaulted by men, and we do this so everyone will feel SAFE.

Yes, maybe I am being "chirpy" about "working together as womyn," but I think everyone can agree that we womyn, at least, do not pose a physical threat to one another. I think we can trust in sisterhood for that.

Best Wishes,
Dorothy

Dear Housemates:

I have detected curiosity from some of you about how I became disillusioned with my career as a high school cheerleader, so I will tell you about it. If you don't know about Texas and football, I'm here to tell you, it's a big deal. It was considered an honor to be on the squad, and I liked rehearsals, and the games were fun. My main objection was this: If we were athletes in our own right, and important contributors to school spirit, why did we have to bake cookies for the football players before every game?

"As a show of support." That's what Suzy Tang, our squad leader, told me.

"Well, if it's so rah-rah-rah, why do we do it in secret?" I asked.

"It's not a secret," Suzy said. "We're just not supposed to tell anybody."

Every Thursday I had to bake at least two dozen cookies, muffins, or brownies and put them in either a decorative tin or a gift box with a ribbon and deliver them, along with a note, to "my" football player, Matt Magoffin, a second-string running back with cystic acne that was not going to be helped, let me tell you, by a fruitcake tin stuffed with chocolate baked goods. (That's when I learned to make my famous blondies, which are like brownies but chocolate-free.)

This was inconvenient, to say the least, as baking sweets is not something you can do in secret in a house with a teenage boy (my older brother Teddy) who insists on eating everything that comes out of the oven, exactly when it comes out. But I probably would have kept baking for boys on the team, as well as getting up at 5 a.m. every morning to blow out my hair with a round brush, if I had not picked up *The Second Sex*, by Simone de Beauvoir, on the recommendation of my guidance counselor, who said I should read some long books if I was serious about going to an out-of-state college. In retrospect, I believe he may have recommended this particular book as a joke. He knew I was a cheerleader and he knew my mother. Perhaps it was not a joke, exactly, but an "impish sowing of mayhem," as the writers among you might say. Anyway, after reading this tome, I realized that my role as a baker for boys was demeaning, since I had potential to be an intellectual. So I stopped. Baking cookies, I mean. I remained on the cheerleading squad and threatened Suzy with exposure if she kicked me out.

I have saved my notes to Matt Magoffin. Here's an example:

Dear Matt,

You are the best! I love to watch you running with that ball! I sure hope you win the game tomorrow against East. Go Injuns! We're all behind you! I hope these blondies make you go "Yum" and encourage you to do your best. I made them from scratch.

Best wishes,
Your Biggest Secret Fan
Cheerleader Who Will
Remain Anonymous

I'd leave them on the doorstep the night before a game. Suzy said it made the boys run faster. I believed her until I read de Beauvoir. Then I thought, *Those stupid fuckers. Someday I'm going to get out of here and live in a women's collective!* Ha, ha, just kidding.

Your friend,
Dorothy

Dear Housemates:

For those of you who have male visitors, remember to ring the Man Gong. It is not optional.

Best,
Dorothy

Dear Housemates:

No matter what you say, I do think there's value to women living only with women (or "womyn") as a way to know ourselves and others, and to learn about justice and equality. Maybe it's not a utopia, but I think it's worthwhile to try to get along and see if there's a different way to think/live, since I guess we all can agree that the patriarchy didn't turn out so well. I know sometimes we are "catty." I have been guilty of that myself. It's hard to be nice to someone just because she's also a womyn, when she might be undermining your authority or saying bad things about you behind your back or shoving Frito bags under your door.

Case in point: my mother's antipathy toward girls, wow. If you could see the glee in her eyes as she talked about teenage girls hemorrhaging after a botched back-alley abortion, you would wonder if maybe she was a serial killer disguised as a Texas Christian housewife with a beehive hairdo, even though those have not been in style since 1965! It's hard to respect this female instrument of women's oppression, and I don't, though I do love her, I guess because she is my mother, and before she started ignoring me in earnest, there was something magical about her, to me at least. Something about the way she could make just a trip to the park seem like a visit to Disneyland, when she turned her attention to me and pretended that I really had caught a fish with the string I flung into the dirty, slime-filled lagoon in the city park. (I was not stupid, just four.)

It is sad when one woman (my mother) is the instrument of oppression for other women (anyone who ever tried to get an abortion in Dallas during the years 1988 to present). When I was a little girl, she used to say, "Oh, I'm going to smush you, you're so cute! I am going to smush you into paste!"

Which is a little aggressive in and of itself.

So we are not immune. But we can try to be better.

Best Wishes,

Dorothy

Dear Housemates:

Please be advised that the student reading tonight at 7 p.m. in Orchard Hall may possibly feature violent misogynist passages from the notorious novel *The Vegetable King*, by Vernon Downs. I advise you to either stay away or join me in a beautiful, meaningful protest in the woods behind the hall.

Dorothy

Dear Housemates:

Thank you to those of you who attended the "celebration" last night! It was a great bonfire, relinquishing violent imagoes of women to flame and retaking our power as subjects, not objects. Not everyone from the house was there, and that's fine. It was a powerful ritual for those who participated! If we could all work together like that all the time, I bet we could keep the kitchen clean.

My thanks to everyone who complimented me on the blondies

served at the celebration. I have made another batch, and everyone who does her chores is entitled to two, and two only. BLONDIES ARE ONLY FOR LAST NIGHT'S ATTENDEES.

The people (person) who was not there probably didn't want to be there, as she was inside at the reading, listening to vile, hateful language about violating the bodies of women. Even if you believe, as some people do, that the novel in question is "satire," and that "sometimes the best way to disarm dickwad asshole men is to make fun of them and their shithead dreams of unlimited power," there is no excuse for a book that takes as its subject the cutting up of women. Is there even a literary category called horror satire?

I had to live the first part of my life listening to my mother talk about cutting up women! I do not want to do the same in the second part.

Yours,
Dorothy

Dear Housemates:

Several people have asked me if it's "about" clean. No, it is not "about" clean. It is about people doing what they say they're going to do. When you signed up for the Womynist House, you signed up for a women's coop with, yes, whole grain granola and patchouli and all the "hippie shit" that goes with it. Even if you are the LONE resident who did not sign up for the Womynist House, it's no excuse for you to be the only person who is now destroying the kitchen on a daily basis, with vigor and glee, and, I am starting to believe, malice.

That said, I do not mean to be unpleasant. I have great respect for people who act as individuals and follow the beat of a different drummer. That takes real courage, even if I do not agree with all of your values. Even just wearing real perfume in a place like Womynist House takes some gumption. I had forgotten what it is

like to stand near a woman exuding the aldehyde snap of a cloud of
Chanel. It is divine.

Yours,
Dorothy

Dear Housemates:

To those of you who say I write too many notes, I say HA,
HA, HA. I love writing notes! I've saved every note I've written
since I was eleven, and in reading them over (as I just did), I have
to say they are often quite amusing; I'm sure the budding authors
among you will be charmed. Here's a funny one I wrote in sixth
grade:

Dear Mom,

*It's okay if you're never there when I come home from school, as long
as I have a key to get inside and there's food in the fridge for me to eat.
Dad said he can't take this anymore and is moving into a condo complex
with a pool. He said it's time for his life to begin and he would tell you
in person but you're never home. I understand this, as you have your
important work to do with Operation Rescue. I agree with your stand on
pro-life, but sometimes I wonder if you don't pay more attention to fetuses
than to your own children.*

Your loving daughter,
Dorothy

To those of you who say making graphic, dripping, bloody
antiabortion posters is as disturbing as writing a book about a preppy
dick who cuts up women, I agree! It is messed up! That brings up the
question: Can women be as messed up as men? Sometimes I truly do
wonder if my mother's obsession with who was getting an abortion
and how far along they were was less about preserving fetuses so
they could grow into Christians and more about her imagining

women getting bloody chunks sucked out of their vaginas. Like she wanted to get inside women's bodies and do violence to them from within—not really, but in her mind. I don't know why I think that, except that she never paid any attention to me and always said how great Teddy was, even though there was nothing great about him. Totally ordinary B student with no good extracurriculars who now goes to Texas Tech with the rest of the dolts. While I was on dean's list, debate team, cheerleading, etc. But Teddy could do no wrong. "What would Teddy like for Christmas? Do you think Teddy will be home soon? Don't touch your brother's used Kleenex. It is sacred." Meanwhile, it's all, "Dorothy, get out from under my feet. Dorothy, did you iron your shirts? You're not sick, go to school, young lady," and so on.

My mother always had to have the bloodiest posters. She said, "It's not effective if it doesn't have a little dripping dead baby on it for all to see. Let's see that baby dismembered and dripping blood!" Ick. The truth is, when I was a little girl, I used to LIKE to protest the clinics with her, that's what's so maddening. I liked it until she MADE ME STOP GOING. This was way before Simone de Beauvoir, but I had already seen that there was something wrong with a mother who wanted all other women to be mothers but didn't have any time to be MY mother.

Not that I'm bitter. Ha, ha, ha.

Anyway, she's a nut. She would never have let me come to Camden if she'd bothered to spend ONE SECOND reading up on it to see how LIBERAL it is. So ha-ha on her. She is a force of nature, however, and it is imperative we keep the kitchen clean for the upcoming parents' weekend. Really. You don't want to mess with her.

My mother, and only my mother, will be coming for parents' weekend. She and my father are divorced.

Your housemate,
Dorothy

Dear ALL Housemates:

What makes you say that these notes are "only letters to Tanya"? They are to *all* of the residents of Womynist House. Yes, some of you may already know my life story. You do not have to read the notes if you don't want to. I happen to think that notes have value. That is why I save them. Someday I will compile my "autobiography in notes." Isn't that a wacky idea? Me and Yoko Ono will work on it together.

Yours,
Dorothy

Dear Housemates:

No, I am not "becoming my mother," and I am not "overly concerned with the domestic sphere of the kitchen." Jeez! Tanya, just because you didn't *ask* to live here doesn't mean you can be so mean, and also, if you didn't want to live here, why is it that you're the big feminist critic now? Who are you to tell me I'm a prissy little Texas lady who wears her hair fried, dyed, and shoved to the side? And that I am destined to give up my lesbianism for marriage to an account executive, whatever that is? Anyway, I have never even kissed a girl, but that is a subject for a different note. This note is about civility. I have treated you with civility and I expect to be treated the same way.

And to answer your question: no, I do not plan to spend my life running around in an apron like Simone de Beauvoir, cutting Camus's croissants into bite-size pieces and shoving them into his little French head.

Thank you very much,
Dorothy Endlich

Dear Housemates:

Some of you have expressed interest in the fact that I save all my notes. Does that mean *all* notes, you ask? Yes, it does. For example, here's a note I found that I wrote to my father when I was in high school:

Dear Dad, please don't leave us. I love you and I want to show you the ashtray I made in art. It has to go in the kiln for three days and then cool down, so it won't be done until next week. You said Teddy would have a room in your new condo, but what about me?

Love,
Dot

He had a room set up for Teddy but not me because he said he didn't know anything about setting up a room for a girl. We only visited once anyway. Isn't that a laugh riot? I bet it soured me on men.

Yours,
Dorothy

Dear Housemates:

Yoko Ono is not an evil witch who "broke up the Beatles." She doesn't deserve that reputation. She was an artist with the art group Fluxus. She probably should have stayed away from John Lennon, though. He was a big star and overshadowed her own creative output, as probably happens all the time when a Creative Woman partners with a Creative Man. Do you know about *Cut Piece*? It is about women's vulnerability, though some of you are probably wondering why I would support a piece of art with a KNIFE in it (scissors). It's because it is used in the service of making a complicated statement about how women are vulnerable, how we expose ourselves to others, hoping for connection. It could be women we expose ourselves to or it could be men. It could be strangers or it could be neighbors. Maybe they will hurt us, or maybe they will be respectful or love us. Okay, that particular piece is a little "sharp," but what I like about Fluxus as a movement is how one thing can be another thing, like

in Dada, where household objects can be art just because someone
says it is. Like a snow shovel. Or a hair dryer. Or a sugar cube. Or
a chore wheel. Sometimes you don't know something is art until it
takes you by surprise and says, *I am more complicated than I seem! I
have a strange, unexpected beauty. In fact, I am art!*

See, I can talk about things other than cleaning the kitchen!
Tanya, if you will have coffee with me, I promise I will not talk
about the Kitchen Question at all. I know sometimes you stay at
your boyfriend's place, but boys can be fickle, so maybe when you
come back, we can have coffee and you will spend more time at
Womynist House. I don't mind at all when you come into my room
to use the light from the window for eyebrow-plucking purposes. In
fact, I find it kind of charming.

> Yours,
> Dorothy

Dear Housemates:

To those of you who have told me and Tanya to "get a room,"
I say first of all, it's none of your business, and second of all, Tanya
has a boyfriend, as you all know by the man-approval process, the
incessant gonging, etc., so it doesn't matter anyway. Yes, she is
intelligent, outspoken, and opinionated (like yours truly), but it is
not to be. It doesn't matter that she said she would kiss me if no one
else will, since it bothers her that I have not passed that milestone,
and she thinks that possibly my "obsession with cleanliness" is a
result of "sexual frustration," which I don't know about that. I'm not
sure if she's kidding. I'm pretty sure she was the one shoving trash
under my door, anyway. That is not love. It is not even like.

To those of you who have complained about my characterization
of Tanya's eyebrow plucking as "charming," I would like to say
that I am also in favor of "going natural." There is also something
charming about women who, if it turns out they have a little upper-
lip mustache, just shrug and go about life while having a little

upper-lip mustache.

Blondies tonight at 9 p.m. for everyone who does her chore on the chore wheel. Gold stars will also be available. Tiaras. A ticker tape parade.

See previous notes for more info.

Yours,
Dorothy

Dear Housemates:

One question that has been posed is this: What is art? What content is allowed, and what should be considered too offensive? When is something satire and when is something actually a veiled celebration of the behavior being "condemned"? Tanya says *The Vegetable King* is not "about" cutting up women. She says it is "a Technicolor Jungian dream pastiche of the dark side of the insecure male imagination," which I guess is a point. I still think that level of violence is for freaks, and I wonder what is in the head of the author, Vernon Downs (though I haven't read the book). Tanya says that the contrast between the bland exterior of the main character and the lurid violence of his interior life is the author's way of making a point that America is like that. It's a way of saying that people disguise their dark impulses even from themselves. Furthermore, Tanya says fantasies of power and aggression are universal, and anything that's universal belongs in art.

"You kind of get a picture of how much people censor out of themselves as writers, you know? When you see someone trying to put in every kind of bad and hostile thought."

To which I said, "No, no, no, no, no." And also, "That just sounds like an excuse to describe people getting cut up."

Tanya tilted her head. "Haven't you ever wanted to kill someone? Put your hands around their neck and squeeze?"

I had to think about this. "My mother said she had to grab my little sister out of my arms one time when I was trying to put her into the dryer."

"Ha, ha, ha," said Tanya, which is funny because that's what I usually say instead of actually laughing, because I have no mirth in me and am full of darkness.

Me: "Maybe instead of writing a book about dismembering women, he could write a book about vaginas and how nice they are."

Tanya: "Hmm. Vaginas don't hurt people."

Me: "Exactly!"

Then I asked Tanya to kiss me and she said "No way!" then did it anyway.

So now I'm totally confused.

Dorothy

Dear Housemates:

I give up! Mess up the kitchen as much as you want! Dismember poultry and spread the innards in a layer on the linoleum floor! Clog the drain with fish heads! Go for it!

The reason I have changed my tune on this matter is that during parents' weekend my mother came to visit me here at Womynist House. Did she freak out when she saw that I lived in a womyn's collective? Did a right-wing pro-life nutjob like Diane Endlich, upon seeing her daughter living with lesbian separatists, panic? No. No, she did not. She was *happy* to see that I was living in gender-segregated housing, or as she refers to it, "a girls-only dorm." She was *overjoyed.* All the things that are special about our house—the novel spelling, the purple paint, the bins of shared beans and cracked wheat, the Man Gong—it all reminded her of her time as a Psi Delt, or whatever it was, when she and her "sisters" swapped sweaters and giggled until they peed in their "knickers" and had to be inside by the 10 p.m. curfew. Which leads me to believe that maybe we should be rethinking our project here at Womynist House.

No, really. If my mother thought it was cool, there's something wrong with this place.

Maybe we should, at least, rethink the Man Gong.

> Yours,
> Dorothy

Dear Housemates:

One question that has been posed is this: What is love? What is a sincere token of affection, and what is simply a way of making fun of people? And why do some people have to feel so sad when birds are singing and the summer light is shining softly through the leaves? For a minute I was glad, but now I feel empty. Tanya is gone. The brief kiss, which I described in a previous note, was some sort of last hurrah, I suppose, a lark or a joke. The Housing Office has moved her into Stokes House. Did she say good-bye to you? Because she did not say good-bye to me. Maybe she said good-bye to someone else, but I haven't heard about it.

Did she leave without a word? No, she did not. She left a note. Does this womyn sound like a creative writing major? Because to me she does not:

I'm moving out. You chicks have been driving me fucking crazy with all your sanctimonious bullshit. I would like some quiet, some privacy, and a window. Thanks for the blondies. They were delicious, so sweet and so moist.

> *Aloha,*
> *Tanya*

She left a few items behind: a T-shirt, a dead fern, some magazines, a ladies' razor, etc. I will be burning them this evening at 7 p.m. in the woods behind the auditorium where the last burning ritual was held. Please join me! It should be a cleansing experience. I do not know if we can rid ourselves of the vestiges of Tanya's being—her insouciance and biting humor, her green eyes and lovely scent. But we can have some fun with flames.

Things are going to be much better around here now. We are all going to cooperate and be peaceful and sing songs and feel good together ALL THE TIME. I guess she was the one eating the blondies. I will be in my room crying, though yes, we are probably better off without her. Ha, ha, ha.

PS: To those of you who say I will someday be embarrassed by these notes, I stridently disagree! These notes will never embarrass me, as I am an adult NOW. Why would I be embarrassed by my enthusiasm for communal life? Youth is for idealism. That's what Thoreau says. I believe we can make this world a better place. I believe that a community is stronger than the individual. I believe that we can lead by example, by hard work, and through notes. To those of you who have supported my work with this project and with the chore wheel, thank you. We will get through this difficult time together. The blondies on the counter are for you.

Love,

Dorothy

Birth of a Fawn

Kenneth Calhoun

ON HIS WAY TO COLUMBIA, DERWIN MACDONALD STOPPED BY THE Black Rabbit in the Village to see if Frank was behind the ancient bar. His old friend wasn't present initially, but Derwin was told he would be arriving in minutes, so he opted to wait. He had a few hours until Gerald's class—until the ambush. At least that's how Gerald would most certainly see it. His plans to pass the time at MoMA, where he would take in the *New Photography* show the *Times* had so strongly endorsed, were not fixed. The photos would be indifferent to his gaze. But not Frank, who would be happy to see him occupying his old perch in the corner—once Derwin's home away from home, back in the seventies, before he abandoned the island for Brooklyn.

The mirror behind the bar, somewhat obscured by bottles, commented with a hint of hostility on the whiteness of his beard and the full revelation of his age-spotted scalp. It was a Manhattan mirror: direct, blunt, annoyed, it would seem, by an aging Englishman pleased to see Double Diamond still offered on tap. For old time's sake, he ordered one from the day-shift bartender, if only to admire the man's brawny arms as he pulled the pint, swiped the head of foam, and slid the dark glass his way.

"A Double Diamond works wonders," Derwin sang under his breath. He took a sip off the top. Same stuff. He hummed the jingle and drummed his stiff fingers on the book he had brought along—

an advanced reader's copy he planned to give to Gerald.

He was surprised at how well he recalled the melody of the jingle, a sonic relic of his British past. Some things had been bolted to the floor, he had come to know, while others—like the name of Gerald's child—had long ago escaped the unbarred window. Was it Kimberly? Must be, what, fifteen years old now? Wait. Katherine? Yes, Katherine! *My God, however did I retrieve that from the murk?* He looked at the dark pint, the suds winking up at him. *It does*, he thought. *It does work wonders.*

Frank's arrival triggered an authoritative change of atmosphere. His status as owner was foretold in the subtle flurry of tightening up and squaring away, wiping down and general tidying, performed with precision by the muscled barman and his lone barback—a stout Dominican who was, to Derwin's eye, too old for his role. Frank failed to notice Derwin at first. The bar owner looked as scarred and weathered as the bar itself—the varnish worn off, the edges dulled— yet, like the old slab of shipwrecked oak, unyielding and enduring. Frank stepped behind the bar, where he fiddled with the register and made some notations on a small clipboard dangling from a nail, stage business of a man in charge. He glanced up, caught Derwin out of the corner of his ice-blue eye, and did a double take.

"The fuck?"

"That's right," Derwin said. "The hens have come home."

"To roost or rust?" Frank said, reaching across the bar. They locked hands, held, released. They were midcentury men—men of handshakes and handkerchiefs, pocket combs and spit shines.

"Rot," Derwin decided.

"Ha," Frank said. "You got that right. Christ, we're old. You look like Moses. Those yuppies finally run you out of Brooklyn?"

"Just taking in the many charms of the city," Derwin said, looking past Frank at the bartender, eyebrow conspicuously raised.

Frank swiveled, put it together. He laughed. "Careful. That's some rough trade."

"I see. Probably best I just go to the museum and look at the pictures like a well-behaved pensioner," Derwin said.

No need to tell Frank about his stupid predicament—his scheme involving Gerald, or rather, Gerald's students. There was nothing Frank could do to help. It was a literary problem. Marjorie Lang was a name known by only a dwindling population, most of them publishing people, and Frank was not a literary citizen, though he could certainly be a character in a book. Still, Frank had helped him in the past, or least attempted. He'd sent him Charlie, for one thing—an aspiring writer who was willing to help with the press in exchange for room and board. And in the early days, when Derwin was running the press out of his East Village loft, Frank had hosted readings in the bar or provided kegs for stealth happenings in the abandoned storefronts of Alphabet City.

"How's the kid working out?" Frank asked.

"Charlie? I don't see much of him these days."

"But he's still helping you, right?"

"Oh, yes. When he's around. He's running with a posh crowd. Seems he's become the right-hand man of Vernon Downs."

"He's that writer, right?"

"Yes. That."

"That one of his?" Frank nodded at the hand-bound book on the bar.

"Fuck no."

"Not your cup of tea, I take it."

Derwin made no attempt to conceal his contempt for the current scene. He failed to understand the appeal of the coke-dusted work being produced, though he coveted the impressive sales, which were reliably boosted by movie adaptations and magazine exposés. Of course, his feelings toward Vernon Downs would have been greatly improved if the writer—by all accounts a shifty yet fantastically famous character—had agreed to kindly blurb Marjorie's book. But he had refused, it seemed. Or at least that's what Charlie said, though Derwin held doubts that Charlie had bothered to make the request. He offered his own antiblurb now: "As Capote once said of Kerouac: 'That's not writing, it's typing.'"

"Meow," Frank said. He took Derwin's pint and poured it out, smiling slyly, then set up two shots of Old Grand-Dad. "We are what we drink."

"Fair enough. But will it work wonders?" Derwin asked.

Derwin took the subway to the Upper West Side and consulted his map of the campus when found himself at street level. People and traffic moved with what he perceived to be a growing urgency. It was the end of the millennium doing it. Somewhere in everyone's mind, or possibly heart, was a single but potent grain of belief that the end was nigh. The signs were everywhere. One only needed to take the time to see them. But he had no such time. He was White Rabbit late, having squandered his time at the Black Bunny, catching up with Frank but not keeping up. Frank had continued to toss back whiskey, though Derwin had begged off after three throat-scorching shots. He felt it in his blood now, coalescing into aggression, but tempered by age and the fact that, normally, he would be napping at this hour, looming apocalypse be damned. His body reminded him of its blood sugar schedule as he moved sluggishly into the manicured grounds.

It had been years since he'd been to the university, and never to visit Gerald. At the time of their Provincetown implosion, Gerald had been a lowly assistant professor at Pace, but an impressive string of publications and a transformative directorship at Hunter had apparently amplified his credibility in the job circuit. Now here he was, firmly entrenched in the Ivy League—finally, an institution equal to his ridiculous silk socks. His elite tastes—a wish-fulfillment affectation of his middle-class past—now befitting his impressive station. Such things could happen in the colonies.

The map had been provided by his mostly AWOL assistant,

Charlie, who, in one of his more useful recent ventures, had visited the campus for the purpose of learning Gerald's office hours, which weren't publicly posted. He had also dropped by the Visitors Center to pick up the glossy map, marking the location of Professor Gerald Stanley's office with what looked like a dab of pink fingernail polish. The mark had puzzled Gerald, as did many other things about Charlie, but he had learned not to ask. In return, Charlie did not ask why he had been sent on a reconnaissance mission to Morningside Heights for the sake of noting the comings and goings of a Brit-lit professor. They had developed, it seemed, an unspoken policy of discretion.

According to Charlie, Gerald should be in his office, door open to student visitors, between 2:00 and 4:00 on Monday and Wednesday afternoons. This appeared to be the case. As Derwin emerged from the stairwell and ambled down the glossy hall, he could see, true to the prophecies, an open door at the far end of the corridor. A student—a young person, anyway—was sitting in one of the chairs just outside this inviting portal, maybe serving as a bouncer or bodyguard, but most likely waiting for his turn to discuss his unworkably broad thesis or maybe to dispute a low grade on an earlier paper. At least, that's what Derwin recalled of Gerald's work complaints.

Derwin considered his options. He could take the seat next to the student and just wait his turn, or he could walk past, continue on, then loop back when the chairs were empty. This would allow him to sidestep the inevitable small talk that could possibly be overheard by Gerald, who would then have time to deploy fortifications. The only risk with the alternate plan was being seen by Gerald as he strode past the door. The other possibility was that he could miss Gerald while making his loop, return to a locked office and an empty hallway after the esteemed professor, perhaps late for his train, dashed out with apologies to the waiting student. A third plan emerged: he would stand where he was, examining every posting on a glass-encased bulletin board, noting that a futon was for sale, that tutoring could be secured, that the women's center was offering free resources, that theater students would be reenacting, word for word, on Friday, an episode of *Friends* that had aired only the night before.

Perhaps, he thought, he should have had some flyers made for Marjorie's launch. He could have plastered them all over the city, and hung one here, among these announcements. But how could he compete with a popular TV show? Or, rather, the restaging of a popular TV show? Once again he was forced to acknowledge that he was of another time, possibly another dimension. He was a book man at the end of the Era of Books. A lowly priest in an abandoned church who had staked the survival of his small press on the resurrection of a forgotten British authoress, only to finally learn, as the launch approached without a single prepub review or mention, that no one cared about Marjorie Lang and, what was more, few cared about the anachronistic format itself: lonely was the irrelevant book, sobbing as it was trundled to the shredder.

On impulse, surely a death spasm, he reached out and tore the *Friends* flyer from the board. He was ripping it up—the book he'd brought tucked under his arm—when he heard his name being called, questioningly, from the far end of the corridor. Gerald. Professor Stanley, standing with two of his students, the befuddlement on his face visible even at this distance.

Derwin waved, the ragged fringes of paper flapping like a wilted pom-pom in his ruddy hand. If only, it occurred to him, he had done the same thing to a certain letter so many years ago. Gerald would no doubt be happier to see him.

"I'm surprised you recognized me," Derwin said. They were now sitting in Gerald's book-crammed office, the students sent away, the open door now closed.

"You have a distinct line," Gerald said coolly, settling back into his armchair—a leather throne that signaled a commitment to certain pretentions. He fingered a sleek cigarette case but did not snap it open, nor did he offer one to Derwin. It was probably empty.

"My *line* is severely distorted at this point, I'm afraid," Derwin said. "More of a squiggle."

"Hardly. Still legible at a distance."

"That's kind of you." It was. He hadn't expected this. But he would soon see if this kindness was merely manners, or if a sufficient amount of water had indeed passed under the proverbial bridge. He attempted small talk, staying away from intimate matters at this point. Asking instead how Gerald was finding Columbia. Were the students markedly different from those at earlier institutions? How was his writing going? And was he in good health?

Gerald answered these questions succinctly, smiling vaguely—tensely—as though through a veil of smoke from an imaginary cigarette. Waiting for the point of Derwin's visit to be revealed, glancing expectantly at the book he held in his lap. When Derwin began, finally, to exhaust the immediate conversational possibilities and lean toward inquiries on more sensitive issues, loading up the girl's name—Katherine—Gerald seemed to sense the shift and cut to the chase.

"What are you doing here, Derwin?" He asked the question, then leaned back and assumed a slanted pose, perhaps borrowed from William F. Buckley Jr., his piercing gaze still holding hurt, or was it contempt? When he crossed his legs, the hem of his slacks rode up, revealing his sock: oxblood patterned with gold diamonds. *Good for you, Professor,* Derwin thought. *Who was it that said character is the product of consistent action? One of the theater Russians, maybe. At any rate, good for you and your socks. Sticking firmly to those silken guns. Admirable, yes, but not a good sign for me. Kind of kills the hope, really.* If only Gerald had been sporting some gym socks, or maybe no socks at all, just sandals, and perhaps more messianic attire in general, one of those forgive-and-forget cassocks. Maybe a beard to fringe the cheek that was turned. Then, possibly—

"Derwin."

"Right." Where to start? He scanned Gerald's shelves, looking for a prop. Marjorie Lang's name among the spines. But Gerald's interests were—academically, at least—firmly male: Angry Young Men, volumes on and by Kingsley Amis, Wain, even some nods to the younger Amis. The occasional detour into Greene—a secondary subject. "Are you at all familiar with Marjorie Lang?" Derwin asked.

The question seemed to throw Gerald. His posture shifted nearly imperceptibly as he absorbed it. So this was a professional visit.

His guard dipped slightly as he said, nearly whispered: "*Birth of a Fawn.*"

Derwin rewarded him with a pained smile.

Yes, the title of Marjorie's celebrated postwar tome about the killing of a Nazi sympathizer by his pregnant wife on the Isle of Man, where Jewish refugees were interned by the British during the conflict. A fearless and astonishingly artful work that was a Nobel Prize nominee, yet eventually forgotten as the flood of postwar novels by men soon stole all wind, ate up oxygen and took the light, buried even the most impossibly beautiful of works by the fairer sex.

Birth of a Fawn.

It deserved a revival, a second life! Believing this, after finding a first edition on a discount cart, then traveling to Brighton and approaching the reclusive author with a plan to reissue, only to be denied *Birth of a Fawn* but counteroffered with a previously unseen, entirely new manuscript featuring some of the characters from the celebrated novel, so that it would function as a kind of sequel, Derwin thought he had found a way to save the faltering press, along with his waning enthusiasm for the business of books itself. But also, here was an opportunity to bring an important undiscovered work from one of the century's most shamefully neglected voices into the spotlight. And the topper was that the book was actually brilliant—same beautiful sentences, same piercing humanity, same timeless urgency. A nearly lost masterpiece, now found, and soon to launch into the uncaring void.

He explained this to Gerald in a mighty rush of words, pausing only occasionally for air and to marvel at the fact that here he was, talking to Gerald after all these years. The encounter summoned regrets, circling overhead like ravens. But he would keep talking. Pushing forward as though no time had passed at all, and no betrayals bruised the surface of their short-lived shared past. The novel's publication date was approaching, he explained, and he had arranged for Marjorie Lang to fly in from the UK, covering all her expenses, but the money wasn't the point of any of this. He wanted Gerald to understand that, right up front. It wasn't about the looming loss, not even fact that he would never recover the absurd advance, which was most of his personal savings, and that, most likely, Obelisk Press would be shuttered over this. He had played the whole thing wrong, underestimating the interest. One would think, what with the Soviet Union dead and the Russians no longer an easy enemy, that Nazis would be fair game once again. People didn't seem to hate Nazis like they used to, it seemed. But that was another conversation.

The point was this: A launch party had been planned. A lavish affair that would include a reading and a conversation between himself and Marjorie, followed by a book signing, then a reception. The hall was rented, the catering arranged, but as the date approached, the book's imminent arrival had made no impression whatsoever in industry press, not to mention the mainstream media, who remained steadfast in their focus on Must See TV. If any ink at all went to the literary world, it was to cover the exploits of Vernon Downs and his rapidly aging-out "brat pack" of scenester word-hustlers. The thought of presenting Marjorie with an empty hall horrified him. Here was a woman whom he had come to see as a kind of neglected saint, a clear-eyed prophet and, ultimately, a kindhearted elderly woman who, like his mother, was in danger of dying alone and forgotten, leaving the safety of her home and garden to fly across the pond, surely with hopes of being greeted by a large, adoring audience—after all, that was one of many promises Derwin had made. Not exactly the Beatles at JFK, mind you, but something, well, celebratory, well attended at the very least. And yet all he could count on, after his calls and queries to press outlets and the big houses went unanswered, was some bookstore friends who would fill a few seats out of pity. Maybe Frank. He couldn't even expect Charlie to be there. No, he needed others. More.

"Is that what this is about, Derwin?" Gerald said. "You want me to attend a book launch?"

"Not so much you, though, yes. Of course. But more so, your students. I'm aware that you currently teach two classes in British literature. The enrollment in your undergraduate course alone could fill the seats. You could send them, Gerald."

"Send them?"

"You could make it an assignment, could you not? So they'll have to come." That came out a bit desperate, Derwin was aware.

Gerald blinked. He looked Derwin over, his gaze starting at the floor, taking in his scuffed boots and loose jeans, traveling up to the faded Pendleton plaid, sleeves rolled up, black tee underneath, sticking for a beat on his white beard, then moving past his eyes to his fully exposed, freckled pate. He must be wondering, Derwin thought, how they, the two of them, could ever have fit their bodies together. Even back then their age difference was pronounced. How could this old troll's ruddy hands, with these knobby, arthritic knuckles, ever have succeeded in smoothing the young scholar's furrowed, conflicted brow, let alone unfastening the buckle of his belt?

Derwin suddenly found the silence between them unbearably oppressive. "You could do that, couldn't you?"

"Do what now?"

"Make it an assignment. She's a valid voice, Gerald. It's not like it's unrelated to your usual syllabus. She *is* British and she's bloody brilliant."

Gerald began to slowly shake his head. "Unbelievable. Fucking unbelievable."

Derwin braced himself. Gerald glared furiously but said

nothing. Again, the prolonged silence compelled Derwin to speak.

"Which aspect?" he said, then grinned at his strained commitment to this obtuse pose he had assumed, hoping it would get him through. It would not, he realized from the scowl on Gerald's face. The slow, shaming shake of the head.

"*Which aspect?* How about, for one, how you ruined my life? Or at least you attempted it."

Derwin said nothing. Only nodded as if to say, *Yes, of course, that.* He had, for many years, practiced a speech for this moment, but as time swam onward, he realized the speech was for himself. A speech that tried to justify one of the cruelest acts of his life. Right up there with abandoning his mother when she began to lose her mind. How he fled, wincing life away on another continent until the news arrived—her body discovered by neighbors on the floor of the loo in her miserable Brixton flat, a bar of soap clutched in her bony hand. "That was, you must know, exactly the opposite of my intention," he managed to mumble.

"No? Not your intention? Maybe you need your memory refreshed," Gerald said. He stood and began scanning the floor-to-ceiling shelves of books. Derwin scanned with him, the titles branded on spines. Most hard to make out at this distance. What book could possibly be relevant to this moment? What quote, somewhere in that sea of words, would shed light on the matter?

Gerald reached out, pulled a volume from a high shelf. E. M. Forster's *Maurice*! He flipped through the pages, then removed something pressed between them. Notes? He held it out. An envelope addressed to the mother of Gerald's child, his ex-wife, Candace. The scrawl issued from Derwin's own, pre-arthritic hand. The letter was inside, he knew. The letter in which he'd detailed his affair with Gerald, essentially outing him to his wife and ending his married life, possibly his straight life. Derwin wasn't sure, since, after all, it had ended his life with Gerald too.

Gerald slammed the book closed and tossed it aside. "I've made quite a career for myself understanding the intentions of authors.

What you wrote—it doesn't take a fucking PhD to see that you were trying to destroy me."

"No," Derwin said. "Trying to *free* you."

"Ha. Is that what you've been telling yourself all these years?"

Derwin said nothing. He stood to leave.

"Sit down."

Derwin remained standing. Gerald glanced around, looking for what? A weapon, perhaps.

"Let me show you something, Derwin. Something that's not in this letter." He went to his desk and opened the top drawer. "This is how old my daughter was when you took it upon yourself to end my family."

He held up the photograph to Derwin's face. A tiny newborn— less than a newborn. It was true. He'd sent the letter days before the unanticipated premature birth, thinking it would arrive before any harrowing trip to the hospital. But as bad luck would have it, the letter arrived when Candace was already home, recovering, while the baby remained at the hospital, struggling to survive in an incubator. "This is what you tried to take from me. But you failed, Derwin. You tried, but you failed. And now here you are, asking for—what? Such a petty favor?"

"I do have regrets," Derwin said.

"Fuck your regrets!" Gerald shouted.

Derwin nodded. "Right."

They stood for another beat of silence, until Gerald said: "Leave."

So Derwin did. If this were an earlier era, he would have shuffled down the glossy corridor, hat in hand. But this was the end of the millennium, the dull edge of time itself, and he retreated with an exposed head and empty hands, the book he had brought abandoned in the face of Gerald's rage.

The most upsetting thing about meeting Marjorie Lang at the airport was the tattered garment bag she clutched as she stepped off the Jetway. They embraced cordially, and he attempted to unburden her. "Please, let me," he said, reaching for the bag.

But she pulled it back. "I'd rather hold on to it," she said. And already, with this utterance, he saw a spark of defiance that he had not seen when visiting her home in Brighton but that was the fiery underpainting of both of her books. Now that glow was in her eyes. Apparently, the imminent publication of her follow-up had worked its own wonders. The small, somewhat hunched seventy-nine-year-old woman—so frail and even mousy—was now, after a seven-hour flight, a petite immortal, striking in a sharp brown wool dress, jawline accentuated by a lavender scarf, her gray hair fluffed and swirled. "This is my gown and I won't have it ruffled."

"Your gown?"

"For the gala," she said. "It was made for me decades ago, and fortunately, it has come back into the fashion. Just in time, really."

The *gala*. His heart sank. There was a small part of him that had hoped she had forgotten all about the promised event. Clearly, she had not. In fact, it was very much on her mind. In the car, she asked, "Would it be possible to reserve some seats? I've written some friends who may attend, if they received my letters. If they are still, in fact, alive."

She laughed at this, and he offered a wobbly smile. It wasn't the morbid humor that unnerved him so much as the assumption of an audience. A need for reservations of seats. When, he wondered, would he break it to her about the lack of response, the grotesque indifference? He had decided that small hints was the way to go. The gentle letdown. He would look for opportunities to begin chipping away at her expectations. But nothing came to him now, so he said, "I'm sure we can find room for your friends in the front row."

"Wonderful," she said.

They rode into the city, and she pointed out the United Nations building. "I spoke there once. When it was shiny and new. When the whole world was starting over again. The folly renewed. You remember those days, don't you, Derwin?"

"I remember playing in smoldering ruins."

"Yes. And what better training could you have had for this life?"

"I suppose you're right," he said.

"I've said it before. One of the most dangerous forms of fallout is hope."

He escorted her by the arm into the five-star hotel he had booked for her months earlier. It wasn't like he could, in good conscience, put her up in his Brooklyn flat. His spare room was suitable for Charlie—who would otherwise have been homeless— but certainly not for a grande dame of letters, especially an unjustly forgotten one. To his mind, she was lost royalty. Had history only been kinder. God, how he wanted the world to see this book! It would put in bend in the canon, he was sure of it. She was a bloody genius. She should be staying in a suite named after her, where she was forced by the inconveniences of fame to use a fake name at the front desk, yet the staff knew to send up her favorite bottle of Veuve Clicquot in a silver bucket.

He left her to settle in, maybe nap, before dinner. She said she had some calls to make. Perhaps to confirm that her few friends were among the living. They would meet in the lobby in an hour. Derwin passed the time wandering shadow-daubed paths in the park. A breeze twirled leaves on the boughs arching over him. Beyond the canopy, the sky was invitingly blue—the exact color of a Hockney pool. Stimulating sights, yet the impending disappointment he would lay at Marjorie's feet weighed heavily. Why had he allowed this charade to go on this long? What was it that she'd said about hope in the car? Indeed, he sighed. He had tried a number of maneuvers, all of them failures. Gerald had been his final, desperate hope. All that particular venture had succeeded in doing was vividly reacquainting him with the terrible thing he had once done—or maybe the terrible thing he had once been. He was beyond redemption, as far as Gerald was concerned.

Derwin's spirits were boosted when Charlie actually showed up for dinner. Derwin felt it was important to show Marjorie that the press had employees, though Charlie barely fit the bill. He was more of an occasional assistant to Derwin than an employee of Obelisk. In truth, there was very little to do these days, though the run-up to Marjorie's launch had required some extra hands. At first, Charlie was often present and accounted for, and capable enough. But his focus soon shifted elsewhere. Lately he had become increasingly scarce as he took up residence in Vernon Down's loft. House-sitting, it seemed. Derwin wasn't clear on the details of the arrangement. He was further confused by Charlie's appearance, particularly a new way of wearing his hair, and the suede blazer that must have cost a small fortune. Clearly, Charlie was wearing Vernon Downs's clothes. What was he up to?

Whatever the motivations behind all of it, the effect of Charlie's wardrobe and grooming—even his newly affected way of crisp enunciation and concise gesturing—was that of accomplishment, of brisk business and high competence. It was possible that this performance was for the occasion, for Marjorie, Derwin realized. It seemed to be working. Marjorie was charmed and Derwin was grateful, temporarily relieved, until Charlie said, "I'm really looking forward to tomorrow's event. It's going to be amazing."

Derwin wanted to kick him under the table.

"I'm going to wear a sparkly gown," Marjorie said. "I'll look like this." She pointed at the bubbles in her flute of champagne.

"That alone will be worth the price of admission," Charlie said.

"Ooh, there's a price. What is the price?"

"A pittance compared to the cost of missing it," Charlie gallantly said.

"What a clever young man you've found, Derwin!"

"Isn't he?" Derwin coolly agreed.

They walked her back to the hotel, arm in arm. She stopped halfway through the lobby and turned to Derwin. "This will be just one of many times when I thank you, Derwin," she said, her eyes going glossy with adoration, "for all that you've done. You've really given an old spinster something to wake up for in the mornings, I must say." She looked, at the moment, very much like his mother, and though he had noticed the likeness before, he was struck by the baldness of his own motivations.

"It was the least I could do," he said, though this utterance did not entirely fit the moment. He tried another pass, this time remembering to address the woman standing before him. "It has been the highlight of my career!"

She squeezed his arm and then continued their journey to the elevator.

At her room, she blew them kisses as the door closed between them. Derwin and Charlie started down the hallway to the elevator. "Thank you, Charlie," Derwin said. "For being here tonight. You were great. A command performance."

"Hey, free dinner," he said with a shrug. The old Charlie was back, it seemed.

"If that's all it takes, then a week of hot meals are on me if you could just show up tomorrow night."

"I was planning on it anyway. She's great." They stepped into the elevator, and Charlie hit the button for the lobby.

"Don't say you're coming and then fail to show," Derwin said. "My heart can't take it. At least when she looks out at the empty seats, there you'll be. She likes you. I can tell."

"What are you talking about? *Empty seats.* She's Marjorie Lang!"

"And when did you first hear of her, Charlie?"

"From you."

"There you have it."

They walked through the revolving door, into the cool evening air, and the porter asked them if they needed a taxi.

"I'm all right," Charlie said. "I'll walk."

Derwin indicated yes, a cab for himself, and the porter blew his whistle, waving in a car from the curbside queue. "I'll see you tomorrow, then?"

"Yes. Look, Derwin. You worry too much."

Derwin ignored this unsolicited advice—or rather, observation.

The advice was implied. That he should worry less. An easy thing to suggest from someone who had never had his heart broken or, worse, never broken the heart of another. He sat in the taxi and lowered the window.

"Bring friends!" he said as the taxi pulled away.

"I don't have friends," Charlie called after him.

The next day Derwin moved within a web of dread. He performed his morning calisthenics before the droning television, his mind playing through scenarios. Of course, there was nothing to do at this point but go through with it all. Still, he could hope that the gods would intervene, perhaps with an asteroid strike. If the world was to end at the millennium, why not today instead? It would be only a few months early. What were a few months in the grand, golden sweep of time? He sat on his bed, holding off the increasingly difficult task of pulling on his boots, waiting to see if the world would graciously implode. He gave it a few minutes, head cocked as he listened for a distant rumbling, the cracking of the world's girding, maybe the angel's horn.

Only street sounds. He sighed and bent to the task at hand.

There was much to do. It required a list. He had to pick up the corrected run of programs at the printer's, box up the books he intended to sell at the event—both of Marjorie's and a few others from his backlist—check in with the caterers, and keep tabs on Marjorie, who was having a Mandarin Oriental spa day at his invitation, and expense. She said she would be dining with a friend, then driven out by car service to the venue. This was a relief, since he needed every available moment to prep. So, yes, the printer's. There was something else. But what? He checked his list. The wine shop! Yes, he had arranged to provide the wine, rather than go through the caterer. A money-saving gesture that he regretted now, if only to have one less item on his list.

The day passed quickly, with Derwin ticking off tasks, only

to discover more tasks in the process. He was too old for this, he recognized. Perhaps that was the lesson here. That it was time. He could not run a press, not without resources and help. He had painted himself into a corner, and maybe deliberately so. His failure needed to be a spectacle for his dim brain to receive it. But did it need to involve others—namely, Marjorie? Must there be—what was that term from Gulf War coverage at the start of the decade? Not shock and awe. The other one. Oh yes, collateral damage.

As evening approached, he was too nervous to eat. He went to the hall and watched the venue employees set up the obscene rows of chairs. "No need to put them so close together, gang," he said. "Spread them out a bit."

He sat down toward the back, knees cracking. The stage, where the podium stood and where they had set up two chairs—one for him and the other for the author—seemed a million miles away.

What he needed, he decided, was to try the wine. He was well into his third glass when Frank showed up. "I was feeling literary!" He was soon followed by Charlie. Derwin was thrilled by their presence, then astonished when more people strolled in and began occupying seats, followed by yet more. Who were they? Not students. Older. Maybe some. There was a mix of ages.

"Did you do this?" he asked Charlie.

"Ha. No, sir."

"Well, I wonder who they are."

Charlie smiled. "Maybe people who've come to see the author Marjorie Lang."

"Cheeky." He reached out to giddily tousle Charlie's hair, but Charlie ducked his hand.

Yet more people poured in from the street, and Derwin soon found himself supervising the setting up of additional chairs. "Tighten up those rows, boys," he found himself saying. To hell with his earlier instructions! The place was filling up, by God!

When Marjorie arrived, people were standing along the back. He ushered her to the greenroom, where she removed her long coat, revealing a smart black dress with a white Peter Pan collar.

"Oh. What happened to the gown?" he asked.

"It was a bit much," she said. "Too Norma Desmond."

"Save it for Stockholm," Derwin said. They both smiled.

Soon they were onstage together, discussing the new book—*A Fawn in the Fight*. During Marjorie's reading of excerpts, Derwin sat in the interviewer's chair, grinning. From there he scanned the audience and was shocked to see Gerald sitting toward the back. He had come alone, it seemed. No, with some students. Or at least one—a young woman sitting beside him. He caught her whispering into his ear and him nodding in agreement. The sight of the crowd, especially Gerald's presence, filled Derwin with a surge of joy. His throat tightened with emotion. Good thing there was no need for him to speak. Marjorie had cast a spell on the audience, who watched her, enraptured, totally unaware of the evening's host, only feet away, pinching at the bridge of his nose in an attempt to hold back tears.

Later, as a line formed for the book signing, Gerald approached him with his student in tow.

"I'm surprised you came," Derwin said. "Thank you."

"I read the book," Gerald said. "You're right about her, Derwin. She's incredible."

"And you brought your student." Derwin smiled at the young girl at Gerald's side.

"Actually, this is my daughter. This is Katie." Gerald hit Derwin with a pointed gaze, trying to press the significance into his mind. The intensity in his eyes like a spotlight on the moment. The girl smiled, revealing braces on her teeth. Yes, too young to be a college student. Here she was: the baby, now grown. "She wants to be a writer."

"I loved the book," Katie said. "Both books. I had to come, to meet her."

"Wonderful! What did you love about them?" Derwin asked.

She gave the question some thought. "That a woman, a pregnant woman, does the things no one else has the courage to do."

"Yes. Absolutely!" Derwin turned to Gerald. "I see she has your brilliant mind."

"You haven't met her mother," Gerald said, nodding at Katie.

He squeezed Derwin's shoulder as they moved past him to take their place in the long line. At the far end, Marjorie vigorously signed whatever was placed in front of her. She caught him watching and waved excitedly. The gala had been delivered, largely by herself, it seemed. These people, she had revealed just before they stepped onto the stage, were the friends she had mentioned. Well, her friends and their friends. And possibly their friends' friends. Plus a critic or two, and it remained to be seen if they were to be considered friends as well.

Derwin sat down in one of the empty seats in the back row. He was tempted to kick off his boots, to lie down and let the night have its way with him. Maybe roll him up in a thousand years of darkness and shuttle him away, depositing him in an incandescent pool of champagne light. The millennial sunrise. But he had made it this far. Might as well stay vertical for the duration. He wasn't dead yet. Nor was Frank, whom he spotted chatting up one of the caterers at the back of the hall. Meanwhile, Charlie was nowhere to be seen.

Derwin looked at the stage, where, only minutes earlier, he had been sitting, imploring Marjorie Lang to say more about her revelatory work for the benefit of the audience. It didn't seem nearly as far away as it did earlier. How was that possible? Somehow, he realized, the world, maybe the universe itself, was getting smaller, not expanding after all. Instead drawing everyone closer.

If This Is Home, Welcome Home

Nina de Gramont

Foreword to Frank Broder's "The Case for *Let It Be*"
by Kyra Broder

June 1989, Modesto, California

"THE FAREWELLS WE PLAN SO RARELY *ARE* FAREWELLS. THE REAL farewells, the ones that truly mean good-bye. Those tend to take us by surprise." So begins Frank Broder's essay "The Case for *Let It Be*," which I've chosen as the title piece for his posthumous collection. If you're a Frank Broder fan, you probably know his choice of *Let It Be* as the Beatles' last album doesn't have much to do with the year it was released. Or maybe you don't. Maybe you read Broder's novel, *Sweet Ulysses on Parade*, and/or saw the movie starring Jack Nicholson and don't know that nonfiction, dissecting the crazy culture of the sixties and seventies, was Broder's first and real passion. "The Case for *Let It Be*" was published long before *Sweet Ulysses*, in a magazine called *Turbulent Times*. I don't know what its circulation was, but based on the way it's stapled together, I'd guess very low.

Instead of being cagey and academic, I am just going to come out and tell you, Frank Broder is my father. Was my father. I have to get used to talking about him in the past tense. Like a lot of writers, Pop was more comfortable on the page than in real life. He never said good-bye, but there were a number of farewells. The days he left (there were several). The day the Martenses' house exploded. The day he died.

The last time I saw him was three years ago. I came home from school midmorning to find him in his study, rummaging around nosily enough—or maybe he was just stoned enough—that he didn't realize I was there. I stood in the doorway, feeling kind of feverish (the reason I'd come home), watching him shuffle through papers and haphazardly toss them into a suitcase.

"Pop," I finally said. I called him Pop because of Willy, my half brother. The first time Pop heard Willy call his stepfather Dad, it broke his heart to pieces, so he figured he'd have me call him something old-fashioned, something not likely to be employed, daughter to father, in these dying gasps of the twentieth century. His words, "these dying gasps of the twentieth century," not mine—you can read them yourself in "Portents from *Portnoy's Complaint*."

I've met Willy only once, on a trip with Pop to New York. Maybe I'd see him again if I went to Pop's memorial service? It makes me sad to think there's a good chance neither of Pop's kids (at least the ones I know of) will be there. But I don't have Willy's phone number or address. He broke Pop's heart, but I'm not sure I ever could have.

"Kyra," Pop said instead of good-bye that last morning I saw him. "What are you doing here?"

I told him about my fever, and how the nurse had called Mom at work and they'd both agreed I could drive home and put myself to bed. Flush from the Japanese translation of *Sweet Ulysses on Parade*, Pop had bought me a new car for my sixteenth birthday, a white convertible Mustang. All my friends were jealous of it.

"Your mother's not coming home, is she?" Pop said. He didn't ask me if I needed anything or put a hand to my forehead, but that wasn't unlike him. I wish he had looked at me in any way that indicated he wanted to memorize my face, at sixteen, clueless to his pending abandonment. Several hours later I'd get the full story and know he'd run off with Marianne, whom Mom would forevermore call "my hitherto best friend." Or sometimes "my erstwhile best friend." Going through these essays, I see that "hitherto" and "erstwhile" are words Pop enjoys. I can't tell if the use is meant to be ironic, the old-fashioned sound of them describing work from an era that rejected all things old. Because Pop died without a will, Marianne is getting all his money—inconvenient timing, as I start Berkeley in the fall, a year late (thanks to Pop's various farewells, I failed three classes and had to repeat junior year).

Later that last day, when I woke up with a clammy layer of sweat on my forehead and a throbbing pain behind my temples, I found a letter from Pop slipped under my door. You might want to say this counts as good-bye, but writing good-bye is not the same as saying it. I read the first few lines, then went into his study, thinking if I found him still packing, maybe I could talk him out of it. The study was a wreck, still jam packed with his stuff, including the suitcase he'd been packing when I interrupted him. It contained the essays for his collection, as well as a letter from an editor who'd agreed to publish it. I've wondered, these past three years, if the reason Pop left it behind was that my arrival made it necessary for him to skedaddle as fast as humanly possible.

"He can come get them himself if he wants them so badly," my mother said when Pop wrote from Santa Monica asking for the essays. It had been my impression that this project, the collection, meant more to him than the novel that had made him (semi) rich and famous. But I guess I was wrong, because he never came back for it.

A new family has moved into the Martenses' house. Not the Martenses' house, really. The house they built where the Martenses' house once stood. I guess it's an improvement? Big, fancy, shiny, new. I liked the old house better. It was sweeter, cozier.

In his essay "Manhood and the Disappearing Father," Frank Broder writes about fathers in the work of Updike and Cheever, how they can be there but not there. A father can be in the house, even in the room, or the swimming pool, or the car, and still be absent. My English teacher Mrs. Fitzpatrick says all narrators, fictional or nonfictional, are either children or parents. Pop wrote "Manhood and the Disappearing Father" after Willy but before me. You'd never know, reading it, that he was a disappeared father himself, with Willy on the other side of the country, calling a different man Dad.

If Pop really wanted an example of a disappearing father, he should have been here the day the Martenses' house blew up, a couple of weeks after he left. We hadn't heard a word from him, didn't even have a forwarding address or phone number. I had been inside the Martenses' house only hours before the explosion, maybe not even two hours, babysitting for their son, Charlie, who was about seven. We roller-skated in the dank, slick basement, where the gas leak started. After an hour Charlie's little head was sweaty, so we walked to Harold's Corner Store for a soda and Fig Newtons. Charlie drooped on the way back, the way a little kid does when he's spent, so I carried him a ways. I heard the explosion like something that had nothing to do with me, far away, and then the sirens. For sure it's the last time in my life I will ever hear sirens and not worry everything's about to change.

In his essay "The Great Pretender," Pop writes about Bob Dylan as a shapeshifter, stealing gestures and phrasing from other artists. In his early performances Dylan copied Woody Guthrie, down to the spasms from Huntington's chorea. Pop was a bit of a shapeshifter himself. I started reading *Sweet Ulysses*, and it seems to me kind of a Tom Robbins rip-off, even though Pop says Robbins is a disorganized hack (see "Psychedelia and the Pseudointellectual"). But maybe that's one reason why Pop never claimed to think highly of his own novel. "My cash cow" is the nicest thing I ever heard him say about it.

Charlie Martens shapeshifted on the day of the explosion from regular kid to orphan in the course of a walk to the corner store. He slipped his sticky hand into mine. The fire trucks and ambulances blocked our view of the house, or rather, blocked our view of the absence of the house. Sunlight was brighter than it should have been, late afternoon. The giant sycamore tree stood in the backyard, newly unobscured, the rope swing swaying like a terrible joke. I scanned all the lawns and sidewalks, the rubbernecking neighbors, for Charlie's mom or dad. And I scanned them for Pop, as if this terrible tragedy could conjure his return. I could feel the little-kid shock radiating from Charlie's body into mine. And I thought, as if the exploded house had to do with me and not Charlie, *Pop's gone. He's never coming back. I'll never see him again.* My bedroom shares a wall with Pop's study. I used to hear his typewriter click-clacking into the night. Now everything's silent, like he was never there at all.

The family in the new Martens house has one child, a boy, just like the originals. I'm guessing he's twelve or thirteen—too old to need a babysitter, and anyway, I don't babysit anymore. The parents are gone a lot. Yesterday I saw the boy, I think of him as Charlie #2, sitting on the stoop after school like he'd locked himself out. I thought about inviting him in, but I didn't. I'm not sure there's been a male in our house since Pop left. Do you know that none of these essays by Frank Broder, left behind in his battered suitcase, are about women? Except for "The Hedonistic Messiah," about Janis Joplin, Jim Morrison, and Jimi Hendrix, and even in that one Joplin gets not the third of the ink she rightly deserves, but barely more than a few lines.

Sometimes a car door slamming will wake me up late at night. I'll think maybe it's Pop coming home, but before I even open my eyes, I'll know it's Charlie #2's father, back from working late or going out partying. Not even Pop's ghost, but someone else's.

I have a new computer for Berkeley, but I haven't taken it out of its packaging yet. At night, despite the summer heat and our lack of air conditioning, I put on Pop's moth-eaten gray cardigan—

left draped over his desk chair—and set to work on his manual
typewriter.

Last night my click-clacking woke Mom. I imagine her sitting
up in bed, confused, thinking Pop had somehow returned. I should
mention that he went away and returned once before, when I was
a baby, so that I actually have a memory of meeting him when I
was around five. "It's your pop," he said, leaning down to say hello,
like his return was a fabulous gift, no apology necessary. I realize a
memory from so long ago, involving a small child's interpretation of
a facial expression, might not be convincing. I realize all my analysis
of his work might be skewed. For how this might affect your reading
of this foreword, please refer to "Franny, Zooey, and the Unreliable
Narrator."

Mom came in and sat down on the old black trunk I used to
take to summer riding camp. "God only knows what he's got in
here," she said, rapping on the dusty lid.

"How come you never went through any of his stuff?" I asked her.

"I already know more about Frank Broder than I want to. And
I never found anything that made me feel better, going through his
things."

"Why didn't you just throw it away?"

"Because it doesn't belong to me." Mom has always possessed a
morality Pop did not. I saw tears standing in her eyes, long elegant
fingers plaiting the hem of her nightgown. She looked younger in
the dim light, her hair loose and mussed from sleeping. For three
years all she'd thought about was how much she hated him, but I
guess sudden death will rearrange a person's memories.

She got up and left and I thought that was that, but she came
back with a bottle of Cabernet and two glasses. The one she poured
for me was half the size of her own. It tasted chalky and deep, like
mashed-up rose petals. I'm not sure Mom's ever given me wine
before, even at special dinners, probably because of my lost year
after Pop left.

"It's a lot of work," she said, nodding toward the typewriter and the suitcase full of essays.

"Right now I'm working on the introduction."

"How's it going?"

"Probably too personal." I took another sip of wine.

"You can edit it later. Frank always said you could be as careless as you wanted in a first draft, so long as you were willing to be merciless with the second." She paused, furrowing her brow. "We should go to the service. I think it would be good for you. For both of us."

"We'll have to see Marianne."

"Fuck Marianne." She downed the rest of her wine and poured another glass.

For the first time it occurred to me to be angry that Marianne had had her sister call with the bad news. What a coward. According to Pop's essay "Siddhartha's Comeback: An Allegory for the Age of Anticulturalism," courage is a necessary trait for rejecting expectations and achieving spiritual enlightenment. When I was eight, Pop took me to New York for Willy's high school graduation even though he hadn't been invited. He brought a copy of *Siddhartha* as a graduation present, messily wrapped in Christmas paper. He sat with it on his knee the whole flight across the country, telling me the story about Siddhartha's quest and the ferryman and the disappointment of riches. Pop said he'd wanted to name me Kamala, after Siddhartha's great love, but Mom shot it down. When our plane landed at LaGuardia, the pilot came over the loudspeaker. "Welcome to New York," he said. "And if this is home, welcome home." Pop thought that was about the funniest thing he'd ever heard. He'd repeat it for years, whenever we walked into the house together.

At Willy's graduation, after we listened to what seemed like three thousand hours of names being called, we fought through the crowd to find him. Willy blinked at Pop, taking a full minute to recognize him, then said "No, thank you" to the presentation of *Siddhartha*. Pop grabbed me by the shoulders and held me out like I was a replacement gift, one Willy couldn't refuse. "This is your sister," he said. "This is Kyra. Your little sister."

Willy knelt down so we'd be face-to-face. Looking back, I think that was very adult of him. He had dark eyes just like Pop's, but without that electric energy. "Hi," Willy said. "Don't worry, this isn't your fault." If Willy was that mature at eighteen, what must he be like at twenty-nine? Maybe I should call Marianne and see if she has his contact information.

Lucia, Pop's original (as far as I know) wife, told Pop he wasn't invited to lunch with them or to the party. "You should have told us you were coming," she said. "We would have told you not to." Pop tried to give the novel to her, but she said, "He already told you, he doesn't want it."

On the plane home Pop drank half a dozen mini bottles of scotch and did a little ranting about literature and life. I tried to listen as hard as I could, but I was only eight years old. We got back to Modesto past midnight, Pop barely able to get from the cab to the house. I had to take the key from his hand to open the front door. Pop threw our luggage down in the front hallway and said, "If this is home, welcome home." He handed *Siddhartha* to me, maybe as a present, or maybe just to get rid of it. I still have it, wrapped in its snowman paper, somewhere in my room.

"I don't want to go to the memorial," I told my mother last night, jutting my chin toward the typewriter, my hands in position on its keyboard. "This is my memorial."

"Dear Kyra. By now you've figured out your pop is not a *Father Knows Best* kind of guy."

That's as far as I got, three years ago, reading his letter. In the midst of putting his book together, I figured I'd give it another try but didn't get much farther before the doorbell interrupted me. It was Charlie #2, with puffy eyes like he'd been crying.

"Can I come in?" he said, without introducing himself. I was glad. I didn't want to know his real name. The original Charlie would be around eleven by now. I wondered where he was, and how screwed up. He'd been a sweet kid, but you don't get through something like that without getting ruined.

Charlie #2 walked bent at the waist, ducking, like he didn't want to be seen through the windows. "Are your parents home?" he asked.

"My mom's at work." Since Pop wouldn't have been here even if he were alive, it didn't seem relevant to say that he'd died. "Is everything okay?"

"You know those kids?" He gestured to the wide window over the sink.

I walked a few steps and peered through the glass at Connor Klam, from three houses over, and his little brother, whose name I couldn't remember. I used to babysit for them back when I still babysat.

"Yes," I said. "Are they bothering you?" I didn't want to say that he was actually bothering me as I tried to put together my thoughts on this intro, having reread "Disappearing Father" and succumbing to a rage that burned every edge of my skin. It was hot for June in Modesto, closing in on eighty-five, and we didn't have air conditioning. Mom said she was going to sue Pop's estate for alimony and to pay for my college. Maybe she'd install central air, too. All the things she couldn't get Pop to do while he was living. Marianne was a less formidable opponent, she said, because her feelings toward her were less complicated, or as she put it, "pure hatred."

"You mean you still have love for Pop?" This was news to me.

"Maybe I'll have love for Marianne, too," Mom said. "When she dies."

Whatever settlement Mom would be able to make with Pop's estate, we didn't have air conditioning yet, and Charlie #2 seemed disappointed by the lack of relief our kitchen provided. I'm sure the inside of his house hums at a constant sixty-eight degrees. "I got locked out again," he said, like he knew I'd seen him locked out before. "They keep offering me cigarettes. Those kids. They say if I don't smoke with them, I'm a pussy." He pointed as he spoke, but toward the floor, like the mere thought of nicotine had destroyed his sense of direction. "Do you think they would hit me?"

"For not smoking?" I took another peek out the window. Connor, about the same age as Charlie #2, was pre-growth-spurt pudgy, with too-long hair. Last time I'd seen him at the corner store, he'd smelled like clove cigarettes and prepubescent sweat. Charlie #2 was already taller than me, slim but not scrawny, muscles and veins on his arms. I thought he might be misinterpreting a twisted offer of friendship, but I didn't want to say so. "You're a lot bigger than them, you know."

Charlie #2 straightened at the waist, as if this hadn't occurred to him. He stopped just short of the window, peering out as if measuring himself against the other two boys.

"You could take them for sure," I said.

"I don't want to take them."

"Then maybe you should remember your key." I opened the window for the breeze, and the scent of mariposa wafted in, along with a stray butterfly. Charlie #2 and I chased it through the house with a plastic cup until we caught it, then opened the back door to let it out. It swirled into the bright blue sky uncomfortably, like it had never learned to manage wind currents.

Back in the kitchen I showed Charlie #2 how to make simple syrup, then dug out the juicer so we could make lemonade. I picked some mint from Pop's garden; it still grew along with all the basil and thistle and dandelions.

"Did you know the family who used to live in our house?" Charlie #2 asked, top lip glossy with lemon juice, along with the faintest shadow of fuzz. He had a pointed face and very clear, almost translucent skin. A gangly little kid, younger than his own body. Nobody had ever lived in his house, brand new and glistening, windows too clean, the sycamore tree cut down to make room for a bigger floor plan.

"Not really," I told him.

In "Forgotten Son" Pop compares John Lennon's relationships with his two sons, Julian and Sean. If you ask me, the essay is pretty presumptuous, cobbled together from song lyrics and interviews. If he'd wanted to make it more personal, he—Pop, Broder—could have tried talking about his own children. Maybe that would have provided a little self-reflection—much needed. Or maybe he'd made it more personal in his original draft, then decided to cut it all out—merciless—in his second.

I did something with the essay that I haven't done yet with any of Pop's writing, not even that stupid good-bye letter. I ripped it in half. Then I burned it in the fireplace. It was another warm day, but I leaned in close. The sweat dripping off my forehead made me feel like all this was having an effect, exacting a change. "The power of late-life metamorphosis," Pop wrote in the essay now swirling up into ash through our chimney.

I had to find Mom's address book because I didn't know my own father's number by heart. I punched it in with one angry finger, each digit beeping short and furious.

"Hello, Marianne?" I said. "This is Kyra. I'd like Willy's contact information, please." Marianne tried to pull me into commiseration, her weepy, grief-stricken voice longing to say the same thing over and over till it began to sound like sense. But I wasn't having it. Pop wrote, "Once Lennon sowed his oats, achieved his glory, he could finally settle down and concentrate on grown-up matters. On family. We forget he was barely more than a teenager when Beatlemania struck his life like lightning."

Pop was fifty-two the day he ran off with Marianne. On his answering machine, Willy sounded like him. "Nowhere is family more evident than in the timbre of a person's voice," Pop wrote, comparing John and Julian's singing.

"Hey, Willy," I said after the beep. "It's Kyra Broder. Your sister? I was wondering what your plans were as far as going to Pop's memorial service. Dad's memorial service. Frank Broder's." I left our number, and as soon as I hung up, I had this horrifying feeling, like what if Marianne hadn't thought to call Willy, and my message was the first time he heard Pop had died?

I came home from the library, driving with the Mustang's top down, to see Charlie #2 standing on his front lawn with Connor. His spine was very straight, and I could see he'd taken what I said to heart, recognizing himself as a good head taller than Connor. I sat in the driveway, heat pulsing through the windshield, spring moving into summer with a film of invisible insects. In just a couple of months I'd be at Berkeley, the air cool with fog. It didn't seem real.

The boys looked over at me, but neither of them waved. I watched to make sure the interaction was voluntary. Sun flattened behind a cloud, and I could see they were cupping some kind of cigarette, passing it back and forth. Maybe I would have said something, but from inside our phone started to ring. We don't have an answering machine, so I ran inside without putting the top up.

"Hello," I said, breathless, just as the other person hung up. It was Willy. I knew it in my bones, his breath through the wire crackling like someone calling from all the way across the country, a sound and sense of Pop even in the careful placement of the receiver.

Through the window over the sink I could see the boys migrating toward our house, like they were checking out the Mustang. At the Stanislaus County Library, I'd spent two hours skimming through a copy of *No One Here Gets Out Alive*, a biography of Jim Morrison whose introduction states flat out that he was a god. I like to think a god would be better behaved, wouldn't claim to be orphaned when his parents were in fact alive and well.

When I went outside to put my car's top up, the boys didn't bother to hide their cigarette anymore, just sat on the curb, passing it back and forth. I thought I could smell the clove scent, which seemed more harmless than other options, but still. The year Pop left was a wasted one for me, hand-rolled joints on my lips, fingers up my skirt, classes missed.

The weather changed suddenly, with descending mist and a rumble of thunder. "You should go inside," I called to Charlie #2 in my best babysitter voice, but he just squinted, then shrugged. Connor did the same, like neither of them remembered who I was.

In "Dead to Me" Pop—Frank Broder—writes about Cat Stevens converting to Islam in a way that starts off like a condemnation but ends up making him into a kind of hero for doing exactly what he wanted, not listening to society, etc., etc., etc. It's a pretty clever structure whether you agree with the central theme or not.

Mom got home from work on Wednesday and barged into the study without knocking. She cranked the window open, mumbling about it being hot and musty, then pressed a hundred-dollar bill into my hand.

"Get something to wear to the service," she said. "It doesn't have to be black. Just respectful."

"I told you I don't want to go."

"I want to go. And I'm not going to let you skip your father's funeral," she said. "You might regret it your whole life."

Obediently, I went to Ann Taylor and bought a black pencil skirt and a filmy black top with tiny beige flowers. Respectful but not funereal. Mom wanted to take her Chrysler on the road trip, but

I made a plea for the Mustang. "We can cut over to the Pacific Coast Highway," I said. "Drive the whole way with the top down. It's what Pop would have done."

"No," Mom said, throwing her suitcase into the trunk of the Mustang anyway. "It's what he'd say he'd do. Then he'd get cold and put the top up. Or get stoned and sleep in the back, with the top up, because the wind gave him a headache."

Mom and me, though. We drove with the top down, wind in our hair, the Pacific Ocean stretching out for miles to the west of us, precarious gray rocks steep and gleaming with sea spray.

"What you remember in later years seldom seems significant at the time," Broder writes in "The Case for *Let it Be*." Marianne insisted on calling the funeral a "celebration of life," which Mom and I agreed Pop would have hated. There was a service at the Unitarian church and then a reception at Pop and Marianne's house. Maybe in a few years, when I look back, what I'll mostly remember is talking to Jack Nicholson about the grossness of maraschino cherries, or shaking John Updike's hand, or letting Marianne hug me and sob into my shoulder. Sooner than that it may be important that I talked to the editor who signed Pop's collection. When I told him I was working on putting it all together, he seemed genuinely interested. And maybe I'll remember a single word of one of the eulogies, all by famous people I'd never heard of before.

There were lots of framed photos in the house, of Marianne's kids, and Pop and Marianne, and their little Yorkshire terrier, but not a single one of me. I went upstairs through the bedrooms, and the hallway, the little dog following me like I was its best bet for food. More pictures but still no me. It was easy to find Pop's study in the finished basement, crowded with books and boxes of paper and an Electrolux typewriter. No word processor, but at least he'd graduated to electric typing. His desk was crowded with books and papers. On a crowded shelf there was one framed picture: of Pop, standing in a swimming pool, holding a little boy parallel to the water. Holding him tight, not letting go, squinting against the splash, both of them smiling, maybe even laughing.

I sat down on a futon draped with a red-and-black Indian rug. The dog hopped into my lap and I petted its head. By the time Pop came back into my life the first time, I already knew how to swim.

A man who could only be Willy—looking a little like Pop, a little like the eighteen-year-old boy I'd met eleven years ago—appeared in the doorway.

"Kyra?" he said after a moment of examining my face.

"Willy," I said, not making it a question. The dog licked my chin. I petted it again.

"I go by Bill now."

I pointed to the picture. "You made it. I didn't."

Willy had long legs. He crossed the room in two strides and picked up the frame. "You know," he said, "I'm not entirely sure this is me." I couldn't tell if he was joking or telling a kind fib. He put it facedown on the shelf and sat next to me. "Are you okay?"

"Yeah," I said. "I think so. You?"

"Yeah," he said, his voice like Pop's but not his inflections. I knew what he was going to say, but inside I prayed he wouldn't. It was just too expected: "I guess for me he died a long time ago."

"Sometimes," Frank Broder writes in "The Pointed Forest: Oblio and Arrow Arrive Where We Knew They Were Headed All Along," "a cliché is the only thing that brings you to the precise truth."

"For me, too," I said. We sat there a long time, both of us trying to think of something else to say.

Finally it was Willy—Bill, I might as well call him what he wants to be called—who spoke. "I guess neither of us knew him very well," he said.

"No," I agreed. "I guess not."

*

Mom and I got back to Modesto on Sunday at the golden hour, streets drenched with blond light and halos of dusk. When I pulled into our driveway, Charlie #2 and his new friends were in the side yard, playing cornhole with bottles of beer in one hand, like they were suburban dads at a barbecue instead of kids. If the old house had never exploded, if his parents were alive and all of them lived next door, would the original Charlie have been similarly corrupted? It startled me to realize I couldn't remember his face. When I tried to picture it, I saw only this new Charlie, with his pointed features and gangly limbs.

"Brazen," Mom said, running a hand through her disarrayed hair. For a moment I thought she'd go over and scold them, take their beers away, but she had already averted her gaze to our front door.

"If this is home, welcome home," I said.

She looked at me, a funny sideways glance, and I realized she'd never heard this before. It had been a private joke between Pop and me. Just moments earlier, when we'd approached the house, a trick of light had occurred. A mirage of rain in the clear, warm evening. Mist gathering—like the way Avalon used to disappear from sight, leaving only a shimmer. As we drove down our same old street, there was a gap in the houses where ours should have been. One brief second, a stunning absence, a hole in the universe.

And then the light shifted back, the golden mist lifted. The house reappearing as if it had never left at all.

Rabbit

Owen King

August 1999

JACKSON'S, WHERE HE KNEW THE GLASSES WERE CLEAN, AND WHICH was right around the corner from the *Post*'s office, was the place Kline normally preferred to meet sources. However, the bodyguard would have attracted notice. Even the most soused of his fellow reporters at the bar would have taken a second look at a six-foot, eight-inch man with bodybuilder proportions. Kline chose instead a restaurant way up in the east nineties called Delta Kitchen for their lunch appointment. While it wasn't Kline's sort of spot at all—they garnished the shit out of the food, so that you practically needed a sniffer dog to find your actual meal, and there was only beer, no mixed drinks—he couldn't imagine that it was any other self-respecting newspaperman's either. The only reason Kline knew about the Delta Kitchen was because Maria, a girl he'd been seeing, had told him she'd once seen Yankee Jim Leyritz there. This had made an impression on Kline. He was a serious Yankees fan.

Conrad was the bodyguard's name. His massive upper body appeared to have sprouted his head. He wore an acre of black suit.

"You know who comes here? Jim Leyritz," Kline said to him after they'd sat down.

The bodyguard glanced from the menu he'd been grimly studying. It was a xeroxed, pamphlet-style menu, and in his huge hands it looked like a Post-it note would have looked in Kline's.

"I don't know who that is."

Kline was a baseball evangelist. He didn't believe in much, and he certainly wasn't a religious man, but he was devoutly confident that inside every person was a baseball fan waiting to receive the good news. "Jim Leyritz is a Yankee. Very important figure."

"Good for him."

"He's not a star, but he's hit a ton of big-game home runs. Mostly a catcher, but he's a Swiss Army–knife type. This current Yankees revival, Jeter and Mariano and Bernie are obviously the centerpieces, but Leyritz's homer off Wohlers in the ninety-six Series, you can make a compelling argument that's the start of it all. He's bounced around a little bit, but now he's back with the Yanks. Real New York guy. If you saw him, you'd know what I mean. Cock of the walk." Kline tilted to two o'clock in his seat and wiggled an invisible baseball bat, imitating Leyritz's batting stance.

They were at a corner table, the farthest from the street, which Kline had chosen on the assumption that it was the one that Leyritz must have taken.

Conrad glanced down again at the menu. Light from the hanging fixtures reflected off his bald head. "Yeah. I don't follow baseball."

"I bet you'd like it," Kline said.

His dining companion frowned at the paper menu. He was really examining the shit out of the thing, little suspecting that he might just as well have brought his own paper sack filled with parsley, because that was what he was going to get. "We just met. You don't know anything about me."

"Just a feeling," Kline said.

They ordered. Once they had their drinks and the waitress had left them, Conrad crossed his arms and stared, unsmiling, at Kline.

Kline wasn't intimidated. He was the one footing the bill. It would be Kline deciding if the bodyguard had any information of value.

Conrad's employer was Mort Spear, the real estate mogul. Morton Spear, who ran around town stamping his name on anything that had a door, all the while nurturing a national reputation for being everyone's favorite rich asshole, marrying and divorcing models, appearing in jokey commercials for Diners Club, and publishing ghostwritten books about building a successful business. Most significantly, Spear had recently fucked Peter Kline over, and recompense was due. Money wasn't the issue, although Spear had cost him money. The issue was the disrespect. Kline didn't at all appreciate being brushed off, treated like somebody who had just wandered in off the street.

He kept repairmen at several of the better apartment buildings around the city on retainer, and in exchange for a small finder's fee, one that worked at Spear Tower had set him up with this Conrad. Spear was on his third marriage, so ideally, the bodyguard had a tip-off about the guy's dick falling out of its zipper.

"So: the hair. Any of it real?" Spear was ugly with a pebbly, lumpy face, but his most noticeable feature was his hair, which was the toxic yellow of Orangina and cupped his skull in a frozen helmet.

"I've never see the man take it off, but"—the bodyguard lightly flipped one of his hands up—"I don't think so. There's a sheen to it."

"You mean like a doll's hair?" Without waiting for an answer, Kline slipped his notebook out from inside his jacket and jotted "doll's hair."

"What the fuck are you doing?"

Kline held up the notebook for the other man to see.

"I didn't say that, you said that."

Kline set his pen and notebook on the table. "Do you want to do this?"

The other man flipped his hand again. In Kline's opinion it was an awfully sassy gesture for such a large person to make.

"Do I? What's in this for me?"

Their food arrived, the respective portions hemmed in on all sides by roughage. Kline fished his hamburger out of the mess and took a bite—overcooked. Conrad didn't touch his salmon, maintaining his arms-crossed position. It was evident that he didn't understand the rules of tabloid economics. Kline began to explain:

"Listen, if what you're getting at is money, I obviously can't pay you. I wish I could, but that would be unethical. Okay?"

Conrad shook his head. "What the hell am I doing here, then?"

"What you're doing here, I hope, is helping me to enhance the public's knowledge, to reveal the truth of what goes on behind a very powerful person's closed doors. And that's a very exciting thing. How exciting?

"Let tell you something about myself: Sometimes I get so excited about a great story, I forget things. It's my journalist's nature. Even cash I forget sometimes, believe it or not, that's how excited a good story can make me. I put my money down somewhere and I wander off, and then I realize what I've done, go back, and damn, it's gone. It's a bad habit, but that's the thrill of a great story."

"Oh." The bodyguard had come around. "So . . . How much cash do you forget?"

"Hundred here, two hundred there. Every once in a great while, I forget five hundred dollars."

"Ever forget a thousand?"

"Not too often, but I have."

"How'd that happen?"

"Well. Let's see. There was an occasion when I heard a story about a famous actor who did gay porn. I was so wound up about that, I misplaced two thousand dollars that day." Kline paused to let that sink in before tacking on the crucial caveat. "That was special, though, because the person who told me, she had a videotape and everything. I'm certain that I wouldn't have misplaced that much money if it wasn't such a convincing, provable story."

The bodyguard's frown broke, and he said all right and relaxed forward in his seat. A few more overcooked bites led Kline to give up on his hamburger. How dare they serve this shit to Jim Leyritz!

Conrad forked his way through the fish and everything else on the plate, right down to the celery leaves.

"All right." Kline picked up his notebook. "Mort Spear. What would people be surprised to learn about him? He faithful to his marriage vows?"

The bodyguard's smile was green flecked. "I don't know about his marriage, but are you ready for this? Spear never wears the same tie twice."

Kline asked him if he was serious.

Conrad chuckled and said he was—never the same necktie twice.

"You great big fucking asshole," Kline said. "That's nothing! No one cares about ties!" He hollered to the waitress and demanded separate checks.

The bodyguard lurched after him to the subway entrance to the 4-5-6, apologetic and breathless. It was dourly satisfying to Kline that Conrad's height and girth had been exposed as an idle threat; he could barely keep up with a reporter in his fifties. The only thing he'd be able to protect Mort Spear from was a rack of ribs.

"I only work the lobby, but I know I can get you something that'll make you forgetful! I promise!" the bodyguard cried as the reporter descended the steps. The words followed Kline into the underground.

2.

Long before he became a *New York Post* feature writer specializing in celebrity profiles, as a sophomore at NYU in the midsixties, Peter Kline staked out a prime position in the basement gym of Main Building to watch intramural girls' volleyball games. He stationed himself on the second bench of the wooden bleachers, right behind where the players sat. From there, twenty-four-year-old Peter Kline had an unobstructed view of the athletic buttocks of all six players on the near team. At the end of each set, teams switched sides of the net, and six fresh asses were arrayed for his viewing pleasure. It was the perfect system.

Saddle Brook–born, the son of a truck driver, Kline had spent four tedious, sniffling years at an army base in Oregon following high school, plagued by leaf mold and manning a teletype machine. After his discharge he had arrived at NYU intending to major in engineering and minor in having sex with hippies, and had been frustrated in both ambitions. He was a C student in his classes, and a spurious campus rumor—probably generated by his regulation brush cut—that he was an FBI plant had poisoned his reputation.

All that had gone right since Kline's arrival at NYU was the discovery of the basement gymnasium, which he had randomly stumbled upon while searching for a water fountain. It was there, on the chipped hardwood of an old basketball court sandwiched between water-stained brick walls, that girls wearing shorts gathered on Thursday evenings to play volleyball. Kline became a dedicated fan, mesmerized by the sight of so much bouncing woman.

This was a decade or so before women's team sports really caught on, but there was a growing interest, and attendance for the games swelled over the winter months of that year, peaking as the teams played in a tournament that they'd organized themselves. By the time of the league's championship game, the gymnasium was packed to the rafters.

Kline made sure to arrive early, though, keen to keep his superior second-row seat from being stolen by some Johnny-come-lately. He sat with his legs comfortably apart and his elbows propped wide to establish a perimeter, and ignored the jostling of his bandwagon neighbors.

But then Kline made an observation that would change his life; he saw that there was, in fact, a vantage even closer than the row behind the bench.

At the very edge of the court, a photographer, a fat guy in a jean jacket, was crouched down snapping pictures. The guy was near enough to the action to lean forward and brush his fingers down a bare calf. Then, between sets, the lucky photographer thumped onto the bench among the players—among the women in shorts and sweat-dampened T-shirts—and sat chatting and laughing with them. A printed card hung on a string around the photographer's neck and identified him as a reporter for the *Washington Square Bulletin*.

Kline never graduated from NYU.

By the time he moved out of his dorm and into an apartment in Fort Greene, he had an overnight shift at the *Daily News*, plugged into a switchboard and transcribing stories for reporters based overseas. Before long they gave him a crime beat, and he remained there for the better part of twenty years. The time passed amiably; he drank Irish coffee and played rummy with cops, wrote up stories on subway flashers and Bowery drug dens. Kline delighted in the access he gained by virtue of his press pass, and gratified by the leeway he earned from allowing officers to edit the stories he wrote about their cases before sending the pages on to the copy desk. Kline liked writing all right, and he appreciated the clap on the back that came with the publication of a splashy story, but the real pleasure of the job was how people let you inside, gave you a seat right on the bench, let you smell their sweat, let you ride along like an official member of the crew. Peter Kline could walk right into any precinct on the Lower East Side and sit down at a free desk in the bullpen and no one batted an eye.

Still, by the mideighties he was ready for a change. Though he was by no means a fastidious man, the proximity to so many murder scenes started to interfere with his peace of mind. He'd be at a Yankees game, enjoying Righetti and a cold Bud, and the first base coach for the White Sox would look like the corpse of a Leggio family bookie that had been discovered in the trunk of a LeBaron at JFK.

That was when he jumped to the *Post*. Originally angling for the Yankees clubhouse gig—a guy could dream, couldn't he?—he settled for the position in features. He'd made his home there since, profiling the shiny types, actors and actresses, models and musicians, debut authors and up-and-coming artists. It was even better than cops. Where he'd had license to stroll through the precinct gates, now he had free rein to attend after-hours cocktail parties at the Met along with Norman Mailer and Al Pacino, to eat at private dinner parties at Balthazar with Robert Altman and Meryl Streep. Kline was on the inside.

3.

As soon as he was at his desk at the *Post*, Kline called the repairman who had referred the bodyguard and informed him that he wanted his fifty dollars returned.

Next he took a call from his older sister. Lisa was a divorced paralegal. She lived in Astoria, just beyond the cursed shadow of Shea Stadium. She wanted him to talk to Neil, his nephew, because Neil said if she didn't take the stray rabbit he'd found in Harlem, he was giving it to a shelter. "Why is this my problem? He's holding this rabbit's well-being over my head," Lisa said.

What the hell were rabbits doing running wild on the streets of Harlem? He made her repeat the story and she told it the same.

"Jesus Christ."

"I know, I know," she replied.

Kline said he'd speak with Neil. While he didn't give a fair fart about rabbits—typical Lisa, wasting energy on a quasi rodent—it was wrong of his nephew to be playing on Lisa's neuroses.

Neil was a peculiar one. He had been a violin prodigy, but he'd been in a chance accident. While he was looking through some shirts on the markdown rack at a Gap, a wall-size mirror had suddenly fallen and shattered on him. This sounded awful until you found out that somehow Neil hadn't suffered so much as a cut from the glass. It had broken harmlessly against his body. Since then, the way Lisa told it, he'd moped around and lived off the settlement. It seemed spiteful to Kline. His nephew could do anything he wanted, go anywhere he wanted, and instead he roosted on his (one assumed) giant pile of Gap money and worried his mother with this manipulative rabbit thing.

His nephew's machine was out of space, so he couldn't leave a message.

He dialed Maria, the girl he'd been seeing, and got her machine, too, but at least she had some tape left. "Kline again. Did you go out of town or something? Call me, I'll tell you about my sister's kid. You won't believe this. There's a rabbit involved."

The phone rang as soon as he hung up, the moronic bodyguard to apologize again and insist that he was going to come through. Kline told him the apology was not accepted and hung up.

Kline went to use the bathroom and noticed that the women's restroom was marked off for some kind of repair work. He went into the men's, had his piss, went back out, and slipped under the tape blocking the women's to see what it was like in there. A couple of Latin guys were chipping off wall tile, and another guy had the floor opened up under one of the sinks. The restroom really didn't look any different from the men's, except no urinals and two more stalls, which made sense. It did smell slightly better than the men's, but not a lot better, not as much as he'd expected. Mostly it smelled like plaster dust.

"What are you doing here?" one of the Latin guys asked.

"I work here," Kline said. "I have a natural curiosity. I like to know what's going on."

"Nothing's going on except for tiling and checking the fittings."

"You do a lot of jobs on women's bathrooms?"

The chippers looked at each other. "Some," the more talkative one answered.

"That's interesting. I thought it would be nicer."

"No, man. Every bathroom is gross." All the workers nodded.

Kline perched on a sink and prompted them on Morton Spear. What did they think of him?

They'd heard he was a chiseler; you had to sue the dink to get him to pay for a lightbulb. Kline had heard that too, and personal experience had confirmed it. One guy thought he was mobbed up. That was another thing Kline had heard whispered, that Spear buildings cleaned money for some of the families. Supposedly, Adolfo Leggio himself had been a silent partner in the new Spear World Casino. Kline asked if they'd ever noticed Spear's ties. They said they never noticed anybody's tie unless it was crazy, flamingos or something. "Right," Kline said.

All the men were impressed that such a weird-looking man could get laid by so many beautiful women.

"Money," Kline pronounced, and they agreed.

The back-and-forth cheered him. He took pride in his ability to make himself comfortable in any kind of group. It was also reassuring, after the disappointment of the bodyguard, to know that other people were onto Spear, the chiseling fucker. If Kline could get something on him, they'd be pleased to hear it.

"Go Yanks," he said to the men as he was leaving.

"Yankees!" they replied in a chorus.

Kline cabbed to a roundtable at NBC for the cast of *Frasier*, the sitcom that centered on the radio shrink. Afterward he cut Kelsey Grammer, the show's star, from the herd and asked him his favorite Yankee. Grammer chuckled. "That's one hell of a question, Pete. I mean, it's dreadfully difficult to select just one, this is a superb team, and every part is an essential cog in the machine. But you say I have no choice, I've got to pick one? All right, very well, damn you! It's got to be Jeter." They shared a laugh, and the NBC publicist kneed Kline in the thigh as she rushed over and swept the star from the room.

He returned to the office and wrote up his *Frasier* piece. The Jeter bit was his lead, the rest of it deftly turning on the idea that Grammer was the star of the show the way that the handsome shortstop was the star of the Yankees.

For an early dinner he ordered in Chinese. While he ate General Tso's, he spoke with his agent, who had been bandying Kline's book proposal for an oral history of an infamous young novelist. The young novelist was a bull's-eye-pupiled fixture on the society pages who had written a novel about shitty college kids that had been made into a movie starring Andrew McCarthy. The proposal seemed to be going nowhere. Kline should have known better than to bet on something as dull as a novelist. It didn't matter how degenerate or horny the guy was, he still plunked a keyboard for a living.

This was the second proposal in a row that had fizzled. Kline's previous proposal had been an oral history of none other than Morton Spear. Over a lunch at Elaine's, Spear had initially been very positive and buddy-buddy with him on the idea. A few days later, without a word of warning, he had unleashed his lawyers and scared all the publishing houses off. This was why Kline felt motivated to obtain some revenge dirt on the cretin.

"What do you think of Frasier?" he asked.

"Good show," said his agent.

"No, the actor. Kelsey Grammer."

His agent said, "You know . . . ," but told him not to write anything for the time being. He'd put out some feelers and see if the market might bear it.

4.

Neil buzzed Kline up to the apartment on 137th. His nephew was in baggy purple pajama pants when he opened the door. Kline stepped into the short hall of the railroad and told the younger man to get dressed; they were going to Yankee Stadium.

"Uncle Pete, you do know I'm a Mets fan?"

Kline pursed his lips and stared at his nephew. Neil looked like he'd been in solitary for a while; his pavement-gray skin was seeded with patchy black beard.

"What?" asked Neil.

"Don't start with me about the Goddamn Mets," Kline said.

With a sigh and a shake of his head, Neil said he'd be a few minutes and walked to the bedroom.

Kline took the measure of his nephew's dim living room. A cheaply framed poster for an opera hung on the wall. There was no television and a turned-off computer on the kitchen table. The rabbit was in a cage on the floor, nestled in wood shavings. Kline wondered if Neil masturbated in front of the rabbit.

He bent down and put his finger through the gridding, but the rabbit blinked and shied away, shuffling deeper into its bed of shavings.

On the train his nephew explained how he'd found the rabbit out on the street, huddled behind a trash can, and felt obligated to take it in before it got run over. Neil hadn't wanted the animal in the first place, and he didn't believe he should have to care for it indefinitely. "I never should have mentioned it to Mom. I just said, 'Unless you want it, I'm going to bring it to the shelter.'"

That made sense; Lisa tended to insert herself into situations. In his school days she'd tried to get guys that gave Kline trouble to back off, which never failed to make it worse.

"Why are you living with the shades drawn like that, though? You've got money from the Gap, don't you?"

"Come on, Uncle Pete. I can live how I want to. I'm not hurting anybody."

"What about the violin?"

"I didn't love it."

"Okay, I understand. But what do you love?"

Neil grinned at him. "The Mets." Kline had to give him the point, and they shared a laugh.

The two teams exchanged runs early on. Pettitte seemed shaky, but New York led 3–2 going into the fourth.

"You know how you love reporting, Uncle Pete? How you love, like, tearing open some story? If I ever had that for the violin, I lost it."

"You don't become a reporter for fame and fortune," Kline said. "That's for sure. Not if you want to be any good, certainly. You have to have a passion for the truth. Right now I'm working on a thing about Morton Spear."

Neil raised his eyebrows in an impressed expression. "He seems like an egotist, the way he puts his name on everything."

"Not the kind of person you'd ever want to be associated with," Kline said. "Unscrupulous. There are a lot of dark rumors. I'm talking to someone who's close to him, so we'll see."

Bernie came up with the key hit in the sixth, his twenty-second homer, and the Yankees went on to bury the Mariners, 11–5. Leyritz played third and went 0 for 4. "It's funny, we run in some of the same circles," he explained to Neil. "So I root extra hard for him."

They each had four or five beers. Kline enjoyed his nephew's company. Neil's imitation of the announcer, Bob Sheppard, was spot-on: "Der-ick Jeet-ahr." He thanked Kline for the ticket and for getting him out of the house, admitting that he'd been blue lately. "Well, for the last two years, really. It made me jumpy, what happened."

Kline patted his nephew's shoulder.

Neil drank down his beer. His chapped lips were wet as he stared into Kline's eyes. "It was like, 'Am I still here?' There's mirror glass all around me, and it's dead silence, and I'm in my body, but at the same time I also can't believe in my body. For a few seconds it was like, 'I must be a ghost.'"

Kline gave his nephew another pat. "You're here, you're alive."

"I know, I know, but I still go back there to that feeling every once in a while. You've heard of PTSD, haven't you? It's when . . ."

Kline began to ponder what they might do the next time. It would be no problem to sneak the kid into a film premiere. . . .

Neil, obviously drunk in the bottom of the eighth, had abruptly confessed that he thought the *New York Post* was a heartless right-wing rag and it made it hard for him to respect Kline. Kline told him that was fine, but when they were leaving the ballpark and Neil begged off from a postgame drink, he changed his mind. Where did he get off? What did he have to be so self-important about?

The kid lived with a rabbit. He'd never done anything except have a mirror fall on him.

"Some people have to work for a living, you know," he said to his nephew.

"I thought we had a good time." Neil sniffled. The crowd on the concourse poured around them. "Your team won."

"You break your mother's heart." Kline drove a finger into his nephew's chest. "You've been whining about this mirror thing too long. You weren't even injured. You need to pull yourself together."

Neil gasped like he'd been slapped, and stormed off.

5.

At home in his own apartment on the Upper West, Kline left a message on Maria's machine to see if they could meet. He'd been having a hard time reaching her lately, but he hoped she around and felt like getting together. Morton Spear, who looked like Andy Warhol's mongoloid brother, could probably arrange a blow job at any hour of any day.

His phone rang a couple of seconds later.

"Kline."

A man with a weary voice: "Peter Kline?"

"Yeah. Who is this?"

"This is a friend of Maria's. She wants you to stop calling."

Kline laughed. He wasn't falling for that one. "Ok, pal. If she tells me that's one thing, but I'm not taking your word for it."

There was a muffled exchange.

"Please stop calling me," Maria said, coming on to the line. "We went out on two dates and you've left me twenty messages in the last month. If I was interested, I'd have called back, you know? You never shut up about baseball and it's boring. Sorry. Goodbye."

The man came back on. "There you go, champ. Now you know."

"What's your name?" Kline asked. His heartrate had picked up and his voice came out half-strangled. "Tell me your name. I want to know your name."

The guy groaned. "My name is 'Stop-Calling-Maria,' man, or else I'm going to lose my temper. I know where to find you and if this phone rings again, I'm coming over, and I'm not in the mood. Understand?"

Kline hung up the phone. He breathed until his heartrate settled. It occurred to him that the Leyritz story was a lie. She'd made it up to impress him. Jim Leyritz wouldn't eat at a place like that. Jim Leyritz wouldn't eat at a place where someone like her went. Fuck her, the fucking liar.

He got up and went back outside.

He poked his head into a bodega down the block from his building. The two old guys were watching a replay of the Yankees game on the television tucked in the corner. Kline got a Budweiser from the cooler, paid for it, and asked the men how they were. One of the old men shrugged. "Eh." The other old man wore a hat and had melanoma on his bottom lip.

Kline leaned over the counter to see the TV better. Bernie was up. "Get ready for it," he told them. Neither of the men responded. Bernie hit his home run. "What'd I tell you?" he said, and they didn't say anything to that, either. He came in here all the time. "I went to the game with my nephew," he said, insisting on acknowledgment. One of the men turned to him and nodded, and smiled, and that satisfied Kline.

Out on the street he drank from his bagged beer and stared down an alley to see if there were any rabbits. He looked under a few cars. He peered into the window of a darkened clothing boutique where a mannequin in a frosted-pink sweater jutted her hip, and wished for the glass to fall outward and break over his body like water. But it didn't happen and he went home, finished his beer in the elevator.

6.

Two days later Kline submitted to a second meeting with Conrad, the bodyguard from Spear Tower. Instead of the Delta Kitchen, they reconvened at the top of the stairs to the subway stop where Kline had ditched him the first time. He didn't expect the bodyguard to have anything meaningful and wasn't about to feed the lug for nothing.

Conrad stood on the corner, sunglasses shimmering atop his bald head, a plastic bag dangling from his hand. "Mr. Kline!" He thrust the bag at him.

Kline accepted the bag and opened it, shifting the handles to inspect the contents. Traffic streamed along Lex.

"They sent me up to carry some luggage down, and I said I had to use the bathroom. I grabbed that out of the can and stuffed it under my coat."

It was Morton Spear's bathroom trash: a Q-tip with a crusted dollop of ocher-colored wax, a length of floss, some crumpled tissues, a *Vanity Fair*, and a prescription tube, flattened and emptied of its contents. Kline manipulated the bag to get a better look at the tube—it was for hemorrhoids, extra strength!

"All right."

While Conrad watched, Kline took three fifty dollar bills from his wallet and slipped them into an envelope. Then he asked Conrad to follow him to a pay phone. Kline placed the envelope on top of the phone box. He took the phone from the hook, listened to the dial tone, nodded to himself, and glanced all the way around. No one was watching them, no one was passing nearby, the traffic on the street was moving steadily. He hung the phone back up.

"See you later," he told Conrad, and walked away, the envelope forgotten.

Back at the office, he screened yet another call from his sister and wrote up a shorty for Page Six. "What real estate titan whose name is on everyone's lips rolled snake eyes at a recent medical exam? His hemorrhoids are causing him tremendous problems. Sad!"

Kline handed it on and retired to Jackson's with the soiled *Vanity Fair* and rewarded himself with a Jameson.

On the last page of an article about Anthony Hopkins's tailor, there was writing in the margin: "8/24 Leggio, Six million, Swiss XR 3993 8380 0044 0782 1."

Kline ordered a second Jameson to keep him company while he figured his next move.

7.

There was someone in service at the tower, Kline informed Spear's lawyer—maybe a maid, maybe a bodyguard—spreading rumors about Morton and the Leggio family. "Something about a Swiss bank account is one of the things I heard. Bullshit, obviously, we both know that Morton is a stickler for doing business on the up-and-up, but he's also a big name and that makes him unfairly vulnerable."

The lawyer thanked him. "Okay. We'll clean house, fire the whole staff, and start fresh."

"Not sure you have any other choice," Kline said.

"I appreciate this, Peter. More importantly, Morton appreciates this. I know he regrets the way things transpired with your book proposal, and I don't want to talk out of turn here, but he's warming back up to the idea."

Kline played it cool. "Right now I'm just trying to be a friend."

Later that week he ate sushi at Nobu with Mort Spear. Between the appetizers and the main course, the real estate magnate brought Kline over to meet the Yankees shortstop, Derek Jeter, who happened to be eating a few tables away, enjoying a rare September day off with a lovely date.

"My favorite player!" Kline cried as they approached.

Big Noise

Jaime Clarke

IT WAS THE BEGINNING OF SUMMER AND I, FOR ONE, WAS GLAD OF it. A string of unsuccessful sublets had visited me in the spring—the share in Tribeca with the divorcee who threw me out when she caught me going through her purse; the warehouse in Brooklyn with the "artist" who turned tricks for drugs; the studio in the West Village that was sublet to me illegally, swindling me out of $650; the hovel on 116th Street in the basement of a building that belonged to a maintenance man for Columbia University who needed to "flee the city"; the vacant one-bedroom I happened upon during an afternoon walk in Astoria where I lived until the real estate agent returned from Mexico. Summer meant the Hamptons, with their late mornings and hazy afternoons spent at the beach. And even though it was already June and I hadn't lined up a summer situation, I remained hopeful that one would materialize. I had yet to find a situation as cushy as my first summer in the Hamptons, two years ago, when I was invited to stay with the Thornleys in Bridgehampton.

I'd convinced the Thornleys that our families, both being from the dust bowl, were related by marriage—a fact that I was vaguely aware was untrue. The Klipspringers were in fact from the dust bowl, as were the Thornleys, but it could have been a different Thornley family altogether. I failed to mention this fact when I met the Thornleys' lovely daughter at Bull & Bear that summer. I was then new to the city, a guest in the Upper East Side brownstone of Mr. and Mrs. Stahler, whom I'd met on an airplane bound for Paris. (I was on my way to visit a nice girl I'd met traveling through Europe the summer I dropped out of college.) The Stahlers were tiring of me, and I faced subletting a shoe box without ventilation in Spanish Harlem or someplace equally disdainful for the rest of the summer.

And then along came Margot Thornley, her butter brown hair just touching her smooth shoulders. Old Man Thornley had promised to meet her there to discuss his favorite subject—when exactly it was she was getting married—and I jokingly offered to propose from across the bar when the old man got there. Margot smiled, and it could've been love at first sight if I hadn't sworn off love—at least for the immediate future owing to a very unfortunate thing that happened to me once, the reason I came to New York. It was then that she introduced herself and then that her old man blew into the bar like a locomotive, just as I went into the incredible coincidence of our being related.

Old Man Thornley unbuttoned his worsted suit, and the gleam left his eye when he realized that Margot and I had just met. "Who have you been keeping a secret?" is what he said when he sat down, which caused Margot a little confusion. "Did you go to Brown?" was his question to me, and I shook my head sheepishly. "Yale," I said. "Class of ninety-four." This was a lie, but I'd just spent a week at the Yale Club on the Stahlers' dime (him finding out about the bill was the initial cause of their tiring of me), and I'd learned a great deal about New Haven from hanging around the locker room on the fifth floor.

"Harvard man, myself," Thornley said, signaling the bartender. An electronic ticker overhead announced the rising and falling stock prices and more than a few upturned faces squinted at it. "I'll have a Beefeater straight up," Thornley told the waiter. "And whatever they want."

By the end of the evening the three of us were suitably blotto, and when Margot slipped away to the ladies' room, Old Man Thornley said to me in a confidential tone, "All Margot needs is a little persuasion. She *wants* to get married, she's just being lazy about it. For Chrissakes, she's a beautiful woman."

I agreed with him that Margot was indeed beautiful.

"Her sister was married at twenty-two," Thornley said. "And it worked out beautifully." He sighed heavily. "If Margot waits much longer, she'll be thirty and forced to choose between Loser A and Loser B."

The waiter slipped him another Beefeater—his fifth—and he came up with what he called a brilliant idea. "Why don't you join us out in Bridgehampton," he said. "We're opening the house this weekend, and all sorts of interesting people are coming over."

Margot wound her way back through the crowd. "There was a line," she murmured. She listed to one side when she sat down.

"Guess what, honey?" Thornley said. "Klipspringer here is going to join us out at the house."

Margot looked at me askance and then a smile spread across her face. "Well, good," she said. "Finally someone *fun*."

Fun was something Margot knew quite a bit about; and as it turned out, she was involved in a little bit of fun with her sister, Pilar, the same sister Old Man Thornley had bragged about that evening.

It seemed Margot and Pilar had befriended a young girl named Shelleyan, who had moved to New York from Phoenix. Shelleyan worked behind the counter at Versace on Madison Avenue (it was just one of three jobs she held when she met the Thornley sisters, but that was all to change shortly). She had moved to New York to become a fashion designer—and to travel in the circles of celebrity. New York was a rude reminder to her that talent isn't everything; flits and flakes who had no formal training, or who had studied at the Fashion Institute in Manhattan, were celebrated over those who truly understood the elements of design. When she met the Thornley sisters that afternoon at Versace, her only contact in the world of glamour was the couple that designed underwear for Calvin Klein on a strictly freelance basis.

Margot and Pilar took an instant liking to Shelleyan. Pilar, being a young socialite and on several junior committees around town, thought she would make an excellent playmate. But it was Margot who came up with the plan to transform Shelleyan from a shop counter girl into a big noise. Since graduating from Brown, Margot had been toiling at the PR firm where she'd had a summer internship during college. Her father hated her working there, but she'd had some limited success coming up with marketing schemes for ladies' handbags and cellular phones. She wanted to try her hand at something more spectacular, something not so . . . *boring*. Pilar agreed to help.

The Thornley sisters searched for weeks for the best venue to announce Shelleyan to their friends and their friends' friends. There was the party down in Soho for the hottest rapper in New York; or the birthday party for the former Democratic senator; or the launch party for the revamped *R*O*C*K* magazine. Pilar wanted to bring Shelleyan out at the party at Veruka for the new line of cosmetics from Estee Lauder. "There'll be a *ton* of celebrities," Pilar reasoned. "And press."

"But there'll be too many wannabes, too," Margot argued. "It needs to be something exclusive, something no one else can get into." Using this reasoning as a yardstick, Margot and Pilar decided on the engagement party of their good friend, Jenny Moore. Jenny's father owned the largest media conglomerate in the world, and *everyone* knew about Jenny's impending marriage to Jonathan Ryan, an executive at her father's company. However, not everyone was invited.

The days leading up to the Moore engagement party were filled with trips to the top designers in the city: Donna Karan, Oscar de la Renta, Gucci, Chanel, and Shelleyan's old place of employment, Versace (her former coworkers were stunned to see Shelleyan among the racks, rather than digging through the returns boxed up in back). The Thornley sisters had an open, revolving credit line with each designer, and more often than not the girls borrowed outfits, having them returned by their father's chauffeur—if the outfits were in a shape to be returned.

Shelleyan liked a dress by Prada, but Margot and Pilar chose a sleek black Armani dress that fit Shelleyan like a second skin. "It makes your ass look delicious," Pilar said.

The day of the Moore engagement party, a Saturday, the Thornley sisters dropped Shelleyan off at Equinox, leaving specific instructions for various skin treatments with the coterie of personnel Margot and Pilar usually required on their weekly visits.

Upon her return from the salon, Shelleyan found Margot and Pilar lounging peacefully in the front room of the penthouse apartment off Central Park West where Margot still lived with her parents. "Wow," they gushed, sitting up on the white leather couch. "That really did the trick."

Even though the engagement party was literally across the street, at the boat-house in Central Park, Margot and Pilar and Shelleyan were driven in the Thornleys' limousine, an extravagance that clued Shelleyan in to how seriously she'd delved into a world not her own. Heads turned when the chauffeur opened the door and the three of them stepped out into the afternoon sun. A photographer snapped their picture and another asked them to pose together. Shelleyan posed for many photos that day. She posed next to an ice sculpture of two dolphins kissing with Suzanne St. Clair, the daughter of Morton St. Clair, who owned the largest chain of drug stores in the Pacific Northwest; she posed with Minnie and Anita Hammersmith, heiresses to the Hammersmith hotel fortune; with George and Jeremy O'Keefe, whose family owned two-thirds of the real estate in New York; with Tonya, Traci, and Tami Campbell— Margot and Pilar called them the Terrible Triple T's—whose mother's grandmother had invented one of the first board games.

Margot and Pilar arranged a group photo with Jenny Moore and Jonathan Ryan, positioning Shelleyan near enough to the couple that if the picture ran in any of the papers, Shelleyan was sure to be seen. It was a photograph that would come to haunt Shelleyan, who fell asleep that night in her cramped apartment in Astoria, Queens, the magic of the party still everywhere around her. The next morning Margot and Pilar placed several strategic phone calls and when the newspapers hit the streets Monday, Shelleyan's face peered out from the pages in bedrooms, offices, and kitchens up and down the island of Manhattan.

The Thornley sisters repeated the same routine at several events over the next few months—a movie premiere at Lot 61; an after-hours party at Moomba for a new CD by Pilar's favorite band; the Velveteen party at Serena in the Chelsea Hotel; the Panty Party at Baby Jupiter on the third Wednesday night of the month; Trans Am at Culture Club; Physics at Vanity; Shag at Shine; and Body & Soul at Vinyl on Sunday nights. By the end of spring, Shelleyan, who had since moved into the Thornley penthouse, was on everyone's call list and was a must-have at any gathering that aspired to reach any significant status.

And so Shelleyan was a permanent fixture in the Thornleys' lives when I met her that summer in Bridgehampton.

I arrived by train, jumping the crowded Long Island Rail Road from Penn Station. The air conditioner on the train had failed, apparently broken beyond repair, so I sprang from the silver tomb the moment we pulled up to the platform. The cool, fresh air dried the sweat on my brow and I looked around, my eyes drinking up the wild green of Long Island.

The Thornleys had sent their limousine to fetch me, and I told the driver to take the scenic route. He obliged, giving the impression that we had no particular schedule to keep, and I stared happily out the window at the enormous mansions set back behind manicured hedges, wondering what marvelous scenarios were developing inside of each—trips to the beach, lunches on yachts, afternoon trips to the movies, dinner parties, nights drinking and dancing at the local watering hole.

At last we pulled into the driveway of the Thornleys' immense house. For a long time all you could see was the gabled roof supported by massive white pillars. The entrance finally came into focus, twin oak doors ornamented with brass knobs that gleamed impossibly in the sunlight. The chauffeur—whose name I'm ashamed to say I never learned—opened my door, and my heels clicked on the polished marble steps leading up to the front entrance. I raised my fist to knock, but the door opened automatically, pulled slowly back by a very old woman who I learned had been the Thornley family maid for over forty years, since Old Man Thornley was in his teens. I announced myself and the maid led me through the cool foyer and spacious front room peopled with extravagantly luxurious couches and expensive wood furniture. A large tinted window formed the back wall of the front room, and I could see Margot and Shelleyan lounging in their bikinis around a table shaded by a yellow-and-white umbrella the size of a parachute. Margot turned her head and I waved, but apparently she couldn't see any farther than her reflection in the smooth glass.

"Mr. Klipspringer to see you," the maid said, and then disappeared.

"Klip, darling," Margot said. "Come kiss me on the cheek. Give Shelleyan a kiss too."

I did as I was told, introducing myself to Shelleyan.

"Very nice to meet you," Shelleyan said.

"We were just debating whether or not we would go to the Tommy Hilfiger party tonight in Southampton," Margot said. "Shelleyan doesn't want to go."

"Why not?" I inquired.

"Because Tommy Hilfiger is a lame designer," Shelleyan said flatly.

"Jesus Christ," Margot snorted. "You don't have to wear his clothes, just drink his booze."

The two bickered about the party, and about some unfortunate thing that had happened at a party the weekend before that resulted in Shelleyan being "accidentally" left at the party, having to catch a ride home with a Pakistani millionaire who tried to kiss her in the driveway.

I asked after Margot's parents, wanting to thank them for having me in their home, but was informed they were at the tennis club for the afternoon and had dinner plans that would keep them out late.

"They'll be at the National tomorrow, though," Margot said. "For some reason my father is looking forward to seeing you again."

I learned the National was a horse show, one of the biggest summertime events in Bridgehampton. Shelleyan seemed particularly excited to see it.

"I had a horse when I was young," Shelleyan explained. "Patches. The greatest horse ever."

"I find them revolting," Margot said. "All that hair. And the smell."

Margot's cell phone rang and she answered it. Shelleyan and I sat silent, awkwardly listening to Margot and the unnamed caller banter about subjects ranging from who was and wasn't coming to the National to the impending Moore-Ryan wedding at the Waldorf-Astoria. The conversation turned embarrassingly affectionate, but Shelleyan pretended like she wasn't listening.

"That was Pilar," Margot said, turning to Shelleyan. "She said to tell you hi."

"When is she coming back from Europe?" Shelleyan asked.

"Two more weeks," Margot answered.

Shelleyan excused herself to watch her favorite TV show on the big-screen television in the front room, and it was then that Margot filled me in about how she and Pilar discovered Shelleyan. She relished the details of the story, and the sun went down before she was finished. Feeling tired from my travels, I excused myself to one of the guest rooms upstairs and fell asleep, dizzy with all the glamorous details of Shelleyan's new life.

*

I woke very early the next morning to the sound of voices and scuffling in the hall. As my head hit the pillow the night before, I fantasized of waking somewhere around noon, sauntering to the kitchen to read the *Times* and sip coffee. But the clock read 6:30 a.m. and I was wide awake.

I cracked open the door and found Margot moving about the hall. She was half-dressed and crazed, dragging a Louis Vuitton suitcase behind her.

"What's the matter?" I asked.

"It's Pilar," Margot said, her face tear-stained. "She's been in a car accident in France."

Old Man Thornley called up from the foot of the staircase, and Margot descended, turning her wilted back toward me.

The house was suddenly empty. The Thornleys took their maid, and the chauffeur never returned from the city where, Shelleyan told me later that morning, he'd dropped Margot and her family off at JFK.

"Did they give any indication when they would return?" I asked.

Shelleyan shook her head. She reached across the polished kitchen table and dug an orange out of the fruit bowl.

"Do you think we should leave?" I asked.

"I don't see why," Shelleyan said, peeling back a strip of rind. "I'm sure Pilar would want a welcoming party here when they get back."

"So they *are* coming back," I said.

"No, dummy," she laughed. "They're going to stay in Europe *forever.*"

I didn't appreciate this sort of mocking. "But it sounded serious," I said.

"It's *always* serious with Pilar," Shelleyan said. She got up from the table and wandered out onto the porch, leaving a small pile of orange rind on the table.

I followed her outside. I was afraid to be left alone in the house until I could resolve the matter of whether or not the Thornleys would return to Bridgehampton, and if so, when.

"What do you mean?" I asked.

Shelleyan plopped down in the same chair she had occupied the afternoon before. "Pilar is a drama queen," she said matter-of-factly. "Last month she called her parents in the middle of the night from her cell phone saying she was going to jump off the Brooklyn Bridge."

"Oh my God," I said.

Shelleyan laughed. "She wasn't even *at* the Brooklyn Bridge. She was calling from Tunnel, high on God-knows-what." She related a couple more stories, each as absurd as the next, and it was obvious that Shelleyan had a great deal of affection for Pilar.

I was beginning to take in the situation, that I would indeed have the run of the house, when Shelleyan asked if I still wanted to go to the National.

"Sure," I said. I could tell it meant a lot to Shelleyan to go, and I started to feel protective toward her, having only the slightest sense that what Margot and Pilar were doing was wrong.

"Good." She smiled. "I don't have a driver's license."

The fact that I didn't have a license either didn't bother me until Shelleyan opened a kitchen drawer and fished out a set of keys to the Thornleys' black Mercedes SUV. I backed out of the six-car garage, careful not to hit the cars on either side, each costing about as much as a small house in my hometown.

"I've been working on my accent," Shelleyan said cheerfully as we zipped down Route 2.

"What's wrong with your accent?" I asked.

"Margot said I should cultivate a lilt," Shelleyan said. She pressed a button on the console between us and the sun roof slid back.

"Do you always follow Margot's instructions?" I asked.

Shelleyan looked at me coldly. "They're just trying to help me," she said. "They know about these sorts of things. They have *expertise*. And besides, I don't want to be who I was. I want to be like Margot and Pilar."

I considered what she was saying and thought to warn her about what she wished for, but I couldn't bring myself to say anything.

Traffic came to a halt a mile or so from the showgrounds. The sun roof of the red BMW in front of us retracted, and a boy who looked seven or eight poked his head through. Shelleyan waved and the little boy's head disappeared back inside the car.

"What about you, Mr. Klipspringer?" Shelleyan asked. "What's your story?"

The question startled me. I quickly calculated the sum of what I'd told the Thornleys, wanting to keep the story straight.

"I'm from the Midwest," I said. "Came to New York about three years ago."

"Why did you come to New York?" she asked.

"I was involved in a sort of bad relationship that seemed in danger of going on forever," I said, which was mostly true.

"So you ended it by moving away," Shelleyan said.

"Something like that," I said.

"Doesn't sound very nice," she said.

Traffic picked up and we sailed into the parking lot of the showgrounds.

"No," I said. "I don't suppose it does."

Shelleyan's pace quickened as we neared the grandstand, which was filled with people dressed in white.

"Look!" Shelleyan said excitedly, pointing at what looked like a black stallion as it cleared a high parallel bar. I half expected Shelleyan to clap her hands and ask me to buy her a pony.

We took a seat on the low tier of the grandstand and watched the parade of horses as they galloped and pranced before us.

"Have you ever ridden a horse, Klip?" Shelleyan asked. Her trying out my nickname endeared her to me, and that old protective feeling returned.

"I once rode on the beach in France," I told her.

"That must've been wonderful," she said, her eyes trained on a pair of Thoroughbreds and their riders. We sat in silence, and then she said, "Who were you riding with?"

"Pardon?" I asked.

"On the beach," she said. "You were probably not riding *alone*, were you, Klip?"

The sudden intimacy stunned me, and I was stuck for any answer beyond, "No, I wasn't." It was the first time in telling this story that I had admitted there was someone else on the beach that day in Nice. It felt dangerous to let that information out into the open.

Shelleyan took her eyes off the horses momentarily. "It's always interesting to me what people *don't* say," she said.

I was about to confess the entire story, that the woman I was with that day in Nice was the only woman I'd ever loved, and that it hadn't worked out for reasons that still baffled me, and that I had no hope of ever recapturing the feelings I had then, when who should pass in front of us but Cheryl and Stephanie Mason.

The Mason sisters, as they would have everyone know, were identical twins. But it was more than that: the sisters were literal mirror images of each other, and no picture existed either where one appeared and not the other, or where the two weren't wearing matching outfits, matching hairstyles, matching accessories, and matching smiles, all of which matched their twin attitude of condescension and their vicious mean-spiritedness. I'd made their unhappy acquaintance my first week in New York, at a fund-raising event at Metrazur in Grand Central Station. I'd conned my way past the security guard and mingled with the crowd. I spotted the sisters (they were wearing matching sequined dresses that night), and it didn't take much to get them to invite me to stay with them at their loft in Soho. I thankfully moved in with them, and for a week the three of us played together in the various downtown night clubs, them always paying with money Cheryl claimed "magically appeared" every month in their bank account. I learned later—after the sisters had unceremoniously kicked me out of the loft—that their father was an investment banker who paid the girls to keep away from him and the rest of their family.

I hadn't seen Cheryl and Stephanie since, and it was a shock to see them standing in front of me, dressed in navy-blue-and-white sailor costumes.

"Well, well," Cheryl said. "Look who it is."

"Is that Klipspringer?" Stephanie asked.

The sisters raised their black Ray-Bans simultaneously.

"And is that Shelleyan," Cheryl asked. She turned to her sister and said, "It really is a high-society affair!"

Shelleyan glanced at the sisters and smiled. "Do I know you?" she asked.

"No, but we know you," one of them answered, adding dishonestly, "and we're *big* fans."

Shelleyan looked at me and I smiled nervously.

"So Klipspringer," they said. "Where are you staying *this* summer?" They tittered and a wave of nausea passed over me. I explained that Shelleyan and I were guests of the Thornleys, and that the Thornleys had been called away to Europe unexpectedly.

"Oh, we know all about Pilar's accident," they said. "She probably called her family *last*."

I was wishing they would go away when a noise I can only describe as terrible silenced the pockets of chatter around us. Everyone turned their heads in the direction of the awful noise and saw a man lying motionless in the grass, his horse dancing nervously around him. A small group rushed to the fallen rider, spooking the horse, which zig-zagged away, finally bolting toward the parking lot.

Shelleyan gasped and brought her hand to her mouth.

"I'm sure it'll be okay," I said. "He was wearing a helmet."

"What will happen to the horse?" Shelleyan wanted to know.

"They'll probably kill it," the Mason sisters laughed.

Just then one of the sisters' cell phones rang, and they walked away, passing the phone back and forth to scream hello into the receiver, and their conversation carried through the hushed grandstand. The rider finally stood under his own power and everyone was relieved, though Shelleyan sat sullenly on the drive back to the Thornleys'.

She spent that night in her room, and, without anyone to keep me company, I sat on the Thornleys' private beach in the dark, pondering the reflections of the stars in the vast, unsettled ocean.

The next morning I heard a concert of voices in the foyer, but all was quiet by the time I reached the landing. I was surprised when, later that afternoon, the house was filled with voices again, the source of said voices being Shelleyan and the Mason sisters fighting over the last Diet Coke in the refrigerator. I avoided them entirely, and we drifted around one another in that enormous house for the next two weeks. By then I'd taken to following around a Swedish au pair I'd met in a bookstore in Bridgehampton, and so it was with great sadness that, upon the Thornleys' return, I packed my bags at their request. They had returned not only with Pilar, who looked none the worse for wear, but also with an unsavory story about me given them by their hosts in France, the McGintys, who were related to the woman with whom I rode horses on the beach that summer afternoon in Nice. Who knew a simple act like giving a witness report to the police about an accident the woman's friend caused would follow me around for all eternity? I did not realize until much later that I'd revealed myself as an outsider, confirming a long-held suspicion by the woman's acquaintances, a suspicion that rippled until I was forced to leave France. But the Thornleys did not ask for a defense or excuse or even my side of the matter, and it was only on my way out to the curb to wait for the taxi that I laid eyes on Mrs. Thornley, who was as beautiful as her daughters.

*

Like everyone else, I read about what happened to Shelleyan in the daily papers. By that time I had taken up with the Oliver woman, who walked in on me playing "Für Elise" on the piano at Russian Samovar on Fifty-Second Street, and I became involved in a matter concerning the Oliver woman and her best friend, so I had all but forgotten Shelleyan and the Thornleys, and the Mason sisters, and the Moore-Ryan wedding—until it was splashed across the front of the *New York Post* and the *Daily News*.

At first you couldn't see the Mason sisters' hands in the whole mess; but once I learned about Margot and Pilar Thornley's active campaign to keep the Mason sisters uninvited to the wedding, what didn't make sense to your average reader—how Shelleyan came to be introduced to Jonathan Ryan and why Shelleyan had a falling out with the Thornleys—made a lot of sense to me. The rest of the story—Jonathan Ryan falling in love with Shelleyan, Jenny Moore catching the two of them at the Peninsula Hotel a few days before the wedding, Old Man Thornley firing Jonathan Ryan—was probably just how the Mason sisters had scripted it.

The papers called Shelleyan all sorts of names, but the Thornley sisters went unindicted. Worse, they provided nasty quotes to the gossip columns about Shelleyan, and one of the last items to appear was a story about how Shelleyan had tried to get into a party at a club in the East Village, only to be turned away by insults screamed at her by Margot and Pilar. The Mason sisters were never mentioned.

A few months after the wedding was canceled, I glimpsed Shelleyan walking down Madison Avenue. I almost didn't recognize her. She was camouflaged head to toe in black, her hair cut short and dyed brown. Her face was heavily made up with eye shadow and lipstick; it was a look that didn't become her, and I started to tell her so, when I noticed something else, the far away look in her eye as we stood talking, a look I recognized from my reflection in the mirror every morning. It was the look worn by those of us who had our dream in hand only to have it thieved without warning, spiraling us into orbit around those who were luckier than we were, or who hadn't yet realized what their dream was. We said good-bye, and as Shelleyan continued down Madison Avenue, I thought of all the unfortunate places she had yet to go.

From World Gone Water

Praise for WORLD GONE WATER

"Charlie Martens will make you laugh. More, he'll offend and shock you while making you laugh. Even trickier: he'll somehow make you like him, root for him, despite yourself and despite him. This novel travels into the dark heart of male/female relations and yet there is tenderness, humanity, hope. Jaime Clarke rides what is a terribly fine line between hero and antihero. Read and be astounded."

—AMY GRACE LOYD, author of *The Affairs of Others*

"Funny and surprising, *World Gone Water* is terrific fun to read and, as a spectacle of bad behavior, pretty terrifying to contemplate."

—ADRIENNE MILLER, author of *The Coast of Akron*

"Jaime Clarke's *World Gone Water* is so fresh and daring, a necessary book, a barbaric yawp that revels in its taboo: the sexual and emotional desires of today's hetero young man. Clarke is a sure and sensitive writer, his lines are clean and carry us right to the tender heart of his lovelorn hero, Charlie Martens. This is the book Hemingway and Kerouac would want to read. It's the sort of honesty in this climate that many of us aren't brave enough to write."

—TONY D'SOUZA, author of *The Konkans*

"Charlie Martens is my favorite kind of narrator, an obsessive yearner whose commitment to his worldview is so overwhelming that the distance between his words and the reader's usual thinking gets clouded fast. *World Gone Water* will draw you in, make you complicit, and finally leave you both discomfited and thrilled."

—MATT BELL, author of *In the House upon the Dirt between the Lake and the Woods*

A Review of WORLD GONE WATER

Kirkus Reviews

A man struggles to navigate his life after a stay in a behavioral rehabilitation center in this character-driven novel.

Clarke's third novel, set years before the events of *Vernon Downs*, returns the reader to the world of Charlie Martens, a self-described "easy-going" man who will "tend toward violence, if provoked." After his parents' deaths, Charlie spent his childhood with various relatives in Denver, Santa Fe, Rapid City, San Diego and, finally, Phoenix, where he emancipated himself. "I am not a good person," Charlie writes in the first sentence of the entrance essay to rehab that opens the book. As if intent on proving this claim, Charlie relives everything from kissing Erica Ryan on the playground in fifth grade to the more recent and far more egregious sexual aggression and physical abuse that brought him to the Sonoran Rehabilitation Center. The gruesome details of his journal entries and essays force the reader to confront his capacity for cruelty along with him and could easily offend sensitive readers. But some slivers of hope still glimmer in the background. His relationship with Jenny, a Mormon and his high school sweetheart, is a brief ray of pure goodness that, though shattered, has a lasting impact on his obsessive and idealistic views of romance. While Charlie is— undoubtedly—*not* a good person, his appeal for sympathy and nonjudgment is warranted. As he states in the close of that opening essay: "You have to feel something to understand it."

Clarke gives us a tortured antihero, a disturbingly self-aware man we might not root for but cannot forget.

Minor Characters from
WORLD GONE WATER

Jane Ramsey, thirties, clinical psychologist who oversees Charlie's voluntary stay at Sonoran Rehabilitation Center. She then has a relationship with him, which ends badly.

Talie, midtwenties, the neighbor to one of the families Charlie lived with as a foster kid. She and Charlie grew close and have a brother-sister relationship.

Jay Stanton Buckley, late sixties, founder and CEO of Buckley Cosmetics. Charlie worked for Buckley as a runner when he was a teenager, a job Talie helped him get, and Jay Stanton Buckley becomes one of Charlie's surrogate fathers.

Jason, midtwenties, Charlie's friend from high school who now owns a bar called Aztecka. Jason employs Charlie upon his release from the rehabilitation center.

Dale, late twenties, Talie's current boyfriend. He is unfaithful to Talie and tends toward violence.

Karine, twenties, a woman Charlie meets in Boca Raton, where he flees to get over the fact that his high school sweetheart, Jenny, marries quickly just after their split. He meets Karine and brings her back to his place. There's some confusion about what happens between them, though later the police are involved. Karine disappears before there can be an investigation, but the police persuade Charlie to enter Sonoran Rehabilitation Center, which he does voluntarily.

Caitlin, late twenties, a sexually secure woman Charlie meets at Jay Stanton Buckley's May/December wedding. They fall fast for each other, and he tags along on one of her business trips, which ends in bitterness on both sides.

Carol Bandes, forties, the reluctant winner of the World Gone Water promotional contest Jay Stanton Buckley has tasked Charlie with organizing.

All the Numbers

Ben Greenman

JAY HAD GONE TO SLEEP IN ONE BED AND WOKEN UP IN ANOTHER one. He would have preferred that it were a metaphor.

But facts were facts. He had gone to sleep at home, with the central air up high to keep the temperature at sixty-seven and the television turned on. What he watched depended on his mood. Some nights it was a business channel. Some nights, sports. If his mood was especially good, he'd permit himself an old movie. He needed his mood to be especially good because old movies, while nourishing, also plunged him into a pit of nostalgia. He would think about what the actors looked like now, assuming they were still alive (most were not), and that train of thought would reach a station and head back toward him bearing its own opposite, which was what he looked like now, despite the fact that his mental picture of himself was of a younger man. This particular night his mood had not been good enough to stomach a movie. He'd settled on sports. There was a golf tournament coming in from halfway across the world, mostly Asian golfers, and he watched as a young man with a bowl cut sank a forty-foot putt, as another young man with long hair hit a long-looking drive, as a third young man, this one bald, shanked a drive and ended up in a footprint-shaped sand trap. That was the last thing he remembered, the bald man scowling, before he drifted off to sleep.

He'd woken in a bed in a white room with a bank of CB radios along one wall. As he focused, he revised. It was not a white room. The walls were painted a pale yellow. The bedsheets were a pale blue. All that was white was the curtains. And the radios along the wall were not radios at all, but various medical equipment that filled in the rest of the story. He was in the hospital. He struggled to remember where he had gone to bed. He had faint memories of television but nothing specific. Had he been watching a movie? He closed his eyes again. In time he sensed a figure at his bedside and opened his eyes to see a doctor, young and Asian, like every golfer he now remembered he had been watching. The doctor was holding a clipboard that could have been charts or maybe a scorecard for his final round. Was this death? He had read somewhere that death, at least initially, seemed like a standard dream, a collage made up of various moments that the deceased had experienced in the moments before passing. It was the universe's way of keeping you calm. "What'd you shoot, Doc?" he said.

The doctor smiled, without enough confusion for Jay's taste. "Mr. Buckley," he said. "You've had a heart attack."

"So this is real?" Jay said, indicating the room with his chin.

"As real as the day is long," the doctor said.

"How did I get here?"

"A friend found you. She said that she had been calling you on the telephone, and that it was strange that you didn't answer. And she had a feeling. You'd be surprised by how many people are discovered by friends who have a feeling. It's one of the things that give me hope for the species. We're all connected in ways we don't quite understand."

"Which friend?"

"Oh, Mr. Buckley, I can't violate doctor-discoverer confidentiality," he said. He tapped his clipboard and laughed. "No, no. Let me see. It was . . ." Jay was suddenly very tired, and went under the waves of sleep before he could hear the name.

It turned out to be not a friend at all, but an ex-wife: Erin. When he woke up, after a little bit of toast and eggs—he wasn't aware that eggs were allowed for heart attack patients, but the orderly explained that these had been stripped of all their harmful properties ("in other words, their flavor," he said, laughing)—the young golfer returned with his clipboard and scorecard. Jay made him say the name twice, just so he was sure that he had heard right. It confused him at first, because Erin didn't make a practice of calling him on the phone, no matter what she had told the hospital. But maybe the other thing was true: that people remained connected to each other via an invisible network. This was a comforting thought, and also a little terrifying.

"Look," the doctor said. "It wasn't a major heart attack. Sometimes people come awake from an episode with cold sweat or pain in their extremities. You were delirious when the ambulance arrived but still able to answer basic questions."

"I don't remember a thing," Jay said.

"That's why I said 'delirious,'" the doctor said. "But we did all the tests and ran all the numbers. The upshot is that you don't have to stay too long. I'm going to put you on some heart meds, and you'll have to change your diet and start light exercise, but this probably ends up being a warning shot more than anything else. You won't be the first man in his sixties to earn another decade or so as a result of a scare."

He was able to drive himself home. Willie Nelson was on the radio, and he snapped it off angrily. He had always hated Willie Nelson, with that fake hippie affect and what was probably the world's foulest bandana. But people were always quick to praise Willie and his authenticity, and Jay had never been brave enough to object. Now he was brave enough. It was a new regime, here in post-heart-attack America.

He went home, knowing that he needed to call Erin and thank her. He picked up his phone, dialed three numbers, and stopped. He couldn't do it. What had she seen when she had come into the house and found him in the bed? Had there been a bluish tint to his lips? Had there been face foam? No matter what she had seen, she had seen a lesser version of him than the version he had shown her during the entire time they were together. That was one thing she always made clear. "You show well," she liked to say.

For a few days he ate according to the doctor's instructions—lean pork, leafy greens, small handfuls of frozen berries—and began to exercise lightly as well. He recovered to the point where he was not afraid to turn on the television before going to bed.

On the third night he dialed Erin again. This time he made it through six numbers before hanging up. There was a reason he could not go further. About a year before, he had been at his real estate office when his secretary had come in to tell him that a prospective seller was on the line. His secretary identified the prospective seller by name, and he remarked that it was close to the name of a famous actress, and she laughed blankly, and he took the call only to learn that his secretary had gotten the name wrong, and that in fact the woman on the other end of the line was the famous actress he had mentioned. He knew her by her voice. Her knew her instantly. She said that she had a property that she was thinking of selling, and he responded with a line from one of her most famous movies, after which she let the line go silent for a moment with what he sensed was appreciation and at least a little bit of irritation, which in his experience only made the appreciation more vivid and more profoundly felt. Back then he had still been expert at making those kinds of calculations. The actress explained that her husband (Jay knew the name; he had been a bigwig in aeronautics glass) had died the previous year, leaving her alone in a large house on a large ranch property. The summer after his death, a wildfire had swept across the valley that surrounded the ranch. The actress's neighbor to the north had lost forty of fifty acres; her neighbor to the south had lost thirty of forty. "We were relatively lucky," she said. "The way the winds moved, we only lost fifteen of our fifty. My husband had planted lots of firewall vegetation before he passed. But it was all too much for me. It requires wearing a bandana over your face against the smoke, shoveling charred wood, and poking at trees to see which ones are still alive. I'm not young enough to—"

Jay interrupted her. "I don't know what else you're about to say," he said. "But you are young enough." She was, he knew, almost exactly a decade younger than he was. He had first seen her at the Ciné Capri in Phoenix when he was twenty-eight. She had been an apple-cheeked ingenue then, playing Marina in *The Dead Middle*, a version of Pericles transplanted to modern-day Wall Street. He had fallen in love immediately, to the point where he didn't even finish his popcorn. At that time, nostalgia had been less pit than platform. Later on, as he built the cosmetics business that would make him his first fortune, he had thought of her often. His products would give other women the belief that they could be as beautiful as her. She had always been there in his mind, elegant and elevated. The collapse of his business had left her untouched. He'd never blamed her. But as he spoke to her on the phone, he felt himself adjusting her downward. He had been taken by her, certainly. He had seen *The Dead Middle* a second time and every movie of hers after that at least once—*Juniper Days*, *The Time of the Rush*, *Past the Last House*, and even duds like *The Chronicle of the Rose* and *Beep*. But had the crush been any more intense than his feelings for dozens of other actresses he had seen in other movies, or for that matter, dozens of other women who were not actresses at all? He had encountered those other women in real life, at a clip of about one every six months or so—there was Melissa, there was Caitlin, there was Sue, there was another Melissa, there was Jane, and so on—until he had allowed himself to be entranced and encircled by, and then legally wed to, Erin. It had been more than six months and seemed like much more. Erin was wonderful, certainly. She was young and beautiful, but he worried there was not much else to her than that. Kindness? Certainly, there was nothing more than youth, beauty, and kindness. He was absolutely sure of that. And yet he had pledged to stay with her for as long as they both lived. At that time, it would be years before he went to sleep in one bed and woke up in another one, and he assumed that it would be forever.

"So would you?" the actress said.

Jay blinked aggressively to return to the conversation. "I'm sorry," he said.

"Would you come out to see it?" she said. He agreed. That should have been the first warning sign. There was a time when all the women had come to see him: some for jobs, some for romance, some for kicks, and he had obliged in every case. A certain number of them had found their way into his house and then into his bed. Few had made it into his heart, or at least that was what he'd liked to tell new women, putting a sentimental spin on the word.

That was what he told the actress. "Few have made it into my heart." This was three days after his phone call, two days after he visited the ranch to assess its value, and one day after he walked into her bedroom, fell into her bed, and plunged into her. Even forty years after he'd seen her on a movie screen for the first time, she still had the ability to send heat moving through his blood, to the point where he thought of her as a human iodine contrast. He must have said so too, because she laughed and laughed. "Wit in a man is everything," she said.

"Isn't that a line from *Past the Last House?*" he said. It wasn't, but it made her laugh again.

That affair flickered on and off—the times when it was on heating him into happiness, the times when it was off making him long for the times when it was on—until Erin discovered it and divorced him, not only writing him a rather formal letter to explain that she was devastated, but refusing to take even a portion of the value of his real estate business in settlement. This in turn devastated him. He knew he had a habit of hurting people, but at least he paid up. It was the only way to keep the ledger balanced. But Erin rejected his offer, demanding not more money but less; and then, when he balked, not just less but zero—after which she moved into a modest apartment complex with a few fists of scrubby bushes and a common kidney-shaped pool. He was confounded and more than a little angry. He asked several times, in several registers, why she would want to live there, and each time she Zenned right back at him. "I want a life that I can understand." Or: "Each decision should be the proper size." Or: "I tried to live outside myself and that did not work, so now I am back inside myself."

Almost every time, after hanging up with Erin, he cursed her name in the most vicious fashion. Who did she think she was, spurning his generosity? He had erred. He had sinned. He had run around on her. He knew the cost of that behavior: it was his marriage. But what was the price of that behavior? Try as he might, he could not believe that there was not one.

Five days after his heart attack, he made himself a health shake, some toast with sardines, and an egg-white omelet; climbed into bed with a travel magazine; switched on the television to the gardening channel; and fell asleep peacefully for the first time since returning from the hospital. He woke in the middle of the night with a twinge in his chest, not near his heart, but close enough. It scared him to the point where the pictures on the television were untenable—they were close-ups of hibiscuses that read as lurid and bloody—and the room felt warm even though the thermostat had been set at seventy and there was no iodine contrast in sight.

The panic subsided, but he was still as alert as if he had just downed a pot of coffee. He turned off the TV and went out into the large yard behind the main house, where he tried to locate the middle of the property. The dead middle. He laughed. He wondered where the actress was these days. They had last seen each other at her house, where they had spent the afternoon in intense sex that both of them knew would be good-bye. The whole time, as his hands and mouth found their targets, and he was in turn targeted by her hands and mouth, Jay had tried to think of a perfect parting line. When you were with an actress, after all, you were always, in some sense, in a movie. She tugged on her underwear to signal that they had come to the end of the road. He got dressed in silence. At the front door he turned back and delivered the dialogue he had written for himself: "Some things get remembered more than others," he said. He was pleased with it—rueful, a little equivocal, maybe a kiss-off, maybe a could-have-been. She put her hand to her chest and blinked slowly, which was even better.

Had he read something about her getting remarried to an older record producer? The man must have been closing in on eighty. Maybe he was seventy-eight. "RPMs," Jay muttered to himself. He laughed again. He was not yet seventy, but he was coming up on it faster than he had ever thought he would. When he was a kid, people had told him that middle age went from thirty-five to fifty, but he had always believed something else: that there was no such thing as middle age, just the beginning and then a long, slow end in hock to time and in denial of its own inevitability. When he was a child, this had been a morbid fantasy. Now it was an equally morbid fact. There had been a newspaper comic once, not a strip but one of the one-panels that ran on the right rail of the funnies page, and it had shown a man in a long robe and beard, holding a sign. THE END MAY NOT BE NIGH, it said, BUT IT'S A WHOLE LOT NIGHER! He had laughed heartily at the strip back then, and he laughed just as heartily now at the idea of the dead middle. His spare tire, another kind of dead middle, wobbled mirthfully around his hips, and he patted it protectively. It would be gone soon enough. He took out his phone to call Erin, for real this time, and then maybe after that he would call the rest of them: Melissa, Caitlin, Sue, Melissa, Jane. He was suddenly flush with strength, a full man again, not a speck lost in the larger darkness of the yard, but the bright center that made the rest of it possible. He was certain, for the first time since he had gone to sleep in one bed and woken up in another, that he could get through all the numbers.

Revere

Mona Awad

KARINE HAD TO ADMIT THAT HER FRIENDSHIP WITH STEPHEN WAS bizarre. Not just bizarre. Creepy? Maybe it was creepy. He was a child, really. And she was . . . how old was she again? These days she had trouble keeping hold of certain facts. Anyway, she was old. Much older than Stephen. *But he's my friend*, she thought mistily. And then she thought, *Is he really my friend?* Was it even a friendship? She couldn't explain Stephen to herself. She could barely explain it to her dog.

"He's kind to me," she told her dog, and there were tears shining in her eyes when she said it. "That's all I want these days is kindness. Is that so terrible?"

Her dog walked away from her. Perhaps he knew she was lying. Since when did she ever want kindness?

Stephen was a young man with a mop of ginger hair and a long, thin nose with a smattering of freckles across the pale bridge. He carried a large knife in the back pocket of his jeans. He was a cashier clerk at Crosby's, a grocery store that Karine had been going to after work of late. It was a terrible place, truth be told. Just off a hideous road that lead straight onto the highway.

Now she here was again tonight, like every night, wandering the sad aisles.

She never bought anything, really. She couldn't really take it in there. Those suicide-inducing white lights. Everything in the store looked like it was dying. The produce was a sea of mottled, unyielding fists. She'd never seen apples so small, bananas so black. The bouquets of flowers were such strange, bright colors. They looked like they'd been spray-painted to conform to someone's terrible, carnival notion of joy. The poor lobsters were piled on top of one another in their cloudy tank of shallow water. The prepared items were all disgusting. Congealed coleslaws in all shades of sick. Rotisserie chickens in halves and quarters that shrank and sweated beneath the heat lamp. She picked things off the dingy shelves at random and dropped them into her shopping basket. The truth was, when she got home from work, she didn't want to eat, let alone cook. She worked at a beauty counter at Macy's. Every day the same little black belted dress, the same hot-iron curl to her hair. The same orthopedic shoes disguised to look like kitten-heeled Mary Janes. The same shade of red lipstick painted onto her cracked lips. "Hello. Hello. Hello." Smiling so hard at people who openly glared at her. It hurt her face by the end of the day. Each night she'd have to take Advil for the pain, maybe a few Xanax. Wine helped too. And vodka. Vodka was good for the humiliation. When customers glared at her when she said hello, she always spritzed them heavily with perfume. Her atomizer was like her little gun, her revenge. She stood in a rank cloud of it all day—freesia, jasmine, green tea, notes of vanilla and bergamot and citrus and rose.

"You always smell so wonderful," Stephen said when she came up to the cash register that night. And he breathed her in like she was mountain air, a spring night. He began dragging her items across the scanner with his customary flourish.

"I do?" she said. She looked at Stephen through her dark glasses. She always wore dark glasses in the grocery store. She couldn't take the bright light. But then, the lights were so terribly bright everywhere, everywhere. "Why can't it be darker everywhere?" she'd once asked Stephen. "Why can't we put a dimmer switch on the world? That's what I want, that's what I'd do if I were God," she'd told him. And Stephen had smiled as if he liked that idea. He liked all her ideas. Every single one.

"Jesus is the light of God, Miss Valentine," Stephen had said. "I bet he'd let you."

"Do I really smell wonderful?" she asked him now. She couldn't believe herself. Blatantly fishing like this. She looked at Stephen standing behind the cash register in his bright blue smock. He was wearing a blue plaid tie today. There was a too-red grocery store carnation in his lapel.

"Oh yes," Stephen said easily, and he breathed it in. "What's that scent?"

She liked that he'd said "scent" instead of "smell." He was sophisticated. A well-brought-up boy. Polite, if a little strange. His elaborate manners had made her laugh at first. The way he bowed a little whenever she approached the cash register, like she was a queen. The way he'd wave wildly at her if he saw her in the parking lot. "Hello, Miss Valentine," he'd say, and he'd wave and wave and wave. He'd be on his knees, cutting the twine off some new young trees with his conspicuously large pocketknife. "Lovely night, isn't it?" It was never, ever lovely. But she always said, "Yes. Lovely night."

And now he was asking her about her scent.

"All of them," she wanted to tell him. "I'm wearing all of them. Every single fucking one."

But what she told Stephen was that it was a new fragrance from a new perfumer. French.

And he was deeply impressed. Or he pretended to be, she couldn't tell.

If her friend Ursula knew about Stephen, what would she say? Probably she would take one look at his long, gaunt, shining face and she would say, "I don't trust that boy." Like Stephen was a child and Karine was an old, stupid woman. But Stephen wasn't a child. He'd told her he was twenty-three when she'd asked that one time. Karine had felt so old at twenty-three. She had felt, in fact, that she was already dying. She'd mope around, reciting "The Love Song of J. Alfred Prufrock" to anyone who'd listen. She loved that poem. "I was going to be a poet," she'd told Stephen one night at the register. And he'd nodded. He could see that about her, he said. She had sort of a poetic way of seeing things, he thought. The dimmer switch on the world and all.

"Plans this evening?" Stephen asked her. He always asked her this. He was still dragging her sad grocery items across the scanner one by one. As usual, she'd chosen random things from the aisles. Cake sprinkles. Coleslaw that looked like vomit. A papaya that would never, ever ripen. Not until long after she and Stephen were both dead. She was terrified of death.

"Things are terrible, Stephen," she said quietly.

"Are they?" he said. He seemed sad for her but also excited by the idea. There was a flush now to his cheeks.

Poor boy, she thought. Would he really make it in the world? Probably not. In that way he was really just like her.

Now Karine was gazing at Stephen from across the table of a dark bar in the middle of the day. It was her day off from the department store. It was Stephen's day off too, apparently. They were at an Irish pub she liked to frequent in the afternoons. She liked how lightless it was and that they played somber music. In her mind's eye she could see the rolling dark green hills, the mist. All from that one lovely instrument, what was it called?

"The harp?" Stephen offered.

"Of course. The harp."

Was he handsome? She couldn't really say he was handsome. But his youth made his skin practically glow in the dark of the bar. She felt a kind of thrill being looked at. She basked in his gaze like a warm light. Probably he did find her attractive in a Mrs. Robinson sort of way. Perhaps he'd seen that film. They were seated in very large armchairs that swallowed them whole. It made her feel as though they were in a play. Or like they were children playing adults. Stephen was drinking a Pepsi. It came with three bright red cherries, which he ate slowly one by one. He kept his coat on in the bar, a thick, woolly tweed thing that made him look like Oliver Twist. When he'd ordered the Pepsi, she'd felt her stomach twist.

"Oh God," she said. "You're not old enough to drink?"

"Oh, no, I am, I am," Stephen said. "Just I've had some trouble with it. In the past." He looked off wistfully into the distance as if it were his past.

"Really?" she said. "With drinking?"

"And other things," he added meaningfully. "But I'm happy to watch you drink. I like to watch people having fun." He smiled. Ate one of his cherries.

She'd ordered a white wine with a shot of scotch on the side.

"Those are great choices," Stephen had said.

Across from her in the bar, he glowed like a moon. A kind moon. Not the cruel night she was used to.

"This is nice," she said. "I like this."

"It is nice," Stephen said. "I like it too."

Who'd asked whom out first? In Karine's mind it was all very hazy. She had been walking to her car after their exchange in the grocery store. She'd been crying; of course she'd been crying. Crying in the parking lot with the bags full of ridiculous inedible items in her hands. She was prone to that kind of thing, ever since she'd left Boca Raton and moved here thinking maybe New England, the gray ocean, the cold damp, the loneliness of the place, would absolve her of something. It hadn't. Still prone to these sudden fits. They'd been happening more and more lately. Every day at least one—breakdown? Yes, she would have to call it a breakdown. Where her face suddenly crumpled into itself like it had been punched. Where the heaviness of her heart became far too heavy, like a bag she could no longer carry. And then there were the tears in her eyes. Falling, falling. It was embarrassing, frankly. And then there had been that voice behind her. "Miss Valentine.

Miss Valentine? Miss? You left behind your . . ." And she'd turned around, and of course she was still crying when she turned around. Couldn't contain it. Great big hideous sobs were coming out of her mouth, the kind that make you hyperventilate. Stephen should have looked embarrassed for her. He should have gone red in the face at the sight of her tears, like a sheepish boy. Probably she looked so terribly old and hideous and pathetic crying in the gray evening light like that. She wouldn't have blamed him even for walking away. "Everyone walks away from me," she would have called after him. "In the end. They use me up and then they walk away. And here I am smelling of all the perfumes of the world, but nothing takes away the rot."

But Stephen didn't walk away. He stood there in the parking lot clutching her wallet. It was patterned all over with tiny corgis. She'd left it at the cash register, apparently. She did things like that a lot these days.

His face stayed pale as he watched her gather herself. Not embarrassed at all. Almost like he'd seen this kind of thing before. He was wearing his bright blue cashier's smock, and it eerily matched his eyes. She looked at the knife sticking so conspicuously out of his back pocket.

"Don't be," Stephen kept saying. Because she kept apologizing: "I'm sorry, I'm sorry, I'm sorry."

"We're friends, aren't we?" he said.

Friends? she thought. *But we hardly know each other at all. And I'm old enough to be your mother.*

Yes, friends. We're friends. And the thought had made her happy.

"I'm going for a drink tomorrow afternoon," she might have said then. "Would you like to come?"

"How about we go for a drink?" Stephen might have said.

One of them had said something like that. And then: "I could come with you," Stephen had said. He had definitely said that. "I'd like that. A lot."

And now here they were. Their first . . . date? No, not a date. A gettogether. That was all. And Stephen was looking at her like she was such a curious and exhilarating dream.

Things were silent between them, but like her crying, the silence didn't seem to embarrass Stephen. At all. He seemed to enjoy staring at her in the dark bar in the middle of the day.

"Tell me something about your life, Miss Valentine," he said to her now. Like he was her priest.

She looked at this boy holding his Pepsi, waiting for her confession. She almost wanted to laugh at his sudden gravity. But then she could also feel herself welling up. All of her griefs were so close to her skin these days. She hated it.

"I've had a lot of shitty men come into my life," she could say. "A lot of shitty ones, Stephen. I could tell you. I could tell you terrible things."

She wanted to tell Stephen about them all. The one who'd stolen her car. The one who'd looked like a frog. At first she'd thought it was her eyes, but it wasn't her eyes. He was green, she wanted to tell Stephen. And yet she'd gone home with him anyway. Found herself in the passenger seat of his Prius, which was green too, just staring out the window at the rushing black outside, thinking, *Why? Why? Why?* She'd sat in his odd living room, staring at a large poster of a vivisected human body he'd hung on the wall, letting him make her cocktails. Aviators first. Then this deep-green-colored drink that had made her sick, that might even have had a drug in it. Though she'd suspected this at the time, she'd taken a sip all the same. She'd drunk the whole thing down, in fact. Staggered into the bedroom with the frog man. One foot in front of the other down his crooked wooden hallway. "Are you sure you're all right?" he'd asked her. "Fine," she'd said. It turned out he had some strange sexual proclivities. And she had indulged him. And now the memory was behind a bolted door in her mind.

Then there was the academic she'd met on Tinder who'd left dark marks all around her neck. She hadn't even felt them at the time. She'd stared at his bedroom ceiling while he did it, marveling at its gritty texture, marveling at all the moths caught in the light fixture. It was only days later when she was gazing at herself in her own grim bathroom mirror that she'd seen them—a necklace of purple-black bruises ringed in yellow like eclipsed suns.

And then there had been Charlie.

And now here I am, she thought. *In Revere. Wandering through my days like they're a kind of limbo.*

"I used to live in Florida," is what she told Stephen.

"Florida," Stephen repeated wistfully. "Palm trees."

"Yes," she said. "And water. And terrible men." She laughed. *Terrible men like Charlie*, she thought. "But then, I guess terrible men are everywhere."

"Yes," Stephen said seriously. "Terrible men are here, too." As if he knew. Had had dealings with the terrible men himself. He leaned forward now, looking at her from across the table. His eyes were far less blue in this coat. They weren't even blue at all, really. They were more like the olive of the coat. He had the kind of eyes that took on whatever color happened to be nearby.

"Why did you leave Florida?" he asked. And there was a hunger in the question. An eagerness she shrank from like a too-bright light.

She had been leaning forward in her chair, but now she leaned back. Shrugged.

"I needed a change, I guess," she said.

Stephen nodded solemnly, respectfully. Of course she'd needed a change. That made sense. Even though he had no idea. Or did he?

"Well, I'm glad you came here," he said. "I like it so much when you come to the store."

"You do?"

"Oh yes. You're like a movie. A sad, strange movie."

A movie, she thought. She liked that idea. Hearing that made her feel like perhaps everything made sense. Florida. And now Revere. Her life had a shape, as it turned out, its sad string of scenes added up to something. They even took on a kind of music then.

"You don't have to call me Miss Valentine," she said.

And Stephen smiled.

He asked her then if she'd like to go for a drive. Would she like to go for a drive?

He wanted to show her something. He thought she might like it. It was a bit of a drive, yes. But so worth it.

It was an old car the color of gold. Brown velour seats inside. Stephen was driving slowly down a dark, winding byway. Karine sat in the passenger seat, watching the strange landscape rush by, the way she had done so many times before in other cars with other men. But Stephen wasn't a man. She shouldn't be afraid to be in the car with him, she thought. That was ridiculous. He was just a boy. Besides, they were friends, weren't they?

And yet she felt a spark of fear. It was the same fear she'd felt when she got into the Prius with the green man. The same fear she'd felt when she saw Charlie behind the bar. Knowing in advance what terrible thing would happen but proceeding all the same. One foot in front of the other. Staggering a little. While they smiled at her and said, "Are you sure you're okay with this? Are you sure you're okay?" And she said, "Fine." Or she said nothing at all. Nothing was like saying "fine" in their eyes, she knew. And she was full of fear. It was a fear not of them, but of herself. Of her own kitten-heeled feet, the click of her heels as they walked her right into the black maw of another terrible night.

The car smelled of cigarettes, which surprised her. There was a pack of Matinée 100s in the cup holder along with a silver lighter.

Stephen grabbed a cigarette then and lit it. Not terribly expertly.

It was funny to watch him smoke. He was probably younger than he'd told her. She shouldn't be afraid. Yet her chest was still tight. Neither of them spoke much. Stephen played a tape of some sort of choir music. It sounded like Gregorian chants.

"When I hear this, I think of you," he said.

He thought of her? Really?

"You shouldn't be thinking of me, Stephen. You shouldn't. I'm an old woman." But as she said this, she ran a hand through her hair like a fool. Afraid. Excited. Excited that she was afraid. Afraid that she was excited.

"I do," he said softly. He spoke so softly.

She thought of the knife in his back pocket. Absurdly large in his too-small pocket, in its suede case.

If he wanted to kill her, if he turned out to be a maniac, it was actually fine, she thought.

Probably her dog was right. Stephen wasn't kind and that was for the best. The movie of her life couldn't possibly end well.

"You attract them," her friend Ursula had said how many times. "They can smell it on you."

"Smell what?"

"That you want to be destroyed."

"Destroyed? That's ridiculous. Who wants to be destroyed?"

And she'd smiled: *You do*, said a voice inside. *You do, you do.*

"That's fine with me," she said to Stephen now, thinking of the knife, of his soft voice, of his feathery hair, which was the hair of killers, she saw it now. And what she was saying then was, *Do it. Kill me or whatever you're going to do. Because what's ahead?* Too-bright light. The glares of Macy's customers. Varicose veins snaking up her shins from standing all day in the perfume cloud. Drugged nights. Afternoons she didn't know what to do with. She just stared at them helplessly through her smudged-up window, her chest tight. Breathing a sigh of relief when at last the darkness fell.

They drove on and on. It was truly dark now. Driving in black, she was used to that.

They were winding their way up a hill now. The road seemed to twist forever upward. She let it twist. A street full of old, impoverished-looking houses. Trees whose branches reminded her of witch fingers. "Where are we going?" she might have asked, but she didn't. She just sat there thinking, *This is the movie of my life. Ending. Finally ending.*

He eventually pulled into what looked like a parking lot and stopped the car.

He turned to look at her in the passenger seat.

"Here we are," he said.

She looked out through the windshield at the black.

"Oh," she said like there was something out there she could see.

"It's just in there," he said, pointing out at the black.

She nodded. Of course it was.

Stephen led Karine through the unlit parking lot. And as he did, she thought, *The end, the end, the end. Finally the end. Here in Revere. On this sad little hill full of run-down houses and witch-finger trees. Why not?* Up ahead she saw there were dim lights. It was a church, it looked like. Creepy. She didn't like churches at all. She could barely make this one out in the dark. Beside it was some kind of gated square. A garden? Cemetery? She couldn't tell. All around the square were tall spikes. What was he going to do with her here? Stab her, probably. Attempt sex.

"Forgot it's locked at this time of night," Stephen said, looking up at the gate.

"Oh," she said. And she thought, *Of course it's locked.*

"We'll have to jump it," he said.

"Jump it?"

She watched as, with shocking agility, Stephen jumped up onto the gate and then, from that height, reached down for her hand.

She looked up at his hand. A white spider glowing above her head in the dark. *He'll do whatever he's going to do to me on the other side of the gate*, she thought. *Inside the square. That makes sense.*

She took his hand and allowed herself to be hoisted up—he was surprisingly strong for a man named Stephen. Once they were both straddling the fence, he jumped to the ground.

She looked down at the pavement below. It was a long way down from this height. Stephen was smiling up at her. "Your turn," he said. His breath coming out of his mouth in twisted smoke. *I'll break my neck*, she thought. She jumped, landing on her feet.

Stephen was smiling. Or at least she thought he was smiling.

"Look," he said softly, pointing at nothing.

"What?" she said.

"Mary," he whispered.

"Mary? Who's—"

"The Mother of God," Stephen said. "Queen of the universe. That statue up there, see?" He waved a hand at the dark.

She looked more closely. And it was then that she could just make out the giant silhouette of a figure against the black sky. It was obscenely tall. It appeared to have a crown of spikes.

"I see," she said.

"She's kind of famous around here. People pray to her and stuff. Wish on her. Ask her for miracles and things. I come here sometimes," Stephen said softly. "I used to come here a lot. When I was in trouble before."

She watched him gazing solemnly up at the statue. Did he want to kill her before the statue as a kind of sacrifice?

"She helps me," Stephen persisted. "She might be able to help you. She listens. At least it feels like she does. And something about her face reminds me of yours. She's always looked really sad to me."

He put his hand on her shoulder then. It felt like nothing at all.

Karine could only just make out the statue's face in the dark. Her spiked silhouette, looming against the black sky. She wasn't smiling. Her eyes were soft blanks. Knowing all the sorrows of the world. Knowing and that was all.

Karine felt Stephen staring at her. He'd never been in trouble before. He wanted nothing dark or terrible from her, she realized then. He wanted to help her. To save her, even. His knife would stay in his pocket. His hand would only ever help her over a fence.

She looked at him. His eyes full of terrible wonder and good intentions. Imagining he could see the statue in the dark. Looking at her, at everything, like it all held such promise.

Looking at the dark like it would be light again and that would be a good thing.

It would all be a good thing.

This was worse than any knife. Worse than Charlie. Worse than anything.

She looked back at the statue she could barely make out in the dark. A blank holiness that waited to take on her broken soul, her tears. Waiting to hear her and heal her.

"Take me home," she said.

On the News

Annie Hartnett

CAROL BANDES HAD JURY DUTY, AND SHE DID NOT FEEL THAT IT
was "a waste of time," as the Coconino County of Arizona website
said was the most common complaint among potential jurors. She
pulled into the Flagstaff town center, up to the courthouse on Beaver
Street, a redbrick building with arched windows and a clock tower.
There was a line out the large green courthouse door. A surprising
number of people were in pajamas. They had not read the website,
which requested appropriate attire. *What universe do these people live
in?* Carol thought. Carol wished her husband were there. Martin
would make her laugh about it.

She got in line behind a fortysomething woman, probably a
few years younger than Carol, although Carol was sure she looked
better. Carol had taken care of herself, a manicure once a week,
regular facials. Her hair was short because Martin liked it that way.
The woman in front of her was in a yellow sweatshirt and Tweety
Bird pajama bottoms, and had penciled her eyebrows on with a
purplish-brown pencil. "Are you a lawyer?" the woman asked.

"No," Carol said. "Sorry."

"Don't be sorry," she said. "You just look like a lawyer."

The line moved forward, and soon they were at the big green
double doors. Once inside, everyone had to go through a metal
detector. Carol was surprised at how often the alarm went off, by how
many people had brought guns to the courthouse. A few knives, too.

*

An hour later Carol was sitting in the juror room, waiting for something to happen. There were about a hundred people in the room, and they sat wedged in wooden pews. It was freezing in the room, and Carol was glad that the website had suggested that jurors wear layers. She was glad for her cardigan. They'd all been told to be quiet, and some of the people had to be hushed several times. A woman wearing a maroon velour tracksuit kept on whistling, didn't think any of the hushes were for her. She was wearing lipstick to match the tracksuit, had her platinum-blond hair in ringlet curls. Her body was shaped like a guinea pig; she was a potato in the middle, with short arms and legs.

A man in a suit passed out a questionnaire. He winked at Carol when he handed her one; maybe he thought she was a lawyer too. It was a list of twenty multiple-choice questions. The final question said: "Are you for or against the death penalty?" The multiple-choice answers were:

A. Yes
B. No
C. Maybe

Carol did not think this case would be a death penalty case. She did not imagine she would be that lucky. She did hope it was a murder trial. A complicated one. A trial that would just about take forever. Carol had shit else to do, as Martin would say.

The man in the suit came around again, took Carol's questionnaire, glanced over it, and handed her a ticket, like they were at a deli counter. He wrote her number on the top of the questionnaire. "If they call your number," he said, "you go into the next room." He winked again. Maybe it was a twitch, Carol thought. Then again, she had always been the kind of woman who was winked at. She had figured it would stop as she got closer to fifty, and she hoped it would. Martin used to go absolutely bananas when another man would flirt with her. It was why she'd left her job at the bank, because her old boss was always making comments about her. Martin couldn't stand it. Her boss had been the kind of man who used the word "heinie" when talking about a woman's backside. She regretted mentioning that to Martin. She really did.

As the man in the suit moved around the room, he looked at the questionnaires and told some people that they were free to go. The woman in the Tweety Bird pajamas was sent out. Then he announced to the remaining people that they should feel free to talk, but not about the news.

No news. Carol was glad of that. She had had just about enough of the news. Martin would have told her to turn that goddamn TV off, but Carol kept it on. She couldn't help it. Of course, the news had stopped mentioning the Snowbowl attack long ago. It wasn't part of the news cycle; it had been over a year. It was April now, another ski season over. Some people in this room might not even know what Carol was talking about if she mentioned the Snowbowl attack. Not everyone had paid attention when it happened, and skiing wasn't for everyone. Many people couldn't afford it, or they lived in Arizona because they hated the snow. Her relatives back in Maryland had been surprised there even was a ski mountain in Flagstaff. But her husband had loved it, the snow and skiing. Since he retired from his job on the railroad, he'd worked at the Snowbowl part-time. He had retired young. Fifty-four. Still had plenty of energy. Their sex life had never been better.

After the man in the suit left with their questionnaires, the room was silent for a moment longer, and then the woman wearing the maroon tracksuit broke the silence with the loud unzipping of her backpack. She pulled out what looked like a small radio, which had somehow made it through the metal detector.

"Oh hell no," another woman said, and got up and moved to the far corner of the waiting room, as far away as possible from the radio.

The tracksuit woman flicked it on.

She just got static, the reception horrible in that thick old building, but she turned the volume up. She did not seem to be looking for another channel, but she kept nodding as if it were the perfect song. She leaned back in her seat.

"Excuse me," the man in the pew behind her said, a black man in a green sweater. "Could you turn that down? I mean, could you turn it off? It's not even playing music."

"Not supposed to be playing music," she said.

"Excuse me?" he said again.

"It's my ghost box."

"It's your what?" the man said. Carol leaned toward the conversation. Of course she was interested.

"Oh, honey," the woman said to the green-sweatered man. "You've never heard of a ghost box? It's like a telephone to the dead. Come over here and I'll show you how it works."

"No thank you," the man said, and turned back to the paper.

The woman looked over and saw Carol staring. She didn't say anything, just beckoned her over with her thick finger.

"How old are you?" she asked when Carol sat down, before she'd asked her name. Carol told her that she'd be forty-eight next month. "You've brought some very old energy with you," the woman said. "I thought you'd say sixty at least."

"Oh," Carol said. "I've had a hard year."

"I can see that. I'm Barbara Anne and I'm a ghost communicator. Don't like to call myself a medium because they don't speak through me. I don't want ghosts inside me, no thanks."

"Amazing," Carol said. Martin would have called this woman full of shit. *Absolutely full of shit.*

Barbara Anne explained how the ghost box worked, that it was a modified transistor radio, and instead it caught the frequency of the dead. So if there was a ghost around and you asked it questions, the spirit could speak through the radio waves. "There should be a lot of ghosts in the courthouse," Barbara Anne said. "There used to be a jail in the basement."

"And the ghosts are . . . angry?"

"Oh, some are angry, sure. But most are just disappointed. That's what I've found in my years of research," she said. "The majority of spirits hang on because they were disappointed by something in their life."

"That's depressing."

"It's a wake-up call, is what it is. Are you disappointed by your life? Then you better figure out how you could be less disappointed while you're still alive."

"Thanks for the advice," Carol said, and it sounded sarcastic. But she didn't mean to be rude to Barbara Anne. She wanted to know more about the ghost box. It was a good thing Barbara Anne wasn't easily shut up.

"You might be interested to learn that Thomas Edison invented the ghost box," Barbara Anne said, fiddling again with the radio dial.

"He absolutely didn't," the man in the green sweater said, putting his newspaper down.

"People *say* he did," Barbara Anne said.

"Who?"

"Forty percent of Americans believe in ghosts, you know," Barbara Anne said.

"Aren't you just full of fun facts," Green Sweater said.

"I should be. I run a ghost tourism business. I drive a bus all around Arizona, and together we look for ghosts," she said, raising her voice now, advertising to the room. She said there were day-trips and overnight options. She took out some business cards and, of course, a pamphlet.

"What a great job," Carol said, but at this point Barbara Anne wasn't paying attention to Carol. She was arguing with the man in the green sweater. He stood up, furious. He said in a very loud radio-announcer voice, "Okay, we've got about one hundred people in this room, right? Do forty of you believe in ghosts? Raise your hands if you believe in ghosts. Raise 'em."

No one raised a hand, not even Carol. Well, of course Barbara

Anne raised her fleshly little paw, with the blue fingernail polish.

A security guard came over then and asked what all the ruckus was, and Carol went back to her seat. Barbara Anne and the green-sweater man tried to explain what they were arguing about, and the longer they talked, the more the security guard looked bored by it all, like he'd heard this one before. The security guard scratched his unshaven face and said they were both being dismissed and they could gather their things.

"I wanted to serve," Barbara Anne pleaded. "I'm an excellent judge of character." But the security guard wouldn't hear it. He looked like he needed a few more hours of sleep.

After Barbara Anne left, Carol looked down at her card. "Barbara Anne Lavoy, Ghost Hunter," it read. Carol wanted to call her. Have her come to the house. See what Barbara Anne could tell her.

It had been a terror attack, that's what the news had called it. Not just *any* terror attack either, when those were so common these days. It was an *eco*-terror attack. Young people trying to make some sort of statement. Carol's mom called them hippies, even though that wasn't what they were, and Carol's mother was batty anyway, locked in a nursing home back in Baltimore. Carol's brother took care of her. Martin was always saying they should go visit if Carol wanted to, but they never did. Carol didn't want to. Carol and Martin just wanted to be alone together. They liked to watch TV; Martin controlled the remote, since Carol could never figure out the buttons. They went to the movies sometimes. They both liked the burritos at MartAnne's. They scratched each other's backs, had sex three times a week. Martin had a few drinks every night, but Carol stayed sober. Carol kept the house clean, absolutely spick-and-span. Martin liked it that way, and she had "shit else to do," since she didn't work at the bank anymore.

Carol slipped Barbara Anne's card into her purse. Then again, Carol definitely didn't need someone to tell her that life was disappointing. One person could fill up your whole life, every inch of it, and then he could be gone and leave you with nothing. Nothing except your spotless house, your close-cropped hair, because that was the way Martin liked it.

While Carol waited for something else to happen in the waiting room, or for her number to be called, she opened the ghost tourism pamphlet to read the testimonials. Carol was so absorbed in it that the security guard had to poke her when they called number thirty-four, and he led Carol into the next room for her interview. Two sets of lawyers were there, and a judge in the middle in the traditional black robe. There was a gavel. There was no defendant in the room.

"Do you have opinions about drugs that would interfere with your ability to be a fair and impartial juror?" the judge asked. That was the first question.

Carol's heart skipped a beat. It was a drug dealing trial. Not as good as a murder trial maybe, but one that might take a while. Break up her life a little. Give her a reason to get out of bed in the morning. Her neighbor Elizabeth had suggested getting a dog. Something she had to walk. A little dog maybe, just one that you have to walk around the block. "Then again," Elizabeth said, "a big dog might be good for protection, since you're all alone in the house and all."

"I don't do drugs, unless you're counting Zyrtec," Carol told the judge. She did not count all the alcohol she'd been drinking. The bottles of Sauvignon Blanc. That wasn't their business. "But I don't have any opinions that would interfere with my judgment."

"Zyrtec, that's good," chuckled the defense lawyer.

"What was your profession when you were employed?" the judge asked, because Carol had written "Unemployed" on the questionnaire. She had thought about writing "Homemaker," but that didn't seem right. She had no one to make a home for.

"I was a bank teller," she said. "But I quit."

"Why did you quit?" the judge asked.

"Well, I was fired," Carol admitted, because she knew a courtroom wasn't a place to lie.

"Were you given a reason?"

"My husband," she said. "He was the reason."

"Huh," said the judge. "That's a new one."

"It wasn't true," Carol said after a minute. "But I was fired all the same."

"What wasn't true?" the defense lawyer asked.

"Well, my boss misunderstood something he said. It wasn't a death threat. Martin was just a bull in a china shop."

"Well, bulls do kill people," the judge said. When Carol had moved to Arizona, she'd been struck by how many cattle lived in the state. Martin always called her his city girl.

It happened then; Carol didn't know what hit her. She started crying. "Sobbing" might be the better word for it.

"I'm sorry," said the judge. "What did I say?"

"I think her husband is dead," the prosecutor said. "It's on the questionnaire."

"Jesus," the judge said. "Ma'am, I'm sorry. I'm sure your husband was not a bull. I'm sure it was a misunderstanding. *This* has been a misunderstanding."

Carol couldn't stop the crying now. She wanted to ask the judge why he had failed her. He hadn't been the judge in Martin's case, but still. He represented the justice system that had failed Martin. The eco-terrorists, four men and one woman, had sawed off the pylons and the cables on the chairlift at the Snowbowl. Martin had been on the first chair of the day, wanted to get on the slopes. He was always an up-and-at-'em kind of guy. Martin had fallen from a great height.

The defense lawyer went to touch her, and the judge warned him not to. Even though she was upset, so upset, Carol could see the judge was on red alert. He knew he had acted out of line. "Thank you for coming in today and offering to serve," the judge said, looking down at his notes. "You are dismissed. Charles will walk you out."

The security guard grabbed her arm and helped her up as she

wiped the snot with her bare hands. He showed Carol to another door, which entered into a long hallway. She stood in the hallway until she could stop crying. People stared. "No one wants jury duty," she said out loud. "I have better things to do," she said to the hallway. But jury duty was going to be something to do. When she had nothing else.

She stopped once more at the front door of the courthouse to collect herself. Next to the door was a bulletin board, littered with flyers, people selling firewood, lost dogs and cats. A part-time director was needed for the community theater summer play. Babysitters were advertising, all the little scraps of paper with the phone numbers pulled off. People with things to do. People with purpose, or at least looking for purpose. Leaving their phone numbers so that a purpose could call.

Carol walked outside the courthouse, and she overheard a man wearing a cowboy hat and Wrangler jeans tell a woman how he was on the way to release twenty-six black-footed ferrets into the wild. "Just waiting on some final paperwork from the courthouse. It's a crime to kill a ferret, you know," he said. "Endangered."

"Aren't they mean?" the woman asked. "I heard they're mean bastards."

"Nah," he said. "Funny little guys, really. I raised them myself in captivity, but it's time to set them free. Help the population bounce back."

Carol loved this man. What a crystal-clear life goal, reintroducing endangered animals to the wild. Something that actually helped the environment, too, not like cutting the wires of a chairlift, killing innocent people, because you were mad about trees that had been chopped down. The other woman walked away; she wasn't interested in the ferrets. She probably had her own purpose, probably had a job. She would probably get picked to serve on a jury.

"Could I come with you?'" Carol heard herself asking the man. "Could I come to release the ferrets, I mean?"

The man looked at Carol, looked at her up and down in a way

that would have made Martin's blood boil. "Sure," he said. "I could use the company."

Two hours later Carol and this man named Hank were in the middle of nowhere. Or in the middle of a ranch north of Flagstaff that had been cleared as a habitat for these endangered ferrets raised in captivity. There were crates of ferrets in the back of the truck; each crate held two ferrets, Hank said. It was enough ferrets to start a colony. The ferrets had been raised in captivity, but they would be fine. The tunnels were predug for them on this ranch. They had been given a head start, and the land would be protected. Coyotes and eagles could still kill them, but humans would not.

Carol looked out at all that land, this land left for the ferrets, and wondered if Hank was the kind of man who would kill a woman out here. He would get away with it; no one knew she was here, not a single soul. What would it be like to be a man, Carol wondered, who never had to think about whether or not he was about to be murdered in the desert or whether he was just going to have a nice enough time? Martin had never wondered if someone was going to kill him until someone did.

Irina. That was the name of one of the eco-terrorists. The female one. Carol thought about that woman all the time. She had printed out her head shot, but her printer wasn't the greatest quality. She would send the photo to Staples, so she could tape that photo up on the wall, look at Irina's face every day, but she was embarrassed. What if the person at Staples asked her why she was printing out someone's head shot? What if she started crying, right there in a fucking Staples? Just like she had started crying in jury duty. What would Martin say? He would be ashamed of her. He would tell her to toughen up. He would tell her not to call that lunatic woman, the one with the ghost box radio. "What on earth are you thinking, Carol?" he would say. "What kind of idiot did I marry?"

Hank was unloading the ferrets from the truck. He hadn't

asked her for help. Many of the ferrets were already released, were exploring their predug tunnels. Some kind of tubing had been used to keep the tunnels open, the kind of tubing that comes out of your clothes dryer. *People are amazing,* Carol thought. *They really are.*

Carol decided she wouldn't wait for Hank to tell her what to do. She went to the truck and grabbed a crate. "Out you go," she said when she opened the cage. There was just one ferret in there. It was so cute. Beady little eyes and a masked face. It looked so curious, and friendly. Carol stuck her hand in to pick up the ferret, and that's when it bit her, and not just a nip, either. There was blood all over the place all of a sudden, and Carol didn't make one single sound, but Hank was now swearing just like Martin would've.

"Goddamn it, fuck, shit, what the hell did you touch it for?" he said, and then he went to his truck. There was a first aid kit in the glove box. He was the kind of man who came prepared. *Probably not a murderer,* Carol decided as he poured alcohol on her hand.

"You didn't even flinch," he said, standing back. "That should have hurt like a bitch."

Carol thought about telling him her husband had died a year ago, last winter, had free-fallen while in a chairlift, had broken so many bones in the fall, but it had taken him seven more hours to die at the hospital. How there was too much bleeding in his brain.

"High pain tolerance," she said instead.

"Sure seems like it," Hank said. "I'm impressed."

Irina had gotten only five years in prison. She took some kind of plea deal. The men had gotten much more, especially the one who had planned the whole thing, but it was Irina that Carol wanted put away. She would have wanted Irina to get the electric chair if it were an option. She should have circled "yes" on the jury duty questionnaire, the last question, about the death penalty. She had circled "maybe."

"Such playful creatures," Hank said, putting a hand on Carol's shoulder. It was a big hand, not unlike Martin's. "I just love 'em," he said. "The ferrets."

Carol reached across her chest to put her hand on top of Hank's, the hand that remained on her shoulder. It was nice to touch someone. They stood there and watched the ferrets dive in and out of the dusty brown earth. They were having such fun.

"Of course, they murder prairie dogs," Hank said. "It's their main food source. That's hard to watch, since prairie dogs are just as cute, if not cuter."

"Everyone murders something else," Carol said. And Hank looked at her funny for a second, but then he told her she could keep being part of the Black-Footed Ferret Arizona Reintroduction Project if she wanted to.

"I don't think my husband would like it," she said.

"And here I was hoping you didn't have a husband," Hank said, winking. *Always with the men winking.*

"I don't," she said. "He's dead. But he wouldn't have liked it when he was alive. He would have thought it was a waste of my time."

"I see," Hank said. "Well. I'm sorry for your loss."

"Do you believe in ghosts?" she asked.

"Nah," Hank said. "My ma killed herself."

"What kind of answer is that?" Carol asked.

"I just think if there was such thing as ghosts," Hank said, "my ma would have showed up by now. To apologize, you know?"

"Maybe," Carol said. "Or maybe she isn't sorry."

"Nice thing to say," Hank said, but he didn't really sound upset. He must be a tough guy, with his cowboy hat and his dead mother who had never come back to apologize.

Martin wasn't the type to apologize either, not when living and not when dead.

"I'm sorry," she said. "I'm not myself lately."

"Don't worry about it," Hank said. "I've heard worse things."

Carol watched the ferrets chase one another in and out of the tunnels. Which one had bitten her, she couldn't tell; which was the one she had set free? She wished she could recognize that ferret, but all the ferrets looked more or less the same. Hank said the males were bigger than the females, but Carol couldn't even tell that. But even if she didn't know which one it was, she knew she had done something good for that one ferret, something really good. Let it out of its cage. Given it a taste of fresh blood. Hank said in captivity they'd had only frozen rats to eat, but out here they'd have to learn to hunt prairie dogs using instinct. Or they'd have to starve. Her ferret had a leg up, Carol figured, had bitten into something still alive, even if the ferret hadn't killed her. The ferret had only wounded her, and not badly, but still. A taste of blood.

Maybe Carol did want to be part of the project, just so she could find out what happened next. Find out if the ferrets lived or died. It really didn't matter what Martin would have thought about it. It really didn't. She was alone in the desert with a strange man, and no one knew, no one cared. No one would be angry with her when she went home, when she walked in the door to nothing but the glow of the TV, the news channel still on. The news channel always left on, because Carol didn't like to be alone in the quiet with Martin's ghost. She didn't like to sit around with his silent disappointment with his life, and with hers.

How thrilling it had been, those two days when the TV anchor had said Martin's name over and over and over, as if the anchor couldn't get enough of it. As if Martin Bandes had committed some crime. Or as if he had lived an extraordinary, newsworthy life. How Carol missed him. And yet how glad she was to have him gone. She didn't know how both those things could be true, until she watched these ferrets, raised in captivity and then suddenly declared wild. You could be two things at once, free and captive forever.

"Let's go home," she said to Hank then, as if they lived together, as if they were both going back to the same house, the same bed, the same living room, the same television remote she still couldn't figure out how to use, after all this time alone.

A Way to Beat Mortality

Shelly Oria

IF YOU WANT TO MEET GIRLS WHO ARE REAL HUNGRY FOR IT, THE psych ward is where you want to go. I say this to my buddy Pete, and Pete says, "That the new bar down on Fifth?" I need to stop wasting my calls on him is what I need to do. "Focus, Petey," I tell him. "Where am I calling you from?" "Oh," he says. "Cool."

The conversation is going nowhere, so I can't even tell him about Cheeky, which was the whole point of the call. Because what was I going to do, bring it up in group? "Fatty over here and me got something we want to share"? Or whisper to my roommates after lights-out, "Cheeky's got a wild side like you wouldn't believe, like no other girl I ever seen"? Say, "Touching her feel like you rolling your whole hot body in snow"? Course not. We all know each other here. That kind of talk would be disrespectful. And if I learned one thing from my relationship with Talie, from her death, from coming so close to death myself that I held it in my mouth and it tasted like rust, like failure, like the end of air—if I learned anything from all that, it's that respect matters. Had Talie and I treated each other with respect, had we respected ourselves enough to respect each other, she'd still be alive. Some things are simple.

Pete can't focus most of the time and it's not his fault; he's got a thing where the left part of his brain checks out if he smokes even half a joint. And what's he going to do, quit smoking? He needs his pot the way I need the hospital. Petey and me, we got in trouble selling a building that couldn't be bought. We had no idea we were doing anything wrong; we didn't mean the illegalities that happened. Turns out in real estate, good intentions don't matter. In a year or two or three, when the investigators decide they've concluded their investigating, we may be able to breathe right again, or we may be facing a jury of our peers. Every time we talk, I say to Petey, "You get yourself some help like I did and you won't have to smoke till you numb." If his head's straight when I say it, he gives me a hard time. "Daley, my man, we both know what help you really there for." He thinks the hospital is my backup plan to avoid jail. Strategizing is what he calls it. "You just strategizing, D." He's not wrong, but he's not right, either.

I show up to group in the afternoon fresh from my call with Pete, and Cheeky's chair is empty. Technically, it's just another chair like any other chair; seats aren't assigned in group, and this is something we're told once a week at least, asked to repeat back—it seems important, maybe because it's bad to indulge the OCDs, maybe for some other reason. In reality we all know which chair is whose, and this is one way in which everyone's respectful. So I don't need to look around; I know right away Cheeky's not in the room. I sit down, and soon as we get started, I say I want to share. What I share is a story Petey just told me on the phone about a girl we know: she got a dog-sitting gig and the dog died. I make this my story that happened in my formative years. I tear up a little describing the dog's eyes going out, touching the flap of his ear for the last time. Stepping out of the vet's cold office, calling my aunt to tell her Donut's gone. And sure, I'm lying, and some people in the room even know it, I bet. But there's a world in which every bit of my story is true, and most of the time that world is where I live. When I cry, it's because I loved that dog. It's because I fucked up.

I often call Pete right before group. "Buddy, give me material for a preempt," I tell him, and he just talks then, talks about anything at all. There's usually something in his words that I can use. I try to preempt with a share if I can, so no one will ask about Talie. These

people love to ask about her, about how she died, even though I
know they know everything. Painted into a corner, I'll say, "Look
it up." This happens in group and also in my one-on-ones. They say
things like, "It might be helpful to talk it through." "Look it up" is
maybe my way of saying "Fuck off" without cursing, which we're
not supposed to do, or maybe it's my way of reminding everyone that
I'm a little bit famous. "What's the difference?" Cheeky asked when
I said all this to her last week. "You're just saying the same thing
twice. Isn't the whole point of fame to keep people at a distance,
have everyone assume you want them to fuck off?"

Cheeky loses her sympathies when I complain about this place.
She says it's my delusions that make her impatient—"delusions" is
a big word around here—that no matter what anyone asks me, I
hear it as a question about my past. But I think she just gets jealous
hearing me talk about Talie. I don't say that, though, because I'm
not an idiot. What I say instead is, "I wish you acknowledged my
reality." And to that Cheeky always shrugs, which I suppose is fair:
she made the same point our very first conversation, months ago,
and back then I responded with gratitude. She cornered me after my
first or second group and said, "New guy, if you listen better, you'll
see most of the time no one's attacking you." I looked at her for long
seconds, and she looked right back at me. The truth is I felt a shift,
the beginning of a stretch, which made no sense—this girl did *not*
look like someone my body would respond to, let's say—and I was
thinking I might be having a reaction to one of the medications.
I said, "Thank you," because it seemed like a good way to end the
exchange.

The reason people around here love talking about other people's
delusions is that it's sort of foolproof; if you accuse someone of being
delusional about something, they can't argue, because arguing would
make them look delusional. That way you're both keeping the heat
off of yourself and supposedly making a valid point, being helpful to
a fellow patient. My tactic with this is to accept the accusation; I'll
say something like, "You're probably right. I struggle with delusions

quite a bit." Then I'll just go on talking. It usually works.

So is Cheeky right, am I just imagining that everyone's fixated on my past? Maybe. But I can tell you this: nine times out of ten, if I don't preempt, I'll get asked about the mess I made after Talie's death, what people like to call a "shooting." And the problem with this type of conversation is you let it start, it's going to continue. That's just how it goes with anything that's ever been in the news: people want to touch it. As if talking about a shooting makes them survivors, as if proximity to violence could make them famous, as if fame is a way to beat mortality. Fame, at best, is temporary distraction from sadness.

People who don't pay close attention conflate Talie's death and the shooting, and I'm not good at keeping cool when that happens. Talie didn't die in a shooting; Talie died in a Dumpster. This isn't a dignified truth, but it's the truth nonetheless. Talie died because she had the kind of friends that get you killed. And the kind of boyfriend, me, who lets death find you. A boyfriend who doesn't say, "Stop hanging with Holly." Who doesn't say, "I swear to God, you fuck around on me one more time . . ." Who sleeps tight, doesn't wake up with a knowing in his chest that something on the south side of town is wrong, because definitely if he did wake up with that type of tightness, he'd listen to it, act on it, wouldn't fall back asleep. He'd go out into the night, into the almost morning, find his girl, and save her life.

"So we're all obsessed with your past and also don't care enough to remember the details," Cheeky has said to me several times. She can sound clever, and a big part of her cleverness is she knows how to twist words around. "No," I say every time. "*Some* people are nosy, and *others* don't use their ears when I talk." The thing about this place is you end up having the same conversations many times. We repeat our words because there are more hours to every day here than there should be. "No one around here thinks your ex died in a shooting," Cheeky says, and usually what I say back is, "Please don't say 'shooting.'"

The main thing to know about the shooting is that it wasn't a real shooting: no one got hurt. Look it up and you'll see "no casualties," but what does that tell you? It suggests maybe no one died but some were injured. It distorts the truth, because lies sell papers. And the thing about a lot of the people here, they're the kind of people who read the paper. Also they are not critical thinkers. You explain to them about the types of distortions the papers are filled with, they say, "Call it what you want, but why'd you show up at that party with a gun?" They ask, but they don't believe there's an answer.

That party was a day or a month or a week after Talie's funeral. I don't know the specifics. A man hugging the floor, wasted with sorrow, high but lower than he'd ever been: what's the difference to him between hours and decades, a week and a day, a lifetime? "I was grieving, is all," I said once about that party, the gun, "grieving and angry." My therapist nodded and closed his eyes. "And you didn't have tools," he said. "That gun was your tool." Tools are what we're learning: how to have them, how to use them. No store sells these types of tools, but anyone can buy them, we're told, by showing up and working hard.

I want to have tools, I do. But I'm in no rush.

"This what you missed group for?" I ask Cheeky, meaning the mashed potatoes she's moving from side to side on her plate. You dating a fat girl, you know where to look when she's missing; nine times out of ten, checking the cafeteria will not be a waste of your time. Cheeky looks up. "What'd I miss?" "Nothing," I say, "I told a story." "Yeah," she says, and pushes her plate away like I just killed her appetite. She shakes her head, a tiny movement, light as a thought. "Didn't need to watch the Dale show today," she says. She gets up to leave like clearing the plasticware is no thing we do. "Baby," I say, "baby." She likes it when I call her that, but she looks at me now like I offered her a taste of poison. "Don't, Dale," she says. Then her back is moving away from me.

This feeling is nothing new: I had it with Talie, had it before Talie, had it every time I put my thing in someone for more than two, three nights. You hold a woman tight enough, sooner or later she'll be asking you questions. What I do now is I grab some stationery—Think Pads, they call them around here, and they're everywhere—and start compiling a list. Ten, fifteen minutes later I am standing at Cheeky's doorway holding some guesses. Cheeky is in bed reading a book. I have no doubt that she sees me, but she won't look up. Instead she pretends to go on reading, or, knowing her, she may actually be reading. That's what I love about her: she gives fewer fucks than maybe anyone I've ever known. I glance at my yellow pages. "This morning," I say, "I brushed my teeth instead of waiting for you to go first. It was inconsiderate." Cheeky's eyes are still on her book. I scan her face, but she's giving me nothing. Probably this first guess isn't right and I should move on to the next, but how can I know for sure? She's so . . . subtle. I think of Talie, the shit she'd have given me on the spot for this kind of move. I mean, you wake up with a woman for the first time and the bed is tight and the bathroom narrow, you don't fucking claim space. You offer up the sink, you offer up the toilet. What was I thinking? Cheeky squints. Her forehead is lines and lines. "What?" she says. So I move on to number two. "Let me preface by saying I very much hope it's not true," I say. She says, "Okay . . . ?" "Are you maybe just wishing we stayed friends and never slept together?" I ask. Cheeky is still squinting. "Last night was fun," she says, and then adds, "The physical part." "Okay," I say, "good. Good." I look at my yellow pad. "Are you reading from a list?" Cheeky asks. "No," I say. Now we are both looking at the yellow pad. "It's not like that," I say. "Okay," she says. "I just," I say, "I wrote down some possibilities for why you might be mad." Something softens in her face when I say this, something opens up just a tiny bit. She sits up, puts her book on the pillow, taps the mattress with light fingers. I walk over, sit by her side. Our bodies are close now, and it takes all my willpower not to kiss her, but I know that would be the wrong move. We look at each other, and then she looks down at the floor. "Tell me," I whisper. She looks back up, right into me, through me.

"Do you really not know?" she asks. We both know the answer to this question. She shakes her head, but it's such a small motion, the motion of a woman who wishes she were more surprised than she is. "For months you pursued me," she says. I want to say, "We pursued each other," but I know that's the wrong thing to say, and once I let it stay in my mouth for a second, two, three, I can also tell that it's untrue. She's right. I have been pursuing her, and for a good while what she did in response was try to convince me to unpursue her. "I just wanted to be friends," she says, and I nod. I hold her hand the way a dear friend would. "If you're not . . . ," she says. "If you don't like . . . ," Her words circle each other and me, forming a knot. I squeeze her hand, but so gentle it's basically like I did nothing. "If I don't like what?" I ask. "If I'm not your type," Cheeky says, and her voice sounds different, sharper, "then . . . why? Why go after me?" We look at each other and I try to think fast, but generally speaking, thinking fast in these types of situations isn't a strength of mine. I probably look like some animal in the wild, realizing that sound in the distance was the click of a rifle. I never said that she wasn't my type, only mentioned that *in the past* she wouldn't have been. It was a positive statement. Cheeky gives up on my eyes now, looks out the window. The windows here are so small. She lingers and lingers and at some point makes a face that's almost a smile, so I wonder, I have to, what she's seeing. Finally she says, "Let me tell you something as a friend." "Yes," I say, "of course." There is no other thing I can say in this moment. Some things are simple: I care more than she does, so she has more power than I do. As long as she's willing to talk, I will be here listening. "Fuck someone or don't," Cheeky says, "but if you do, then make no apologies." I narrow my eyes at her. "I don't understand," I say, though for the last few seconds a part of me has been replaying our whole conversation from last night, and I'm hearing it for the first time. "You don't need to understand," Cheeky says, "just don't ever tell a woman that you feel proud of yourself for fucking her."

I'm moving fast after that, changing clothes, passing through hallways and doorways, signing a piece of paper at the front desk, something titled Voluntary Patient Temporary Leave, and Reviva says, "You okay, Dale? Maybe discuss with your doctor first?" and I say, "I'm cool, Reviva, I'm cool," and she smiles at me like she believes in me, or maybe I'm so desperate for someone to believe in me that I'm willing Front Desk Reviva's smile with my imagination. She says, "You haven't filled out this part," her finger pointing at a question on the form, and I say, "I won't be gone very long," and she says, "You need to be more specific," and I chuckle like this is a joke we always tell, turn around to leave because this question feels suffocating, but Reviva's face is saying, *Answer my question or I'm not buzzing you out*, so I say, "Four, maybe five hours," and then I turn my back to her and then the main door, a heaviness I didn't expect against my muscles, and for a quick moment it seems my upper body isn't up to the task and I think, *Maybe this is a mistake?* Then I'm out.

The outside world is quiet, and I know it has quieted down just for me. I'm not being sentimental. It's just what happens, the soundtrack of silence piercing through the air. I also know it won't last; these gestures between Universe and Man, they are always brief. I'm not wrong, of course: a moment later I look around and everything is too much. The world has never been this beautiful, has never been this ugly, has never been this boundless. It is spilling, spilling all over. I see every detail all at once, and the thing is that the resolution is off. My eyes want to shut but I force them to stay open, then force them to imagine cubes, rectangles, sharp lines dividing the landscape. I can breathe again now, and what I do next is that I say hi. I say it out loud. I say it to the skies, to a tree, to the concrete under my feet, and the way that I say it is a flirt. I say hi like there's a girl in front of my face that no one else can see. *Hey, you.*

Thirty minutes later Petey opens the door, saying, "What the . . . ?" I hug him and try to explain about the world. I say I felt attacked by the air but I fought back and maybe I won. I say something about pixels. "Don't they ever let you go outside?" Petey asks. His question makes my body go small. It reduces my spiritual moment to exactly what you'd expect from any type of inmate. "There's a backyard-type place," I say, "but it doesn't feel like it's even outdoors at all." Pete nods. He looks different, maybe bigger or maybe just pastier, and also his eyes seem to have moved a bit forward, no longer sinking into their sockets like tired bodies collapsing into a couch. He definitely hasn't smoked today, maybe hasn't smoked in some time. I wonder how I didn't notice this change on the phone. He gives my shoulder a squeeze. "It's good to see you, Dale," he says.

In Petey's living room, over a beer that goes to my head like I'm pubescent, I talk about Cheeky. The room is as stripped as it's always been: tall white walls, no furniture except the worn-out sofa we're sitting on, not even a coffee table for our beer bottles. But looking around, I do notice one new thing, a strange thing: a small plant on the windowsill. If I didn't know better, I'd think a woman got Petey this plant, but he'd have told me if he was dating. I try to explain why in one sharp moment I had to leave the psych ward. I say "psych ward" when I talk to Pete, but it's not an accurate name for the place that's been my home in the last few months; no name feels accurate. Cheeky always says "the institute," which I can't bring myself to say. When I stop talking, Petey is looking at me like he's a detective working a case and I'm one of the suspects. I know that look; it means he's trying to gauge if I can take what he has to say. He's probably had that look for some time, but I kept my eyes on the floor or the plant the whole time I was talking. Now I'm looking straight at him, but he still seems unsure, so I have to verbalize. "Hit me," I say. He nods. Then he says, "You're an asshole." This makes me laugh even though I know Pete isn't joking. "I'm serious," he says. I say, "How am I an asshole?" Pete says, "Dale, crawl outside your own ass for one minute and think." I look at him, then I look away like I'm thinking, then I shake my head, quick gestures, the kind where if you do them too long, people think it's a seizure. I suppose I'm trying to communicate something like *Fuck if I know!* without using the actual words, which for some reason I can't locate. "Pete, I know the moment she was talking about, okay? I'm not an idiot.

I just don't get why it was so wrong to say what I said." I can't read Pete's eyes in this moment, but I know I don't like what I'm seeing. Still, I say the thing I didn't dare say to Cheeky earlier, not because it's a lie—it isn't—but because I feared her response in a way that I don't with Petey, in a way that you never do with blood. "I gave her a fucking compliment," I say, "someone else would have said thank you." Petey chuckles. "You're fucked in the head, D.," he says. I say, "Well, then it's good I'm in the loony bin," and we laugh. It's a nice moment. Petey's laughter is open and deep. I look at him and I see that he loves me the same whether I'm an asshole or a saint. This thought makes me tear up. I close and open my eyes a couple of times to dry up the tears without touching my face. "I care about this girl, Petey," I say. I start to explain something about Talie, but I stop myself. Instead I say, "I haven't felt this way in a long time." Petey nods and takes a swig. Then he nods again. "Then you gotta show her you get it," he says, "none of this compliment shit." "Okay," I say. The problem with showing Cheeky I get it is that I don't really get it, and Petey can see this problem on my face. "Thinking you're awesome for finding someone attractive is one of those things," he says, "like a logic loop?" I stare at him. "The fact you're celebrating this proves there's nothing to celebrate," he says. "But there is!" I say. Pete shakes his head. "Think of it this way, Daley," he says. "If this girl said to you, 'You know, I never imagined I could be attracted to a dude with such a tiny dick, but I've really grown as a person, so now I don't mind,' would you feel . . . complimented?" I say I don't think it's the same at all. I say it's a ridiculous example, considering my girth. And then I say thank you. I say I get it now. "Do your thing," Petey says, because he can tell I'm suddenly itching to head back. "Glad I could help."

On my way out I say, "So, what, you into greenery now?" I point with my chin toward the plant. "Oh, that?" Pete says. "My sister got it for me." "Mel's talking to you!?" I say. Pete chuckles. "Guess she decided to believe the whole thing wasn't our fault," he says, "or maybe once her douchebag was out of the picture, she figured better to lose money than lose money *and* your brother." I know it's my turn to laugh now, but I can't laugh. "She forgave you," I say, "Mel forgave you." "Yeah," he says. "I suppose she did." I look at Petey. "This makes me want to cry," I say. "Don't cry," he says. "It feels like we're going to be okay," I say, "like there's not gonna be a trial." "I really don't think this proves that," he says. "I'm so happy I came here today," I say. I can see now that we're both starting a new chapter. I give him a hug. Going down the stairs, I shout to him, "There's still hope for us, Petey!"

Entering the institution is much easier than exiting was, much less dramatic. I walk in like I went out for groceries and the store was closed. "Hey, Reviva," I say. She looks up. Her hair is a funny color, something between purple and blue, and I wonder how I never noticed before. "Did you go to the salon while I was gone?" I ask her. I'm half joking, half thinking maybe that's what happened. Reviva looks at me with concern, so I give a quick laugh. She smiles at me and my quirky sense of humor. "Sign here, sweetie," she says. She looks me up and down with kind eyes. "Any new acquisitions for safekeeping, sweetheart?" There's a gray plastic box to her left where any contraband should go. Cracking a joke about a hidden gun would likely be a bad idea. It's possible that for the rest of my life I'll never be able to mention the word "gun" without putting people on edge, which is unfortunate, considering all the work I've done on myself, all the progress I've made. "Nope," I say to Reviva, "nothing new." "Good," she says, "because you know if that thing starts beeping, it beeps for days." She nods at the metal detector as if I'd be confused otherwise. I shake my head. "Welcome back," she says.

I wait for the elevator, and when it doesn't come, I remember that it's not coming; it's been out of order for days. The stairs to the fourth floor are a mountain, and right now, it turns out, I am a careful climber. I see myself like you would see a movie—this happens sometimes, and generally speaking, it's not a good sign. I am still me, but I also see me. I look like a man who's lost his gumption. I can tell: each step is costing me confidence, taking a toll of spirit. The man who left Pete's place an hour ago was going to run to Cheeky's room so fast he'd feel the strain in his muscles. He knew how it would all play out: she would notice the change right away—something in the man's eyes, something in his shoulders—and she would hug him. But as she hugged him, her arms would be soft, cautious, because she wouldn't be ready to forgive him, not yet. But then the man—because he felt something for her that wasn't *bigger* or *stronger*, precisely, than what he felt for Talie, but different, more centered, the feeling of getting back on the hiking trail after a long roundabout through the woods—he would find the right words. Or really, the words would find him. This would happen with such ease, it would be hard to believe there was ever any hardship. He would keep it simple, the man. He would say something like: "I'm so sorry. I was a jerk. What I said had nothing to do with you and everything to do with my bullshit. You are gorgeous and I could not be more attracted to you." When he was done saying these simple words, he would see their effect taking shape, and that shape would be the shape of the woman he loved opening up. She would take his hand, then the rest of him. They would move out of the ward eventually, of course. They would gain custody of her daughter—she has a daughter, he remembers now, whom she hardly ever mentions, but he figures that has to be important, the custody part, because what mother wants to leave the care of her child to strangers? So they would get custody. And sure, they would fight on occasion, disagree on some stuff involving finances and sometimes the laundry. Nothing is perfect. But this man and this woman, theirs would be a happy ending.

This confident man must have died on the way over and somehow I didn't notice. Because the man I'm watching now climbing up the stairs—I mean, are you seeing what I'm seeing? The slow rhythm of his body, the bad posture? This man is going to fuck everything up, same as he did before; if he's lucky, this time at least no one will die. When he arrives upstairs, he will exude hesitation. He'll speak nonsense. And Cheeky, here's what she'll say: "I love you, Dale. But you have so much growing to do. And if I'm going to be somebody's mama, it should be my baby girl back home, not a six-foot-tall man." Hearing her words, the man will feel himself start to shrink: a loss of mass, a shortening of the bones, not by an ax, not by any violence. Through the physical power of memory, his body will morph back into its old form, its true form. The man—you can see this, right?— he is in fact a child. And in this moment he'll wear the body of a child. The woman talking to him, she is enormous. Her size is her strength as much as his smallness is his weakness. What can either of them do with this truth?

The woman will see what her words have done, and maybe some part of her will wish that she'd stayed silent. She will take the child's hand and squeeze it—gentle first, then hard. The child will move their hands toward her thigh and lean into her, waiting only for her invitation. But what kind of woman lets herself open to a child? What kind of woman allows her body to lead such a small body into herself—even if it would be just this one time, this one last time? She shakes her head. "No," the woman says. "No, Dale. No."

So much air is leaving my lungs when I hear this word, and at the same time new air enters, waves and waves of oxygen. I'm at the top of the stairs now, I am back inside my body, I am riding the oxygen all the way up until there is no more up ahead. *Fuck all that*, I think. This thought blasts like music, and for a second I think I cursed out loud. *I'm* a child? Me? I let out a laugh. I've lost the love of my life to a senseless death. I've expressed my anguish with a weapon and managed to hurt no one. I've avoided jail more than once, collected garbage at the side of the road while humming a tune. I've made fortunes in real estate, lost fortunes in real estate. Even at my lowest I still got my clothes dry-cleaned. I've broken the law, yes. Some people paid money and got no property in return, good people like Pete's sister Mel. Even her douchebag was a good man, if I'm being honest, not someone who deserved a swindle. So yes, for my most recent mistake, I may lose my freedom. A part of me thinks that kind of payday would be just fine, offer relief. I'd make good on my moral debt with time served and be absolved, reborn. Another part of me says, *Hey, Dale, if you're your own enemy, who you think will be your champion?* Every day I get out of bed and talk to both voices. I show up to group. I do the work. So say what you will about me, but I've lived a full life. I am a grown-ass man. And if Cheeky can't see it, well, that must be all the sugar in her bloodstream making her thoughts a little loopy. And to that I say, her fucking loss.

Day of the Fragheads

Lauren Mechling

CAITLIN PAULSON WAS ON THE VERGE OF FORTY-FIVE, WITH caramel eyes and cheekbones that ran across her face like a couple of shelves. She was an attractive woman by any measure, yet she was among the least beautiful in the Marriott ballroom—nobody's fault but her own. As the lead consultant organizing the Fragrance Foundation's annual Fragrance Awards luncheon, Caitlin had been responsible for assembling the crowd. She'd approached the industry heavyweights and medium weights, the executives and beauty editors, the YouTube personalities and television actresses (for there were no actors), then spent the ensuing months following up and circling back and resurfacing and, in a few cases, hounding until she could assure her client that every single seat in the third-floor hotel function hall would be not only filled, but filled with people wielding the right kind of influence.

Caitlin had assigned herself a seat by the left rear exit door, at a table with supplier representatives and publicists from low-ranking brands. But Olivia Dubrow, an Influencer of the Year nominee, had brutally cut herself while shaving her legs and needed to go to urgent care. In her time as an event coordinator, Caitlin had dealt with her share of last-minute bailing. This usually took the form of mysterious disappearances and next-day apologies. She was surprised that Olivia's agent, Tina, had sent Caitlin an up-to-the-minute update, and even more surprised that Olivia wasn't using this fiasco as an excuse to skip the luncheon altogether. She'd already gone through hair and makeup, Tina explained, and she planned to come straight from the clinic. By the time Caitlin learned all of this, the cocktail portion was wrapping up, and there hadn't been time to orchestrate an elaborate reconfiguration and insert another high-profile guest in Olivia's spot. So Caitlin was now in the fertile crescent of stages warming the chair of the Influencer of the Year shoo-in.

Notes of bergamot and Egyptian amber infused the ballroom's recycled air. Caitlin knew this for sure because the scent had been custom-created by Paul de Falaise, a past Nose of the Year recipient. Outside, the city was under a heat advisory, and Caitlin could still feel the film of dried perspiration clinging to her skin. She glanced up at the stage, where Susan Diehl, president of the Fragrance Foundation and bane of Caitlin's existence for the past three weeks, was giving her opening remarks. Notes on "sustainability" and "diversity" were hit while images of beetle-browed chemists in goggles and lab coats shuffled past on the white screen in the background.

Caitlin felt a buzzing in her lap and glanced down. It was a text from her sister, Denise, who was in Maplewood, watching the girls. Caitlin's daughters were between school and camp, and going through a truculent stage, suddenly opposed to doing anything constructive or cooperative. Caitlin's nine-year-old, Ruth, had claimed she had a migraine, a word she had only just learned, thwarting the original plan to come into the city with her little sister and aunt and hang out in the hotel room that Caitlin was preapproved to expense.

Where do the spatulas live? Denise asked. **I don't want to bother Ethan.**

Bother him all you want. I'm the one who's working :)

Caitlin tucked her phone underneath her napkin and looked up at the man seated to her left, a graphic designer named Anton who'd masterminded the Tom Ford gender-fluid campaign. He looked no older than thirty and must have been well raised, because he actually smiled at Caitlin and introduced himself. His eyes were green and a little bit crazy. Extending her arm, Caitlin wondered what he would have made of her back when she started out in the industry, when her hair swished down to her elbows and was thick enough to grab in a fist. When Caitlin had been offered the job at Buckley Cosmetics, her cosmetics bag had contained some Wet n Wild products and a sample-size bottle of Clinique lotion that her dance school friend had given her. Caitlin used to thin it with drops of warm water to keep from running out. But Caitlin had a quality, something that surpassed any amount of beauty know-how. She could break people down, bend their desires in under five minutes. Her focus never faltered, and she hit her target numbers month after month. By her second year she'd placed second in the Southwest regionals. She was unstoppable in other respects too. She spent half her nights in hotels like the one they were in now, never at a loss for companionship. The jerks used to be her favorite perks.

Caitlin had been slinging serums for seven years when she met Ethan, at an event at Saks Fifth Avenue. He was tagging along with his coworker, a snobby bond trader named Peter. Ethan was an inch shorter than Caitlin and wearing a tie patterned with expensive-looking turtles. He got her number and asked her to meet him the following Saturday—for brunch, a move that she mistook as a sign of quirkiness. He was forthright in his desire to settle down, which she liked. She also liked that he was Jewish, which had always struck her as the height of sophistication.

Ethan turned out to be indifferent to sex, which didn't terribly bother Caitlin. It was almost exciting, to put all that behind her. Their wedding ceremony had been a salvation, airlifting Caitlin out of her life and delivering her to a pasture of adulthood and respectability. Her travel schedule lightened up, and when Ruth was born, Caitlin called the head office and put her job on hold, like a library book. Ruth was less than two when Caitlin had Janie.

Caitlin stopped smoking cigarettes, and stopped thinking about them. There was a good stretch when Caitlin's only connection to the beauty world was watching contouring videos on YouTube while she nursed. She missed it, the brightly colored bottles, the sugar rush that came with triumphing over self-erasure.

The waiters had descended with the salads. The woman on Caitlin's right, a Lancôme executive, removed a spray bottle from her purse and spritzed the leaves. "Nutritional yeast," she muttered to nobody. Anton checked with the server to make sure the salad contained no dairy, and Caitlin pretended not to notice. Instead she asked him about his work. He had a way of speaking that might have come across as half ironic but Caitlin recognized as flirtatious. She rested her chin on her hand as she listened and brushed her knee against his. She was curious about how long it would take him to pull away.

Ethan had lost his job five months ago. He was treating his search as his new job, which meant annexing Caitlin's home office, so she had to set up her laptop on the kitchen counter, amidst the household coloring books and dirty coffee mugs. One afternoon not long ago, she'd come home from barre class and opened the office door to find Ethan staring at an image of a naked woman on a yacht. The woman had long black hair and a butt that looked like a basketball split in two. It was not Ethan's time wasting that bothered her. It was the pathetic look he'd fixed her with when he'd whipped around and confirmed that his wife was standing there. Much as Caitlin tried, she could not forget that expression on his face.

Anton must have been more bored than Caitlin realized. His leg remained touching hers through the Lifetime Achievement and Home Fragrance portions. Anton surprised Caitlin when he ran his hand along the top of her thigh before raising it to snatch a rosemary roll from the bread basket. Caitlin felt a stab of disappointment when she saw the message on her phone. "Olivia is in her Uber," she reported to the table. The Lancôme lady pretended not to care.

Caitlin had tried to meet Ethan on his level. The previous

weekend, when the girls were at gymnastics, she'd looked up videos and ended up watching a young woman masturbate while she ate an orange. The actress's method was bizarre—she bit into the citrus as if it were an apple, then used her front teeth to wrest bits of flesh away from the peel. It took Caitlin a moment to recognize that the woman's pubic hair was thick and exaggerated, like the eyebrow pieces in her daughters' puppet kits. Only then did Caitlin notice the name of the channel: HairyHotties. Repulsed as she was, Caitlin forced herself to watch the girl take another bite of orange. Caitlin sat still and waited for a dribble of juice to work its way down the actress's chin before she clamped her laptop shut. The whole thing left her cold and disgusted.

Even when Caitlin had been at her friskiest, porn had never been part of the picture. There had certainly been requests, but Caitlin was on an expense account and wasn't going to submit smut fees to her employer—the minibar charges were suspect enough. Besides, it wasn't as if supplemental entertainment was ever required. Caitlin was an artist, and the men who got to be with her were entranced and energized.

"Omigod!" A fried voice came from behind, and all the faces at Caitlin's table froze with delight. Olivia Dubrow had on an itty-bitty dress. Caitlin saw no sign of any shaving accident. "I can't believe I made it!" Olivia said. She eyed the place card in front of Caitlin and waited for the anonymous seat warmer to slither out of the chair. "I didn't miss my category, did I?" Olivia said as she took her place. "Today has been crazy. You won't believe what happened to me. . . ."

Anton moved to say something to Olivia—yet he looked over at Caitlin and gave her a wink. She felt a jolt of electricity shoot through her throat and was reminded of Operation, a board game she hadn't played since she was a kid.

Caitlin located table twenty-seven and saw her seat, empty and unappealing. She found a spot with the assistants, who stood rigidly in front of the piles of leaving favors. Caitlin had worked with the graphic designer and ordered the goody bags from a printer in Indianapolis, had personally hit up all the potential partners who might want to donate branded product for the guests to take home and, with any luck, post with the #FragFoundFever hashtag. Caitlin watched an Australian fitfluencer read the nominees for Body Care of the Year award.

Caitlin mouthed gibberish to one of her minions, who nodded dourly. She slipped past the door and into the corridor. It was brighter out here, and it took her eyes a couple of seconds to adjust to the lighting. At the reception desk, Caitlin set her credit card on the counter and requested the room she'd been approved.

She swiped her key card and waited until she was on the other side of the door to locate Anton's Instagram account, @AntonBlue. It was a grid of selfies, most of which were taken next to models. There was something metallic about his self-presentation, cool and chemical. But there was no denying how hot he was.

hi

Caitlin paced around the room while she waited for Anton to reply.

yo. I don't c u. what table are you at?
room 912

Misbehavior felt so good. Caitlin couldn't believe she had waited this long.

lol
for real, she typed. **wanna hang out?**
that might be rude ;)
when it's over ;)
hmm tempting

Caitlin smiled to herself and lay belly-down on the bed, where she spent the next hour refreshing the hashtag and watching the event from her phone. She wasn't needed downstairs. At this point her job was to be as invisible as possible. If Susan texted for some reason, Caitlin would be there in a flash.

Olivia took a video of the cheering crowd from her spot on the stage as she accepted the Influencer of the Year award. The Lancôme lady posted her dessert, a fondant cake sculpted to look like a bottle of Calyx, one of five Classic Comeback nominees. Anton tossed in a selfie of his and Olivia's flushed faces pressed together like two sides of a panini. Thanks to Bronx Fragrance Lover's live video, Caitlin could watch the crowd funnel out of the ballroom. Her pulse raced as she made out the back of Anton's head moving toward the exit.

Caitlin gave it half an hour before she allowed herself to let go of her last shred of hope. He wasn't coming. Maybe he never planned on it. She called down to Chloe, the most trusted of her assistants.

"Everything okay?"

"Totally, we're just trying to figure out what to do with the goody bags."

"You can leave them there for hotel staff. I'll touch base on Monday."

She considered texting Ethan and telling him that she had a hotel room—Denise was there to watch the girls, after all. But he'd respond about the city-bound Lincoln Tunnel traffic, or some other depressing reason not to come. Caitlin examined her reflection in the elevator mirror on the ride down. She looked ragged, but in a sexy way. Caitlin touched her hair. What the hell was she going to do? She wasn't going to leave Ethan and walk out on her daughters. It was an addition, not another subtraction, that she needed. Maybe she'd find a full-time job, somewhere a long drive from home.

The ballroom was unrecognizable without the flower arrangements and mood lighting. A team of hotel workers with bus tubs held against their waists cleared the tables. Caitlin helped herself to one of the remaining goody bags and walked out.

The hotel's main floor was crowded, likely on account of the heat. She recognized a few of the fragheads lingering at the lobby bar. A porcupine-haired man who was working on a beer and had nothing to do with the event managed to look simultaneously at and straight through Caitlin, stirring up her hunger and rage. She headed into the bathroom and turned the goody bag upside down. Its contents made satisfying ricochet sounds as they tumbled onto the counter. She sprayed Urban Decay's's new perfume on her neck and hair until it made her sneeze, then ripped open the miniature Benefit lipstick and swiped it across her mouth. Anna Karenina was a honking red that did not suit her. She dabbed her lips with a tissue and puckered her lips, now a slightly tamer shade. She opened the bareMinerals travel compact and used her fingers to daub on blusher and eye shadow, availing herself of all the colors in the palette. Finally, she squeezed a travel-size Angel Gloss into her palms and applied the glittery gel to her forearms and décolletage, running her palms over her skin to smooth down the lumps. She took a step back and felt a rush of glee. Who could stare through this.

The Serial Lover

Jaime Clarke

THIS ONE, THE ONE WITH JAMES NOW, HER NAME IS RITA. I NEVER knew James liked those Latin American women (or wherever she's from). Even though I heard James say her name into the hall phone—the phone under the beveled mirror his parents gave us for our wedding—I didn't put together that she was Latin American. She could be Spanish. Or it could be that the salsa music and the rum are making me think she's Spanish.

James sees me and his face goes flat.

"I'm sorry, Jane," he says to me. "I didn't know you were going to be here."

James kisses me on the cheek. He's been smoking cigars.

"Barbara decided she didn't want to see a movie," I tell him. "So this place popped into my mind. I didn't know you were going to be here, though. Isn't that remarkable?"

A smile comes across James's thin lips.

"It *is* remarkable," he says.

"Well, I'm going," I say, hopping off the tall chair at the bar.

"Will you be up later?" James asks.

"I'm pretty tired," I admit.

"Okay," James says, and turns back toward his table, back toward Rita, who I think now might be Cuban.

A glass breaks behind the bar and everyone looks. It feels like everyone is looking at me, the same feeling I had when James first brought me here. We strolled through the low door together, arm in arm. James wore a new suit from H.T. Crouch & Sons, the clothier in Scottsdale he started working for right out of high school. (He actually started in the flagship store in downtown Phoenix and worked his way into the tonier suburb.) He's their number one salesman.

James had a friend, Patricia somebody, who worked in the women's department at Sak's Fifth Avenue, and she had fit me with a beautiful strapless silk dress. When I reached for my purse, this Patricia somebody shook her head.

"This dress was lost in shipping," she said.

It was like that. James knows a lot of women and these women, most of whom I know only by name, are friendly and giving as sisters if we meet. Even Patricia touched me in a familiar way, and I figured out later what I didn't know then: she was more than likely one of James's mistresses.

"You can't fault a man like James for his fine sensibilities," Barbara says. "The man simply appreciates beauty. He has an eye for it. He saw you, didn't he?"

He *did* see me. The world is full of endless possibilities that provide freedom and excitement, James is always saying. He seemed shy when we first met—me sulking at a bar over a bad break-up, him celebrating a milestone at work. I could be shy too. (My mother said I was weak in a social way. "It'll be your end," she used to say.)

My mother was strong. Like me, she married late in life. My father was a wanderer who didn't go anywhere. That's what he used to say about himself. He itched to be in the world like James, but for his own reasons he never went out. For his own reasons, too, he hanged himself in the garage.

"It seems like the only possible ending," my mother said when it happened. I understood then she knew more about loss than I imagined I ever would, or that I ever wanted to.

Barbara's been with James, too, a few years after we were married. James apologized, though—the only time he has.

"It really wasn't right," he said. "But it was just casual. Have you noticed how deep Barbara's eyes are?"

I had noticed and told him so. He likes this about me. He likes that I can see what he sees. I see beauty too. I understand how it fills James up to take in beautiful things. He's no good when he's run down.

Once he sat on the back porch looking at the rotting creosote bush in the corner of our yard. I was taking care of the things around the house that never seem to take care of themselves no matter how long I leave them. I'd check on James now and again, but I didn't bother him with foolish questions like some wives do. If he wanted something to drink, he'd get up and get it. Or he'd ask me. I pride myself on not bothering James with silliness.

So I went to check on James again and he was gone. I searched the backyard, but he wasn't there. Peeking out the front window, I saw him in the neighbor's flower bed, trampling the petunias and daisies. A look of complete concentration was drawn across his face. The neighbors were away in Mexico on summer vacation, so I didn't rush out and stop him or ask him what he was doing. I can sense when he is run down.

Someone at the bar makes a joke about Juan, the bartender, being drunk.

"If you want to stay, we'll leave," James says. "She isn't feeling well anyway."

"What's wrong with her?" I ask.

James shrugs. "You know, it's just general."

Rita is slumped over their table, watching the flame of the candle flicker inside the clear candle holder. She tips the glass and the candle floats from one side to the other on an ocean of melted wax. Suddenly Rita stands up and rushes into the ladies' room.

James follows her with his eyes and strains to see after the ladies' room door closes. He looks at me, and I can tell he wants to ask me if I'll go see if she's okay, but he knows he can't ask me that.

"I think I'll freshen up before I go," I say.

James smiles his appreciation.

Rita is running water down the sink and spitting into the rushing current.

"Are you all right?" I ask.

She looks at me in the mirror, and what can only be described as real terror comes across her face. I've seen the look before. They always assume they've been caught in an elaborate lie, but the truth is more elaborate than they could understand. James doesn't make a show of his women, but he doesn't dishonor me by telling lies.

I know the corrosive power of a lie. Every year H.T. Crouch sends James to Vegas for a convention where James catches up on everything new in the world of clothing. It's a small convention; the attendees don't even fill a hotel to capacity, and the gathering is really a fraternity. Men need that. They need to come together once in a while, leave their familiar surroundings and entertain their thoughts in a new, wild environment. I'd be lying if I didn't admit to a certain anxiety every year when the convention nears, but trying to guess what James is doing when he's out of my sight is a losing game. I have to rely on James's account when he returns, an account filled with the extreme behavior of Alex from Saint Louis, or Harry from Pennsylvania. Sometimes I wonder if James exaggerates the others' behavior to make his own seem small and rational. I've never been able to know how James considers himself.

James took me to the first convention, a gesture of kindness and a show of solidarity in the face of the scowls of the others. None of them wanted to be reminded of marriage, reminded that there was such a thing as a wife.

The others started going out at night without James.

"You can go if you want," I remember telling him.

"I don't want to go with them," he said. He meant it too. Whenever I am alone with James, I am the only one anywhere around. But I feared James would regret bringing me, so I volunteered to visit my sister Arlene, who lives in Payson. I live in fear of regret of any kind.

"I can drive you," James offered.

I assured him the bus was fine. I liked looking out the window, I told him.

The most powerful lie in my relationship with James is my own. But it's too late now to confess. It would only reveal my deceit. Maybe I really felt put out by what happened in Vegas. I'm like that. I sometimes say things I don't mean. I sometimes don't stand up for what I'm thinking because I don't trust myself. Maybe I was tired—for the moment, at least—of James and his women. The ramifications of that thought are unthinkable. I sometimes get upset thinking about Barbara.

Whatever it was, I let the guy at the Pine Tree Inn waltz me around the dance floor while my sister watched from our table. She's lived her whole life without a husband. "But I love men," she says. "The older I get, the more I love them."

I let the guy at the Pine Tree Inn take me up to his room, too. It's so easy when there isn't anyone to check your actions. My sister certainly wasn't going to say anything, and like I've already said, I don't verbalize what I'm thinking until I've had a chance to think it to death. I was thinking it to death while the guy did what he did to me in his room at the Pine Tree Inn.

After, the guy offered to drive me home and I said I wanted him to take me to my sister's house. I wasn't too clear on the directions, but Payson is small enough you can drive around and find everything sooner or later. We made a wrong turn at first and ended up on a dark stretch of highway that led back toward Phoenix. The guy pulled the car over to check his map and we got out. My eyes adjusted, and even though there were no streetlights, the moon was so bright everything appeared fluorescent. It was the first time all night either of us had stopped the locomotion of our actions, and the unexpected moment made me appreciate all that had transpired. What the guy said and did to get me to his room at the Pine Tree Inn was what every woman expects a man to say and do. And women need men to say and do those things so that a familiar, comfortable atmosphere is maintained. Ask any man who is unsuccessful at romance and you'll find out he is trying too hard to be original. All men should know this. James knows this.

Rita shuts off the faucet. Excuses are working their way down from her brain to her lips, but she's too stunned from being seen in the light to say anything. She mumbles something about a bad dinner, an incomplete sentence of simple nouns and verbs, and the thought occurs to me that Rita might not speak English that well.

"Look, it's okay," I say. "I know who you are."

Rita's eyes grow wide.

"Do you know who I am?" I ask.

She nods, and it seems she doesn't speak English until she says, "Yes, I know who you are." The words are as clear and cool as an October night.

"James is worried about you," I say.

"Aren't you worried about *him*?" Rita asks. Her question seems confrontational.

I stare into Rita's face and see her incredible youth. At a distance she looks like a woman of about thirty. Up close, however, she has the face of an angelic child, a girl who might draw a hopscotch game in colored chalk on the sidewalk in front of her house.

"How long have you been seeing James?" I ask. I already know the answer, two months, but this is always a good test to see how on the level they're going to be with me.

"I don't think I should answer that," Rita says. Her childlike beauty is momentarily erased, replaced by hard edges. She wants to push past me, but I'm blocking the door.

"Two months, right?" I ask.

Rita stares at me incredulously.

"It's not a secret between me and James," I tell her.

"He tells you everything?" The question is more like a gasp.

A young black woman bursts through the bathroom door, drunk. She catches herself on the sink, and Rita is pushed aside, so that I can see myself in the mirror. My reflection is angrier than

I imagined I looked, and I'm unsettled by what I'm giving away. Rita pretends to be watching the drunk woman, who is checking her makeup, but Rita is really staring into the sink, wondering what she's going to say next.

The woman keeps glancing up at me in the mirror, and the uncomfortable silence makes her turn away from the sink without her purse.

Rita sighs heavily, perhaps surrendering herself to me.

The small brown leather purse spreads like a stain on the corner of the sink.

"Don't go in there," the drunk woman says to someone outside the door.

"Did James tell you about me?" I ask, asserting my superior position. As confident as I'm feeling, I never know the answer to this question.

Rita nods tentatively.

I expected the answer to be no, so my curiosity overwhelms me. "What did he tell you?" I ask coolly.

Outside the door we both hear the drunk woman say, "Shit, I forgot my purse in there."

"Just go in there and get it," a voice, another woman, says.

Rita glances at the purse. "He was very complimentary," she manages to say, her coolness matching mine. "He said he loves you. Don't you think that's shitty? That he can be with me and he still has the nerve to say he loves you?"

Oh, my dear Rita. My dear, simple Rita. I'm dialing up the words to make Rita understand, trying to come up with something she can get her tiny thoughts around that will illuminate for her how complex relationships can be, when she starts to fidget with the paper towel dispenser. "How do you know James and I aren't planning to run away together?" she asks without looking up at me.

I stifle a laugh. I'm not sure if Rita is trying to be mean or if she is under a delusion. "James is married to me," I say. "And he always will be."

"I'll go in and get it for you," another voice says.

The door opens, and Rita and I are expecting a stranger, but James walks in, startling us both. He appears like a giant in the fluorescent light. He shifts uncomfortably. "There's a line outside, and Juan says he's going to have to come in if you two don't come out." James looks at me when he says this, and Rita stares at him, waiting for acknowledgment.

James backs out of the bathroom without looking once in Rita's direction, and I'll admit this gives me a small pleasure. Rita charges after him, and they're both lost beyond the crowd waiting outside the bathroom door. By the time I make my way to the door, they've vanished.

On the way home I can't stop thinking about my mother. No words about my father's affair were ever spoken between us, but we both know the other knows. I actually knew first. My father and Candy Howard were caught by the innocent interruption of a child sent home sick from school. I knew right away that the naked body under my father wasn't my mother and the enormity of Candy's bare feet frightened me. The callused undersides of her feet made me gasp, and my father scrambled to find clothes for the both of them. When I think of my father's affair, Candy Howard's callused feet and my father wrapped in my mother's robe remain as the images of what can result from elaborate lies and deceit.

It's more complicated than that, I know. My mother wouldn't have been able to live with Candy Howard in her life. And Mr. Howard wouldn't have stood for it either. I loved my mother, and I didn't want my parents to divorce like everybody else's parents, but there was something dishonorable in the way my father scrambled when he was caught. I'll admit to dishonor, too, when I used his secret for favor and personal gain. In that instance, everyone behaved badly.

At the stop sign two blocks from our house, I hear Rita's question again. I'm thinking about that ugly robe and those callused feet, and suddenly I'm hearing Rita asking me how I don't know she's not going to run away with my husband. A mild alarm colors my perception, and not only can I not answer that question, I can't figure out how James and Rita disappeared so quickly outside the ladies' room at the club.

I narrowly avoid a trash can the wind has blown into the street as I race home. I can see the driveway a million miles before I get there and I'm disappointed that James isn't home but surprised at the strange station wagon in the driveway.

"Hello?" A small man emerges from the dark shadows the house is casting under the moonlight.

"Can I help you?" I ask officiously. The sight of this dwarfish man is startling. He keeps putting his hands in his pockets and pulling them out.

"You don't know me," he says.

"Do you know me?" I ask.

"No," he admits.

"What are you doing at my house?"

The small man looks at the ground. "I'm looking for my wife."

I try not to give away what I know, but the picture of this small man and Rita on their wedding day appears in my imagination, and I think of Rita and think: *It's no wonder.*

"I can't see what I have to do with your wife," I say. "Do I know her?"

The small man locks his gaze on a cement seam in the driveway. He's trying to be delicate. He doesn't know how to say what he has to say. The air of weakness around the small man actually shrinks him until he is so pitiable I am about to tell him that his wife is, in fact, with my husband but that there isn't anything going on that he should be worried about when the small man says, "I found this."

He hands me a square of paper that falls open at its worn folds.

"I'm running away," is all the note says.

"And this," he says, handing me a folded-over photo. A crease runs across James's face, giving him a double smile. Rita is standing next to him, looking off as if someone called her name right as the camera flashed. A small, one-armed totem pole stands like a sentry in a curio cabinet behind them. "That's in my house," the small man says. "After I found that, I started following her around, and the man in that picture lives here." He jams a thumb violently in the air.

Calmly, without allowing an awkward pause, I redeem the currency of the graceless note. "Is Rita your wife?"

The sound of his wife's name startles him, and he involuntarily leans forward.

"I just had dinner with her," I say. "And with my husband, James. She's a very charming woman." This cover, this lie, will be the small man's only compensation for his devotion to Rita, and it fills me up to pay him.

Unanswerable questions fill the small man's mind, but instead of asking them, he just stands still, looking past me into the street. He knows I'm lying, probably could produce more proof than the photograph, but he realizes it's useless and doesn't try to persuade me further about my husband. If James and I stand together, we can resist all accusations.

My mind drifts to Rita and James, the postcard-perfect picture of them hanging off the bow of a ship, sailing into a yellow horizon but somehow sailing *toward* me. My lie is still floating in the air, and I have to say, it never occurred to me that the small man's reward might be mine, too.

James pulls up in his car, the one he got when he traded in my father's old car, the passenger side empty.

"Hi, honey," James says to me, kissing me loosely on the mouth.

Honey, this is Rita's husband," I say.

"Oh, hello," James says, powerfully shaking the small man's hand. The small man wants to make a protest, wants to take back his hand and point and accuse, but James's charm overwhelms him and all he can say is, "Well, okay . . . goodnight."

James watches the small man drive away, and I tell him about the note.

"She's left him," he admits.

I feel sorry for the small man as his car disappears at the end of our street. The streetlights flicker once and then snap out, leaving James and me standing in the darkness outside our house. Before my eyes adjust, James's figure is as unrecognizable as a stranger's. I remember the name of the guy from the Pine Tree Inn, and the same thought occurs to me now that occurred to me then, standing among the moonlit trees: *I don't find freedom and excitement in these endless possibilities.*

From Garden Lakes

Praise for GARDEN LAKES

"It takes some nerve to revisit a bulletproof classic, but Jaime Clarke does so, with elegance and a cool contemporary eye, in this cunningly crafted homage to *Lord of the Flies*. He understands all too well the complex psychology of boyhood, how easily the insecurities and power plays slide into mayhem when adults look the other way."

—JULIA GLASS, National Book Award-winning author of *Three Junes*

"As tense and tight and pitch-perfect as Clarke's narrative of the harrowing events at *Garden Lakes* is, and as fine a meditation it is on Golding's novel, what deepens this book to another level of insight and artfulness is the parallel portrait of Charlie Martens as an adult, years after his fateful role that summer, still tyrannized, paralyzed, tangled in lies, wishing for redemption, maybe fated never to get it. Complicated and feral, *Garden Lakes* is thrilling, literary, and smart as hell."

—PAUL HARDING, Pulitzer Prize-winning author of *Tinkers*

"Jaime Clarke reminds us that if the banality of evil is indeed a viable truth, its seeds are most likely sewn among adolescent boys."

—BRAD WATSON, author of *Aliens in the Prime of Their Lives*

"In the flawlessly imagined *Garden Lakes*, Jaime Clarke pays homage to *Lord of the Flies* and creates his own vivid, inadvertently isolated community. As summer tightens its grip, and adult authority recedes, his boys gradually reveal themselves to scary and exhilarating effect. In the hands of this master of suspense and psychological detail, the result is a compulsively readable novel."

—MARGOT LIVESEY, author of *The Flight of Gemma Hardy*

"Smart, seductive, and suggestively sinister, *Garden Lakes* is a disturbingly honest look at how our lies shape our lives and destroy our communities. Read it: Part three in one of the best literary trilogies we have."

–SCOTT CHESHIRE, author of High as the Horses' Bridles

A Review of GARDEN LAKES

Kirkus Reviews

Charlie Martens recounts an ill-fated high school program that haunts him into adulthood.

Clarke (*World Gone Water*, etc.) develops the memorable protagonist of his previous two novels while crafting a story that stands on its own. The novel proceeds through two interwoven narratives. In one, Charlie, a junior at Randolph, an all-boys prep school, is selected to participate in a summer leadership program at Garden Lakes, an unfinished housing development in the Arizona desert. In the second, an adult Charlie is a successful newspaper columnist in Phoenix. Undercurrents of greed and self-interest unite the strands of the novel, from the creation of the fellowship on property donated by a Randolph graduate trying to keep it from being seized by the government to Charlie's career-defining investigative reporting, which sparked legislation but was predicated on deception. . . . As the summer progresses, old and new rifts divide the boys into fighting factions. Abandoned by their advisers and with a heat wave reaching unbearable levels, the structured schedule breaks into fast-paced chaos reminiscent of *Lord of the Flies*. Charlie, an orphan and transfer student, does not appeal for pity. Still, we see that he is implicated in these events largely in an attempt to fit in.

An intriguing cross-section of loneliness and power in the world of boys and men.

Minor Characters from
GARDEN LAKES

Mr. Hancock, sixties, the disciplinarian teacher that students fear. He is one of the two faculty administrators overseeing the Garden Lakes summer fellowship for high school juniors. He is unexpectedly called away from Garden Lakes for a family emergency.

Mr. Malagon, thirties. The young, hip history teacher at Randolph College Prep that all the students admire. He is one of the two faculty administrators overseeing the Garden Lakes summer fellowship for high school juniors. His disappearance creates the first crisis for the fellows that summer.

Dave "Figs" Figueroa, seventeen, a Garden Lakes fellow who will one day cover up an embezzlement at his firm, shifting the blame to an innocent department head at his father-in-law's insistence, resulting in the department head's firing.

Roger Dixon, seventeen, a Garden Lakes fellow who will one day be court-martialed for taking a platoon of men in Iraq AWOL and killing one of them after the soldier is wounded by enemy fire and begs Roger for a mercy killing.

Duane "Hands" Handley, seventeen, a Garden Lakes fellow who will one day lead his family's sixth-generation brewery to ruin.

Casey "Smurf" Murfin, seventeen, a Garden Lakes fellow who will one day successfully slander a female colleague with whom he cheated on his wife.

Vince "Assburn" Glassburn, seventeen, a Garden Lakes fellow who will later die plunging into a frozen lake somewhere between Canada and Detroit, after driving across the ice while smuggling counterfeit game systems in order to raise bail money for his best friend.

Warren James, seventeen, a Garden Lakes fellow who will later be unwittingly implicated in an Internet Ponzi scheme.

Axia, eighteen, a girl who has run away from home to hitchhike around the West. She is staying with Native Americans in the desert when she stumbles upon Garden Lakes. Her sudden appearance at Garden Lakes creates another crisis for the fellows.

Rebecca Clement, seventeen, a high school student at Randolph's sister school, Xavier College Prep, who spurns Roger's invitation to the winter formal but makes an effort to be nice to him after. He invokes a shun against her and prints up cards that say "He-Man Becky Haters Club" and passes them around liberally, causing Rebecca to transfer to another school.

Mr. Baker, late thirties, the construction specialist who periodically visits Garden Lakes during the fellowship to help direct the construction the fellows are tasked with. His kidnapping brings about the novel's culmination.

Hiawatha

Neil LaBute

THE WATER WAS COLD AND DARK. IT BIT AT THE WINDOWS AND began to seep in through the door frames and the carpeting at his feet. The car had stopped sinking by this time and was resting on the rocky floor of a remote mountain lake, although he could only see this thanks to the thin beams of the headlights that were somehow still working (God bless stolen foreign cars). Assburn knew this couldn't last for long just like he knew that he too couldn't last for long, not down here, not under the ice in freezing cold water. No, this was probably the end for Assburn and he realized that ('probably' because most human beings feel somewhat immortal during their lifetimes, continuing to live out their days on Earth with a false sense of immunity while those around them die of throat cancer or old age or murder or a thousand other atrocities but it's always someone else . . . until it isn't). Now it was Assburn's turn and this is how it looked like he was going to go out, trapped in a stolen Audi under the ice of a lake whose name he couldn't pronounce (it was some kind of 'Native American' word) in a state he'd never been to before. That was just his luck, dying this way . . . and how ironic, for a guy who'd been born in the beautiful state of Minnesota, home to some ten thousand lakes . . . but he was going to die in this lake instead. Forgotten. Unseen. Never found. Well, his skeleton might be discovered some summer, years from now, by recreational divers or someone like that, but it was quite possible that he would simply cease to exist, skidding off an icy country road, never to be seen again (and barely even thought of by anyone that he knew who was still alive). His cold fingers worked at the seatbelt that held him fast but the locking mechanism wasn't giving way and his mind was wandering as he pulled on it . . . Assburn was trying to remember just how he got himself into this particular mess in the first place. Oh, that's right, he was trying to do a good thing: running an illegally obtained stash of video game consoles north to Canada for resale (in a desperate attempt to raise bail money for an incarcerated—unfairly, from his point of view—friend of his). His 'best' friend, if he was pressed to say it, if indeed Assburn had anyone in his life who could be considered a 'best' friend. At this point, now that the headlights had shorted out and he was alone in the freezing wet darkness, Assburn fully expected to see his life passing before his eyes, fully anticipated a flood of memories to rival the lake water making its way into the brand-new SQ5 he was currently trapped inside of. But nothing came. No burnished, slow-motion images of his relatively lousy childhood or those malignant high school years of his or the wild, endless days spent up at Garden Lakes with his would-be friends. Nothing. His mind drifted back to how he got his nickname in the first place—when his real last name was 'Glassburn' ("Your 'Christian' name," his mother would mistakenly say)—and even in this situation he nearly smiled at the memory. Eighth grade, 4th period lunch, and someone had challenged his boast that he could actually create a torch using his farts and had provided him with a cheap blue Bic to sweeten the deal. Assburn could never pass up a bet and certainly not one that might make him a buddy (or at least get him noticed for a minute or two), an attitude that had brought him a lot of trouble and heartache and detention in his teenage years. He promptly laid himself out on a lunch table for all to see, pulled his legs up to his chest and let one rip while he controlled the flame with a free hand. Trying to do everything himself is what cost him the victory: instead there was a flash of light, his jeans caught on fire and there and then he earned the moniker of 'Assburn' for ever more. He shook off this flashback as his teeth began to chatter and his fingers stopped working at the safety belt that held him fast in place (his digits were frozen solid now). Instead of fighting, Assburn sat back in his luxury leather seat and waited for death to come. Death with a capital 'D,' in fact, as Assburn was the kind of guy who—having grown up on Stephen King and *Goosebumps* and the like—fully expected some bloated, rotting ghoul to appear at the windshield, smiling in at him as he fought for a final breath as the inky black water rose slowly over his head. Or even the Devil himself (or herself, for that matter, for that's one thing that Assburn was not—sexist—he was completely open to the idea of the Devil being a woman). Not today, though . . . not even a corpse or Satan (him or herself) would visit Assburn in these, his final minutes. He tried once more to shift his body to one side and then the other, hoping against hope to free himself and break the safety glass (with the tiny red hammer he'd seen in the glove box during a cursory check of the stolen car) and then swim up and up and up to safety . . . but nothing. These German cars were not kidding when they trumpeted their commitment to safety and Audi was no exception: Assburn was not getting out of this one. Several plastic game controllers were floating around the cabin of the SUV now, bumping into each other like ducks in a baby's bath. Assburn had some kind of switch go off in his head because of this, some memory of his mother's face, smiling down at him as he splashed about in a warm tub, and for a moment he grinned and felt safe and knew that no matter what happened next, everything was going to be okay. Those feelings slowly slid away, however, as the water rose above his neck and then his mouth and finally above his nose until only his eyes were left unsubmerged. He'd already taken in his last gasp of air and Assburn's eyes widened as he looked out at the dark glass in front of him. Was someone out there? Staring in at him? He was sure he could see the outline of a person, the waterlogged face of a man—or was it a woman—floating there in the void, watching him. Smiling in at him. Waiting.

*

His last attempt at a breath was more like a scream but there in the dark and the wet it was impossible to tell which was which as the two things blended into one and then, finally, inevitably, disappeared completely beneath the surface.

Goth Music

Andrea Seigel

WHEN ROGER ASKED REBECCA TO THE WINTER FORMAL, HE kneeled in front of the courtyard fountain between their schools, holding out red roses in one hand and a boxed necklace in the other. Her immediate thought was, *I can't wear that necklace.* It was a palm tree on a silver chain. Rebecca didn't know what it meant other than that Roger had some picture of her that was wrong.

They hadn't ever talked that much before, just in groups, but Rebecca knew it would be a lot of work for her to shop for a cute formal dress, track down cute matching shoes, smile for pictures next to Roger's parents' pool, go to a fancy restaurant where the adult patrons told them they were cute, fast dance to a bunch of songs, and slow dance at the end of the night, all the while keeping her interactions with Roger on the same impersonal level as the palm tree necklace. Rebecca wasn't attracted to him, and she didn't see the point of school dances, so everything in her body was screaming, *WHY, THEN?*

Turning up her hands, she said, "Sorry, I wasn't planning on going to winter formal in general."

Rebecca felt bad that Roger's friends were watching, that her friends were watching. Roger looked at her with such hurt that she immediately wished the two of them could disappear. Not together. Just both evaporate to different places at the same time. Roger dejectedly threw the necklace in the fountain but kept the flowers, walking off. What did it mean? Rebecca was the most intrigued she'd ever been by him.

After Rebecca rejected Roger's invitation, she treated him like he didn't exist, which was what she would have wanted if their roles had been reversed.

The dance came and went.

On the first day of classes after winter recess, Rebecca and her friends Helen and Noelle were about to pass by Roger and his two friends, who were sitting on the fountain before the first bell, when Noelle accused Rebecca of going out of her way to be a bitch to Roger. "A ton of time has passed, and now you're making it awkward," Noelle complained.

Rebecca and Noelle were getting on each other's nerves because they'd spent too much time together over Christmas, since their other friends had mostly gone out of town.

"Fine, fuck it!" Rebecca snapped at Noelle. Then she made herself switch over to a more casual, breezy tone, turning to yell over her shoulder, "Hiya, Roger!"

Rebecca knew it was a mistake as soon as she saw Roger's look. He didn't answer, didn't even acknowledge her, just got this look like she'd cheated at something they were playing together. Before, Roger had been accepting that he'd eaten it and the two of them would likely never speak again. His vibe had been, *Sometimes things just go that way. You give life your best, shoot for the stars, and it sucks when you land on your ass, but that's all part of the game.* The attitude was a sports thing, as Rebecca understood it. Now she saw that all bets were off.

Rebecca never heard anyone say that Roger had told them to stop talking to her, but either that's what happened, or it was just his example that was enough to force the change. His friends stopped saying hi to her when she said hi to them. Then it became friends of friends.

Then, in early spring, the He-Man Becky Haters Club cards started to appear. Guys that even Roger didn't talk to were flashing them. Roger had printed out the cards at home, then gone through the trouble of having them laminated at the copy shop.

The effort really blew Rebecca's mind at first—she realized Roger had discovered some feeling of purpose and was actually thriving. It reminded her of when her mom had switched jobs from answering phones to bookkeeping at her real estate office; Patricia had started waking naturally and didn't need to set an alarm clock anymore. Roger now seemed to be inwardly driven in a similar way, and Rebecca knew if she stayed at Xavier, her life was only going to get worse and worse.

She was coming up on her senior year and needed to focus on keeping her grades steady and working on her college application materials, which would be due in the winter. But now Xavier had begun to feel like poisoned ground, like if she stayed there, she was going to lose sight of what she really cared about, which was her future. She didn't need to be crying in bathroom stalls. She didn't need to be discussing the brewing situation indefinitely with her friends. She didn't need to be spending time after school on the counselor's couch he'd brought from home. She didn't need to be putting energy into printing out her own dot-matrix cards and organizing the girls on the opposite side.

Rebecca asked her parents if she could transfer.

They were surprised by the question because Rebecca had never mentioned Roger. As far as Patricia and Tom knew, Rebecca kept her distance from guys because she was too mature for them. Which was disappointing—to Patricia, especially, who'd been boy crazy when she was younger. She'd looked forward to helping her daughter navigate her crushes and heartbreaks. But Patricia and Tom had never caught Rebecca talking on the phone to a guy, had never been asked to drive her to meet a guy at the movies, had never seen her get excited about Tom Cruise, Jon Bon Jovi, or anyone cute and famous. It wouldn't have occurred to them that anything of this intensity could have been going on between Rebecca and Roger.

A big part of the reason that Rebecca had never tried to date (she'd hooked up with guys at parties and had sex semi-by-accident in the neighborhood community pool) was because even if she really fell hard for someone at her age, it would still only be puppy love. That bothered her.

The way Rebecca felt about the time she was in right now was that she could already feel it gone. The friends she had, the things she liked, her favorite shade of L'Oréal lipstick, the songs on the radio, the thousands of facts she'd memorized for tests—she couldn't get out from under the awareness that they belonged to the current phase of her life and wouldn't ride out the next. Once, Patricia told Rebecca that when Rebecca was born and handed to her, she immediately felt sad about Rebecca not being a newborn anymore, even though Rebecca was still a newborn. Rebecca's feeling about high school was very similar—there was a melancholic sheen over the whole thing. But instead of clinging to the present with a premature nostalgia, Rebecca just constantly felt kind of mournful, like she was living inside of a memorial for someone who'd lived until 102. The death was expected, but the fact of death still got to her. Sometimes she'd get choked up, feeling trapped by her perspective. For instance, when she went to see *Cocoon* and profoundly overrelated to the senior citizens.

"Why do you want to transfer?" Tom puzzled. Rebecca was sitting at the kitchen counter, and he and Patricia were chopping onions for pasta. "You're doing so well."

"I'm asking if you can just trust me," Rebecca said. She had a feeling they would, because she'd never given them reason not to, aside from having sex in the community pool, which they wouldn't have approved of but didn't know about.

"Well, you've always been able to make good decisions for yourself . . . ," Patricia said, contemplating Rebecca.

Rebecca began attending Rancho Solano, which was in Scottsdale, so that added about a half hour to her drive. But she didn't mind it so much, especially in the mornings, because she'd started listening to a goth show called *Eternal Slumber Party* on the college radio station. She'd found the show by accident but really taken a strong, immediate liking to the music, which was alternately romantic and pounding.

All thoughts went to her future. High school was about college. Instead of further developing new friendships and keeping up with her old ones, she took a part-time job as a clerk at Sam Goody in order to make some spending money for college next year. During her interview in the back room, Rebecca felt like a fucking idiot as she tried to sound adult to sell herself to the fortysomething manager, Tyler. She felt stiff and fake and like she had absolutely nothing to offer.

When Tyler asked her what her worst quality was, she said that she was a perfectionist. Which wasn't her worst quality. Her worst quality was that she couldn't take any interaction at face value, and also that she found it nearly impossible to admit when she didn't know how to do something. The latter was why Rebecca was so bad on the register for the first couple of weeks. A handful of customers got free stuff because she couldn't remember how to go back and add an item after she'd totaled a purchase.

On one Sunday night Rebecca was working until close, it was pretty dead, and she'd put "First and Last and Always" by the Sisters of Mercy on the sound system. She was singing along quietly to the title track and organizing the Top 20 wall when she noticed an older guy in an office shirt stealing looks at her while he browsed.

She could tell he wanted to talk to her. But instead of doing that, he also started quietly singing along to the title track without looking at her again.

At a quarter to ten Rebecca shut and locked one of the front glass doors, giving the signal that shoppers should wrap it up. The other worker on shift with her, Abe, had the vacuum out at the back of the store. He'd been told so many times to stop vacuuming at the feet of customers, but he was part of a local rap crew and was constantly rushing to rap battles after work.

The guy in the office shirt brought his cassettes to the empty front registers. He stood there, not looking at Rebecca, who was just to the side of the registers, organizing the blank tapes.

"Are you all set?" she asked.

"Yep," he said.

She walked around the counter and took the cassettes. The guy was buying *Black Celebration* by Depeche Mode, *Twitch* by Ministry, and *Tinderbox* by Siouxsie and the Banshees.

"I know two of these," Rebecca said.

The guy tipped his head back. "You're into this kind of music?"

"Yeah, I just found out about it this year." She scanned his cassettes.

"Wow."

"What?"

"You look like a normal high school girl."

Rebecca had her hair half up, and she was wearing a tank top and a jean skirt underneath her Sam Goody apron.

She began removing the cassettes from their security holders. "I mean, what's normal, anyway?"

"No. There's definitely normal." As he said this, the guy hooked both hands on the edge of the counter, leaning back, and that action lifted the cuffs of his work shirt enough to show that he had gray-scale tattoos. They looked like part of something bigger that probably ran up both arms. Rebecca couldn't make out any definite figures, but one side might have had a vertebra.

"I don't know," she said.

"I do. I've been alive longer. You're how old?"

"Sixteen," said Rebecca, bagging his tapes.

"Right. I've got about a decade on you."

That would put him somewhere in his midtwenties, but Rebecca thought he could easily be midthirties. His skin had a weathered quality. His cheek-length hair was dyed a blue black, but the texture gave her the impression that there might be salt-and-pepper underneath.

Rebecca totaled his purchases on the register. The process had become second nature now, and she never fucked up anymore.

"Okay, that comes to twenty seventeen, Grandpa."

Rebecca wasn't exactly trying to flirt with the guy by adding that last part. She just hated being reminded of how little she counted in the world yet. But she was also aware it sounded kind of flirty.

The guy huffed, but not unhappily, as he handed cash to her.

Rebecca pulled a brochure from next to the register. "Do you want to sign up for our customer loyalty program? If you spend—"

"Do I have to fill out a form?"

"Yeah, just basic info."

"Life lesson: you don't ever, ever give any of your information voluntarily to a corporation." Abe was vacuuming toward the front of the store now, and the guy had to talk louder to carry over the whirring.

"They make us ask," Rebecca said.

"The overlords."

"Yeah."

The guy nodded, accepting the bag from her, looking like he wanted to say something else. He settled on "Have a good one" and left.

Walking past the glass front of the store, the guy glanced back and nodded again without stopping.

The following Sunday the guy came in again toward closing, acting surprised, but in a nonchalant way, to see Rebecca. As he purchased headphones, he asked if she'd heard of a local industrial dance band called Sixteenth Ghost. They were playing a venue by ASU later that night; she should check them out.

When Rebecca stepped out of her car at the venue, which was some kind of student union, a crazy wind was blowing, whipping her hair in her face, and she could hear the driving beat of the music from the building. It was the beginning of summer but felt like fall, felt like that heightened combination of fresh school supplies and paper skeletons on doors.

Inside there were only maybe thirty people. The guy was by himself near the makeshift stage, wearing a black T-shirt and black jeans. His dance move was to keep one foot forward, shifting his weight back and forth, his head dropping forward each time he lunged. He didn't spot Rebecca until he broke to grab some water, and when he did, his eyes lit up. It was too loud to talk. He gestured, *Hey, do you want to go outside?* He led her to a side patio for smokers. He didn't smoke. The wind was still going crazy.

There was nowhere to sit, so they just stood around. Even under the moonlight, he could definitely have been in his thirties.

Rebecca learned his name was Kane. He worked in an office doing network security for a small telecommunications company. His boss was a conservative guy and asked him to wear long sleeves because of the clients, which Kane thought was bullshit, and he had made known to all his coworkers he thought it was bullshit. Now that he was in a T-shirt, Rebecca could identify a long alien, like from the movie *Alien*, going down his right arm, and what looked like a wad of circuitry going down the left. Kane didn't trust his boss, didn't trust the company, didn't trust banks, and when he talked about these things, his voice got louder with skepticism.

Rebecca told Kane about how and why she'd transferred schools, because he didn't know any of those people, so it didn't matter. Kane said that Roger sounded like a real punk. Rebecca said yeah, but also that Roger felt like the kind of person who was going to mail her a long, remorseful letter in about five years. Kane said she was weirdly wise for her age. He said she saw that there was more out there. Rebecca liked him telling her this and thought it was true, although at the same time it embarrassed her to like it.

The wind got so intense that it knocked over one of the planters lining the patio. The two of them righted it together. Then Rebecca said she had get going, without mentioning her curfew. Kane walked her to her car. The music in the background, with its crashing beat, made Rebecca picture a naked woman with gigantic bloodred jewels on her neck rowing the ferry across the river Styx in a shimmering fog. The image just came to her. "Can I hug you?" Kane asked. She scoffed, hugging him.

The next morning Rebecca started her lone summer school class at the community college, a Brit lit seminar that would count as a senior elective at Rancho. That way she could get out of school at one o'clock during her final semester.

The first time Rebecca and Kane hung out in a planned way was to get coffee in the shopping center after she closed at work. She ordered hot chocolate. Kane teased her for it as he paid. Rebecca dryly joked, "Sorry I'm not as edgy as you," and he immediately pulled her into a hug.

The second time they hung out was during a weekend afternoon. Rebecca told her parents she was going over to Noelle's, then she followed the directions Kane had given her to his stucco apartment complex. She parked in a guest spot under the pergola and locked her car twice because Kane had mentioned he and his roommate had their cars broken into two times each in the past six months.

Inside, the apartment was boring, just white walls, tan carpet, vertical blinds, black pleather furniture, zero architectural or decorative surprises. Rebecca briefly met the roommate, a blond man who also worked with computers. He made a point of explaining away a stuffed sheep he kept on his bed, even though Rebecca would never have noticed it if he hadn't brought it up.

Kane's bedroom was the master in the back of the unit. He had a fan going by the open window and the ceiling fan on too. He asked Rebecca if she felt like watching a movie he'd rented. She said sure. He shut the blinds and put on *Return to Oz*, and they lay on his bed with a foot between them in the darkened daylight.

Partway through the movie Kane's phone rang on his nightstand. All that Rebecca could follow was that it was some kind of work emergency. Kane began talking his colleague through a code they needed to type into the system. In the middle of this, seeming as if it were a casual thought, he picked up Rebecca's hand and took it in his.

Still on the phone, Kane mouthed to her, "Is this okay?"

It was impossible for Rebecca to make sense of how she could be startled by this development when she'd always known it was coming. Similar to how she felt the first time she got her period.

"Yeah," Rebecca said.

They lay there holding hands as Kane finished giving instructions to the person on the phone. "Okay, talk to you later," he said, and then he went to kiss Rebecca. That fast: hang up, lean over, kissing.

From the moment they were kissing, Rebecca knew that she would never be able to fall for Kane. It was something chemical. Instead of losing herself in him, she was clocking everything physical that was happening. Thoughts came like, *My tongue is under his tongue, now it's over his tongue.* The only romantic stirring Rebecca had was that she felt flexible. Flexibly minded, in that she knew she didn't want this relationship between them to go anywhere, but was open to riding it out for a bit. Flexibly bodied, in that she understood that hooking up with a grown man with an apartment, a job, white button-down shirts, and sci-fi tattoos was going to be a different kind of experience than she'd ever had. Although Rebecca hated being exposed for what she didn't know how to do, something in her was trying to grow.

Kane removed her bra and took in her chest, staring, audibly inhaling he was so turned on. He said, "I never preferred big breasts until right now."

"Isn't that the default preference?" Rebecca asked genuinely.

Kane sucked on a nipple. "I'm constantly forgetting you're at an age where you're surrounded by a bunch of idiots who think they all need to do and like the same things." Then he sat up, now having reminded himself of her age. "We can't have sex," he said. "I could go to jail."

The next weekend, after Kane got Rebecca topless again, he took off his own shirt to reveal four barbell piercings straining against the skin of his chest. He asked if he could slide himself between her breasts, which seemed simple enough in the abstract. But then Rebecca felt silly when Kane had to show her how to use her hands to keep her breasts squeezed around his dick to create the right friction. His shaft had two more barbells in it. As he slid toward and from her chin, the barbells making a clickety-clackety sound from rolling, like some type of tiny mouse car rolling up her sternum, Rebecca inwardly debated whether she was supposed to be doing more. Eventually she stuck out her tongue so that Kane met it every time he thrust. Kane groaned from above, but the combo of his penis hitting her tongue like a buzzer and the clickety-clackety of the barbells made her feel like she was in a pornographic *I Love Lucy* bit. Rebecca busted out laughing, and Kane tackle-hugged her, burying his face in her shoulder.

They didn't always stay in his master bedroom. One evening Kane wanted to take Rebecca out to dinner at the Old Spaghetti Factory, but then when they got there, he seemed angry. Not at her. Just worked up at the way other people were behaving, which was something she'd seen in him before. Rebecca made a few halfhearted attempts to probe at the story of his underlying anger, but she never got very far because Kane refused to talk about his past. His denial of it was so full that she only accidentally found out he'd been born with a different name when she saw a bill in his car that said "Matt." She just picked up on old injuries as they blipped in and immediately out of their conversation. A bad mom. Grew up poor.

Another evening, while walking along Saguaro Lake, they ran into Donnelly, who had been one of the friends sitting on the fountain the day Rebecca said hi to Roger after their mutual freeze. Rebecca was surprised when Donnelly stopped to talk to her. Now she intuited a brew of curiosity, confusion, and awkwardness compelling Donnelly to ask her what she'd been up to as his eyes nervously darted between her face and her hand, being held by Kane. Rebecca and Donnelly shot the shit about their upcoming plans to go look at college campuses—it was the end of July, and Rebecca was going on a two-week trip with her parents at the tail of August to Vermont, Massachusetts, and New York, while Donnelly was tagging along with his older brother to Texas and Florida. Kane didn't say a word the whole time, just stared at Donnelly in a way that seemed prickly.

"Is it weird for you that I'm in high school?" Rebecca asked Kane when they continued their walk.

"I don't think of you that way," he said.

They were lying in Kane's bed, Kane examining the side string of Rebecca's underwear from Contempo Casuals, when he said, "There's always been something I wanted to do."

"What is it?" Rebecca asked.

"I don't want you to feel like I'm pressuring you."

"Just say what it is."

"It's a fantasy that's maybe going to sound out-there." He said "out-there" with a swing of anger. The same tone he used to talk about his shirts for work.

"Okay. Go," she said.

Kane stayed concentrated on her underwear string. "I have a fantasy—it's just a fantasy, remember that." He paused to make sure that sank in. "Of having sex with a dead woman, but you and I obviously can't have sex because of the age issue, so it would be a modified version of that. You'd drop your body temperature with an ice bath, just as much as you can stand, and if you hate it from the first second, we stop. That's the end of it. But you'd drop your body temperature and then you'd lie in bed, not moving, with your eyes shut. I'd come and lie on top of you. Feel you, kiss you, rub against you, whatever. It's a fantasy, not something that translates into a real-life desire."

Rebecca thought this was a weird fantasy and wasn't at all titilated by it, but something in the exercise struck her as worthwhile. "I would do that," she answered.

"You would?"

"Once."

Rebecca stayed behind to review her underlined sections and marginalia in *Tess of the d'Urbervilles*, while Kane went to the grocery store to buy party ice. She was taking her final in her summer school class the next day. When Kane returned, he dumped six bags of ice into his bathtub-shower combo and filled the tub halfway with cold water. As soon as Rebecca put in a foot, she realized this was going to suck more than it had in her imagination, but she'd always been goal oriented, so she challenged herself to the fifteen minutes.

Kane sat on the toilet seat to keep Rebecca company and told her she was amazing. Her teeth chattered, but she read, memorized, silently quizzed herself. In order to push past regret, it was better just to focus on the novel. She had to ask Kane to stop talking to her. When his watch beeped, Rebecca got out of the bath, went over to the bed, splayed herself across it, shut her eyes, and pictured stillness (trees and streets in the middle of the night) and steadiness (the hum of an invisible freeway).

Kane put Depeche Mode on his stereo. He got on top of Rebecca, kissed her. She didn't have to kiss him back. She found she didn't miss kissing him back. Then she knew their time together was wrapping up. She wondered if Kane had felt it before it crystallized for her. Maybe he'd taken this dead-girl leap because he was trying to grab that one last thing from the burning building. Or maybe it was his funny way of saying good-bye. He came quickly on the outside of her thigh. When Rebecca finally moved, opening her eyes and turning toward Kane, she saw his face and thought, *Oh, he's really falling for me.*

The next few times they saw each other, a chant had started in Rebecca's head that went, *Dump me, dump me, dump me.* But Kane didn't. He maintained his patience even when she experimented with being snippy and distant. He saw the bigger picture, but it wasn't accurate from her side. She talked a lot about her upcoming trip to the East Coast, which was being taken for the purpose of deciding where she would move somewhat soon. Where she would leave to. At the beginning with Kane, when Rebecca had pictured how they would go their separate ways, this silly fantasy had come to mind of her on a cruise ship and Kane on a dock, waving, already remembering her fondly. She hadn't thought it would go down like this, being dragged out, considering all Kane had cementing him to his grown-up life—his office, his salary, his benefits, his apartment, his favorite goth clubs—and the known fact that she was at an age where she couldn't be doing anything besides just passing through. But the possibility finally struck her that Kane would wait for her, as long as she was going to return.

So Rebecca finally asked Kane to come meet her after her closing shift, knowing she had to break up with him directly. Tomorrow she was flying with her parents to New York. That night, as she worked stocking cassettes, six teenagers came in on what seemed like a group date. They flirted by pushing each other, messing with each other's hair. One guy hopped up on his girlfriend for an impromptu piggyback ride, and the girl tried to carry him around for a few seconds. Rebecca couldn't help but wonder where she'd gone wrong.

Her manager, Tyler, walked out of the back room holding a piece of printer paper. "This fax just came in addressed to you?" he said, confused but mostly entertained.

Rebecca looked and saw this on the page.

After the doors had been locked, she counted the register drawer. She felt Kane outside even before she looked up to check for him. He was standing in front of the shopping center fountain, backlit by its blue glow. Tyler came to the counter to double-check her cash and worriedly noticed the guy watching them. He was always on high alert when handling money. Rebecca told Tyler not to worry, that she knew the guy.

The drawer came out even. Rebecca hung up her apron in the back room as Tyler shut off the lights and activated the alarm timer. They walked toward the glass front, Kane straightening upon seeing Rebecca about to exit. Tyler put the key in the door, looking back at her incredulously.

"Wait . . . is that the guy who sent the fax?" he asked.

Feeling watched from multiple directions now, Rebecca stared outside. *Oh boy. Unnnnnh. Fuck.* She wished from the bottom of her heart that Tyler just hadn't said anything. The existential dread came barreling down upon her: the weight of time, space, humankind. The deeply heavy smallness of humankind. As she considered Kane, the fountain, the rose he'd sent, the palm trees waving in the background sky, she thought, *My life is going in circles.*

Malagon's Proverbs

Daniel Torday

NO ONE EXPECTED TO HEAR FROM FRED MALAGON AGAIN AFTER his ignominious departure from public life. If they did, they expected, say, an apology because it was the eighth step. A court-ordered mea culpa. A drunken final plea for return, as, say, the assistant field hockey coach. Testimony at the trial of some Trumpist.

The last word from Fred Malagon came instead in the strangest form possible: an annotated copy of Proverbs. Fred Malagon—Fred Malagon of all Malagons, of all Freds, for that matter (agon)!—was not a reader of the Bible. And yet. On a Tuesday afternoon in late July he found himself alone, in his tiny Crown Heights one-bedroom, bored by all novels, bored by all nonfiction, bored by all tweets, all internets; and the copy of the Stone Bible he'd lifted off a stoop on the other side of Eastern Parkway just looked so . . . big. Black. Big and black and full of words. So he had a look at what was inside. Recto was just a bunch of ancient Hebrew garble, so that he would have to ignore. But verso was English. First he learned that these were sayings from Solomon, whom he vaguely knew to be wise, because you couldn't live in the culture for long without knowing that Solomon, whomever he had been, he had been wise.

So he proceeded to read. The thing was, it was one long rejoinder to, well, him. Fred. His worst behaviors, all of which were pretty bad. The nose-picking, the rage-honking, the front-in-parking-spot-stealing, the teenager-ogling. The things he couldn't speak himself. And now here were the words of Solomon, who wouldn't even let a baby be split in half. In the first chapter there were just some small tremblors—"incline your heart to understanding"—that sounded fine. But as he ranged deeper into the book, and Proverbs on its own was a short book, just thirty-one chapters, it got at him. At his heart, a thing he didn't like to admit he had. "If one is drawn to the scoffers, he will scoff; but if one is drawn to the humble, he will find favor." Fred Malagon was a first-rate scoffer, and a first-rate first-rate-scoffer-lover. He remembered a series of scoffs—at his fellow teachers at Randolph, at the papers on historiography he found lacking, at the way not one of his students could seem to spell "desiccate," except Katie—and how he and Katie had scoffed at her fellow students in his office, and scoffed again when they fled Garden Lakes together in the cold, dark paleness of a dark, pale night, scoff-scoff-scoffing all the way.

Fred Malagon scoffed at the fascists as well. But it occurred to him as he read through Proverbs that this was one long rejoinder both to him *and* to the fascists, and that that might make him one. One of the fascists. That was the trouble with living in a country where a plurality of one's fellow citizens had chosen to elect a fascist—it might reveal that you were one too. Fred put down the Stone Tanakh, and then he just couldn't help scoffing at, well, himself. Picked it back up. "The path of the righteous is like the glow of sunlight," Solomon said, "growing brighter until high noon, but the way of the wicked is like darkness, they know not upon what they stumble." *Well, fuck,* Malagon thought. *I am wicked. I know that much. But that I'm a stumbler too?* He threw the book across the room. He'd learned long ago from a Jewish friend that if a prayer book hit the floor, you were supposed to kiss it, so he stood up and walked the thirty feet across his apartment, picked up the book, kissed it. On the way back to the couch, stumbled.

Fuck.

He made it only as far as Proverbs 6, if you want to know the truth. Most people don't want to know the truth, so if you'd like to stop listening to Fred Malagon now, stop. Stop reading. It'd do you fine. One way to stop listening to fascists is to stop listening to fascists. But that doesn't mean Fred Malagon didn't quake when he read 6:12-14: "The lawless man is a man of iniquity: He goes forth with distortion on the mouth; he winks with his eyes, shuffles with his feet, points with his fingers, duplicity in his heart; he plots evil all the time; he stirs up strife." And here's the thing about Fred Malagon, alone, in this apartment: he knew it. He wasn't just a scoffer. He was a winker, a mouth distorter. He was a shuffler with his feet. He was a finger pointer and he had always been a finger pointer.

But here's the other thing about Fred Malagon: he knew it. He knew it now. And he had a single realization, sitting there reading Proverbs, reading Proverbs 6:12-14 in particular, a verse that ends, "Therefore, his undoing will come suddenly; he will be broken in an instant." It wasn't forgiveness he needed from those he'd hurt. He had apologized and would apologize more. What he needed, Fred Malagon, pointer of fingers, shuffler of feet, was to undo the duplicitousness of his duplicitous heart. He looked up "duplicitous" on Dictionary.com just to be sure he knew that it meant what he thought it meant, and it did. This was what he needed, this was what Solomon long dead wanted of him in this thirty-one-chapter-long rejoinder. And it was, above all things, the one thing he didn't know how to do. It made him—and probably you knew this—sad. The one thing you cannot do, though, you who've stayed here with Fred Malagon through to the end, was as clear to Fred Malagon as it is to you. DO NOT SCOFF. No scoffing. No finger pointing. No mouth distorting. No, no, no, no scoffing, friend.

Do not.

And so with what little strength was in him after reading up to the sixth chapter of Proverbs, Fred Malagon decided there was one thing he could do. He opened his Google Chrome to where his Twitter was linked to his Facebook was linked to his Insta was linked to his duplicitous heart. And he pushed the little blue button with the feather on it. And he typed: "I am a lawless man of iniquity. But I am trying to stop." And he hit . . . send. Sat back. Was his heart less duplicitous now? Did he feel something else? Less finger-pointy? Less scoffy? Less whatever it was in the mouth? In the trespasses big and small, ripe and rotten, of his long un-Solomonic life, had Fred Malagon found a way past, a way around, a way through all he'd done? Coulda, woulda, might a Fred Malagon find a path forward? Hit it, Fred. Hit it again. Send. Send. Send.

Forsaken

Joseph Salvatore

IT WOULD BE THE HOTTEST DAY OF THE YEAR, THE TEMPERATURE just right, my life coach and I well knew, to allow my cremaster muscle (the one muscle that I could not build to perfection) to relax and let descend, from inside this hard body, my anxious scrotum. Within the expandable folds of my cherry-red satin scrunch-back posing bikini, as my life coach and I well understood, my shy scrotum would indeed descend and welcome with open arms this, the hottest day of the year, the day my life coach and I had been anticipating and preparing for throughout the last six months: the day I would step back onstage after my three-year hiatus, a hiatus that, in the press and on social media, I claimed I had embarked upon so that I could focus more on family and building my brand, but which, in reality, my life coach and I well knew, had actually been taken as an emergency measure because I could no longer step onstage in that satin bikini without suffering a full-blown nervous breakdown. This was no mere case of stage fright, and my life coach was the only person who understood. He said he knew from past experience how one might feel the desperate need to escape one's circumstances. The hiatus was his idea.

But little did I know then, on that sweltering day, that those previous six months would be the last time I would ever work with my life coach. His disappearance would dismantle everything for which we had worked together. I wouldn't understand the devastating effects his departure from my life would bring about until much later. And by then my ex-wife would be remarried; my daughter would be moved out of the Figueroa family compound, having packed up herself and all her many things, loaded them into a U-Haul, and driven far, far away; and I would be ruined. Little could I have imagined, given the success we had attained, that upon his disappearance, I would be, yet again, adrift, un-self-embraced, totally out of harmony not only with my scrotum and groin, but with my entire body. I would lose the me that he and I had worked so hard to regain for those six short months. He would abandon me and leave me forsaken.

Perhaps I should have done more research on him before handing over my fragile, fractured psyche so completely to a stranger. But I had not then the wherewithal to do anything other than the exhausting repetitive daily routine (work out, create content, post videos, eat, practice posing, rinse, repeat) that I had been doing for so many years, both on and off the road, and that had served in its comforting familiarity to preserve whatever sanity I still outwardly maintained, but which my life coach helped me to realize was nothing more than a constant existential hamster wheel, functioning as what he called a "dopamine-driven feedback loop," a continuous distraction drip keeping me anesthetized from facing the real and difficult work I should have been doing all along—i.e., dealing with my shit. I drove by his office on one especially dark day and then turned around and stopped in for a consultation. An hour later he said calmly and convincingly that he could save me, and that promise, along with his firm handshake (despite his advanced age, his grip was as strong and hard as my father's cast-iron vise, and he stood as straight and tall as a man half his age), was all I needed.

I am a professional body builder, a five-time Mr. Olympia (the youngest to win that title in the IFBB Pro League back in 1993, when I took first at age twenty), the owner of a multinational sports nutrition supplement empire as well as my own line of gym wear and gym gear, and one of the internet's most well-known and well-subscribed-to health-and-fitness experts and influencers, with a staggering amount of YouTube subscribers and Instagram followers—with all of that, it often comes as a great surprise to many people when they learn that I have what my doctor and other sexuality experts would call an "average-size" penis. It's best that we be clear about this: Not small. Not large. Truly average. *Utterly medium.*

Given my girth, and the size of my calves, and the span of my lats, and the swell of my traps, and the natural, God-given thickness of my wrists and ankles, and the size of my hands and feet, and the unusual (and some have said "sexually suggestive") length and shape of my fingers, and even my head of overly thick, very shiny and wavy black hair—given all of this, my average-size penis is often the elephant in the room when I take off my clothes to be with a woman, nude and natural, precoitus.

Then, about four years ago, this intimate performance anxiety, if you will, spread to my professional life and became, for me, a full-blown pathology: an "unhealthy preoccupation" with something that was completely average. Totally normal. Statistically insignificant. Neither exceptional nor nonexceptional.

If you saw me walking down the street, you'd understand: everything about me screams, *Huge penis.*

Having grown up in Queens, New York, with a brood of only brothers and a father who was a foreman on a construction crew, all of us losing our beloved mother, Patricia, to ovarian cancer while we boys were still in grade school, I have found it difficult throughout my life to talk openly with women, not only about my penis (which, precisely because of its intense averageness, some women have assured me is, for them, in fact, a nonissue in our relationship), but also about my many anxieties and bodily insecurities. My ex-wife says I "keep it all in." The ability to open up and share my pain and fear with my partners, my life coach assured me, is the key to unlocking my romantic potential and conquering my scrotum-tightening stage fright and sexual performance anxiety. Only by

talking frankly, he said, about my insecurities and fears can I ever
hope to achieve what he called full "self-embracement," to make
myself open and vulnerable and ready to welcome success and love
and authentic intimacy into my life. He even encouraged me to refer
to my penis as, simply, "my penis," which, for much of my life, I
have always felt more comfortable calling "my package." But my life
coach said a package was something we used to cover something up,
to contain something, maybe something really special if we'd only
be brave enough to show it to the world. He thought I should let my
penis out, release it from its "package," and show it off to the world,
wave it like a flag, a flag of my burgeoning self-embracement; only
then, he said, would I be free from my paralyzing anxiety and truly
come out of hiding.

I should add here that of course he was being figurative when
he said I should "let it out." He was referring more to my *inner penis*
than to my actual outer penis. If you haven't worked with a life
coach before, you might not understand all the lingo; it took me
a little while. See, my dad and brothers, we never talked like that.
And being a half-Spanish, half-Italian kid from Elmhurst, and a
high school football and wrestling star, I only ever knew one coach,
my *coach* coach, whom we always called simply Coach. Whereas
my life coach urged me at every session to stop calling him Coach,
but rather by his first name, Mike. Mike, who despite being an
octogenarian, looked like a fierce, giant, bald drill sergeant, but
who could be, at times, as soft and supportive as a satin scrunch-
back posing bikini. Mike, whose disappearance from my life would
doom every member of my family; he said we were both equals in
the agreed-upon safe space of his coaching office, colleagues, he
called us, fellow conspirators in our mission to liberate the real me,
the real Gerry Figueroa. Not the Gerry Figueroa that my millions
of fans referred to as the Quadzilla from Queens, but rather the
flesh-and-blood man standing, at six feet five, in nothing but a
satin bikini on life's grand stage, nearly four hundred pounds of
pure muscle and 7 percent body fat and one extremely average-size

penis—quivering, sweating, muttering Catholic prayers to stave off yet another panic attack.

But try as Mike might, I still feel paralyzed, both onstage and in the bedroom. For it is because I am so large and striated and cut and lean and ripped and dry, even during the off-season, that my penis is often a distracting blip on the romance radar screen, and I find myself, especially now that I'm divorced and my daughter is in college, dating young men who have posters of me hanging in their home gyms, I find myself obsessing about this "nonissue." It was especially difficult in the months after my wife left, when I briefly reentered the dating scene. I am "fixated," to use my Mike's word, on that moment when, in the bedroom before coitus, I unlatch my belt, unbutton my trousers, and bend over to lower my pants. I know full well (or think I do; Mike called this belief "projection") what my partner's reaction will be when she sees the utter averageness between my legs. I can practically feel the complete lack of noticeable response, the nonplussedness, masking the deeper disappointment, even if she is unaware of it on a conscious level. Who would want me, and why would I want to be with someone so in denial about my averageness that she would actually want to be with me? And yet I always submit to participating in this choreographed charade because, as Mike helped me to understand, I somehow believe it might be different this time.

I have actually perfected a trouser-lowering technique, in such erotic instances, that conceals my penis until the last moment, when my pants, having been lowered to the point where my arms can no longer reach, drop to my ankles; and I must finally stand up and step out of them, flexing my hairless, waxed quads and tightening my waxed and deeply tanned and dry and striated buttocks muscles. Often at that moment of full nakedness, I'll do a few little warm-up jumps on my toes, a jaunty little boxer's hop, to instill some sense of confidence. It's something I started doing onstage back at the 1994 Arnold Classic, when I began what was to be my unstoppable winning streak for nearly a decade, and which, when I do it naked in

front of a woman in a bedroom before coitus, bounces my penis up
and down just a bit, loosening the tendons and relaxing the cremaster
muscle and allowing enough blood to flow through and elongate it
just a little bit, and though it is often limp from the anxiety caused
by my horrible, secret awareness of the upcoming reveal of my
average-size penis and the ensuing trauma of my lowered trousers,
that little hopping routine manages nonetheless to elongate it just
enough to keep me from dropping to the floor and curling up from
the unbearable self-consciousness of my penis's sheer and utter and
gruesome averageness. Mike used to say, before his disappearance
that would doom us all, that I shouldn't have to live like that. Mike
said it was my birthright to be happy and successful and fully self-
embraced.

But he had his work cut out for himself, Mike did. It's bad
enough that I am built the way I am. But add to it that I am known
for my body. *I am my body.* So much so that I am a brand, not a
person. Kids at the gym, getting ready to step under a bar and squat
five hundred pounds, don't say, "Fellas, in preparation for this squat,
I'm going to ingest a bioavailable amino-membrane-permeable
caffeine-protein substrate." No, you know what they say? They say,
"Hold on, dudes, I gotta pop a Gerry." That's my preworkout product
slogan and trademarked branding tag line: "Pop your Gerry." Well,
I'm that Gerry—Elmhurst's own Gerry Figueroa—and my clothing
line is called Gerry Gear, and my highly successful sports nutrition
supplement empire is called Gerry-Rigged; I am an internationally
recognized brand name, and yet I am the owner of an indisputably
average-size penis, and it has ruined my life and my career. And the
only person who ever helped me get close to overcoming this curse
was Mike. Coach Mike Hancock, whose departure would send all
of us to our doom.

Needless to say, I never made it back to the stage. The last
day I was to see Mike was a week before the competition. It was
sweltering, and I was late for our appointment. I entered his brightly

lit office to find him hunched over a small white plastic container. Mike did not look up from what I could now see was a pineapple-flavored yogurt. I apologized for being late. He continued eating, his bald dome shining in the afternoon light from the window next to his leather recliner. The air conditioner was on, but it had little effect on the heat.

Finally he said, without looking up from his yogurt, "I don't have to tell you, boy, that deviation from the schedule will not be tolerated."

"I know, sir; I'm sorry," I said. "But I had an emergency call from my cousin. His firm is going through some restructuring, and he needed some information from me, which I had to find on my phone for him. Took me a minute to figure out how to find it. Fuckin' Dave wouldn't let me get off the phone while I did it. Won't happen again, Mike." I remained standing, but I noticed his facial expression change to one of bemusement. Was it my use of the curse word? Mike's face drained of color, and consternation replaced the bemused look with which he had held me during my explanation. He cleared his throat.

"Today it's 'Mr. Hancock,' son, till I say otherwise. We save 'Mike' for when you earn it." He crushed the yogurt container in his large freckled hand, and a few small white drops of yogurt dappled his leather loafers. He reached down with his massive hand to wipe away the drops, then licked his fingers clean and tossed the crumpled container into the trash can next to his desk. "Gonna ask you to come back next week, Gerry. I need to take care of a few things."

"I'm sorry, sir? Didn't we have a session today? The Arnold is next week." I felt my groin cinch.

"Today's session is cancelled, son."

"But why?"

"Must I remind you that I do not need to have a reason, Figs?"

He'd never referred to me in that way before, never once during the entire six months. The tone of familiarity with which he said it felt intimate and accusatory at the same time. "What did you call me, sir?"

"Never mind. Come back tomorrow, son. We'll playact the stage routine here in the office."

"Should I wear my bikini?"

"Won't be necessary; boxers will do."

The next day was hotter than the day before. I arrived at Mr. Hancock's office at noon, our usual time. Mr. Hancock liked to eat while we began our sessions, often wrapping up the uneaten bits carefully afterward and lifting it like a baby through the air to place it gently, rather than tossing it, into the trash. Which was why yesterday's yogurt spill and brash trash can toss were so unusual.

After passing the security guard (a guy named Kelvon, who asked for my autograph twice when I first met him) and taking the elevator to Mr. Hancock's floor of office suites, I found his door was unlocked. Heat radiated from inside the office. His air conditioner was off. Mr. Hancock had left his office impeccably clean; only the mess of stuffed animals we'd used for playacting my inner-penis trauma work remained scattered in the corner near the trash can. A couple of clean plastic spoons and tiny unused paper napkins on his desk suggested his absence was accidental. I trained my eyes on the clock behind Mr. Hancock's desk chair. I contemplated whether or not Mr. Hancock would materialize, and while I ultimately believed otherwise, I vowed to work on my stage routine myself alone until Mr. Hancock returned. I left the AC off; the heat helped my confidence level rise. I was pepped at being able to stave off a potential panic attack.

I went through my routine nearly a dozen times, each time finding my concentration pulled more and more down to my penis. Finally there came the sound of a key working to open the door. Mr. Hancock hadn't ever been late. Never once. I worried that what had seemed to bother him yesterday was causing some problem for him—and, by extension, for me. But it wasn't Mr. Hancock; it was Kelvon.

"Whoa, sorry, Gerry. Wondered if you were still here. Didn't see you leave. Mr. Hancock called to say he had family business to attend to. He told me to tell you he'd be back in time to see you at the Arnold." He stared unapologetically at my quads. People always do this: stare at various parts of my body without any shyness, which always causes, on my part, an involuntary flexing of that body part's muscle. The only place they never stare is the one place I can't flex. Denial is as deep as the deepest-running river in Egypt.

"Thanks, Kelvon. I'm using the space to practice my routine. The heat makes it so I don't need baby oil."

"That's just pure sweat all over you, Gerry? Damn, you glistening. Lock it when you leave."

The day of the Arnold arrived, the weather perfect for my scrotum and, by extension, for my penis. I'd stopped by Mr. Hancock's office before I left for the event, but Kelvon said he'd not been back. I asked if I could leave something for him in his office. When Kelvon left me alone after opening Mr. Hancock's door, I walked over to his desk. I looked down to the corner of the room at the stuffed animals that had, once upon a time six months ago, reactivated and then released and, finally, somewhat relieved my unrelievable pain. I looked on the shelves of his white IKEA bookcase, at the brightly colored plastic bins in which were stored the talking sticks and talking mirrors, and the clay and the colored construction paper and crayons and markers and building blocks we'd used for art therapy. I raised my right arm in a classic biceps pose, and then I extended my arm over his desk. I unclenched my fist and let drop to the desk my expandable cherry-red satin scrunch-back posing bikini.

I knew the casino and resort hotel where the competition was being held would be overrun with people. Many of whom had paid a lot money to stare at my body, whether I was onstage or not. The place would be overrun with those people. All of them wanting to stare at me. None of them Mr. Hancock.

Lindy

Jaime Clarke

WHAT YOU HAVE TO DO TO GET IN HERE: SET FIRE TO YOUR FAMILY while they sleep; lock a small child in an old refrigerator abandoned to the earth by its owners; lay wooden posts in the path of an Amtrak Sunset Limited; remove the stop signs at an intersection near a grade school; dump hydrochloric acid in a public pool; lure neighborhood boys and girls into your house for cookies and movies and store their body parts according to size in a reach-in freezer; order a Big Mac at a McDonald's and open fire on its patrons—all of these things will get you sent to the Arizona State Hospital, usually for life. Whereas I thought I would spend at least six months there, I ended up lasting only a day, the most bizarre day in my then eighteen-year-old life, because Lindy had no sooner introduced himself than he was dead.

Of the number of venues for serving your mandatory Christian service, a graduation requirement heartily endorsed by the priests and lay people of Randolph College Preparatory, there were two: the children's crisis center or the state mental hospital. And on the authority of generations of graduates before—an authority based on tales of crazy women shedding their clothes while walking down the hall, men who tried to shove eating utensils in various orifices, human beings acting like animals, performing for the benefit of craven teenagers whose hair was, at all times, cut above the collar—the hospital was the place to volunteer.

My assignment that first and last day, a day which seemed forever in coming as I waded through a series of checks (fingerprint, background, etc., as well as various interviews with doctors whose peculiarities paralleled their patients'), was a large man with a stone face who looked about forty, his dull gray crew cut meticulously maintained. "Thomas Major Hill," his chart read, along with an ominous instruction to "keep the patient out of the vicinity of any activated television."

"Call me Lindy," Thomas Major Hill said. "My friends call me Lindy."

"Is that a nickname?" I asked.

"Sort of. I'm Charles A. Lindbergh Jr.," he said. "I'm the baby Lindbergh."

Lindy seemed exceptional in his incarceration. He hadn't violated someone else and become a criminal; his brain just wouldn't unhinge itself from an assembly of facts: that he was born in 1930 to Anne Morrow and Charles A. Lindbergh; that he spent the first year or so of his life at Next Day Hill, the Morrow estate in Englewood, New Jersey ("That's En-glewood," Lindy said. "Not Inglewood, as in California. I've never been to California. I hate California"); that his real nickname was "Hi" because of something cute he once said; that he missed his nurse, Betty Gow; that his father was a great pilot. Lindy said he'd been separated from his family since he was young— when I asked him what had separated them he nodded vaguely, saying "Yep, exactly"—but that he'd tried several times to reunite with his sister, who lived in Hawaii. Apparently it was these reunions that caused Lindy to wind up in the loony bin.

"My sister has a magnificent house," Lindy said. "She has three children with her husband, Tom, who is a lawyer. They have a maid, their house is so big. I had a picture of them, but it got taken away."

I told Lindy I once lived in Hawaii, and his stone face softened with a big smile. "How did you like it?" he wanted to know.

"I loved it," I said.

I wondered where Lindy was from. When you meet someone, it's interesting to guess at who their parents were, what their childhood was like, etc. I figured it wouldn't do any good to point out that mathematically Lindy wasn't old enough to be the Lindbergh child. Plus, to do so might enrage him, a feeling substantiated by something I learned later from Stillwell, Lindy's doctor.

Stillwell told me about another patient who came to the hospital claiming to be the son of Charles Lindbergh. Lindy was understandably irate. He publicly challenged this Lindbergh to prove his claim. This Lindbergh told a long-winded tale in the cafeteria one lunch about how Bruno Hauptmann snatched him from his crib, then handed him off to Al Capone, who changed his name from Lindbergh to Salvatore. This Lindbergh—now Salvatore—grew up under Capone's wing, managing several casinos in Las Vegas under the name Bugsy Siegel. When Lindy pressed this reputed mobster for details verifying his birth, this Lindbergh admitted he wasn't in fact the baby Lindbergh but Colonel Lindbergh himself. The colonel hinted that little Lindy was the bastard child of Mrs. Lindbergh and one of the construction workers who built the Lindbergh estate in Hopewell. Further, he hinted that the worker and Mrs. Lindbergh conspired to have Hauptmann abduct the bastard child and kill him. This sent Lindy into a fit, and luckily he was restrained after cutting the impostor with a sharpened toothbrush Lindy carried in his sock. By the time Lindy came out of isolation, a long hall of dank rooms in the windowless basement, the Lindbergh impostor was gone, transferred to a facility in Georgia.

I told Lindy about when I was sixteen, how I spent the summer with my aunt in Macon. Bobby Haynes lived next door. Bobby Haynes and his girlfriend, Beth, took me out to the lake with them on those hot summer nights. I kicked rocks around the lake while Bobby and Beth listened to the radio. After a while I got to where I could time when I could come back to the car. The three of us would go to the Dairy Queen if it wasn't too late. There was an even calm to those nights, a calm shattered when they found Beth face down at the lakeshore, her lungs clogged with red mud. Everyone, including my aunt, thought Bobby did it, that he probably got her pregnant. They were satisfied in this when Bobby's mother found Bobby hanging in his closet by his rhinestone belt. He'd removed the silver buckle with the engraving of a cowboy lassoing a bull and put it on his dresser. My aunt sent me home shortly after that.

I didn't actually tell Lindy the part about them finding Beth and Bobby. Lindy spent the rest of that day playing chess with Old Sam Strumm, who claimed to be the greatest chess player in the history of institutionalization. The cause of the riot that day, the riot in which Lindy would end up dead, wasn't a disagreement of any kind over the chess match. The riot started because Martha Easton opened the piano when it was quiet time in the common area. I was still learning the rules of quiet time myself, so I wasn't sure that piano playing wasn't allowed, but the orderlies said, "Now Martha," and flipped the lid down. Martha flipped it up and started playing, and one of the orderlies slammed the lid down on Martha's fingers. Martha yelped and jumped up, the top of her head catching one of the orderlies on the chin so hard he opened his mouth and spit blood. As you can guess, in a minute everyone was up and screaming. Orderlies from other halls flooded the common area. For my part, I tried to pull the orderlies off Martha, who was cowering near the pedals of the piano, but I was so new I wasn't sure what to do. The sound of glass breaking hushed the room, and when an orderly stuck his head through the broken window, which had a shard of glass hanging like a guillotine blade, he looked down and saw Lindy crumpled on the sidewalk, ten floors down.

Or something like that. Who could re-enact that melee? With all the flailing arms and screaming, it's a miracle more people didn't get hurt. It's all true, though. Everything I said happened did happen. Well, except the part about me being an eighteen-year-old volunteer. That part was a fib. I wish I had the luxury of being an eighteen-year-old buttfuck volunteer, laughing at all the crazies while leaning against a new sportscar Daddy bought me, worrying about whether or not I was going to get blown Saturday night after the dance. Eighteen for me was graduating from high school and being drafted into the army. Eighteen for me was worrying that I might not live to do the things these punk volunteers take as their holy God-given. Eighteen for me was being in the jungle.

The jungle was a bad place for a war, was the first thought I had on Vietnamese soil. The jungle is really all I see when I remember back. I can't remember anything I ate, or the places I slept, or anyone's face except Renshaw's and Kim Li's. And of course what happened.

Private Renshaw was my shadow on my first tour. Everywhere I went, he went. He was from somewhere in Kansas, and whenever we came upon a rice paddy, he'd shield his eyes and peer into the distance and say, "This ain't no wheat field." That sounds like a sweet, innocent thing to say, but that was just part of Renshaw's shtick. He might've looked like a corn-fed dope, but he had hellfire in him. At night in the foxholes, the sound of monkeys and who-knows-what echoing all around us, he'd tell about what he and his buddies would do back home after the Friday football games. Renshaw was a defensive lineman, which he had us understand wasn't a glory position necessarily, but he was also the quarterback's best friend, and to hear him tell it, boy, those cheerleaders couldn't line up fast enough. He amazed everyone in our platoon—Riker, Macdonald, Seeley and Sergeant Roberts with his tales of conquests. All his storytelling sort of backfired on him, though. He opened his mouth so much the others used to kid him. "Watch Renshaw around that grenade launcher," they joked. "Don't get too close to that beer bottle," was another one. Or: "Lock up your pets." Renshaw grew to hate the kidding, but he never let on. I sort of kept my distance from him in the foxhole, too. I knew the fag jokes wouldn't be far behind.

Vietnam wasn't anything like boot camp, let me tell you. In South Carolina the sky was quiet and filled with the colors of the rainbow at sunset. When you looked up in Nam—*if* you looked up—you didn't see the sky, but you saw the helicopter patrols that buzzed day and night in your ear. And the screaming. Everyone screamed. I got so I was afraid to take a step forward.

Renshaw knew of a place to unwind. A couple hooches near our post housed ten or more girls, and one of the girls' mothers ran a shine bar out of a third, adjoining hooch. The thatched roof was so low Renshaw couldn't stand upright, which was okay because we never stood around for very long.

This one particular night, the night in question, Renshaw grabbed a girl and headed for what he called "the Renshaw Suite." It didn't matter which girl you chose; they all knew us and they all knew we went back into the dirt-floor rooms and either gazed over the mud windowsills or closed our eyes and thought of girls back home. Still, we got to know all the girls, and some of the guys could even talk about them by name.

Maybe Renshaw was getting Dear John letters from home or, more likely, he couldn't stomach another day of the smell of killing. The best way to explain what happened is to figure he just snapped. No one heard the girl's screams but me. I knocked on the wall of the Renshaw Suite to make sure everything was okay. You always checked on your buddy. The screams stopped as I reached the burlap bag splayed and hung in the doorway. I peered around it and saw the girl, her wrists tied behind her back. Renshaw'd stuffed one of his socks in the girl's mouth and was forcing her head down while he sodomized her. I could smell his sweat. Renshaw pulled the sock out of her mouth, but before she could scream, he shoved her head down on him so hard she gagged. He held a gun to her head and told her to take it nice and easy.

I stood watching. I realized that, through the tears, I recognized the girl. Kim Li Phan. Renshaw rolled his eyes in his head and nodded forward, relaxing his grip on the gun. He jerked up when Kim Li accidentally bit him, and he slapped her hard, knocking her into the corner. Renshaw stuffed the sock back into Kim Li's mouth and turned around, seeing me in the doorway. "This gook bitch bit me," Renshaw seethed. He yanked Kim Li out of the corner and asked me to help him get her out of the hooch. I followed them down the noisy hall, Kim Li moaning and sobbing. "Don't fuckin' follow me," Renshaw warned, pointing his gun at me. "Just stay where you are." I stared at Kim Li helplessly, and her sobs faded into the dark as Renshaw dragged her into the jungle.

Things happened quickly after that. I was reassigned to a desk in a supply camp. The government needed me alive because I was the only witness. They never found Kim Li's body. Renshaw swore his innocence at the trial, telling everyone I was making the whole thing up, but when you had the sort of reputation Renshaw had, it was easy for people to believe how he got from A to B. In the tradition of military justice, Renshaw was convicted of rape, but because there was no body, not murder. He got eight years and was hauled off to Leavenworth. I never saw him again. The war ended and I went home to North Dakota, got married, and settled down. Maybe you saw the movie *Casualties of War*—that was based on me, partly.

Well, tried to settle down. Not in North Dakota, though. I don't know why I said that. I *did* go home to North Dakota, that part is true. Got a job as a night manager for Pete's Fish & Chips. You never saw a bigger bunch of morons than the guys who worked there. My main responsibility was to count the receipts and make sure the money matched and deposit the blue bag with the locking zipper in the night deposit slot at the bank.

The bank parking lot wasn't that well-lit, and I guess I shouldn't have been surprised when I got jumped. It was three or four guys at least who came out of the bushes. One of them had a gun. I didn't get a good look at their faces because another of them conked me over the head with a baseball bat. When I regained consciousness, the little blue bag stuffed with $3,000 was gone. Mac, the day manager, didn't believe my story and fired me. Who knew the bank had the parking lot under surveillance twenty- four hours a day? He gave me the same look Bobby and Beth did when I said I really did have sex with Mrs. Jones, the woman who cleaned my aunt's house. I had to say something. Who can take the kind of kidding Bobby and Beth gave me when I came back to the car too soon and found them naked in the backseat? I was just kidding when I said earlier that Bobby and Beth are dead. They're not. I wished they were when Bobby told me he asked Mrs. Jones if what I'd said was true and Mrs. Jones said she was going to have a talk with my aunt, who sent me home right after that. Bobby and Beth still live in Macon. My aunt told me they got married and had children.

I got married too. In Sacramento. North Dakota was too small for me anyway; and California is a dreamer's paradise. I dreamed of finding a woman to love and to make a home with on the Pacific shore. When I met Jill, she was waitressing during the day and taking law school classes at night. Not law school really, but criminal justice classes at the community college toward a degree so she could go to law school. You never saw so much ambition. It made me ambitious too. I got a job in the admissions office at the big state university. My coworkers liked me and we all got along fine. Jill started to make plans to transfer to the state university. We were also making plans to get married, which we did in a very low-key Vegas ceremony. "We'll do it big when we have lots of friends and paid vacations," she said.

People always say you should know someone inside and out before you marry them, but I found it exciting to find out about Jill along the way, sweet discovery after sweet discovery. The only discovery that wasn't so sweet was learning that Jill was in a secret competition with her best friend, Helen, who lived in New York. Helen was the fashion editor for one of those big glossy Madison Avenue magazines. Jill and Helen had grown up together outside of San Francisco, and Helen had gone to college right away and moved to New York after that. Helen's husband was a literature professor at Columbia and had published a big-to-do book on Shakespeare. Our autographed copy carefully supported the towels and sheets in our linen closet. Some days Jill seemed impatient with our ascent.

Then, out of the blue, I started to rise through the ranks at the university. One of the history professors found out I was a Vietnam vet and asked me to give a lecture in his class. I did and the professor was so impressed that he recommended me for an adjunct job teaching a course on military warfare. Of course I had to lie about being a college graduate to get the job, but who wouldn't? Jill was able to quit her job at the restaurant, and she transferred to the university as a full-time pre-law student. I took on a couple more courses, freshman Western civ classes.

Jill talked about having children. We talked about getting out of our useless apartment and buying a house. Things were going well, but an uneasy feeling settled around me. Helen and her husband continued to write with fantastic details of their life in New York, about parties and museums and openings—all the things that get shallow people so excited they can't talk. What those people know wouldn't fill half of Jill's brain. She wouldn't see it that way (if you saw a picture of Helen, you'd understand Jill's agitation, though; Jill wouldn't admit that had anything to do with it). Jill grew agitated by the sight of me.

Then fortune knocked. Jill and I came home to a letter on embossed stationery. A big publisher in New York wanted to publish my book on the history of the world. "I didn't know you wrote a book," Jill said, but she was so happy she hugged me until I was blue. She called Helen immediately. The story of me blowing up in my editor's office and throwing the only copy of my manuscript out the window reached the status of legend with my immediate circle of friends. It still makes me laugh.

The guards are good sorts, and when there's a lockdown they always give me the same room, the one with the corner chipped away, which I did when I was eighteen. You figure it worked for Clint Eastwood, why wouldn't it work for your average Joe? "Hey, Lindy, how are ya' doin'?" the guard says and it reminds me of that show with what's-his-name on it, the one where he looks at the outside from the inside and wishes he was on the outside. You know the one.

A Story About Warren James

Christopher Boucher

THAT WINTER, MY FRIEND JAIME CLARKE E-MAILED ME ABOUT writing a story for his anthology *Minor Characters*. The idea, as he explained it to me, would be for writer friends of his to craft a story using one of the characters in his novels. I told him I was happy to be included, and he sent me a list of characters to choose from. I perused that list and chose Peter Kline, a journalist who appeared in *Vernon Downs*. I'd met Kline only once, at a writers' benefit dinner, but he was nice enough to walk over to my table and introduce himself to me and my then wife. We even talked about working together sometime in the future. When I sent Kline's name to Jaime, though, he wrote back: *Sorry, Kline's taken. Hey, hear about Vince?*

Yup—so awful, I wrote back. *Any update?* Vince Addition was a character we all knew—one of those characters who's friends with everyone—and he appeared in a draft of one of my very first short stories. He'd collapsed a few days earlier while raking leaves in his backyard. Then I wrote: *Re: anthology—how about Derwin?*

Ken's got Derwin! Jaime responded. *Let me know if anyone else catches your eye!*

I made a mental note to review the list again. That very afternoon, though, I received an e-mail from an address I didn't know, brightfuture971@gmail.com:

Dear Mr. Boucher,

I don't know if you know me, but I'm the character Warren James from Jaime Clarke's novel Garden Lakes. *I'm told that Mr. Clarke is curating a collection of stories about characters from his novels, and that you've been asked to write one of the stories. Have you chosen a character yet? If not, I'd like to throw my hat in the ring. I've yet to be contacted about the collection, which I'm guessing is because of my recent financial mishaps and the difficult turn my life has taken. I can assure you, though, that I'm a good character with many as-of-yet-untold experiences.*

In the wake of my recent misfortunes—whereby I lost my life savings, watched my marriage dissolve, and lost most of my friends—I have invested wholeheartedly in G. R. Virely's ideas regarding "directive energy." I'm not sure if you're familiar with Mr. Virely's work, but his book Manifesting Yes *has been a lifesaver for me. Among other ideas, Mr. Virely suggests that we all have the ability to change our circumstances by locating those moments in life where we can "turn the dial to yes," as he says, and steer ourselves toward pockets of positive energy. I see YOU as an energy pocket, Mr. Boucher, and THIS VERY E-MAIL as the kind of "dial" that Virely writes of.*

In other words, I've had a tough year. From what I hear, you have too. This could be a boost for both of us.

Light the spark,
Warren James

I didn't know Warren personally, but I recognized the name—I remembered his optimistic, naive appearance in *Garden Lakes*. In retrospect, I should have taken a few minutes right then and there to thank him for his e-mail and tell him I'd give it some thought. Had I done so, I would also have told him that, from my perspective, his misfortune was likely out of his control. I mean, the "mishap" referred to in the e-mail—the Ponzi scheme by which he lost all his money—was mentioned in *Garden Lakes*! The poor guy never had a chance.

Instead of doing so, though, I texted Jaime. *Hey guess who I just heard from*

> *Who?*
>
> *Warren!*
>
> *Ah shit*, Jaime responded. *He wrote to David too.*
>
> *Not responding to him.*
>
> *Good, don't. Guy's a leech!*

Two days later I received another e-mail from Warren.

You haven't written back, so I don't know if you received my first e-mail. If you DID receive it, though, you know that DIRECTIVE ENERGY is very important to me, and that I pay close attn to whether that energy manifests as POSITIVE or NEGATIVE. And man, the no e-mail back thing is very NEGATIVE, it's just sitting there in the bottom of my heart, and only through the spiritual discipline which I learned from G. R. Virely's teachings have I been able to KEEP THE +ENERGY CHANNELS OPEN, and to maintain faith that you're a GOOD PERSON, and to therefore give you ANOTHER CHANCE to make the right decision and pick me as a character for your story in Minor Characters. *At least meet me for coffee, Mr. Boucher. Give me the chance to explain myself, and to tell you some of my ideas for stories.*

Light the spark!
Warren

I was reading Warren's e-mail, though, when my phone rang. It was my ex-wife, Liz. "Hey," I said.

"Chris?" She was crying. "Oh, it's so terrible."

"Is it Vince?"

She started crying harder.

"When?" I asked.

"Earlier today," she said.

*

We all went to the funeral—Jaime, Mona, Vida, Carol, Liz, Ken, Mary, Wanda; everyone in the greater Boston writing scene was there. When I paid my respects at the casket, I couldn't believe how thin and gray Vince looked. I said a prayer for him—*God*, I prayed, *how could you?*—and then rushed awkwardly past Liz and over to Ken and Mona, who were talking to Kline. "Jesus Christ," I whispered to them. "He's so thin! It's like he's barely there!"

"He was in a coma those last days," Mona said.

"This isn't right," I said. "Couldn't anyone do anything for him?"

Kline shrugged. "Who could *do* anything?"

"What I mean is, the authors . . . "

But then people started taking their seats for the service, and I settled in toward the back for a long series of tributes. Jeannie spoke, and then Wanda, and then Vincey's brother Gregorio, and then a few other characters I didn't know, and then the famous author Varna D. Fall. "Once I remember," said Varna, her face folding over itself, "Vincey signed up for two novels at the same time. Remember, Marcus?" From his seat in the back, a teary Marcus Houston smiled and crossed one leg over the other. "His scheme," said Varna, her lip quivering, "was to appear in both novels without telling either of us about the other project. But one day . . . one day he showed up to . . ." She stopped to collect herself, then said, "Marcus, tell them."

"Vincent showed up to my novel in the wrong costume," said Houston.

Everyone started laughing.

"That was Vincey," said Varna. "Ambitious. A little crazy. But absolutely passionate about contemporary literature. He loved being a character, and he was a great one."

When the service was over, I found Jaime and Mary, and we walked out of the funeral home together. As we stepped into the bright morning, though, I saw a character who was smoking a cigarette in the parking lot stamp out the butt and jog toward us. "Mr. Bowcher?" he said.

Jaime stopped. "Dude," he said.

"Yeah?" I said to the guy.

"Mr. Bowcher, I'm Warren James," said the character.

"You can't do this, man," Jaime told him. "We're at a fucking *funeral.*"

"I don't mean to bother you. I just saw you both and figured I'd . . . I've written to you repeatedly, Mr. Bowcher—"

"It's Boo-shay," I said.

"Boo-shay, forgive me—"

"This isn't a great time," I said.

"And it's caused this negative *soup* inside me, and I've read all your books, and I thought maybe we could—"

"Warren?" said Jaime, advancing on him. "Get the fuck out of here."

"Just have coffee or something."

"Right now," burred Jaime.

Warren looked to Jaime and then back to me, and then he held up his hands, spun on his heel, and walked across the lawn of the funeral home. We watched him disappear, and then we got into Jaime's car and drove to the cemetery. Jaime apologized for Warren's behavior as we drove out of the lot, but we didn't discuss him after that—we focused our attentions on the very difficult task of burying our character friend.

Jaime and I didn't talk about the anthology again either—not that day, nor in the weeks that followed. I'm sure Jaime knew about the writing drought I found myself in after Vince's death—it was literally months before I could write a paragraph—and he didn't want to push me. It's not like Vince and I were close, but I'd never had a character die on me before, and it completely disarmed me.

My mind-set eventually improved, thankfully, and after a few months of false starts I decided to go back to the story I'd been writing for Jaime. I called the character Figs, another schemer from *Lakes*, and we met for a beer at Brewer's Union so I could tell him my idea. But in the midst of my pitch—for a story in which Figs, in the wake of framing a coworker, transforms into an actual picture frame, his limbs cornering and starting to gild—he leaned over the café table and said, "Don't take this the wrong way, Bowcher? But no way, man!"

"Why not?" I said.

"It's too fucking weird! That's why no one wants to work with you! I mean, listen—you've always been weird. But since your divorce you've really gone off the deep end."

"Wait—what does my divorce have to do with anything?"

"Plus, a story where I become a frame? Who wants to go through something like that? You're talking prosthetics, a weight regimen—"

"Wait," I said. "Let me tell you how the story ends—"

Figs put a hand on my shoulder to stop me. "No thank you. Okay?"

With most of the other characters taken, I swallowed my pride and e-mailed Warren a few days later. I told him I was sorry I'd never responded to his earlier messages, and that I was still willing to meet if he was. When I didn't hear back, I texted Jaime. *Hey, know how to get in contact with Warren? Emailed him yesterday, but no reply*

Don't hold your breath, Jaime texted back. *Dude's in the clink!*

What? Seriously?

Owed a lot of people a lot of money, Jaime wrote back.

So I decided to drive out to Millington to see Warren in prison. I signed in, sat down at a filthy table in the visiting room, and tried not to eavesdrop on the other inmates' conversations. Finally, after ten minutes or so, Warren appeared. He looked like shit—he had a ratty salt-and-pepper beard, and his hair was a construction site. When he saw me, he walked over to the table and stood next to it. "I didn't believe it when they told me," he said.

"Hey," I said. "How are you?"

"Oh, I'm fantastic," he spat. "What do you want, Bowcher?"

I gestured to the bench across from me. He looked at it, breathed heavily, and sat down.

"How's it going in here?" I said, trying to sound compassionate.

"Like you care," he said.

"I absolutely do care," I said. "That's why I'm here. I heard what happened to you, and I felt bad—"

"Ha!" Warren slapped the table, and a guard in the corner looked over at us. "Don't you think I know what you're doing? Characters *talk*, Bowcher. You're here because you need a *story*."

I acted shocked. "I am here," I said, leaning toward him, "to try and *reverse the current*."

Warren's face brightened slightly. "You read Virely?"

I hadn't—I'd just Googled him—but I nodded. "And doesn't he say that the currents can change with one simple gesture?"

"One *purehearted* gesture," said Warren.

"Listen to me," I said. "If you work with me? I can write you out of here. Right now—today. I'll write a story where you're pardoned. Or where you escape!"

Warren smiled sourly and shook his head. "It doesn't work that way, man. Don't you get it? The story's already happening. And here's how it goes. You try to save me, but the charged opportunity has passed—I'm already soaked in negativity. Then I leave this room, and you're forced to confront yourself. In what Virely calls an 'ionic epiphany.'"

"No," I said, confused. "I'm the author. And it's not too late for us to change your—"

"I'm starting to think it was always too late," said Warren. Then he stood up, regarded me with pity, and walked out of the room. "Warren!" I said, but he didn't turn back—I watched him walk through one windowed door, and then another, and then another, until I couldn't see him anymore, and could see only my own reflection in the glass.

Appendix
We're So Famous

Praise for WE'RE SO FAMOUS

"Jaime Clarke pulls off a sympathetic act of sustained male imagination: entering the minds of innocent teenage girls dreaming of fame. A glibly surreal world where the only thing wanted is notoriety and all you really desire leads to celebrity and where stardom is the only point of reference. What's new about this novel is how unconsciously casual the characters' drives are. This lust is as natural to them as being American—it's almost a birthright."

—BRET EASTON ELLIS

"Daisy, Paque, and Stella want. They want to be actresses. They want to be in a band. They want to be models. They want to be famous, damn it. And so . . . they each tell their story of forming a girl group, moving to LA, and flirting with fame. Clarke doesn't hate his antiheroines—he just views them as by-products of the culture: glitter-eyed, vacant, and cruel. The satire works, sliding down as silvery and toxic as liquid mercury."

—ENTERTAINMENT WEEKLY

"Jaime Clarke is a masterful illusionist; in his deft hands, emptiness seems full, teenage pathos appears sassy and charming. *We're So Famous* is a blithe, highly entertaining indictment of the permanent state of adolescence that trademarks our culture, a made-for-TV world where innocence is hardly a virtue, ambition barely a value system."

—BOB SHACOCHIS

"Clarke seems to have created a crafty book of bubble letters to express his anger, sending off a disguised Barbie mail bomb that shows how insipid and money-drenched youth culture can be."

—VILLAGE VOICE

"Darkly and pinkly comic, this is the story of a trio of teenage American girls and their pursuit of the three big Ms of American life: Music, Movies and Murder. An impressive debut by a talented young novelist."

—JONATHAN AMES

"This first novel is plastic fantastic. Daisy, Paque and Stella are talentless teens, obsessed by Bananarama and longing for stardom. They love celebrity and crave the flashbulbs and headlines for themselves. The girls become fantasy wrestlers, make a record, get parts in a going-nowhere film, then try to put on big brave smiles in the empty-hearted world of fame. Sad, sassy and salient."

—ELLE MAGAZINE

TO: Joseph Apodaca/808 Films
FROM: Jaime Clarke/Little Girl Bay Prods.
RE: WE'RE SO FAMOUS

Dear Joseph,

I was able to find a working fax machine!
Very excited about working with 808 Films
on WE'RE SO FAMOUS. Was very impressed
with you and Jules and your commitment to
the challenge of bringing my first novel
to screen. As you both noted, the decades
between the novel's publication and now make
the time period of the novel seem quaint,
but I'm sure you'll agree the premise of
the talentless seeking fame has remained
unchanged (unfortunately) and, I'd argue,
has even accelerated with the aid of new
technologies. But we'll get into all of
that. For now: thanks for the nice lunch.
Look forward to hearing your notes on how
to proceed. And at Jules's request, I'm also
attaching the short story the novel is based
on, which was first published in the literary
magazine, MISSISSIPPI REVIEW, edited by
Frederick Barthelme. The writer Mary Robison
selected it as a finalist for their annual
story contest.

We're So Famous
By Jaime Clarke

Me and Stephanie have always wanted to be famous. In the fifth grade, we lip-synced a Beatles song for our entire class and we loved the attention. Before we dropped out of high school, we were famous as party chicks, known famously as Masterful Johnson. No one in high school could appreciate the irony. We have famous names, too. I'm Paque and she's Daisy.

You've probably heard of us. The guy who discovered us saw us dancing in a bar and told us he liked our moves. We thought he was just some pervo who wanted to take us back to his place in a big car and make us fuck each other and him, too, but he turned out to be a really sweet, sad kind of a guy who just wanted to make us famous.

We started out doing these gigs for his friends. He knew a couple of guys with a recording studio in their house and we started partying with those guys. One night we were all sitting around, fried out of our gourds and one of the guys says, "Why don't you guys record a few songs?" Me and Daisy thought that was a pretty good idea, so we recorded eight songs that we just kind of made up on the spot.

Music was something we never practiced, so we found out that night that neither one of us could play an instrument and our voices caused everyone in the room to bring their hands to their ears in a weird, involuntary reflex. But we got the songs down (my favorite was one Daisy wrote called "I'd Kill You If I Thought I Could Get Away with It" and I also wrote one with this dude Jeffrey called "Do Fuck Off," a sort of mellow love song).

One of the dudes who owned the recording equipment made copies for everyone, and me and Daisy played it for a few friends, who told us frankly they didn't care for it. We were hurt at first, of course, but we never really wanted to be musicians anyway. Only famous.

We went on crashing local events, sometimes going to other

cities to hang out and pose with people who knew the people we hung out with last. We'd practically forgotten about our record until we climbed into this limo paid for by these really cool Japanese girls in L.A. When I heard Daisy's voice, I looked at her, thinking she had broken out in a little ditty; but her lips weren't moving. Suddenly the Japanese girls cranked the tune, one called "We Love Goo," a sort of rock anthem that I didn't particularly like. We all started bobbing our heads, and me and Daisy didn't say anything about the fact that it was us.

Well, that was only the beginning of our recording career, but it was pretty close to the end, too. Some people from *R*O*C*K* magazine came to our apartment and took pictures of us on our yellow vinyl couch. Before we knew it, we couldn't go anywhere without seeing that picture, me leaning back on Daisy, our platinum hair all mixing together. They made posters for the bus stops, billboards; I even saw it in a friend's dorm at school when we went to visit her.

And the magazines. That picture was on every cover in the supermarket, it seemed. There was only one problem. Me and Daisy noticed that the articles in the magazines didn't mention anything about us being a band. The stories were about us doing all these things we'd never done.

Like we were supposed to have slept with all the guys from Hey!, some gay-ass punk band from New York; and one said we trashed a hotel in Paris and had to pay $10,000 in damages. The one we liked the best was how we both were in kiddy-porn movies when we were, like, seven or eight. We cut these out and stuck them under the fruit magnets on our refrigerator.

Now everyone wanted to hang out with us wherever we went. We'd go out to see a movie, and people waiting in line would come up for our autographs. The same thing happened if we were at McDonald's, or at the record store, or if we we're just walking back from the grocery store with a sweating gallon of whole milk and a carton of half-and-half (Daisy makes these killer dairy drinks called whiteys).

One day the dude that said he wanted to make us famous invited us over to his condo for dinner to tell us that he was leaving town. Me and Daisy were sad about this, and we asked where was he going. He said he had to go take care of some things and that we were going to be taken care of. That's when he told us about this corporate sponsorship he set up. He said we were never to tell who it was because the company didn't even know they were sponsoring us; he said he set it up through a friend of his who would keep it a secret as long as we would.

We asked him why he was doing all this for us, and he got too drunk and admitted that it started out as a line to try to fuck us like we first thought, but then he said it was a "great joke," and then he got super drunk and started cackling in our faces in a mean way, and me and Daisy left without saying anything.

At first we started getting these checks in the mail from the corporation, mailed from Dallas. Then these shiny gold plastic credit cards came, engraved with my and Daisy's real names.

Right after we got the credit cards, something really awful happened. Daisy went back to Ohio to visit her parents, who called after they saw our picture in the supermarket, and when Daisy got off the airplane, this girl screamed out her name, and she whipped around and looked just as this rush of teenage girls surrounded her on all sides. She called me that night, sobbing into the phone, telling me she couldn't breathe very well with all those people around her and no matter which way she tried to walk, there they were, blocking her way. Since then Daisy has not been the same. She gets very quiet when people yell out our name, and she stands close to me when people come up to us in public.

Somehow the story got out that me and Daisy made a movie called *Sprung*. We gave an interview to this movie magazine, and the interviewer was a real dipshit chick who kept calling us Masters and Johnson. I don't know where the idea got into her head that we were actresses.

So agents and then studios started calling about making a

sequel to "the wildly popular cult movie". Exactly three weeks after that article appeared, a script for *Sprung II* arrived at our apartment. Me and Daisy had a good time acting out the parts for our friends Anthony and Kurt, a couple of skater guys we met hanging out one night.

Those dicks Anthony and Kurt wanted to act out the love scenes with us, but we told them no way. We noticed that there were a lot of love scenes, or scenes where me and

Daisy were naked, and we laughed pretty hard at this. Anthony and Kurt kept trying to talk us into just one scene, and finally me and Daisy told them we had boyfriends so they'd leave.

Sometimes we wish we had boyfriends. It's been difficult for me and Daisy to keep them, though. Most guys get jealous about our fame, always wanting to know where we're going and who we're going with. I dated this guy, Jim, who wouldn't take me to his house because he was afraid his parents would find out he was dating "that disgusting girl." He told me that.

Daisy dated this real sweetheart, Daryll, who used to bring her a present every time he came over. He'd bring her little things he made out of scraps he'd find, and always he'd spell her name on it somewhere. He was heartbroken when he found out Daisy wasn't her real name. He called her a filthy liar and never came back. Daisy cried for a few days, until she cleared all his gifts off her dresser. They're in the bottom drawer now, and sometimes I walk in and Daisy has the drawer open, just staring down at all the little things.

Daisy thought it might be Daryll when the door buzzed. We were surprised when the mailman had us sign for an invitation to the L.A. premiere of *Sprung II.* The studio sent a movie poster for each of us, and these two chicks that looked like me and Daisy were standing there, about eight feet tall, with knives in their hands (my knife had blood dripping from it).

The movie studio flew us in from Phoenix and sent a limo to our hotel. When we got out at the theater, we got mobbed by reporters and people just standing on the street. Daisy ducked back into the

limo and just sat in there until everyone went away. Which everyone
eventually did.

The movie was pretty dumb, but the girls who played the main
chicks were dead ringers for me and Daisy. We noticed that those
chicks weren't at the premiere and that's why everyone thought we
were them. We didn't meet any of the studio people. On the way out
of the theater, this guy rolled up his shirt-sleeve and showed me his
tattoo of me and Daisy.

For a long time after that, things were pretty quiet. Me and
Daisy bought records and listened to them, bought clothes and wore
them, bought food and ate it.

Then one day Daisy told me she didn't want to be famous
anymore. She said she liked not doing anything, but it was a drag
to have everyone staring at you all the time. I told her I agreed, but
that there wasn't anything we could really do about it. We were
famous and that was that. We couldn't become unfamous.

A doll company sent us a contract along with a check for
$50,000. They wanted to make Paque and Daisy action

figures and wanted to get them out for Christmas. I asked Daisy
what we should do, and she said we should cash the check and not
sign the contract. I tried to read the contract out loud to her, but we
had trouble understanding it.

Finally we decided not to do it. Daisy thought it would only add
to the problem of people recognizing us on the streets. We didn't
cash the check, and it expired.

That Christmas the stores were filled with Paque and Daisy
action figures, but they didn't really look like us, so we weren't too
worried about it. We even bought a few for our relatives and sent
them back home. We tried to buy some other things for Christmas,
but the cashier told us our credit cards had been canceled. Me and
Daisy wondered what to do, but we knew we couldn't call anyone.

The checks quit coming in the mail too. We didn't really notice
until the first of the month, when the rent was due. We waited for
the little yellow envelopes to arrive, but all that came was junk mail

and late Christmas cards. The situation got worse when we started to run out of food.

So me and Daisy decided to get jobs. I applied for this job as a secretary, and Daisy found an ad for a cashier in a record store. At my interview the guy, Harry, couldn't get over the fact that I was "that girl from *Masterful Johnson*." He asked me for my autograph.

Daisy came home in tears and told me that the manager brought out old copies of our album and asked her to autograph them while he played *Combat* on an old Atari in his office.

Our landlord gave us a thirty-day notice thirty-one days ago. Daisy has packed all her things in milk crates she stole from behind the grocery store. We've been living off stolen produce and water. We called home for money for plane tickets, but no one seems to believe we really do need money. My parents laughed, and Daisy's parents thought it was a joke, too. I wonder what our options are as me and Daisy sit at the kitchen table, Daisy drawing "SOS" in spilled salt with her fingers.

MEMORANDUM
TO: Jaime Clarke/Little Girl Bay Prods.
CC: Jules White/808 Films
FROM: Joseph Apodaca/808 Films
RE: WE'RE SO FAMOUS

Dear Jaime,

It was great to meet you, too. Lunch was our pleasure. And thanks for persevering with respect to the fax machine. We're still reeling from the e-mail breech, and until faith is restored in our computer system, we're all off e-mail.

Everyone at 808 believes in WE'RE SO FAMOUS, and I personally have no doubt that this can be a successful series. The story is timeless, as you suggest, and the novel is full of wonderful story line possibilities. And we believe viewers will easily and readily identify with Paque, Daisy, and Stella as they try to grasp what eludes them.

To that end, I thought we'd jump right in: the obvious question to tackle is the point of view. The novel deftly tells the story from each of the three girls' POVs, each picking up the strand of the narrative as the other leaves off. It's very effective in the novel and could be replicated on the screen, but that decision will dictate how we move forward. How do we want viewers to think about this narrative? Are they rooting for a single protagonist, or two protagonists who play off each other? More than two protagonists is an

ensemble piece, which plays well in the new
era of anthology TV, but it would likely mean
threads of the plot will be picked up and
dropped and picked up again as we go. So as
you see, <u>how</u> we tell this story will dictate
a number of things.

I think that's it from me. You may hear
from Jules, but we're trying to streamline
communication to you through me. You know
what they say about too many cooks!

MEMORANDUM
TO: Jaime Clarke/Little Girl Bay Prods.
CC: Joseph Apodaca/808 Films
FROM: Jules White/808 Films
RE: WE'RE SO FAMOUS

Dear Jaime,

Hello! I'm so excited about this project! I was reading parts of the novel out loud to my partner, and he was laughing like a hyena.

I wonder if it isn't prudent to put how the story will be told aside for a moment and address the elephant in the room: the fact that we need to update the story to account for the twenty years since its publication. I'd love to hear your thoughts on the subject.

MEMORANDUM

TO: Jules White/808 Films
CC: Joseph Apodaca/808 Films
FROM: Jaime Clarke/Little Girl Bay Prods.
RE: WE'RE SO FAMOUS

Dear Jules,

Thank you for this thoughtful query. I have
a little insight, perhaps, as I was privy to
the same conversation as it relates to the
off-Broadway production from ten years ago.
The producer and playwright tackled the same
question. For the play, it was determined early
on that using the time period from the novel
was not viable, as the narrative would simply
seem dated. Not enough time had passed, and
there was a general fear that the play would
seem like a B-movie rather than the spirited
criticism of celebrity culture the novel aspires
to. As you may know, the producer and playwright
opted just to revise the pop culture references
to make the play seem up-to-the- minute.

I do recall a brief flirtation with the idea
of setting the play in the 1950s, not just to
utilize references from that era of Hollywood,
but also to skirt the question about various
technologies that were obviously not available
at the time of the writing of the novel.

I wonder if, twenty years on, we could
present the novel as it is with the hope that
the production would have a retro feel. The
1980s and 1990s are a bit in vogue, still,
would you agree?

MEMORANDUM
TO: Jaime Clarke/Little Girl Bay Prods.
CC: Jules White/808 Films
FROM: Joseph Apodaca/808 Films
RE: WE'RE SO FAMOUS

Jaime,

What would the novel look like if you were writing it today?

MEMORANDUM
TO: Joseph Apodaca/808 Films
CC: Jules White/808 Films
FROM: Jaime Clarke/Little Girl Bay Prods.
RE: WE'RE SO FAMOUS

Dear Joseph,

An intriguing question! And timely. I was
just reading a profile of a guy who makes
half a million dollars a year playing video
games in his apartment while fans can log in
and watch, and comment on his social media
feeds. Apparently, the gamer has a worldwide
following. I can't fully wrap my mind around
the idea, just as I couldn't all those years
ago when I read that article in DETAILS about
the two girls who seemed like they were
famous for being famous, also a novel idea (at
the time). But the gamer would be a character
in the novel. As would the aging talent agent
recently in the news who tried to blackmail a
studio boss who had sexually assaulted one of
his clients into giving his clients more roles
at the studio.

What else? Oh, the celebrity murders re-
enacted at the dinner theater in the novel
by Stella would perhaps be updated to include
the OJ Simpson story, and Robert Blake.
(Though probably Stella would dabble in social
media influencing rather than dinner theater.)

When Alan Hood tries to help Paque and
Daisy capitalize on their sudden notoriety, it
would likely involve some sort of social media

campaign rather than a reality TV show.

Thematically, the idea of becoming famous for the sake of being famous has exploded far beyond anything that was around when I wrote the novel in the late 1990s. Things didn't go viral then, if you catch my meaning. Also, someone might've been a renowned astrophysicist or cellist or what have you, but the average person wouldn't have heard of them. (Now they'd have a social media following!)

So the notion captured in Bret Easton Ellis's blurb for the novel, about how the characters consider fame a birthright, is no longer singular. If I were writing the novel today, the narrative would instead be about how to harness existing technologies to compete against a crowded field of wannabes. And how infamy and fame are often confused for the same thing now. Either will do, seems. Previously, infamy was the tarpit under the pursuit of fame, where you'd land if you aspired to be famous but missed the mark.

MEMORANDUM

TO: Jaime Clarke/Little Girl Bay Prods.
CC: Joseph Apodaca/808 Films
FROM: Jules White/808 Films
RE: WE'RE SO FAMOUS

Dear Jaime,

Brainstorm: What if we cast the leads with actresses in their sixties or seventies? To make a pointed comment about the pursuit of fame.

MEMORANDUM

TO: Jules White/808 Films
CC: Joseph Apodaca/808 Films
FROM: Jaime Clarke/Little Girl Bay Prods.
RE: WE'RE SO FAMOUS

Dear Jules,

My immediate reaction? Love this idea! Did a quick internet search, and any of these would be terrific: Meryl Streep, Helen Mirren, Diane Keaton, Sally Field, Jessica Lange, Sissy Spacek, Susan Sarandon, Dianne Wiest, Sigourney Weaver, Faye Dunaway.

The brilliance of this idea is that it brings across the novel's main theme, how ridiculous fame obsession and the pursuit of fame for fame's sake is. The novel is constantly suggesting the idea, but the visualization of any of these actresses above in the various scenes from the novel would be a powerful advertisement for said theme.

MEMORANDUM

TO: Jaime Clarke/Little Girl Bay Prods.
CC: Jules White/808 Films
FROM: Joseph Apodaca/808 Films
RE: WE'RE SO FAMOUS

Dear Jaime,

    Jules and I conferred on the phone, and
this idea is off the table.

MEMORANDUM
TO: Joseph Apodaca/808 Films
FROM: Jaime Clarke/Little Girl Bay Prods.
RE: WE'RE SO FAMOUS

Dear Joseph,

It's been a few weeks since I've heard from you or Jules, and I thought I'd check in. Did you get your e-mail fixed?

To keep busy, I worked on a new short story that's tangential to the ideas in WE'RE SO FAMOUS, called "The Oswald Sightings." The title derives from a historical footnote I read about how during the first moments of the Kennedy assassination, there were Lee Harvey Oswald sightings everywhere. The footnote reminded me of when Paul McCartney's first wife passed away and there were conflicting eyewitness reports that put her final days both in Tucson, Arizona, and in California. Both anecdotes speak to how people clamor to intertwine stories about the famous (and infamous) with their own lives. Anyway, a little distraction. Hope you like it. And hope to hear more soon about the project.

The Oswald Sightings
By Jaime Clarke

OKLAHOMA CITY, OK

Swear to God. Standing there plain as day, just as you are, his arm around my girlfriend Peyta. Peyta introduced him as Ozzie, which I just assumed was kind of like a nickname, like the way Peyta called me "kid" and I called her "sis." It was in January 1960—maybe '61, '62 at the latest, because I remember staying home for New Year's 1963 because of what happened with Peyta's car.

Anyway, it was January '60 or '61 or '62, and Peyta had just come back from Cuba—she liked to take her vacation days all at once, usually to some exotic locale south of the equator. She flew free on account of her being a stewardess with TWA. Peyta would always bring me back something nice, since my second husband, Gerry—a pilot for TWA—never took me anywhere.

At that time Raleigh's was *the* place to go for dinner. It was swank, for Oklahoma. But not swank like California. "Order whatever you like," Peyta told me, insinuating that Ozzie was going to pick up the check, though she didn't seem surprised when he emptied his wallet to cover the tip. Peyta charged the whole meal on her shiny new gold Visa card. "It doesn't have a limit," she told me. I caught Ozzie admiring it before Peyta slipped it back into her wallet.

Raleigh's was empty that night for some reason, which was unfortunate because on a normal Raleigh's night Ozzie's whiny voice would've been drowned out by the hustle and bustle. But dinner was practically ruined by Ozzie's monologue about a book he'd just read, *The Rise of the Colored Empires.* I remember the title exactly because he wouldn't shut up about it. On and on and on about *The Rise of the Colored Empires* and how we all (by which he meant us whites) had to watch our backs. I wanted to talk to Peyta about Dawn, the new flight attendant on Peyta's crew, and to ask her point-blank if Gerry and Dawn flirted on the job. Gerry and I had known Peyta for years, and he never said two words about Peyta outside her presence; he'd been flying with Dawn for only about two months, and though I'd never met her, I knew from Gerry that she was witty, charming, and extremely intelligent, and that she was an amateur photographer. Our dinners were punctuated by Dawn's witticisms or insightful observations on this or that. I couldn't get a word in edge-wise, though, on account of Ozzie's lecture about *The Rise of the Colored Empires*. I never chewed a steak so fast as I did that night.

Anyway, Peyta broke up with Ozzie by the summer, calling him boring and ill-mannered. I was a bit surprised at this as I hadn't seen hide nor hair of her since our dinner at Raleigh's. I had assumed she and Ozzie were having the time of their life; she didn't even talk about him on the job, apparently, because Gerry had no idea who he was when I mentioned him to ask if Peyta was still seeing him. Gerry screwed up his face. "Peyta has a boyfriend?" he asked. I said "Sure she does," just as you are. "I'm pretty sure she doesn't," Gerry said, and I couldn't convince him otherwise before he buried his head in the sand and quit listening altogether.

Things were pretty back to normal by summer; as I say, Peyta began picking up some extra shifts in order to save money for a flower shop she wanted to start somewhere near the downtown galleria, but she squeezed in a girls' night out as often as she could. The best was the two tickets to a Bob Dylan concert she got for flirting with Dylan's tour manager on a flight from L.A. to Nashville. The tickets were great, too. Dylan wasn't any farther than here to there, swear to God.

That was the summer I started my book club, which I envisioned as a sort of social club for other ladies like myself whose husbands were gone for long stretches of time. I began to notice familiar faces down at the local branch of the library, which is what gave me the idea. I handpicked the ladies I wanted to join and paid a calligrapher to do up a nice invitation on some silver paper I picked up in the bargain bin at the five-and-dime.

"Oh, I don't know, honey," Peyta said when I asked her if she wanted to join. "I'm not much of a reader."

"You and Gerry both," I laughed, the dig oddly satisfying. The summer had seen a spike in amusing anecdotes about the ever-charming, ever-astute Dawn, who Gerry assured me was very popular with the other flight attendants.

"Yeah, she's great," is all Peyta said when I asked her about Dawn—not the commiserating I was hoping for. (I learned the word "commiserating" from the book club, among many, many others.)

I gave Peyta a copy of the first book for the book club—*Tess of the d'Urbervilles*—and I even wrote her name inside it and put a smiley face next to it. I did the same for each subsequent book—*Wuthering Heights, Heart of Darkness, Alice's Adventures in Wonderland*, etc.— even though Peyta made it to only one in three meetings, usually for the books that were short or had been made into a movie. Gerry felt threatened by my book club; he called it "ihe Hen Club."

"Cluck, cluck, cluck," he'd say if he caught me reading on the couch, or at night before going to bed. Jealousy is what I thought it was when I found a copy of *Alice's Adventures in Wonderland*— the book club selection for that particular month—packed in with Gerry's dirty clothes upon his return from a fishing trip to Lake Overholser with some other fly-boys. These trips were of no interest to me, and they got Gerry out of the house at least once a month, sometimes twice depending on the weather.

I held up the copy of *Alice's Adventures in Wonderland* and chuckled, delighted that I could give Gerry a good ribbing and maybe even a hard time about taking an interest in my so-called Hen Club. My delight lasted just a moment, though, when it sank in that Gerry was trying to horn in on my book club, a thing that was mine and mine alone. I believe I actually turned red. I remember putting my hand on my cheek to feel if I was flush. It was almost a relief, then, when I opened the cover and saw Peyta's name in my handwriting, the smiley face staring up at me, mocking-like. I slipped the book into my nightstand without thinking and walked around the house in a daze.

What made me follow Gerry in my own car—a baby-blue Thunderbird that my first husband had bought for me, a car Gerry refused to ride in—I don't know. Maybe I was still in a daze. That's the best explanation. All the times I had suspected Dawn, I never once thought to back the T-Bird out of the garage. Funny, Peyta's betrayal stung worse than Gerry's. *How could she?* All the nice things I'd ever done for Peyta bounced around my brain as I tailed Gerry to the Commodore Motel, out by the airport. A sickness came over me when the young clerk behind the counter greeted Gerry with a salute. The sickness spread when I spotted Peyta sitting in her red Corvette in the parking lot. Gerry made a big show of driving around to the back of the Commodore, taking the stairs slowly, as if he were just a single man nonchalantly checking into room 203. I remember he looked younger that day, spry in a way he hadn't acted in the whole time we were married. I felt a jealousy rise up inside me: I wished it were *me* he was taking into that motel room, which is crazy, I know, but just as you are, I felt it. I imagined Gerry making the most spectacular love in the world inside room 203, and I fantasized about walking into the room before Peyta could get out of her car. Gerry would make up some excuse, and I would pretend to accept it, and we'd make love like teenagers on prom night. The fantasy seemed a real possibility, but it grew fainter and fainter as Peyta climbed the stairs to the room. I'd grown so insignificant in their lives that neither checked over their shoulder when Gerry opened the door, a big, goofy grin on his face. They stood chatting like neighbors before Gerry invited Peyta inside and the door slammed shut on my second marriage for good.

The sound of the door slamming echoed in my head as I pressed the accelerator on the T-Bird. The first hit popped the trunk on Peyta's 'Vette. I backed up and rammed the car again, this time smashing out the back window. All the doors of the occupied rooms at the Commodore flew open, all except room 203's. A small boy in a cowboy hat held onto the second-floor railing, and I waved at him as I threw the T-Bird into reverse, taking aim at the driver's side door. The Corvette was slowly streaked with blue and vice-versa. That's what I think of when I wonder where Gerry is now—blue on red, red on blue.

BURLINGTON, VT

He introduced himself as Jack, but I knew that was a lie. I can tell when someone's lying. But what did I care? I think I told him I was James, but I might not have. It was a seven-hour bus ride, and I intended to ignore the person in the seat next to me regardless of whether his name was Jack, Joe, Tom, Mike, or Lee Harvey Oswald, as it turned out to be. We were roughly the same age, so I can see how he thought we might have something in common, but the reality was I was a freshman on scholarship at Columbia University and he was a loony tune aimlessly riding the bus to God-knows-where. I doubt he even knew where Columbia was, or how prestigious a scholarship to Columbia was. I would probably have had to explain it to him like I did the hayseeds at my high school, or to Lily Mackenzie, that snob, who pretended not to know anything about the programs of study at Columbia after she was accepted early to Yale—even though I know she applied to Columbia. I was pretty sure they'd turned her down, based on the arrogant interview she gave the local paper for a story about how Lily and I were going away to big-time colleges. My mother bought ten copies of the newspaper, even though they forgot to mention that I was going to Columbia on scholarship.

I wasn't eager to see my mother's face, or Lily Mackenzie's, for that matter. They wouldn't know anything about it, and they could all shove it if they had something to say about it. I felt like saying that to Oswald when he asked me why I was headed home—and him clueless that it was the middle of the academic calendar. What made me want to tell him is that he sort of looked like Professor

Thompson, who was the reason I was on that goddamn bus to begin with. It creeped me out plenty, sure. I could still hear Professor Thompson's offer to become his teaching assistant—I knew students like me were offered such positions, but my love for nineteenth-century British literature wasn't the most ardent in our class, so I was surprised at the suggestion. I accepted, of course, owing more to Professor Thompson's being a graduate of Harvard, where I hoped to do my graduate work than anything else.

The assistantship was as boring as anything Oswald had ever done in his life, I'll bet. The sheer volume of papers that need shuffling, files that need filing, books retrieved and returned to the campus library, just to keep a professorial office running is bone numbing. And the endless phone calls and notes from students wanting this or that. That the world is full of people who want something or other is the only thing I really learned during my short tenure.

That and the fact that Professor Thompson, who made a great show of being the distracted, rumpled teacher, was actually savvy enough to use two different exams so that students in one class couldn't pass answers to the later class. So when Sheila Gardner gave the exact alphabetical sequence of answers for the midterm she didn't take, it wasn't hard to trace it back to me. Maybe Oswald would've guessed that ending for me; I felt it a little too, when I first discovered the answer key by accident in Professor Thompson's top desk drawer, the As and Bs and Cs and Ds listed neatly next to their respective question numbers.

Oswald would probably have pointed out how much Sheila Gardner resembled Lily Mackenzie, but you can't ever take the word of lunatics. Maybe they did look alike, but Sheila was nicer to me than Lily ever was. I wanted to talk that one out with Oswald, who had fallen asleep with his greasy forehead against the window, to parse my memories for the exact moment Lily and I transformed from being the two smartest kids in school to being academic adversaries, pitched against each other in everyone's minds until we

were convinced we were natural enemies. The last good memory I
had surfaced as Oswald began snoring: Lily swooshing by me on
the late-afternoon bus, her orange-and-blue plaid dress whispering
around her knees, her skin brushing against my hairless leg, a warm
tattoo where our skin had touched evaporating as the ancient bus
cranked to life.

Baton Rouge, LA

Wasn't me that shot him, no. He got me caught, but I didn't
shoot him. Give me another life sentence if I'm lying. Didn't you
read the history books? It was Jack Ruby that shot Oswald, not me.
I shot John Alexander Hamilton, not Oswald. Ask around. How'd
he get me caught? That's another story. No, wise-ass, it's not in the
history books. I'll tell it to you, since you asked.

It was the night I killed John Alexander Hamilton, my girlfriend's
ex. They were just separated, actually, but they were working on their
divorce. She was working harder than him, though. She kicked him
out because the house was in her name—he'd owed a lot of money to
the federal government when they got married, some failed business
or another before he met Jennifer, so they'd kept everything separate.
Jen and I met the summer of '61 at the annual Fourth of July picnic
they have in Sanders Park. I was there with a buddy from back home
that flew in for the weekend. He was married, but he hooked up
at the park pretty quickly, just left me on my own. I wasn't really
wanting a girl, but when you come across a girl like Jen, you have to
stop. She was there with a couple of friends and I remember this blast
of pecan pie hitting me when I saw her. Now, normally I would've
been too shy to go up to a group of girls like that, but I had to. Truly.
Had to. I walked up and just said my name. Like that. Jen looked at
me like I had the wrong person, but I had the right person, all right.
Boy, did I. How I got Jen away from her friends is just as much of a
mystery to me as how I came to shoot her ex. It just happened. We
walked around until it got dark, just talking. She told me about her

ex right up front, but she didn't say "ex." She said "husband." But she dropped in the ex by the time the fireworks started. "You passed the test," she said.

She asked me to move in shortly after that. I gave up my apartment, no problem. Jen's house was small but cozy. The walls were empty, since her ex had taken all the pictures and mementos. "The mirrors broke in the driveway, actually," Jen said. "That's his bad luck." I tried to sweep the little pieces of glass out of the cracks in the driveway, but you could still see some when it was a sunny day.

Jen worked days as a secretary for a law firm in downtown Baton Rouge—that's who represented me when I got arrested—and I was working nights as a short-order cook at Harry's, a chat-and-chew off the highway. Thursdays and Sundays were my days off, so we really only had one day together during the week. Thursday nights were the one night during the week her ex would never come knocking. At first it was real innocent-like—her ex would drop by on his way home from his job down at the port switchyard, where all the cargo is taken off ships and put on trains because of how low the Huey Long Bridge is, to pick up something of his that he'd said Jen could have, but then changed his mind about. Stupid stuff like the toaster, or a set of towels he'd bought on his credit card. Jen was annoyed, but what could you do?

Next he came to my work, ordering a big meal and making a real production out of it. I noticed him right away but thought it was a coincidence. I didn't spit in his food or anything, truly, even though he kept sending his order back, claiming it wasn't fit to eat. I kept re-making his order because Burt, our manager, was off somewhere doing God-only-knows-what. I wasn't sure how it was going to end, but I knew he wouldn't pay his check when he left, which he didn't. Burt took the check out of my pay, and I didn't say anything. It went on like that. Phone calls late at night. Tires screeching out in front of the house. The worst of it was when Jen's ex switched the utilities off, telling the power company and the phone company to

shut down his accounts. Jen forgot the utilities were in his name—
she just continued to pay them every month—and so we had to
check into the Holiday Inn for a night that summer while we got
the utilities fixed. I was thinking about the look of humiliation on
Jen's face when the van—one of those VW vans hippies get high
in—smashed through the wooden rail and plunged into the river.
Actually, I'd been thinking about that look on her face ever since
the night at the Holiday Inn. A heat I'd never felt before just burned
me when I thought about how much humiliation her ex caused her.
You make one little mistake, Jen would say, trying to make a joke about
it, but it wasn't really that funny. If you make a mistake, you pay for
it and that's that. You don't keep on paying for it over and over. I
didn't tell that to Jen, but I hope she knows that's why. All I meant
when I called her ex out of that crappy, unlit bar of his on Main
Street was that he should pay for what he'd done. Her ex knew it
too. He didn't even act surprised when I leveled my shotgun at his
chest. I think he expected to finally pay, if you ask me.

Anyway, back to the van. I thought the damn thing would bob
along the river, but it landed on its roof, the back wheels spinning
like Ferris wheels. Me and this other guy—Oswald, as it turns out—
pulled over and rushed down the riverbank, which was slick with
moss because of a recent thaw. I could see this woman trapped in
the driver's side, but she looked okay to me. I thought about getting
out of there when I saw the look on Oswald's face. Maybe I thought
jumping into the river would wash away Jen's ex's blood—I was
surprised at the blood spray, or I would've thought to bring another
shirt. Can't really say what I was thinking. I jumped into the water,
which was cold as cold gets, probably. Oswald jumped in after me,
but I lost sight of him as I tried to get this woman, who turned out
to be bigger than I first thought, over my shoulder. She was dead-
like, and I thought she might be, but she moaned when I lost my
footing and we came crashing down. The cold water woke her up,
and just as I laid her out on the dark riverbank, I heard Oswald
shouting. Night fell just like flipping a switch, and I could hardly

make him out, holding on to a plastic bag full of garbage someone had dumped, screaming about how he couldn't swim. What kind of person jumps into a river if he can't swim? Get me? I started shivering as I waded back into the middle of the river, yelling out for him to kick his legs. I got in up to my waist, and my body starting heaving, the smell of Jen's ex's blood heavy in my nose. I wasn't sorry, that much I knew. I thought about how much better off Jen was going to be from that day on—even if it meant that we couldn't be together. Oswald kicked his way over to the riverbank, splashing like a wild animal. The air was suddenly loud with police sirens, and I emerged from the river, soaked and shivering, ready to embrace a life made up only of the past.

Dutch Harbor, Unalaska, AK

This Oswald he come on board for Coolie, the cook's assistant. None of us liked Coolie, so we didn't give a damn, but this Oswald was a lazy S.O.B. Lay in his bunk for two days till Cap'n said, "You ain't sick, get up," and this Oswald got up and started work in the galley. I paid him no mind and he paid me the same. Shoot—after nine, ten hours cutting on the line, I hardly noticed anything 'cept my plate at dinner and my pilla at night. Not even the stank from the feet of one Mr. E. S. Townsend, the government inspector we picked up when we picked up this Oswald. Why Cap'n bunked 'em both with me, I did not know. He was P.O.'d at me and Buck for bringin' the ship up late from Seattle. I told Cap'n it were Buck's fault—was him that showed up a day late—but Cap'n had it in for me ever since we pulled in late.

I didn't mind bunking with Townsend—but this Oswald was on me from the get to help talk Cap'n into giving him a spot on the line. He'd come in and switch on the light while I'm tryin' to sleep, saying he'd only turn it off if I promised to talk to Cap'n about putting him on and givin' him 1 percent like each of us on the line got when we docked and the haul was counted up. This Oswald followed me everywhere—up on deck for a smoke, down in the film room when a couple of us wanted to watch one of the three reels of war movies Cap'n kept for our entertainment, even in the pisser, where you had to hold yourself up by the wall because of the chop. The only place I were safe from this Oswald was in the wheelhouse, where I went to call home ship-to-shore. This Oswald wouldn't go into the wheelhouse 'cause Cap'n hated his little skinny ass for playin' sick and makin' the cook do everything them first days.

Cap'n didn't mind my tryin' the phone on my breaks. "You either smokin' or callin'," Cap'n said in his broke English. He put his thumb and finger together on an invisible ciggy with one hand and held a phone like with his other. Us cutters got real good at speakin' Dutch English 'cause that's where Cap'n and his crew were mostly from. Us cutters were mostly Americans, as a certain percent of us had to be from the God-blessed U.S.A. in order for Cap'n to pull up fish from American waters.

I probably spent more time with Cap'n than any other cutter, which is why this Oswald got on me right away, I figured. Cap'n didn't listen to anything I said, though, just laughed when I picked up the phone and dialed my house in Idaho to say, "Hello, baby, it's me," before my wife, Betsy, hung up. Them ship-to-shore calls costed ten dollars a minute, and when I got my paycheck every two weeks, it was always minus two-eighty, my twenty-eight one-minute calls—two a day—itemized on a scrap of paper stapled to my check.

I went to writing letters to Betsy to try an' explain why I had to run off to Alaska and leave her and the baby in Pocatello. Cap'n gave me the letters back in a bundle at my farewell party. He'd wrapped them present like and had a good laugh when I opened it and saw all my letters marked "Return to Sender" in Betsy's scrawl. I expected a present from this Oswald, as he was getting my spot on the line, since Coolie was back from wherever he went off to. I read them letters start to finish on the plane ride to Anchorage. Some of 'em I wish Betsy had actually read, but some I was glad she hadn't. Like the beginning ones where I said I had to go to Alaska because of money. Betsy knew we had money enough, so she'd'a sniffed that as a lie. The second letter I said I had to clear my head and I was embarrassed to read it. I went back to talking about money in some other letters, not saying 'cause we needed it, but saying it was a man's job to make money and I couldn't make no money in Pocatello or anywhere else 'cause of my run-ins with the judges of several states. I was glad, too, that Betsy didn't read the letter where I said I was afraid of the baby. I was embarrassed about that, too, but not like I was embarrassed about saying I needed to clear my head—that wasn't true. I *was* afraid of that baby, though. What that baby gonna think about a daddy like me? What he gonna tell his school chums about a no-good like yours truly? It is a burden to go through life aware that you are an embarrassment. The only place no one was embarrassed of me was on the boat. And all I had to do was kick a little ass now and then to keep it that way. That's what made me turn around in Anchorage and go back to Dutch Harbor, to find another boat. Before I left, I wrote one more letter to Betsy—paid a girl at the airline counter to type it out so Betsy wouldn't know it was from me. I said I knew my leaving was just one sorry act in a life full of sorry acts and that it was okay for her to stay P.O.'d at me. I said I knew I was in no position to ask a favor but if she ever wanted to do me a favor, it was this: when she was comfortable with a new man who was a real man, and the baby was all grew up into a real man who maybe was raising a real man of his own, would she just put aside her anger for five minutes and dredge up some pity for them who was cowardly and knew it?

TO: Jaime Clarke (jaimeclarke@hotmail.com)
FROM: Robert M. Stevens Jr. (rms@abn.com)
RE: WE'RE SO FAMOUS

Dear Jaime,

As you know, 808 Films has sold its interest in *We're So Famous* to the American Broadcasting Network. Let me assure you that ABN is very excited to develop this series. Everyone is looking forward to working to make *We're So Famous* a successful series.

As we discussed last week at lunch, ABN's vision for this series is to have a single protagonist, rather than all three from the novel. Can you tell me if your initial reluctance to this idea has evolved?

Many thanks.

RMS

TO: Robert M. Stevens Jr. (rms@abn.com)
FROM: Jaime Clarke (jaimeclarke@hotmail.com)
RE: WE'RE SO FAMOUS

Dear Mr. Stevens,

Thanks for lunch, and for your e-mail. I appreciate your suggestion, and know you feel it's right for the series. I'm happy to argue against it if you think it will sway anyone's opinion. The three narrators in the novel, to me, are so distinctive and vital to the narrative that I can't even fathom choosing one over the other. But I also acknowledge ABN's right to adapt the novel as it sees fit.

Jaime

TO: Jaime Clarke (jaimeclarke@hotmail.com)
FROM: Robert M. Stevens Jr. (rms@abn.com)
RE: WE'RE SO FAMOUS/Bryan Metro

Dear Jaime,

ABN's legal department has a question about the intellectual rights to the character Bryan Metro, which we understand to be a character from another novel.

Thanks.

RMS

TO: Robert M. Stevens Jr. (rms@abn.com)
FROM: Jaime Clarke (jaimeclarke@hotmail.com)
RE: WE'RE SO FAMOUS/Bryan Metro

Dear Robert (if I may),

Bryan Metro is a character from *The Informers* by Bret Easton Ellis. I have borrowed the character with Bret's blessing. If this makes ABN's legal department skittish, I can point out the specific details I used from *The Informers* so that we can alter them to make the character more generic and thus original for our use to illustrate Stella's celebrity worship and her subsequent downward spiral.

Jaime

TO: Jaime Clarke (jaimeclarke@hotmail.com)
FROM: Dana Reynolds (dana@abn.com)
RE: WE'RE SO FAMOUS

Dear Mr. Clarke,

Bob Stevens has asked me to provide you with some notes for ABN's development of the series. There is a ton of excitement to transform the material in the novel into a series featuring the Apple Scruffs, the groupies who would hang around the Beatles' Apple headquarters. They started their own fanzine, too, which could be a device we could use in the series. The idea is that the Scruffs are fame chasers during the day, but amateur sleuths by night. And we'd play on the close personal relationships between the Scruffs.

Let me know if any of the above doesn't make sense.

Best,
Dana Reynolds

TO: Robert M. Stevens Jr. (rms@abn.com)
FROM: Jaime Clarke (jaimeclarke@hotmail.com)
RE: WE'RE SO FAMOUS

Dear Robert,

    I received an email from Dana Reynolds of ABN. Can you tell me who he is?

    Thanks.

Best,
Jaime

TO: Jaime Clarke (jaimeclarke@hotmail.com)
FROM: Dana Reynolds (dana@abn.com)
RE: WE'RE SO FAMOUS

Dear Mr. Clarke,

Bob Stevens asked me to respond to your email: I am the executive in charge of development for this series. (And I am a she.)

Best,
Dana Reynolds

TO: Dana Reynolds (dana@abn.com)
FROM: Jaime Clarke (jaimeclarke@hotmail.com
RE: WE'RE SO FAMOUS

Dear Ms. Reynolds,

Very nice to meet you! Some correspondence must've gotten derailed, as I didn't know you were aboard. Look forward to working with you, though I admit confusion about this Beatles interpretation of the material. Wouldn't it be expensive to use Beatles music, for a start? Also, I understand the worldwide appeal of the Beatles, but this would be set in London? Would an American audience embrace a series set overseas? Would there still be three main characters, or a group of main characters? And what kinds of mysteries do you envision them solving?

So many questions!

Best,
Jaime

TO: Jaime Clarke (jaimeclarke@hotmail.com)
FROM: Dana Reynolds (dana@abn.com)
RE: WE'RE SO FAMOUS

Jaime,

ABN has drawn up a profit and loss statement, and based on a number of factors, including shooting a series abroad, and licensing of Beatles-related images and music, we have decided against the idea. There was some enthusiasm for setting the series during the golden age of Hollywood, but historical dramas can be as expensive.

Best,
Dana Reynolds

TO: Dana Reynolds (dana@abn.com)
FROM: Jaime Clarke (jaimeclarke@hotmail.com
RE: WE'RE SO FAMOUS

Dear Ms. Reynolds,

Thank you for your last email. I was driving home from work the other day and it hit me: What about the series in the style of a mockumentary?

Best,
Jaime

TO: Jaime Clarke (jaimeclarke@hotmail.com)
FROM: Dana Reynolds (dana@abn.com)
RE: WE'RE SO FAMOUS

Jaime,

    I appreciate your enthusiasm for the mockumentary idea, but it would drastically reduce the audience for this series. ABN is looking to create something with broader mass appeal.

Best,
Dana Reynolds

TO: Robert M. Stevens Jr. (rms@abn.com)
FROM: Jaime Clarke (jaimeclarke@hotmail.com)
RE: WE'RE SO FAMOUS

Dear Mr. Stevens,

    I hope this finds you well. I'm writing, as it's been over a month since I've heard from Dana Reynolds. Does she still work for ABN? My e-mails to her have gone unanswered and I'm eager to move this project forward.

    Thanks.

Jaime

TO: Jaime Clarke (jaimeclarke@hotmail.com)
CC: Robert M. Stevens Jr. (rms@abn.com);
Dana Reynolds (dana@abn.com)
FROM: Knox Wallace (kw@abn.com)
RE: WE'RE SO FAMOUS

Dear Mr. Clarke,

I'm writing to inform you that ABN has decided to put *We're So Famous* in turnaround. The idea is an intriguing one, but ultimately it's not quite right for ABN at this time. If circumstances change, we'll reach out again.

ABN wishes you luck with all your future endeavors.

Sincerely,
Knox Wallace

Afterword

The Salinger Principle; or, A Writer You've Never Heard of Calls It Quits

Jaime Clarke

IN THE LATE 1990S, WHEN I WANTED MORE THAN ANYTHING TO BE a famous writer, I took a job as assistant to J. D. Salinger's literary agent at Harold Ober Associates, the oldest literary agency in the country. Walking into Ober's offices in midtown Manhattan was like climbing through a wormhole: Overhead lighting was eschewed for desk lamps, the ceiling tiles were yellow with cigarette smoke, and the drinks cart would make an appearance on Friday afternoons (except in the summer, when Fridays were half days). The office was also alive with the clattering of typewriters—typing was a prerequisite of the job, and my boss was somehow surprised that I had taken typing in high school and could center words on a page without the aid of a computer. Ober had computers, but the Internet was available only on a common terminal in the middle of the office, which made checking your personal e-mail an open declaration that you weren't, in fact, working when you should be. All Ober correspondence was dictated into Dictaphones, and I became expert at working the foot pedal—left to rewind, right to fast-forward, my boss's voice in my ears with the day's business. As a recent graduate of the MFA program at Bennington College, I'd made a few friends who lived in New York, who warned me that the thousand dollars I'd saved working at a family print shop in Phoenix was not enough to move to the city, but I was impatient to live the literary life. And when Ober answered the resume I'd faxed to every literary agency in the city, I had no inkling they represented Salinger, or James M. Cain, or William Faulkner, or Sherwood Anderson, or Agatha Christie, or any of the other storied writers on their roster, save for F. Scott Fitzgerald, one of my favorite writers. (I'd read through the letters between Fitzgerald and his editor, Maxwell Perkins, which mentioned Harold Ober. Spending my lunch hour in the Ober conference room poring over the bound drafts of *The Great Gatsby* taught me more about writing than my undergraduate and graduate degrees combined.)

I'd visited New York once, the previous fall, before committing to the move. The Bennington MFA program was low residency, and I'd fly back and forth twice a year from Phoenix to Vermont. My interest in Bennington stemmed from my infatuation with the novelist Bret Easton Ellis—or rather his being a young, famous novelist, my own ambition at that time—and for my graduate lecture at Bennington, I wrote Bret a letter asking if I could interview him by mail. Instead, he called and asked if I wanted to fly to New York to do the interview in person. As the plane circled LaGuardia Airport, the entire metropolis I'd only dreamed about lay out before me, an adult Disneyland full of noise and lights. After our interview, Bret walked me out, and his parting sentiment was, "New York is a great place to be a writer," which settled the matter in my mind even though I had no idea how to go about undertaking such a move. So I just did it. Not long after I arrived, I looked Bret up, mostly to say I'd taken his advice. He invited me to book parties at KGB, as well as dinner with other writers at places like the Bowery Bar and Grill, and offered to read the novel I'd written, a largesse I quickly learned extended to a whole stable of young writers, all of us envious of Bret's career and fame. When Bret asked about my job at Ober, he seemed amused by its quaintness. Bret's world appeared to exist in another dimension from that of Ober, my days filled with transcribing royalty reports into a coded form that would be typed on color-coded index cards, or comparing an author's new contract with her last contract to look for discrepancies (read: rights grabs by greedy publishers), or granting permission for the various requests to reprint material written by Ober authors, save for Salinger, whose work couldn't be reprinted in any way under any circumstance, etc., while a large portion of my spare time was dedicated to the get-famous-quick come-on of New York City. These were the days of Puff Daddy, the moment before the explosion of reality television.

Toiling at Ober was a calming reprieve from my baser instincts, namely those of self-promotion in service of my ambition to be a famous novelist. My mentors at Bennington were powerless against the impression, honed over years of growing up in the culture of spectacle, that you could catapult yourself to the world's attention if you tried hard enough. I began writing what would be my first published novel, *We're So Famous*, with just those ideas in mind, churning out pages on my lunch hour, or after hours, or on weekends spent in the Ober offices. Writing a novel about talentless fame seekers in an office lined with classic books by famous literary writers was a study in extreme contrasts, surely, and as I mined my personal biography for all the attention-seeking things I'd ever done—the time I converted to Mormonism for my high school girlfriend; the job I took with Charles H. Keating Jr., the infamous Lincoln Savings and Loan owner; the sudden trip to Alaska to strike it rich in the fishing industry, e.g.—I was glad for the safety of Ober. I recognized that while the outside world might consider Ober a relic of days gone by, there was something religious about their desire to be faithful to old-fashioned business values, especially in a business like publishing, which appeared to be seduced more and more by youth and technology, like the film and music industries before it. Letters instead of e-mail; hand-delivered manuscripts to editors rather than electronic attachments, etc. One day, no doubt, the world would breach the walls of Harold Ober Associates, but for the moment it was a safe haven for me, not just from the impending millennial world, but from my becoming an inveterate trickster, someone more satisfied with the con than the gain. My life had been a litany of stunts, perhaps small and harmless, but stunts nonetheless.

I knew I hadn't completely reformed when I became fascinated with the stunt J. D. Salinger pulled when he moved to the woods of New Hampshire and left his publishing career behind.

I'd loved *The Catcher in the Rye* like every other teenager, but had read nothing else of his work. Eventually I read and admired *Nine Stories* while answering the Ober phones on the receptionist's lunch hour, but a sampling of *Franny and Zooey* and *Raise High the Roof Beam, Carpenters* was enough to know that on balance Salinger's work wasn't for me. What was of more interest was the volume of mail Salinger received in care of Ober, considering he hadn't published a book since the early 1960s. Nearly forty years. That, to me, was remarkable. Perhaps Salinger had invented the lexicon all future young adult novels would imitate, but that wasn't a literary legacy large enough to engender the absolute cult built up around him. The only explanation was his shunning the world, his declaration that he wanted not to be a famous writer but to be an ordinary citizen, causing the exact reverse to become true. A part of me argued that it had been Salinger's intention to do just that. The coming Internet age would prove true that a little mystery goes a long way. Even after I left Ober, I harbored the thesis that Salinger was more like Madonna than anyone could guess.

I spent the next decade working on my writing, and editing *Post Road*, the literary magazine I cofounded with friends. I floated back to Arizona, then to California, then to Boston. I got married. My wife and I worked on *Post Road* together. We ghostwrote some books. I edited a couple of anthologies. We rescued a failing bookstore. We started a family. Through the bookstore, I met a writer who wanted to start a small publishing company, and he agreed to publish the trilogy of novels I'd written when I wanted to be a famous young novelist. I also met a British writer who put me in touch with his editor at Bloomsbury, in the UK, the same publisher that published my first novel. The editor agreed to bring my new novels out in the UK as well, and eventually became the sole publisher of said novels, with the small publisher's blessing. As I revised the manuscripts, I found myself thinking of Salinger. Friends and writers were impressed that I was able to write and publish novels while coparenting a toddler and helping run an independent bookstore. I unreservedly copped to the reality that the books had been written in what seemed like another lifetime, though I admitted I was grateful for their publication. I hadn't had the impulse to write another word in years, and when friends inquired if publication would inspire more books, I answered truthfully: that I'd said what I had to say, and more books would just be my making the same arguments (albeit with differently named narrators in differently set locales), namely, that you and I are essentially alone in this world, and that we could be better people, less selfish, more understanding, that we could do more to look out for each other.

It struck me that the same might've been true for Salinger. The world awaited more work from him, but the only tangible proof he was still writing came in the form of his entering and ultimately breaking a contract to publish a revision of his story "Hapworth 16, 1924," first published long ago in the *New Yorker*. It was a fair assumption that Salinger had said what he had to say, and I revised my opinion of his disappearance from a publicity stunt to an organic understanding of himself as an artist.

Writer friends consoled me on the loss of my ambition, but it hardly seemed sad. I certainly wouldn't miss the intense examination of human motive and behavior that had seemed so compelling at the outset, but that had ultimately poisoned my general outlook. The lure of trying to illuminate the sadness in the world only led to a fetish for sad books, sad movies, sad songs. Once writers begin cataloging sadness, they see it everywhere.

An amateur diagnosis is that once becoming famous became beside the point, my ambitions were so modest—I was never interested in winning awards, giving lectures, writing book reviews, or acquiring any of the decorations of the writing life—that they were too easily satisfied: study creative writing with authors I admired; start a literary magazine; publish a handful of short stories; work in publishing; publish some novels, and a memoir; edit some anthologies. Plus all of the unexpected nice things writers get to do: give readings, appear on panels at literary festivals, be invited to teach, contribute to magazines, make book trailers. My only real want along the way was to illuminate something about the human condition in a voice and from a point of view that could belong only to me. And if a bid for posterity beats in the heart of every writer, mine is alive with the possibility that long after I'm gone, someone will discover an old paperback of my work and say, "What's this?" But whether or not that happens is independent of the volume of work a writer publishes, so what's done is done.

I sometimes daydream about the notion of learning how to write the kinds of books that capture the popular imagination, "entertainments" the novelist Graham Greene called them, without prejudice. I know how to write character-driven books where language is paramount, but popular fiction is far removed from what I gleaned from MFA programs and literary magazines. In my quest to become a Writer with a capital *W*, I failed to learn the essential elements of storytelling that these books require. I often fantasize about creating a pseudonym and becoming that writer, akin to creating a pop-star persona and becoming its principal songwriter. But the attraction is mostly me daring myself to start from scratch writing-wise, to learn how those writers do what they so successfully do.

The dissipation of my literary ambition is more freeing than anything else. Perhaps just as it was for Salinger. No more reading both to scavenge, with my own work in mind, and to keep hacking away at the forest of Great Literature too populous ever to clear. Owning a bookstore is positive proof that there are more books published than anyone can possibly read—if you think the stack on your nightstand is mocking you, try working in a bookstore—

and the defeat is liberating. The stress of literary ambition demands that you at least attempt some sort of relationship with those books and authors labeled canonical, never mind the contemporary writers you haven't read, or writers in the zeitgeist. When my ambitions vanished, so too did the anxiety that yet another good or even great book demanded my immediate attention. My prevailing assumption is that the bookstore will keep stoking my reverence for writers—as well as allow me to continue to promote them and their books—and that a desire to read as I like, just as the patrons of the bookstore do, will replace a desire to write, a nice irony.

For me, Salinger's isolation was too complete, too much like death. Writers are born of a kind of benevolent arrogance; the notion that you, and you alone, can tell a particular story that will reveal something hitherto unknown about humanity is the engine that fires the imagination. It's a fire that can burn so brightly that it consumes itself, and sometimes everything and everyone in proximity. That's one explanation, anyway. After spending two-plus decades striving to be just one thing, I was surprised to look back and see my ambitions far in the distance, struggling to keep up, ultimately falling back, leaving me open and available to welcome whatever is next.

Contributors

Mona Awad is the author of the novel *Bunny* and *13 Ways of Looking at a Fat Girl*, a finalist for the Scotiabank Giller Prize that won the Colorado Book Award, the Amazon Canada First Novel Award, and an Honorable Mention from the Arab American Book Awards. The recipient of an MFA in fiction from Brown University and a PhD in English and creative writing from the University of Denver, she has published work in *Time*, *VICE*, *Electric Literature*, *McSweeney's*, the *Los Angeles Review of Books*, and elsewhere.

Christopher Boucher is author of the novels *Big Giant Floating Head*, *Golden Delicious*, and *How to Keep Your Volkswagen Alive*. He teaches writing and literature at Boston College, and is the managing editor of the literary journal *Post Road*.

Kenneth Calhoun's stories have appeared in *Ploughshares*, *Tin House*, the *Paris Review*, and the *O. Henry Story Prize* anthology. His novel, *Black Moon*, was long-listed for the PEN/Robert W. Bingham Prize for Debut Fiction. A native of Southern California, he currently lives in South Boston.

Nina de Gramont is the author of eight books, including *The Last September*, *Gossip of the Starlings*, and the story collection *Of Cats and Men*, which was a Book Sense selection and won a Discovery Award from the New England Booksellers Association. She is the co-editor of an anthology called *Choice* and the author of several young adult novels. Her next novel, *The Mystery Writer*, is forthcoming with St. Martin's Press. She teaches in the MFA program at the University of North Carolina–Wilmington.

Ben Greenman is a *New York Times* best-selling author and *New Yorker* contributor who has written both fiction and nonfiction. His novels and short story collections include *The Slippage* and *Superbad*, he was Questlove's collaborator on *Mo' Meta Blues* and *Something to Food About*, and he has written memoirs with George Clinton and Brian Wilson. His writing has appeared in *The New Yorker*, *The New York Times*, *The Washington Post*, *Mother Jones*, *McSweeney's*, *Rolling Stone*, and elsewhere.

Annie Hartnett is the author of the novels *Rabbit Cake* and *Unlikely Animals*. She has received fellowships from the MacDowell Colony, Sewanee Writers' Conference, and the Associates of the Boston Public Library. She lives in Providence, Rhode Island.

Owen King is the author of the novel *Double Feature* and *We're All in This Together: A Novella and Stories*. He is the coauthor, with Stephen King, of the novel *Sleeping Beauties*; coauthor with Mark Jude Poirier, of *Intro to Alien Invasion*; and co-editor, with John McNally, of *Who Can Save Us Now? Brand-New Superheroes and Their Amazing (Short) Stories*.

Neil LaBute's plays include *bash*, *Reasons to Be Happy*, *The Money Shot*, and *The Way We Get By*. His films include *In the Company of Men*, *Your Friends and Neighbors*, *The Shape of Things*, *Some Velvet Morning*, and *Dirty Weekend*. Television includes *Billy & Billie* and *Van Helsing*. He is a Lucille Lortel Playwrights' Sidewalk Inductee and a recipient of a literature award from the American Academy of Arts and Letters.

J. Robert Lennon is the author of eight novels and two story collections. His fiction has appeared in *The Paris Review*, *Granta*, *Harper's Magazine*, *Playboy*, and *The New Yorker*. He lives in Ithaca, New York, where he teaches writing at Cornell University.

Jonathan Lethem is the *New York Times* best-selling author of eleven novels, including *The Fortress of Solitude* and *Motherless Brooklyn*, winner of the National Book Critics Circle Award. He is the recipient of a MacArthur grant and currently teaches creative writing at Pomona College in California.

Lauren Mechling is the author of the novel *How Could She*. She has written for *The New York Times*, *The Wall Street Journal*, *Slate*, *The New Yorker* online, and *Vogue*, where she writes a book column. She's worked as a crime reporter and metro columnist for *The New York Sun*, a young adult novelist, and a features editor at *The Wall Street Journal*.

Shelly Oria is the author of *New York 1, Tel Aviv 0* and the editor of *Indelible in the Hippocampus: Writings from the Me Too Movement*. In 2017 *CLEAN*, a digital novella Oria was commissioned to coauthor, received two Lovie Awards from the International Academy of Digital Arts and Sciences. Oria's fiction has appeared in *The Paris Review* and been read on *Selected Shorts* at Symphony Space; has been translated to other languages; and has won a number of awards. Oria lives in Brooklyn, New York, where she has a private practice as a life and creativity coach.

Stacey Richter is the author of two short story collections, *My Date with Satan* and *Twin Study*. Her stories have been widely anthologized and have won many prizes, including four Pushcart Prizes and the National Magazine Award for Fiction.

Joseph Salvatore is the author of the story collection, *To Assume a Pleasing Shape*. He is the books editor at *The Brooklyn Rail* and a frequent contributor to *The New York Times Book Review*. His fiction has appeared in *New York Tyrant*, *Open City*, *Rain Taxi*, and *Salt Hill*, among others. His criticism has appeared in the *Los Angeles Times; Routledge International Encyclopedia of Queer*

Culture; *Angels of the Americlypse: An Anthology of New Latin@ Writing*; *110 Stories: New York Writes After September 11*; *The Believer Logger*; and elsewhere. He is an associate professor of writing at The New School in New York City, where he received the University Distinguished Teaching Award and was the founding editor of The New School's MFA literary journal *LIT*.

Andrea Seigel is a novelist and screenwriter. She is the author of the novels *Like the Red Panda*, *To Feel Stuff*, *The Kid Table*, and *Everybody Knows Your Name* (with Brent Bradshaw). Her films include *Laggies*, *Handsome: A Netflix Murder Mystery*, and the forthcoming *Silent Twins*.

Daniel Torday is the author of the novels *Boomer 1* and *The Last Flight of Poxl West*. He is a two-time National Jewish Book Award recipient and winner of the 2017 Sami Rohr Choice Award for *The Last Flight of Poxl West*. Torday's work has been on NPR and appeared in *The New York Times*, *The Paris Review Daily*, *Esquire*, and *Tin House*, and has been honored in both the Best American Short Stories and Best American Essays series. He is the director of creative writing at Bryn Mawr College.

Laura van den Berg is the author of three story collections, most recently *I Hold a Wolf by the Ears*, and the novels *Find Me* and *The Third Hotel*, which was a finalist for the New York Public Library Young Lions Fiction Award. She is the recipient of a Rosenthal Family Foundation Award from the American Academy of Arts and Letters, the Bard Fiction Prize, and a PEN/O. Henry Award, and is a two-time finalist for the Frank O'Connor International Short Story Award. Van den Berg is a Briggs-Copeland Lecturer on Fiction at Harvard, and currently splits her time between Massachusetts and Florida.

Author photo by John Laprade

Jaime Clarke is a graduate of the University of Arizona and holds an MFA from Bennington College. He is the author of the novels *We're So Famous*, *Vernon Downs*, and *World Gone Water*, editor of the anthologies *Don't You Forget About Me: Contemporary Writers on the Films of John Hughes*, *Conversations with Jonathan Lethem*, and *Talk Show: On the Couch with Contemporary Writers*; and co-editor of the anthologies *No Near Exit: Writers Select Their Favorite Work from Post Road Magazine* (with Mary Cotton) and *Boston Noir 2: The Classics* (with Dennis Lehane and Mary Cotton). He is a founding editor of the literary magazine *Post Road*, now published at Boston College, and co-owner, with his wife, of Newtonville Books, an independent bookstore in Boston.

www.jaimeclarke.com

www.postroadmag.com

www.baumsbazaar.com

www.newtonvillebooks.com

What Was the Question Again?

Charlie Martens

I WAS AT A PARTY ONCE, YEARS AGO, WHEN THE MOVIE *MAGNOLIA* was on everyone's lips, and someone across the room started waxing on and on about what a great film it was. I'd spent the better part of a Martin Luther King Jr. holiday watching it, and it has some nice moments, but more interestingly the film provides a fun and easy litmus test to weed out the pretentious in any crowd. Just ask, "What's up at the end with the frogs falling from the sky?" Then count up the silent but pitying looks and you'll know who is who.

The reason I remember that it was Martin Luther King Jr. Day is that it was over a hundred degrees that day, hot for Arizona in January, the earliest in recorded time that the desert had boiled over. So a darkened theater seemed the perfect cloak from the heat. After the showing, I lingered in the bathroom until the next showing and watched it again just to be indoors. The theater was the Valley Art, an old pink and neon Art Deco gem on Mill Avenue in Tempe dating back to the 1930s. For most of the time I lived in Arizona, it was the only place besides maybe Ciné Capri in Phoenix where you could see interesting movies.

Tempe is the college town outside Phoenix that Arizona State University ("Go Sun Devils!") calls home. Around the corner and up the street, more toward campus, is Sun Devil Stadium, the collegiate arena where ASU's football team does battle. Way back when I was in high school, the Irish rock band U2 played a couple of sold-out concerts back-to-back at Sun Devil Stadium so they could film scenes for their rockumentary, *Rattle and Hum*. Tickets to the show were five dollars, and most of us attended the show both nights. Those of us who grew up in the desert in the late '80s believed deeply in the myths promoted on U2's album *The Joshua Tree* and, further, believed the album was about us collectively. Even when I close my eyes now, the haunting keyboard intro that gives way to the brain-tingling guitar riff evokes the desert after a rainstorm, or the smell of orange blossoms after midnight, in summer, when it was cool enough to go for a drive with the windows down.

The Joshua Tree began the period of time when the lead singer, Bono, became Saint Bono, and while you sometimes laughed at his pretentiousness, you were still a member of the congregation. On the previous album, *The Unforgettable Fire*, Bono famously muffed the time of day Martin Luther King Jr. was killed, saying it was early morning when in fact it was just after six o'clock at night. So he was still human, in his way. There are plenty of song lyrics that aren't factually true anyway. "Thunder only happens when it's rainin'." "Only the good die young." The notion that doves can cry. And then there are completely untrue lyrics like "Every little thing she does is magic." Or this false chestnut: "I don't care about spots on my apples / Leave me the birds and the bees." Spotted apples are the last ones people reach for at the grocery store. Don't most people sort through the apples, touching each one, looking for those without imperfections? And probably not just apples.

Bono had low-hanging fruit at those two concerts for *Rattle and Hum*. The governor of Arizona, a Mormon used-car salesman who won without garnering a majority of votes, made his first order of business to cancel the Martin Luther King Jr. Day holiday. "Blacks don't need holidays, they need jobs," he said. By the summer a petition to recall the governor was circulating, and Bono encouraged everyone to join the fight. You got the impression that Bono *lived* in Phoenix, that it was personal, such is his gift.

He is that mesmerizing personality who looks you in the eye when he's speaking and later you have dreams about him, and still later it seems strange that he's no longer in your life, save for his voice coming through your speakers.

Ever see that duet Bono did with Frank Sinatra? Think it was for a gimmicky album where Sinatra and other famous artists sang Sinatra classics, but they didn't sing them together—they were actually in separate studios, and the magic of editing made it appear they were singing to each other?

I met a kid in a community college class way back who claimed she had a million-dollar idea for a card game called Who Sucks More? The idea was you'd flip two cards off the deck to reveal a couple of names, X and Y, and the game was for you to argue that X sucked more than Y, or vice versa. I asked how you would score the game to find a winner, and she said *persuasion* would be the judge. The winner would be obvious. I said, "Okay, let's give it a try." She said, "Who sucks more: Sinatra or Streisand?"

I equivocated, secretly hoping to please her, trying to read her expression for a tell about who *she* thought sucked more. But in truth, I knew nothing about Barbra Streisand, except for that people my age thought she was uncool, and sometimes confused her for Bette Midler. I had more of an opinion about Sinatra and opted to argue the case that he sucked more. The Sinatra duets project seemed to me preposterous, and I began my answer with how pathetic it was, but I was surprisingly loquacious on the subject of Sinatra, betraying a lifelong bafflement about ol' Frank's popularity. I went on a pretty solid tear about him being merely a personality, one you either dug or not. The *idea* of Sinatra was more important to fans than any of his dumb songs or his lame attempts at acting. If you were a Sinatra fan, God help you, it was because you liked the insertion of his familiar face and voice into whatever was before you. Sinatra was comfort food for an entire generation, their macaroni and cheese and mashed potato dinner, and though I probably intuited that *every* generation had its equivalent, I tore into Sinatra, the words tripping off my tongue. Then I went for the win with the lines from the David Mamet film *Heist*:

"'Nobody lives forever.'

"'Frank Sinatra gave it a try.'"

The Empire State Building was lit blue when Sinatra died, a silent tribute. I heard about it a year later, on a brief stay in New York. "New York, New York" blaring from every open bar door. If you can make it there, well. The same drunk nobody who related that bit of trivia in the Black Rabbit said the Empire State Building had also been lit in tribute to Jimmy Stewart, who had died at the age of eighty-nine.

"Who sucks more: Jimmy Stewart or Bing Crosby?" I asked the nobody, who got a horrified look on his face.

"Just kidding," I said, to the nobody's relief.

I consider myself a Jimmy Stewart fan, though I admit he's a personality player like Frank Sinatra. When you watch a Jimmy Stewart movie, you're signing up for Jimmy Stewart's personality over whatever story is being told. There are shades, of course, like Sinatra. Jimmy in *It's a Wonderful Life* is a shade lighter than the Jimmy of, say, *Rope* or *Rear Window*. But it's still Jimmy.

I once got into a heated discussion in a bar in New York with a different set of nobodies about Hitchcock movies, about how great they are, but how every single goddamn one of them has a little thing that drives you crazy.

Take *Vertigo*, for example, which is always at the top of the best-of lists. So much of it is terrific, but in the back half of the film, that part that ties it all together, we're supposed to believe that Judy, poor Judy, was so terrific an actress as the double for the murdered wife that she had to go back to her job as a salesgirl? C'mon, son. That dipshit husband would've had to *pay* her to bring that deception off. He's gonna skate off to Europe and leave her roaming the streets of San Francisco and take a chance that no one would put it together, let alone Jimmy Stewart, a former cop? Also, it has to be said, a girl with that much talent for deception is probably not a salesgirl. No offense to salesgirls. Hitchcock movies are full of things like that, drive you crazy.

There are no perfect films, I guess. What's the closest? Actually, there's a film that's nearly perfect, and it's Hitchcockian, though it's probably not fashionable to say because it was directed by Roman Polanski. *The Ghost Writer*. Seen it? Every beat, every scene, every character, is perfect. Its only flaws are minimal, like how Ewan McGregor turns left at the New York Store in Provincetown on Cape Cod after getting off the ferry, when that only takes you farther down Commercial Street rather than to Boston, where the OnStar lady is trying to direct him.

I only know that because of my one trip up to Boston, a twenty-dollar bus ride from New York, back in the day. Get on in Chinatown, fall asleep, wake up in Connecticut to pee when the bus stops, maybe grab some McDonald's, watch the landscape go by like a verdant zoetrope until you're deposited in a different Chinatown, one less threatening than before, ride the trolly system in Boston that stands in for a real subway. A friend I'd made in the first days of my first move to New York invited me to come up anytime. Sometimes in life you meet instant friends like these. I boarded the bus as a lark, desperate to escape the city. If you've ever been to New York in the summer, you know it's just tourists and garbage strikes that leave the streets stinking to high heaven.

I'd made the friend at a show at CBGB (this was New York back before every corner had a Starbucks and a Duane Reade pharmacy). Her name slips my mind, but I remember her father was a financier of note. "Financier" is a word that never carries a positive connotation, amiright?

Back in Arizona we had our own infamous financier, Charlie Keating, who was in the papers every day. Keating was a real estate developer who bought Lincoln Savings and Loan in California, and may or may not have tricked senior citizens into investing their life savings in junk bonds, which are high yield but high risk, in order to get cash to invest in his real estate empire. Our guy Charlie was raking in cash and investing it in developments in Arizona, the kind that have grass where there shouldn't be grass, all financed by Lincoln Savings and Loan, made possible by the government's relaxation of the rules surrounding savings and loans.

Ever press your fingernails into your gums until they bleed? It's an oddly satisfying sensation. After the second *Rattle and Hum* concert in Tempe that December before Christmas, a girl who claimed to be a vampire sat on a stolen futon in an apartment I couldn't find again with a gun to my head and cut herself on her upper arm, under her sleeve, and her boyfriend slurped the blood that ran in tiny rivulets down her arm. When I press my fingernails into my gums and hold them there, I think of the aspiring vampire and wonder what she's up to now, or if she remembers that night.

I shouldn't have said how much I like *The Ghost Writer*. The fact that Roman Polanski's victim, now an adult, defends him is no defense. You can't speak for someone else's pain, but you can speak for yourself, and speaking for myself, the idea of a grown man doing what he did to a thirteen-year-old girl, no matter who he is, or whose house he was at, drives me to the brink. And yes, I've seen *The Ghost Writer* at least a dozen times, and every time I feel guilty about it, and at least a dozen times I've tried to convince myself that if all the actors in the movie thought it was okay to associate themselves with Polanski, it's okay for me to like the movie. Which, of course, is . . . what's the word?

But you have to overlook a lot of stuff to merely function. One foot doesn't get in front of the other if your scorecard is heavily marked up. Forget about the flaws in the films of Hitchcock; by all accounts, he was a questionable human being. What he did to Tippi Hedren? Oh, sorry, what he *allegedly* did. If your coworker behaved in a similar fashion, he or she'd be on trial and you'd be a witness.

Was thinking about that very thing when I was last at Taliesin West, the place in Scottsdale where Frank Lloyd Wright founded a school back in the late 1930s. The American West is famous for those seeking reinvention. Wright was no different. His family had just been murdered by a paranoid Barbadian chef, a tragedy that might've crippled an ordinary life, but even before that he'd created trouble for himself by abandoning a wife and running off with the wife of a client. On down the line. So the sun-tinted red rocks of the Valley of the Sun must've been a welcome reprieve.

The heavy mythology surrounding Wright—he was essentially a pop star at the end of his life—wants to obscure the inconvenient fact that he might've been an arrogant pseudointellectual. The beaming smile on the tour guide's face faded when I posited just such a question, and before the guide could answer, someone else on the tour, a hayseed from nowhere, made a quip that bailed out the tour guide and I didn't get an answer to my query. The better question, for tour guides everywhere, is this: Why do we generally overlook the terrible personalities of quote-unquote geniuses? Does the world need more brilliant art, books, architecture, what have you, or could it use another decent person? The nervous jackasses among us will be quick to point out that the two aren't mutually exclusive, but what about the preponderance of examples that prove the opposite?

I mean, I dig Frank Lloyd Wright. I've purposely traveled to many of his creations. Stood at Fallingwater. Climbed the pulpit at Unity Temple when I was in Chicago. Looked out at Lake Erie from the windows of the Darwin Martin House in Buffalo. Something about the clean lines of Wright's work appeals to me on a base, childlike level. Have to admit that. And though all the furniture and all the rooms I've stood in, including those at Taliesin, appear wildly uncomfortable for everyday living, they have a movie-set quality that gets the old goose bumps popping.

I shouldn't've said Frank Sinatra sucked more than Barbra Streisand. That was childish. I should've been courageous enough to say that I hated the way fans co-opted Sinatra's music and incorporated it into their personal mythology. Everyone quote-unquote doing it their way. Nauseating. Guessing the same could be true for fans of Streisand, but how would I know?

Or Bob Marley. My innards curdle when I hear the opening notes of any Bob Marley song and my mind shuts down; but upon reflection, it's not Marley I'm reacting violently to, it's all the white kids I knew in Arizona who sprouted dreadlocks and got high because Bob got high, or adopted Bob as their pot buddy as cover. Or, worse, the plain vanillas without any personality of their own who started smoking pot and listening to Bob Marley to *borrow his personality.*

Know who else is an inveterate pot smoker? You'd never guess, or maybe you would. Rick Steves. Know this motherfucker? Travels the world with nothing more than a backpack slung over his shoulder? If Rick Steves isn't in real life the nicest guy you'd ever want to meet, we are all of us kidding ourselves about our day-to-day realities. It's clear that if you're in Rick Steves's company, nothing bad is going to happen to you. Rick Steves isn't going to find himself in a hot tub at Jack Nicholson's house with a thirteen-year-old girl. Rick Steves isn't going to run off with a friend's wife. Rick Steves is proof of decency. And he can't be the only one. It's hard all of the time not to be overwhelmed by the filth inflicted upon us by the lowest common denominator.

In a game of Who Sucks More? you should pray Rick Steves is always the second choice. The other person undoubtedly sucks more. That's just math.

But Christ, I like the movie *Chinatown*, too. Have seen it as many times or more than *The Ghost Writer*. A thriller about water rights! Nicholson at his finest. Faye Dunaway stealing every scene. John Huston giving a career-capping performance.

But then you're thrown back into the other thing: Roman Polanski at Jack Nicholson's house, where he lived with John Huston's daughter, Anjelica Huston, who wandered into the surely criminal scene of Polanski and the drugged thirteen-year-old girl in the hot tub. All the elements of a compelling film, but also details of a terrible criminal and immoral act.

How much can one person be expected to overlook? And for how long?

Well, but. Polanski pled guilty and actually served more than a month in prison for his crime and only fled to Europe when the tables were turned on him by the judge overseeing his case, who was shown a photo of Polanski with his arms around some underage girls postconviction. The judge was allegedly a publicity junkie—it was LA, after all—and swore a campaign against Polanski rather than honoring the plea agreement.

Life is full of plausible deniability, but doesn't said deniability say more about the denier than it does about what is denied? An immoral act was committed, without question, and in its attempt to offer justice, the meager justice system, never up to the challenge of regulating what is morally right and wrong, created enough false narratives to provide cover to Polanski, so that three decades later I'm transfixed watching Ewan McGregor, whose ghost writer character is never named, come to grips with the morally reprehensible person whose memoirs he's ghosting.

When you hang a Louie at the New York Store in Provincetown on Cape Cod in the summer, you're treated to a carnival featuring drag queens, homosexuals, and saltwater taffy stores. After hopping off the Chinatown bus, I made the last ferry from the seaport and kicked my feet up on an empty seat while the bow cut a direct line across Massachusetts Bay. My CBGB friend's parents had a house in Provincetown for reasons that are still unknown to me, as the house was, according to my friend, always empty. I never saw the house, though, and before we lost sight of each other that night, we had an unpleasant experience at a darkened bar blaring some of our favorite tunes. The sunlight drained from our eyes as we entered the cool, low space, and when my pupils adjusted, the first thing I noticed was a shirtless man dressed as a centaur, which, hard to believe maybe, was not an out-of-place sight. Of course there'd be a centaur in the bar! My friend and I pulled ourselves up to the wide plank bar and ordered some cold beers. But we'd drunk only half of them before a friend of the centaur's politely let us know that women weren't allowed in the bar. My new friend giggled, as if this custom of the country was an amusement, but I could feel a tightness grip me. The reservoir of goodwill I'd built up high-fiving drag queens on Commercial Street drained in a sudden rush. I was apoplectic that, having faced discrimination practically everywhere and from everyone, the patrons were practicing reverse discrimination in the Shangri-la built as a celebration of the gay lifestyle.

My friend tried to distract me from my rage, but as the sun began to cast long shadows, she mentioned that the last ferry back to Boston left soon, as if remembering something she'd mentioned earlier, as if that had been the plan all along.

How many people think Martin Luther King Jr. was assassinated in the early morning based on the U2 song, do you think? Not that it matters. The enormity of the act, and the emotions the song conveys about the assassination, are more important. But a century from now, the lyrics may come to stand in for common knowledge, the facts of the history books lost on the general populace. Like the Oliver Stone movie *JFK*. Me and my generation know the movie so well, it's as good as a documentary to us. We believe the CIA and the military-industrial complex were involved. We're sure Lee Harvey Oswald was a patsy. The summation by Kevin Costner as Jim Garrison at the end of the movie beautifully sows the seeds of doubt about an entire generation's understanding of the murder of their president. The line "Who grieves for Lee Harvey Oswald?" feels seditious if you don't fully embrace the movie and its mission to finally solve a generational mystery.

Is it any wonder that baby boomers love conspiracy theories? The assassination of President Kennedy was the first chapter in the novel of that generation's upbringing. Sirhan Sirhan may or may not have assassinated Robert F. Kennedy in the kitchen of the Ambassador Hotel five years after his brother was gunned down in Dallas;

Martin Luther King Jr. was shot the same year; the United States landed men on the moon (maybe) the following year; then came the terrible cover-up by President Richard Nixon of the markedly lame crime committed at the Watergate office complex. Too many conspiracies for one generation to bear.

Paul Harvey, the radio star, lived out most of his final years in a mansion at the Biltmore Estates in the Camelback Corridor in Phoenix, his red Ferrari sometimes parked in the driveway. It was rumored he had a studio somewhere in the mansion where he could record his famous broadcast, telling everyone "the rest of the story." No small wonder that his audience was so large, those who were sure there was always more to the story, something that wasn't being said, a conspiracy of silence.

Up the hill from Paul Harvey's estate is the Wrigley Mansion, built by the chewing gum magnate back in the day. Ever hear the one about how chewing gum stays in your stomach for seven years? The children of the baby boomers carrying on the tradition. A penny dropped from the Empire State Building can kill you. *Disney on Ice* is a nod to the fact that Walt Disney is cryogenically frozen somewhere, waiting to make his triumphant return. Elvis Presley once stayed at the Wrigley Mansion. Who sucks more: Elvis Presley or Rick Steves?

The crown jewel of the Biltmore Estates is the Arizona Biltmore Hotel. Many of the expensive homes line the hotel's golf course. There's a common misconception that Frank Lloyd Wright designed the hotel, because it bears a resemblance to his previous works. Wright *was* a consultant on the hotel for a few months, but he is not the architect of record. That honor goes to a draftsman who worked for Wright. But the Biltmore Hotel has been Wrightified over the years. A stained-glass window fabricated from a design of Wright's was installed at some point. And then of course the various bars and restaurants throughout the hotel are named with a nod to ol' Frank. Too bad for what's his name, who actually designed the hotel.

The worst moment of my life occurred in a hotel. Nothing like the Arizona Biltmore Hotel. Farthest thing from it. A hotel off the westbound I-10, past the I-17 interchange. I met a girl, Madeline, the summer after high school while working as a caddy for the golf club at the Arizona Biltmore. Her father golfed at the Biltmore, and she would sometimes sit in the clubhouse snacking on Cheez-Its and Diet Pepsi, playing solitaire with a deck of Uno cards, while I followed her father around for eighteen holes, pointing out his ball in the rough, sometimes pretending to discover it on the lip between the fairway and the course. Madeline always seemed out of reach, lost in her own thoughts, but she laughed at a random aside I made while passing her table and we became fast friends.

We both liked the new AM alternative music station, KUKQ, and she somehow snagged us tickets to the first Q-Fest, a music festival the station was hosting at Big Surf, a cheesy water park in Tempe that featured a wave pool. They claimed it was the *first* wave pool in America, which seems like a pointless distinction. Though apparently when it first opened, you really could surf on surfboards, before someone realized that might be dangerous and put the kibosh on it. Madeline said Pink Floyd once played Big Surf, in the '70s, and I teased her about secretly being a fan of the Q's sister station, KUPD, which played hard rock. The morning DJ at KUPD was a bit of a local legend. People called him the Morning Mayor and turned out for concerts by the band he fronted, the Sex Machine Band. The Morning Mayor was always courting controversy and was an early prototypical shock jock, perhaps. One of the bits his fans couldn't get enough of was a segment called "Spelling with Darnell." Darnell was a semiliterate character who would successfully spell a word like "dictates" and then use it in a sentence: "I asked my girlfriend how my dictates."

The lineup for the first Q-Fest included just four bands: the Red Hot Chili Peppers; Mary's Danish; the Sidewinders, a local band from Tucson who later had to change their name to the Sand Rubies after another band called the Sidewinders sued and won; and Camper Van Beethoven. Big Surf could hold only about ten thousand people, and Madeline bumped into a few people she knew, introducing me as her friend. I wanted to be more than friends and endeavored to be as clever and funny as I could as an audition to becoming her boyfriend. The problem was she was cleverer and funnier, by far, and I could feel myself being relegated to sidekick.

I finally made my move when Madeline expressed interest in learning sign language the following semester at Arizona State University, where she was studying psychology. She knew I wasn't in school but never asked me about it, though there wasn't much to tell. I'd given community college a try after obtaining my GED, but it didn't stick.

Anyway, I went to the campus library while Madeline was in class and found a sign language chart to photocopy and cut up, then pasted together a note proclaiming how much I liked her. I slipped the note into her hand, and she gave a look before slipping into her Powerpuff Girls book bag.

A few days later her father appeared at the Arizona Biltmore for his tee time, but Madeline wasn't with him. She didn't always show, but she usually alerted me if she wasn't going to be there. I thought nothing of it until the end of the round, when her father asked me to drop by his hotel that Saturday, to talk. I was besieged by panic, which was magnified when I couldn't get a hold of Madeline for the rest of the week.

Madeline told me her parents were divorcing and that her father was living in a hotel, but the extent of the situation wasn't apparent until I was parked in the hotel lot, next to her father's vintage Corvette. The ragtop had a tear in it that I hadn't previously noticed. I once overheard him telling someone in a golf foursome that he kept a handgun in the glove box. The other members of the foursome did too, and someone cracked that most of the glove boxes in Phoenix likely had a *pistola* inside.

My emotions in the days leading up to Saturday were all over, and by the time I was behind the wheel and driving to the hotel, I was exhausted and ragged from a bout of insomnia the night before.

But as I mounted the exterior steps up to Madeline's father's hotel room, I turned back and looked at the Corvette. Moments later I was at the top landing of the stairs with the handgun from the glove box tucked behind my back, under my shirt, my sweaty skin sticking to the cold metal. It was like walking with a short metal pipe where it shouldn't be, but a powerful feeling came over me as the father's numbered door came into view. Everyone has to decide what kind of person they are, and Madeline had confided to me in the early twilight hours after Q-Fest, both of us drunk on Southern Comfort and Diet Pepsi, that her father had decided that he was the kind of person who would do things to his daughters that most would, and all should, not. She regretted saying it immediately, and I pretended not to have heard it, or to understand, and never brought it up again, though it consumed my thoughts on the golf course as her father had the nerve to joke and banter with the others in his foursome, as if he weren't a perverted scumbag. I was haunted by her confession, and the powerlessness I felt in the face of it. How could I let it slide, knowing? I pictured her father on his knees on the dirty hotel carpet, me towering over his small frame, pressing his gun into the back of his head. A fever gripped me as I approached his door. The gun was warm now from my body heat. No one knew I was meeting him, not even, presumably, Madeline. Maybe she would know it was me, maybe not. My exit strategy, if implicated, would be to ask Madeline to provide me with an alibi. Regardless of where things stood with her, I was sure she would help. My mind reeled thinking about all the terrible things the father had done to her and her sister, amplified by who knew what other horrible things he'd done in his life. He'd made his choice, had decided what kind of person he was. Long ago I'd decided too. My life had been made harder by the decision to be the kind of person who didn't look the other way, who didn't let things slide, who always said something without regard for whatever would follow. And because Jesus Christ was just a historical figure to me, nothing more, I would have to deal only with the laws of men, if that. I barely knew Madeline's father. I wasn't always his caddy. Who would put the two of us together at a hotel off the freeway? Who would believe it? Surely there were more-plausible suspects in her father's life.

I knocked on the motel door. A high-pitched shriek I recognized filtered through the air. The door flew open and Madeline smiled at me, her father waving from the far side of the tiny motel room. An old black-and-white Christmas movie was playing on the television. I stepped from the blazing December sunlight into the cool room, which had been converted into a bachelor's apartment. Outside of the two single beds, you could easily have mistaken it for a dorm room. The gun felt like a boulder on my back, and I spent the next half hour or so worried the thing would fire when I was offered a chair to watch the last of the movie.

The Red Hot Chili Peppers were the headliners for Q-Fest, but me and Madeline hadn't heard of them. They weren't the ubiquitous Seussian rockers they are today. We just knew the one song, "Higher Ground," which the band saved as an encore, because it was on the radio. It was probably another decade or so before I realized that "Higher Ground" was a cover of a Stevie Wonder song. The Chili Peppers certainly didn't mention it that night. So many times I've been fooled by bands presenting songs as their own on the assumption that I'd know it was a cover:

Like "Red Red Wine" by UB40.

Or "Blinded by the Light" by Manfred Mann.

Or "I Love Rock 'n Roll" by Joan Jett.

Or "Tainted Love" by Soft Cell.

Or "Twist and Shout" by the Beatles.

Or "Cum on Feel the Noize" by Quiet Riot.

Or "The Tide Is High" by Blondie.

Or "It's All Over Now" and "Time Is on My Side" by the Rolling Stones.

Who sucks more than the Rolling Stones? Though in their defense, how did American radio listeners ever know they dug rhythm and blues until the Stones appropriated it and packaged it in some poses and bad acting?

I purposely left out the detail that Madeline was Hispanic. It isn't important, and you know how people start discounting what you're saying when they learn this or that extraneous detail. Her father was not Hispanic, but her mother, whom I never met, clearly was. Madeline insisted when that she wasn't Mexican, but Hispanic. I was too dumb to know the difference and was worried that it was a subtle form of racism, but she said, "Mexicans live in Mexico, dummy," and that's all it was.

I remember the motel had a Thomas Kinkade painting on the wall, the one that looks like the sun is setting in Venice. Those paintings are a trip! You swear they are battery-operated. Ever see the ones that look like it's raining? The only artist, guaranteed, whose works are sold in shopping malls. So what? You bury them in the ground for hundreds of years and who knows what people will be saying about them in the future? How many artists hanging in fancy museums today were the laughingstocks of their age? Losers and weirdos. Reliant on the patronage of this rich person or that . Not our man Thomas Kinkade. Every fifth house you enter in Arizona proudly displays a Kinkade. He even had the good business sense to die an artistic death from booze and drugs, leaving his wife and girlfriend to fight over his estate.

That lameness about how the Arizona Biltmore Hotel tries to fool everyone into thinking it was designed by Frank Lloyd Wright, rather than one of Wright's students, is exactly like how the disciples of Christ try to put their words on Jesus.

What's funny—and funny ha-ha, not funny queer—is how Jesus and Saint Nicholas are both historical figures who, by all accounts, were kind and generous, but at some point in our lives we are told to double down on Jesus and start thinking about Saint Nicholas as a fairy tale, saddling him with magical realism involving a sleigh and reindeer. Even renaming him Santa.

Speaking of gifts: Madeline's father had asked me to meet him in his hotel room because he understood from Madeline that I was deeply in debt and was having a hard time making any headway with my life because of it, and he offered me an interest-free loan to help me get my head above water. It's true the job caddying at the Arizona Biltmore was mostly about the tips, but I secretly also hoped to apprentice myself to one of the businessmen from the Phoenix 40, the annual list of the richest Phoenicians, to start me on an upward trajectory.

But the worst moment of my life played out in that hotel room when I accepted a check for a couple thousand dollars, Madeline beaming as her father wrote it out, me never considering not cashing it, or repaying it, the handgun cold again like a block of ice down the back of my pants.

Everyone has to decide what kind of person they're going to be.

Madeline never said anything about my note, and she never appeared again in the clubhouse while her father golfed. I quit my caddying gig a month or so after the loan was given, before the first payment was due.

John Huston's line in *Chinatown*, when he says to Jack Nicholson's character, "Most people never have to face the fact that at the right time and the right place, they're capable of *anything*," meant one thing before I met Madeline and another after. Truthfully, I could never watch that film again, but that line is in my marrow now. As someone who moved around a lot as a kid, I lost the sinuous connection to the everyday human condition that binds people together. But I know I'm not capable of anything. I spend too much time thinking about my limitations, and worrying over any lines I'd be willing to cross.

Some lines you can't know you'd cross until after you've crossed them. I was prepared to put a bullet in Madeline's father's head that day. I was. I was sure it was the right thing to do. There was a moment that afternoon when it would've been cowardly not to. That's how quickly wrong becomes right. I still carry immense shame that I didn't follow through, regardless of the circumstances.

For a long time after, I fooled myself that the loan I'd accepted in place of my thirst for murder was a lateral impulse, but forever afterward the memory filled me with shame, and at some point I convinced myself that I'd never borrowed the money, or that I'd borrowed it and paid it back.

Do you sometimes wonder whatever happened to people whose paths you crossed, if briefly? The ones the internet can't help you hunt up because you don't know a last name, or never knew a name to begin with? The face of the aspiring vampire who sat on the purloined futon has faded, and I never knew her name, but what remains of her essence always invades my brain when I hear the opening of the song "Never Let Me Down Again" by Depeche Mode, from the *Music for the Masses* album. The cutting and the bloodletting began as that song blared through the expensive sound system in the apartment where I found myself, swept along as I was in a stream of concertgoers after the *Rattle and Hum* show at Sun Devil Stadium. My clearest recollection is that the apartment complex was a new stucco construction, painted pink and turquoise. And only college students lived there, giving the place a campus feel, or that of a co-ed clubhouse. I've driven the streets of Tempe searching for any glimmer of the pink and turquoise, but it's clear that the complex was either razed or painted over.

The vampires floated through my mind when my CBGB friend and I filtered into that bar on Cape Cod, the Depeche Mode blaring as if on cue. I shouldn't have said what I said to the centaur and his friends. Anyone who knows me knows I'm slow to anger, can laugh off almost anything, or offer a tasteless joke or cynical comment in an attempt to deflect the ugliness that is always lapping around the edges of every conversation, every circumstance. Never give anything power over you. But when the centaur asked us to leave, and said why, I was one foot up on the steps of Madeline's father's hotel again, the same blackness rising, and the rush of anger crested and crashed in an instant. The centaur and his friends gave a fearful look, as if their bubble had been pierced by a lethal virus. The return ferry to Boston that night was mostly empty, the boat whooshing through the darkness as it carried me back to my exile.

One of the centaur's friends was wearing a pink T-shirt with a white linen coat and pants, and espadrilles, a look popularized by Don Johnson's character Sonny Crockett on the hit television show *Miami Vice*. I'd had a similar outfit and worked it into the rotation my freshman year. This was when I was living in San Diego. All the streets in my neighborhood were named for writers. The foster family I was living with, the Wallaces, lived on Sterne Street, next door to an inveterate pot smoker who owned a string of successful hat shops and who was always blaring Pavement albums on the weekends. The pot smoker razzed me from his porch on one of my Sonny Crockett days, but we would get high and watch *Miami Vice* every Friday night. He'd had a long-running dispute with the Wallaces, the nature of which I never learned, and I sometimes thought he was cultivating me as a double agent, though he never asked me about them. Maybe he just sensed a deeply unhappy freshman who, for some reason, liked to dress up like Sonny Crockett.

Legend is that the then head of NBC scribbled the note "MTV Cops" and the idea for the series was born. As legends go, it's too predictive to be taken as truth, but there wasn't anything else like it on television. The slick cars, the hit-radio songs, the fashionable clothes, the perfect interplay between Crockett and his partner, Ricardo Tubbs, played by the winsome Philip Michael Thomas. And the guest stars! Phil Collins as a con artist–cum–game show host (and Kyra Sedgwick as his accomplice), Pam Grier as Tubbs's old girlfriend, Helena Bonham Carter as Crockett's girlfriend, John Turturro as the leader of a prostitution ring, Julia Roberts as a drug dealer's girlfriend, Gene Simmons as a drug dealer, Ted Nugent as a drug dealer, Bruce Willis as an arms smuggler, Liam Neeson as an Irish terrorist, George Takei as a money launderer, Chris Cooper as a dirty cop. Eartha Kitt, Little Richard, G. Gordon Liddy, Frank Zappa, Leonard Cohen, Willie Nelson killing it as a Texas Ranger.

The show was edgy, too. One of the episodes from the first

season has Crockett running into Evan, a former vice cop he came up with who is now undercover with an arms dealer. Crockett begs off the investigation that has brought him back into Evan's orbit, but no dice. Tubbs wants the backstory, but Crockett gives him an icy stare and tells him to drop it, which of course Tubbs doesn't, instead pulling Evan's file, where Tubbs learns that Crockett and Evan went through the academy together with a third officer, Mike Orgel. Tubbs's snooping around chaps Crockett's hide, and they decide here near the end of season 1 not to be buddies, but just to do the job together and leave it at the office. As it was the show's first season, it was highly believable that this partnership might not work out. (Unless you were a television executive, I guess.) But in the inevitable scene where Crockett seeks out Tubbs and they make up, Crockett relates how the third officer, Orgel, tried to beg out of an investigation he and Crockett and Evan were on that required them to infiltrate gay bars. Evan started giving Orgel shit, saying things like, "Mike's afraid someone will recognize him ." The way dudes did in the '80s, calling each other "faggot" or "queer" and saying this or that was gay. Crockett tells Tubbs that Orgel *was* worried he would be recognized, that Orgel was indeed a homosexual, and that Orgel walked into a police situation with a shooter shortly after and was shot dead. "Suicide," Crockett says. And ever since, Evan has been volunteering for every kamikaze assignment in the hopes of meeting the same fate, such is his guilt. The anguish on Crockett's face when he tells Tubbs all of this relayed to all of us viewers that he, too, has been carrying the same guilt for forever and, by extrapolation, that it is important to always do the right thing, to stand up for someone else's rights and beliefs, regardless of whether or not you share the same rights and beliefs.

It was a powerful television moment. And it flushed to the forefront of my mind when the centaur asked me and my CBGB friend to leave the bar on Cape Cod. And even though I shouldn't have said it, the words "You're no better than those who hate gay people" left my lips before I could check them. The disservice done to whatever suffering he and his friends had had in their lives as homosexuals had been delivered. Some things when spoken become tattoos, and mine has been an indelible part of me since that night.

When I was living in Florida in the early 1990s, there was a buzz one day that Magic Johnson was going to make an announcement, and in the pre-internet days there wasn't much more information than that until, at a seemingly hastily arranged press conference, the Laker point guard announced he was HIV positive and would immediately be retiring from basketball. The next night he was a guest on his friend Arsenio Hall's talk show, where the pair talked expansively about Magic's new life and his role as a spokesman about the virus, especially within the black community, where HIV was spreading at an alarming rate. We had the television on in the bar where I was bartending, and there was an odd moment where the idea that HIV was strictly a gay disease was dismissed and Magic said something like, "I'm as heterosexual as they get," and the crowd whooped and hollered their affirmation and appreciate for the fact, as if the average person were so invested in the sexual preferences of one Earvin "Magic" Johnson. But you knew you were witnessing an important television moment, and—unlike the fiction of *Miami Vice* but just as powerful—all of us watching could sense that there'd been another shift in our understanding of the world at large, and how important it was to be inclusive rather than reductive.

How many people believe John F. Kennedy was a progressive threat to the Establishment because of the Oliver Stone movie? Not sure the history books bear that out, but they don't bear out much of what's in the film. Too much of history is too boring to craft compelling cinema from. But it wasn't until many years later that I learned that the whole enterprise was essentially factless. The tip-off should've been that even with all that compelling evidence— the testimony of the characters brilliantly played by Joe Pesci, the aspiring priest who ended up a CIA mercenary and confesses to his role before being murdered; Kevin Bacon, the young homosexual who was the object of the affections of Clay Shaw, played by

Tommy Lee Jones, who may or may not have been in the CIA, and witnessed many of the characters plotting Kennedy's assassination; and Donald Sutherland as a nameless government official who breathlessly reels off a tight narrative of the entire conspiracy and how high it went—the trial ended in a not-guilty verdict. Others have been convicted on less. And then the crazy magic bullet theory, with its impossible ballistic logic.

Joe Pesci's portrayal of David Ferrie was Oscar-worthy, and Ferrie's paranoid ambivalence before confession felt so emotionally true that you as the viewer needed Kevin Costner as Jim Garrison, the New Orleans district attorney who charged Clay Shaw with the conspiracy, to come through. But then it turns out that in real life David Ferrie always said he was innocent, that he didn't know anything about anything, and that Pesci's amazing performance was just a trick. Imagine if Ferrie had still been alive (he actually died of natural causes and wasn't murdered) when the film was made. Oliver Stone would've had to buy his silence, or pay libel.

And the conspiracy narrative Sutherland spools? It's taken directly from what *The Guinness Book of Records* considers the Most Famous Literary Hoax, the book *The Report from Iron Mountain*, which was cheekily published as nonfiction but was always fiction, like the magic bullet theory, which isn't really built on the laws of physics or any other science. The reverse of what the film suggests about the movement of Kennedy's head has been proven in scientific re-creations, which confirm the same in the Warren Commission report.

What's remarkable about the movie, though, is not that my generation believed its presentation as a near documentary, but that so many who grew up in the Kennedy era believed it too. You could charge Oliver Stone with gross insensitivity for exploiting the unhealed wounds of those who had to live through that and other assassinations of the '60s. Viewed strictly as a piece of art, the movie has a conspiratorial, antigovernment vibe that feels historically accurate, and you can hear its echoes in conversations with baby boomers, who essentially mistrust the Written Record, or What Is Told. Their children, by comparison—my generation—simply don't care if it's true or not. Our parents' paranoia bred our indifference.

Which likely accounts for the dearth of Generation X politicians.

Another trial that seemed like a slam dunk, though lacking in cinematic style, was the murder trial of O. J. Simpson. The case had Hollywood elements—a former football star–turned–actor, beautiful victims, outraged family members demanding justice, all the defense lawyers money could buy, and the same judge who had previously put Phoenix financier Charlie Keating in custody—but all the acting was terrible, and save for the twist ending, it might've gone relatively unreviewed. The trial confirmed a few widely held suspicions, paramount among them the idea that the rich and famous are not necessarily as intelligent as or smarter than the rest of us. That their privileged lives shelter them from real-world consequences we all would face if we behaved similarly. Or didn't have the money to maneuver around egregious mistakes.

But rich and famous or not, murder is a heinous and serious crime, and so we all watched, riveted to our television screens as the so-called trial of the century played out episodically. The mistake most of us who were surprised by the verdict made was that we believed the jurors were telling us that O.J. didn't commit the murders. That was a head-scratcher in view of the evidence and the slim mathematical probability that anyone else might've done it. It would be a long while before we heard what the jury was trying to say about racial injustice in general and racial injustice specifically at the hands of the Los Angeles police. The verdict as a form of protest would come to make sense down the road, and everyone would have to settle for themselves if freeing O.J. was the right bargain.

A by-product of the Simpson trial was that finally the line between fame and infamy had been crossed forever. Previously, infamy had been the last-place prize for those who had aspirations of becoming famous but who had reached for the brass ring and felt their fingertips brush it on the way down. Or those who had never even sniffed the brass ring. For example, you might think that appearing on the world stage as a college dropout who fit the description of a surfer frat boy right out of central casting might expose you to ridicule, as it did Kato Kaelin, the witness who'd lived in O.J.'s guest house and heard a thump against his wall on the night in question. And you might think, previously, that you'd spend the rest of your life trying to undo that image of yourself, to no avail. Once Kato the aspiring but ultimately failed actor, always the aspiring but failed actor. You might expect that appearing at a local car show, or in a spoofy national commercial during the Super Bowl, might be the best someone like Kato Kaelin could dream of after the lampooning he took in the media. And, previously, you would've been correct. But Kato Kaelin was able to parlay his appearance as a witness for the prosecution, and not really one of their main witnesses, into a long television career. It must've been strange to move effortlessly into a Hollywood orbit larger than the one O.J. could provide him. It was a remarkable rise even for the fickle demarcations in Tinseltown. Whether or not his television career was based solely on his trial personality is not for me to say. Hollywood does love to typecast.

Or is it that we the audience require typecasting? They say the mark of genius is the ability to hold two opposing ideas in your mind at the same time. But we're not a society of geniuses, by the strict definition, so is Hollywood just reacting to the reality they've been given, as tabloid newspapers always claim? And, more disturbingly, are we faux-outraged at the concept but secretly relieved by it?

Are we generally satisfied with Orville Redenbacher as the folksy spokesperson for a beloved brand of popcorn, or can we also admit that he was a pioneer who made an important contribution to agriculture by creating the strain of popcorn that served as the foundation for his empire?

How did the rest of the United States House of Representatives treat Gopher from *The Love Boat* and Cooter from *The Dukes of Hazzard* when the actors were elected to their hallowed ranks?

So many times a beloved actor in a celebrated TV series has a hard time convincing the public that he or she isn't the character we've come to love. Don Johnson was able to shed Sonny Crockett to become Nash Bridges, as well as a handful of believable film roles. Or maybe we were always thinking, *That's Sonny Crockett.* Was Ted Danson believable as Dr. John Becker for those 129 episodes, or were we thinking, *That's Sam Malone playing a doctor in the Bronx?* Same for Julia Louis-Dreyfus—Elaine from *Seinfeld*, my generation's *I Love Lucy*—in *The New Adventures of the Old Christine?* The geniuses among us would allow for both, I suppose.

We forever want Molly Ringwald to be the girl from the John Hughes movies; we don't even care which one. We just want her to remain America's sweetheart. Never mind her subsequent career in film or her endeavors as a writer. It makes it a lot harder to take the "Which John Hughes Character Are You?" quiz after we've had a few too many.

What's fascinating about the painter Thomas Kinkade is how vehement his detractors and critics were. The arguments proffered for his artistic illegitimacy were many but hardly cohesive. He sold his paintings on QVC. He didn't actually paint the paintings. The so-called Kinkade glow in every painting was a gimmick. He only painted similarly styled cottages and landscapes. His paintings sold not in art galleries, but in shopping malls.

It's a sure bet that those who turned up their noses at Kinkade are fans of the film *Magnolia.*

It wasn't that long ago that another artist commercially produced his art, conceiving of the original idea and having apprentices complete the finished product. And instead of glowing paintings, his gimmick was to create meaningless art out of the meaningless products of everyday lives. Soup cans, celebrity portraits, boxes of Brillo pads. When asked what the work represented, Andy Warhol shied away from answers, which enhanced his pop star aura. We're all old enough to know that the level of fame Warhol achieved required cunning, and silence. A mystery is preferable to all else.

Warhol collectors, *Magnolia* fans all, wouldn't see or acknowledge their kinship with Kinkade fans, but both admire technical mastery and gimmickery.

And by rights, both would be fans of the original commercial artist, Albrecht Dürer, whose mass-produced engravings made him wealthier than any of his contemporaries, who likely were in the service of their patrons. (Learned that from Rick Steves.)

The unspoken, sometimes spoken, central objection to Kinkade's work was that the fervently religious saw God in his paintings, and their religiosity was the basis for Kinkade's popularity. And while it might be okay for tourists to flock to museums around the world to gawk at paintings from centuries past that either depict religion outright or seek to express a belief in God, it's not okay for your grandparents to fight traffic and shuffle through the food court on their way to find the paintings that soothe and comfort them.

Many of the shopping malls on the west side of Phoenix, the older section of the city, as well as in the suburb of Mesa, populated mostly by Mormons, had Kinkade dealers. Not so the malls in the richer suburbs, such as Scottsdale or Paradise Valley. Or, of course, Tempe, the college town.

Before upscale malls were developed in Scottsdale, the toniest shopping center in Phoenix was Biltmore Fashion Park, built along Camelback Road, dubbed the Camelback Corridor, so named for being in the shadow of Camelback Mountain, a nearby geological red rock wonder in the shape of a camel. Biltmore Fashion Park abutted the aforementioned Arizona Biltmore Hotel, giving the outdoor shopping center a proximity to luxury.

Across Camelback Road from Biltmore Fashion Park in the 1980s and 1990s was a complex of buildings known as American Continental Corporation, the headquarters of financier Charles H. Keating Jr. Before Charlie Keating came to symbolize the naked greed of the time, he was a pioneering antipornography crusader appointed to an antiobscenity commission by President Richard Nixon. When the commission confirmed in its report that pornography did not corrupt morals and lead to an escalation in crime, Charlie was the lone dissenter. The Nixon administration gave Charlie help with writing a rebuttal in the form of speechwriter Pat Buchanan. However, the rebuttal was widely mocked by both political parties. Undaunted, Charlie took the experience back home to Cincinnati, where he waged war against filthy movies, filthy plays, and hotel chains that featured filthy in-room programming. He even produced his own documentary about the dangers of perversion.

One of the clients at the law firm where Charlie worked was a financial services holding company, American Financial. Charlie ended up leaving his legal career to become an executive at American Financial, and over the years he was the cleaner, whose job it was to fire employees of the companies that American Financial acquired. But soon there was an SEC investigation, and Charlie was charged with filing false reports and defrauding investors. Charlie resigned from American Financial, and the same year he turned up in Arizona, ready for reinvention.

Phoenix was a small city then, ripe for the kind of real estate expansion Charlie envisioned. It wasn't long before American Continental was the biggest home builder in the valley. Soon after, Charlie bought Lincoln Savings and Loan, a California bank whose conservative investments made it a perennial loser, though a safe bet for its customers. The federal government deregulated the savings and loan industry, meaning S and Ls could use their deposits for riskier financial projects, and soon Lincoln's profits increased fivefold. But the government quickly realized the downside of said investments, namely that they exposed the government's guarantee to depositors to potentially crippling risks. So the savings and loans were reregulated and ordered to reduce their risky holdings.

But Charlie said, "I don't think so," and went to war with the government. He enlisted a handful of United States senators, known colloquially as the Keating Five, to plead his case with the government. At a hastily organized press conference at the Arizona

Biltmore Hotel, Charlie was famously asked if he expected a return on his investment of campaign donations to the senators, and he said, "I certainly hope so."

But it didn't work out, and Charlie was indicted and ultimately convicted and sent to prison, his company liquidated by the government. The Phoenician, a luxury hotel he built in the side of Camelback Mountain with marble imported from Italy, among other lavish touches, was sold to a group of Kuwaitis for twenty-five cents on the dollar and still stands as a monument to Charlie's opulent lifestyle. Near the entrance of the Phoenician is the Jokake Inn, the facade of which was used as the home of the fictional Nathan Arizona in the film *Raising Arizona*.

There are a number of terrible Nicolas Cage movies, but he's made so many that it's just the law of averages that some are mediocre or not great. But the breadth of roles Cage has played over the years puts him in the never-boring and almost-always-surprising category. Everyone likes risk takers—we cheer when they win, and deride them for trying when they don't, but they don't go unnoticed by us.

My first stint in New York City, in the late 1990s, gave a glimpse of what it would be like to live among an entire city of risk takers. The top whatever percent of ambitious people from all the hometowns across the globe seemed to have found their way to New York. I was only chasing a girl I'd met in Arizona, still an ambition, but a low-level one by comparison. My first couple of days in New York, I wandered Manhattan, unsure of how the subway system worked and feeling a little exposed as I ebbed and flowed with the throngs of people mobbing up and down the island. Back in Phoenix, you'd see everything through your windshield. Drive to where you were going, see the place, get in your car and drive back. But the ribbons of pavement in New York brought me into the mix.

I found myself in Lenox Hill, on the Upper East Side, along with a constant crowd of onlookers at the "grave site" of an illusionist who had buried himself in a plastic see-through coffin as a feat of endurance. Another see-through box filled with water was placed on top of the coffin, and I wondered what we all looked like to the illusionist peering up through the water. People waved and took pictures. Someone said that the stunt was a tribute to Harry Houdini, who was an idol of the illusionist's and who'd had plans for a similar stunt but died before he could perform it.

I also stood at the makeshift memorial of flowers and messages in front of the building in Tribeca where John F. Kennedy Jr. had lived with his wife. Kennedy and his wife and sister-in-law had been on their way to a wedding of another Kennedy on Martha's Vineyard in a plane piloted by JFK Jr. when the plane went down short of the Vineyard. A Coast Guard search finally turned up the plane and its passengers in the cold waters, and everyone's hearts broke for the handsome son of the assassinated president and his beautiful wife and sister-in-law. We get spooked when tragedy befalls those who lead quote-unquote charmed lives. It confirms our vulnerability, that we're out here on our own, without advantage of wealth or pedigree, and that more likely than not, we won't escape tragedy. Dying in your sleep of old age is mostly a myth.

The near-universal acclaim for *Raising Arizona* was a welcome surprise to those of us toiling in the desert heat. Especially given that the state had turned into a punch line since Evan Mecham, the Mormon used-car salesman who had become governor, was an undisciplined, uneducated racist. Blacks weren't the only object of his prejudice: he told a Jewish delegation that America was a Christian nation, and relayed to a local Kiwanis club how on a recent trip to Japan he gave a golf club as a present to the head of a prominent bank and how the banker "got round eyes" when Mecham told him how many golf courses Arizona boasted. And then, of course, he said on the television program *60 Minutes* that homosexuality was illegal and that he wasn't prejudiced against gays, just that their lifestyle broke the law, a line his supporters relied heavily on when defending him. But like all things, to not see it is to not want to see it.

A recall of Mecham was initiated on the 181st day of his

administration, the earliest date as prescribed by law , and it didn't take long to collect the signatures needed. Shortly after Bono and U2 left town, a recall election was scheduled. Mecham decried the "homosexuals and dissident Democrats" trying to turn him out of office, but the special election set to recall the governor never took place, as Mecham was convicted on an obstruction of justice charge related to one of his aides making death threats against a witness for various investigations into Mecham, as well as "high crimes, misdemeanors or malfeasance" for diverting state money in the form of a loan to one of his Pontiac dealerships. Upon conviction by the Arizona State Senate, Mecham was removed and the secretary of state, Rose Mofford, whose beehive hairdo was legendary around the state capitol, became the first female governor of Arizona, presaging a time two decades later when every elected high office in the state would be held by women.

So it was fun to see Phoenix and the surroundings up on the big screen. Though there were plenty who thought maybe the joke was on Phoenicians, and because of the national headlines about the Mecham saga, politicians worried that the film was more oxygen for the bonfire consuming the state's reputation. In the wake of the Mecham antics, there was a boycott of the state by Stevie Wonder, the rap group Public Enemy released a protest song called "By the Time I Get to Arizona," and the NFL withdrew the honor of Phoenix's being a host site of an upcoming Super Bowl. The Super Bowl situation dragged on for more than half a decade, until voters finally passed a paid Martin Luther King Jr. holiday, mostly, some felt, to win back the right to host the Super Bowl and reap the economic windfall. Arizona was indeed the site of Super Bowl XXX; or rather Tempe, as the game was played at Sun Devil Stadium, since Arizona didn't have a professional football stadium then. Plans for the Cardinals to have their own stadium had to be shelved for nearly two decades, owing to the financial upheaval of the savings and loan crisis.

Still, how cool is it to see something familiar in a movie? Not just

Sun Devil Stadium in the football game scene at the end of *Raising Arizona*, but Lost Dutchman State Park in Apache Junction, where H.I. gets into a fight at a family picnic, and the gas station on Deer Valley Road where he famously steals the Huggies. Every time after, whenever you'd pass near any of the filming locations, you'd get a jolt that Hollywood actors knew where you lived, had seen what you'd seen, and you were dying to know what they thought of everything that was swirling in the background of their minstrel show. Maybe that sounds silly, but it's akin to when someone is suffering with a diagnosis and a celebrated person announces to the world that he or she is similarly diagnosed . Magic Johnson's announcement that he was HIV positive made a tremendous difference not just in how the virus was perceived, but in how people who had contracted the virus were regarded. When the actor Mandy Patinkin tells the world that he had to have a double corneal transplant, it makes the procedure a little less scary for the person who needs the same and whose friends have never even heard of such a thing. Even if the celebrated person is forced into confession before being exposed by the vile tabloid press, the calming effect is the same. For a moment we get amnesia about the socioeconomic differences that might dictate the variable quality of treatment and just revel in the connection. Suffering anonymously feels so ignoble and lonely.

New York City is the ultimate movie set, and you can't help but think of all the films you've seen that have New York as a backdrop when you visit or live there. The skylines in *On the Waterfront*. Fifth Avenue in *Breakfast at Tiffany's*. Before the Dakota on Central Park West was known for the terrible murder of John Lennon, it was the backdrop for the couple in *Rosemary's Baby*. Gene Hackman's wild pursuit along the D train through Bensonhurst in *The French Connection* reveals the chaotic madness of New York maybe better than any thing else. *Saturday Night Fever's* John Travolta trucks into the city from Bay Ridge to reinvent himself, but a thousand Travoltas materialize on the streets of Manhattan after dark. The Broadway of *All That Jazz*. The East Village of *Desperately Seeking*

Susan. Spike Lee's Brooklyn in *Do the Right Thing.* The New York of all of Martin Scorsese's movies is alive both then and now. Who can blame Charlie Sheen's intoxication with the wealthy as he inhabits enclaves like 21 Club and Tavern on the Green in *Wall Street*? Glenn Close on the Upper West Side in *Fatal Attraction* is maybe less frightening than the spoiled brats on the Upper East Side in *Metropolitan.* And, of course, the iconic scene with Meg Ryan and Billy Crystal in *When Harry Met Sally* has tourists in line at Katz's Deli at all hours.

When I finally made my way back to New York, leaving Phoenix for good, the city was constantly reminding me of the Scorsese cult film *After Hours*, a black comedy about a character played by Griffin Dunne trying to find his way home. I'd crashed out of my job as a columnist in Phoenix, and New York was an unscratched itch. One hot and sticky night in August as I packed up the meager belongings in my one-bedroom apartment in Phoenix, I e-mailed the girlfriend who had led me to New York, a British woman named Olivia, and the cosmos aligned when she e-mailed back to say that she would meet me in New York if that was the plan. I assured her it was, and there was suddenly a sense of urgency and logic to my moving east.

Olivia kept her word, though it was a bit of a cheat, as she had business in New York in her capacity as a purchasing agent for a London pharmaceutical company. So what if I was flying thousands of miles to see her, and she was making a transatlantic journey *both* for me and for business? At least I was in the mix, which was more than I had going in Phoenix. But the reunion was marred by the fact that we were complete strangers all these years later, which we discovered over drinks and dinner in the East Village. Whatever passion had fueled our romance almost a decade previous was a mystery to us as we droned on at dinner about our respective lives, our jobs, the subtext being how we both were still searching for life answers but that we were essentially strangers to each other.

After Olivia caught her flight back to London, I was left roaming the streets of New York. I'd seen *After Hours* at the Valley

Art cinema back in Tempe during a film festival celebrating cult films of the 1980s, and while I'd dug it, the landscape had seemed completely foreign. But suddenly I was trudging similar New York streets, unmoored, desperate to get back to my temporary home, a room built of four walls in the middle of an artist's loft in Soho. The desperate need to find his way home is the brilliant suspense of *After Hours*, but in my case it was less a sense of urgency than a foregone conclusion. The artist's loft was teeming with people at all hours, and even within the confines of my four walls there was never any peace. I'd come to live in the loft only as a matter of convenient rent, but there had been obvious trade-offs on the first night, when the artist invited the acrobats in a traveling circus to stay with us for the week they were in town to perform.

The first few months back in New York, wandering the streets and watching my savings decline, I worried that there was nowhere left for me to run. That I was able to hang in for a couple of years, long enough to meet the woman who would become my wife— in the other room of our Chelsea apartment now, winnowing our possessions to the essentials for our move to the Hudson River valley, close enough to visit the city anytime we'd like—redefines "miraculous." I can't say how I hung in. That's how it is for the underclass in New York. One day at a time, like an alcoholic seeking redemption. And I almost refused the invitation to the garden party at the brownstone in Brooklyn where Vanessa and I met. I remember that week had ended on a particularly down note, with my being fired from a temporary position as a researcher in a bankruptcy law firm in Midtown. It was my plan to grab a Styrofoam container of General Tso's chicken from the corner place near my apartment on the south side of Williamsburg and gorge on the salty-sweet flesh and rice, but before the fluorescent lighting of the Chinese joint could pull me in, I bumped into the guy I'd interviewed with at *The Wall Street Journal* when I thought about continuing my career as a journalist, not fully appreciating how burned my bridges were. His name escaped me, and I accepted his invitation to the party as a courtesy, planning to duck out at first chance, but not before I could overhear someone mentioning his name, which no one ever did. Had I left fifteen minutes earlier, I would've missed meeting Vanessa, a recent graduate of the School of Visual Arts who was as unmoored as I was. My empty stomach was baying, but I kept as still as I could as I peppered Vanessa with questions about her mixed-media art, stretching the limits of my knowledge of her world before telling her how tremendous it was to meet her, hoping that we would see each other again. "How about now?" she said, and it wasn't long before I moved out of my Williamsburg apartment and into her rent-controlled one-bedroom in Greenwich Village.

It was a nerve-racking few months for me, as it had been a long time since I'd courted a love interest. Olivia a decade earlier, and before that, what? High school? But New York was an easy place to be in love, and we ate in cheap restaurants, drank watered-down well drinks in dive bars, scored discount tickets to Broadway shows, and spent a lot of time in Central Park. I was anxious about relating too much of my chaotic past and tried to dole out my story anecdotally, but the pieces shot randomly from a cannon began to seem . . . unbelievable. A nd one night, late, after we'd smoked more than a few joints in the roof garden of her apartment building, I tried to tell it chronologically, and while the end result was still a patchwork quilt, Vanessa peered at me across the darkness, a look of not just comprehension but understanding on her perfect face, and I never needed to say another word about it. Her own upbringing, in Ohio, had been as stable as growing up in Ohio sounds to outsiders. She had very few complaints. Her parents had owned a stationery store, where she'd work in the summers to make extra money. Her job at a bookstore near Grand Central Station was as much about the stationery they sold as it was about the employee discount on books.

Vanessa thought I was kidding when I told her that I'd published a novel. There was an awkward moment where, when I said I'd *written* a novel, she thought I'd come to New York to find an agent and a publisher. But I assured her that I'd moved to the city with no such ambition, or any ambition really. To prove to myself that I didn't care what I did for money, I took the test at a temp agency, dumbed down my past experience, and happily went wherever they sent me. Working nights in the print shop of a well-known cancer hospital in Midtown. Writing catalog copy for a tool company in Brooklyn. Mostly proofreading legal briefs at law firms all over Manhattan and sometimes in New Jersey. In each place I was just an anonymous face, a passing curiosity.

The temp agency sent me to the offices of a free weekly alternative newspaper, and by chance one of the editors had just read my novel and recognized me from my author photo. He offered me a job as a book reviewer. That gig was even easier than being a temp, and the salary and benefits were welcome, but I grew to hate the assigned books on sight, and right when I was contemplating quitting, the editor who had hired me called me into his office with a hangdog expression and announced that the Arts section was being shuttered in favor of paid advertising and would I accept a buyout? I pretended to be as bummed about the change as he was, deposited their check, and celebrated my good fortune at a string of bars on my way home.

Vanessa ordered a copy of my novel, and it was a bit of a thrill to see it in her bag. She prodded me about what was true and what was fiction, and I just shrugged. "After a while you can't really tell anymore," I said. She encouraged me to write another book, but what I couldn't say was that I didn't have the key weapon all writers need in their arsenal: the ability to see all sides of everything at once. That's not just the ability to hold two opposing ideas in your mind. It's something else entirely. My former training as a newspaper columnist had encouraged me to choose a point of view and run with it.

Jimmy Stewart's apartment complex in Hitchcock's *Rear Window* was meant to be Greenwich Village. On one of my wanderings I found myself traipsing along Christopher Street near the building that was the model for the movie apartments. A film crew was set up in front of a couple of Federal-style brownstones, and I could hear the talking head saying something about how Hitchcock had had the courtyard the buildings shared photographed in all manner of weather and light in order to re-create it back in Hollywood. "Jimmy Stewart would've never made it up these stairs," the talking head laughed as the camera panned to one of the building entrances.

The most satisfying and least aggravating Hitchcock films are the ones that have the feel of a stage play—*Rear Window*, *Rope*, and *Dial M for Murder*, the latter two of which were actually based on stage plays. What Hitchcock gets right, always, is a character's obsessive nature. In *Rope* and *Dial M*, the murderers have considered every detail and are consequently quick on their feet when variables challenge their version of events. *Rope* features the added stress of the murder dredging up a bitter fracture between the two murderers, which their onetime teacher (Jimmy Stewart again!) senses, leading him to deduce what has really happened. The Jimmy Stewart in *Rear Window* similarly pieces together a murder, though the exercise is not as existential as it is in *Rope*.

Phoenix features in the opening sequence of *Psycho*. After the credits dissolve, you can see Camelback Mountain in the distance as the camera shows the skyline. A nifty camera pan brings into focus the original downtown, much of which still exists: the Hotel San Carlos; the Adams Hotel; the Jefferson Hotel, where Janet Leigh and her boyfriend are holed up. The building with the giant antenna remains, though the antenna does not. A different antenna exists in the same general area and is often confused for the one in *Psycho*.

It seems like utter nonsense that *Psycho* is not named as Hitchcock's best film, over the likes of *Vertigo*. Perhaps the inherent snobbery of the Magnolias against horror films is to blame. But there's little doubt that the DNA of *Psycho* is in every subsequent horror movie, especially slasher flicks. The shot-for-shot remake of the film by Gus Van Sant, though a terrible failure, was terrifically successful at pointing up just how revolutionary Hitchcock's version was in its time. Cinemagoers in 1960 were rightly shocked, and possibly understood that the stifling culture they lived in was being criticized in the bargain. By the time the Van Sant version arrived almost four decades later, the audience was neither shocked, nor sympathetic to the culture being critiqued. Instead the film is more revealing as a meta exercise in recycled content. Everything comes from something, but the remade *Psycho* proves that the pivot away from the original source material is key to a successful homage.

Hitchcock forbade cinemas from allowing late seating at *Psycho* showings, which you can appreciate if you've ever suffered through shadowy figures filtering in long after a movie has started. It's unreal that in the old days of cinema, patrons were allowed to join a movie in progress, allowed to watch until the end and then stay for whatever they might've missed from the beginning. But Hitchcock was insistent that the beginning, middle, and end were paramount to the full thrill of *Psycho*, and he undertook a campaign to convince theater owners, who largely abided by the novelty.

Ever hear this little chestnut: "Who are you to judge?" You know whose favorite refrain that is? Selfish people's. It's the ultimate cover story.

But there are some easy calls. You don't have to be pure of heart to point out that the drowning of untended children in swimming pools every year is the result of bad parenting. Or that drunk driving is a careless, selfish act. Same for animal cruelty. You can probably judge O.J. Simpson's guilt or innocence pretty easily. There's a low-level current of everyday selfishness that has become so commonplace that while we might get angry at the driver who cuts us off in traffic, we've been told so many times not to cast the first stone that we can't admit the obvious to ourselves: that driver is a selfish person and, by extension, a terrible citizen. What's good for them is good for them. Who cares about *you*? Perhaps it's nostalgic to think there was once a time when people weren't so blatantly selfish, when we might go out of our way to disguise our worse impulses. We're forever telling children that it's okay to make mistakes, which it is, but when mistakes are habitual, they cease being mistakes and become conduct. A lot of violence has been done in the service of religion, but the saying "Let he who is without sin cast the first stone," derived from the Bible verse, has done as much or more damage as any other biblical passage, as it lets us all off the hook. We're no longer held accountable, except by the laws of man. (And, of course, God, if you like.)

You're thinking it, so I'll say it: a further problem, unpopular to even think, forget about uttering aloud, is that not all people are created equal. That might sound like a Magnolian thing to say, but it's just a factual statement and not an emotional one based on race, religion, money, or social status, so it's not an excuse for discrimination. The root cause of this inequality depends on where you land on the nature-versus-nurture argument.

Plus, all those commonsense product warnings and disclaimers belie the unspoken truth. "Once used rectally, the thermometer should not be used orally." Or: "Never iron clothes while being worn." You might think that's just lawyers being lawyers, but if a base doesn't need covering, the players on the field will hold their positions.

There are some disadvantages in life so extreme that it's not fair to judge that person against someone who hasn't suffered similarly, but what about the person who has not only overcome those disadvantages, but has been so assiduous with the handling of his or her own life that he or she has excelled? Exception to the rule, or a poor reflection on the person who didn't excel? Can we have an opinion about that?

Even if we admit that people have complex inner lives, and that their own personal web of experiences and emotions influences their decision-making, does that ever allow people to behave selfishly and not for the greater good? Did the person with the complicated life story who repeatedly [insert selfish act here] just make a mistake? Or is it okay to call out his or her behavior?

O. J. Simpson?

Roman Polanski?

Frank Lloyd Wright?

Charlie Keating?

Easier if we just fit them for a black hat and move on with our lives.

In truth, we spend a lot of energy judging one another, subconsciously but also consciously. But in both cases silently, either out of fear that a society that openly judges itself will live under a depressive cloud of paranoia, or out of a sense of superiority. And so we make little judgments only to ourselves, casting stones left and right, all the time, but claiming the opposite in polite conversation, insinuating that we all of us live in glass houses.

Related: turning the other cheek. For the same reasons re lack of accountability. Don't get me started.

Before Olivia caught her flight back to London, she mentioned that her old friend Shelleyan was living the high life in New York. Olivia called Shelleyan "our mutual friend," but Shelleyan was exclusively Olivia's friend from our days at Glendale Community College back in Phoenix. I've never settled with myself whether Olivia was oblivious to Shelleyan's taunts directed toward yours truly, or if she just looked the other way. At the time I was so desperate for Olivia's affections that either was acceptable to me, but sitting across the table from her in the well-lit and decidedly unromantic restaurant Olivia had chosen as the site of our reunion, the former seemed impossible and the latter seemed like a benign cruelty.

I actually knew Shelleyan was living in New York, as I'd bumped into her on my first go-around. I had avoided her then and was surprised when Olivia brought her up again. I could sense in Olivia's casual tone that she was fishing to see if I was somehow in touch with Shelleyan, and I imagined, perhaps spitefully, that Olivia had tried to reach out to Shelleyan but to no avail. That Shelleyan was quote-unquote living the high life in New York was a burning curiosity, but the old buried bitterness sprang from deep within me and I couldn't bring myself even to raise an eyebrow, or to hear Olivia's speculations on what it all meant.

Olivia made her life in London sound terrific, and who knows, perhaps it was. I remembered a time early on in our relationship when she confessed to me that the worst thing that could happen to her was that she'd end up back in London, living close enough to all her relatives to see them at holidays and birthday celebrations, working a job she marginally cared about to meet her monthly obligations, punctuated by the occasional nights out with friends. She'd flung herself halfway across the globe in an effort to exorcise those demons. A problem with her visa flung her back, but she swore she'd return to Arizona once it was all straightened out. But she didn't. Now I charitably hoped that she'd forgotten about those early ambitions of flight. But who ever does? Shelleyan had gotten out, and the case could even be made that I had too, though it was my second attempt, and at that point things were going about as well as my first effort. Olivia showed me one last kindness by not asking me too much about my new life in New York. The sheer wonder and excitement of the limitless possibilities someone feels when they move to a new place is absent upon a second try at the same move, and I wouldn't have had it in me to invent a narrative plausible enough to be believed.

What's remarkable about past cinemagoers wandering into a film whenever, and watching until the story was complete, is their willingness to piece together what was being told, rather than demanding the beginning come before the middle, or the middle before the ending. Some must've stumbled upon a film's conclusion and wondered what it was all about until the opening credits appeared. The most remarkable part, though, is how that sort of in-medias-res approach is truer to life than the artifice of beginning, middle, and end, if only because, absent death, how can any of us know when we're being presented with the beginning or the middle or the end of something? We mark our birthdays, sure, and we're told that the X years are for this, and we can expect these things in the Y years, but that's just another artifice. If we're lucky enough to reach old age, we can look through the lens of retrospect and understand certain things that happened, and why, though perhaps too late to learn anything from the retrospection. But a remnant of Hitchcock's legacy has to be shaping our narrative expectations, which I'd argue has created a sense of incompleteness in our lives as we intuitively clamor to know where we are inside our own stories. You could say we're all in the middle, all the time, but that's of no use as we try to make sense of the world around us.

Crime stories offer us the narrative structure we've been conditioned to favor. There's a comfort in learning the events leading up to a crime and then following the investigation that reveals, hopefully with satisfying twists and turns, who committed the crime and why, as well as the guilty party's requisite punishment. Unsolved mysteries like, say, the Kennedy assassination, challenge and delay the dopamine rush we experience with the arc of crime stories, so we invent conspiracy theories as the potential endings we're being denied. Less satisfying, sure, but still made to conform to our expectations.

A funny crime story with a predictable outcome in Arizona involved state legislators who got caught up in a sting operation called AzScam, named after the FBI sting Abscam a decade or so before. The plot of AzScam starred a thrice-convicted felon and purported midlevel mafioso, a handful of lobbyists, and about a tenth of the Arizona legislature. The felon posed as a lobbyist wanting to legalize gambling in the state and began meeting with and bribing legislators over the issue, all while a hidden camera was rolling. As painful as it was, Arizonans saw how easily their elected representatives could be bought, and the sting exposed the lawmakers as small, petty, and ultimately selfish people interested in improving their own lot at the expense of their position. Of course, the jig was up, and of course the nightly news had a wealth of footage to show for weeks and months leading up to the trials. Clever extrapolators opined in the national news that AzScam would shake what little faith cynical voters had in their electoral process, which would threaten to dramatically reduce the voting rolls when it might matter most. But Arizonans had been made electorally cynical by the national elections of years past, mostly when the Big Three news networks would project winners before most Arizonans could leave work to vote. Somewhere along the line that was all smoothed out, but it was then forgotten with the 2004 election, when, for the first time, modern voters were confronted with the truth that the definition of a winning candidate was not the one with the most votes, but instead the one who used a map of the United States as a game board, plotting out the states that mattered most in the quest to win the electoral college. In the aftermath of the 2004 election, a powerful essay called "Why It's Okay Not to Vote ," written anonymously, began to circulate on the burgeoning World Wide Web, though its popularity was sustained mostly by photocopying.

My first week back in New York, I happened to be passing the Whitney Museum of American Art on one of their free admission days. It was early and there weren't too many takers yet, so I sauntered into the imposing building and wandered into a room celebrating photocopier art by artists who had formed a collective called the International Society of Copier Artists. You think you have a handle on just about everything, and then you see something that you wouldn't have dreamed existed, and it takes you aback. Someone thought to use the enlarge and reduce buttons on a photocopier, as well as the dark and light functions, to create art. A lot of someones. Wild stuff, too! Cut-and-paste seemed to be another tool in the photocopier artist's arsenal too , along with a whole host of ingenious ways to manipulate images. An image's replication seemed to be at the heart of a lot of the pieces, the idea that a copy of a copy of a copy of a copy could suddenly become an original of its own.

I took in the rest of the museum that day, but my mind kept wandering back to the photocopy art, the brilliance of it. And the democratic nature of being a photocopy artist. While not everyone could afford a photocopier of their own back when they first appeared, anyone could gain access to one. No expensive studios to rent, or oils and canvases and all other manner of art supplies to buy. Any demographic was welcome to step up and give it a try. No cumbersome patronage required. I imagined several photocopier artists staying late in the offices where they slaved to pay their bills by day, the office turning into an idea factory at night, the floor strewn with drafts in search of a finished artistic expression.

Why do you think it is that it's okay to commission a painting, or for filmmakers to fund their own movies, or for bands to underwrite the production of their albums, but that any self-published book is immediately under suspicion as being complete garbage ? The paradox feels like a Magnolia-backed one, though it's more likely one they simply condone. If you happen to be at a party where the subject comes up, mention that Dickens self-published *A Christmas Carol* and that all those Peter Rabbit books were self-published too. Muse aloud about when exactly cultural gatekeepers were suddenly deemed so essential.

Something about me that people, especially my wife, find astounding is that I've known very little of death in my own life. If you don't count my parents, that is, who died in a house explosion when I was seven. I guess you could argue that their deaths were enough trauma for a lifetime, and that the carousel my life became after ensured I would only be passing through people's lives, not staying for the final curtain. Once, when I was in high school, I caught a whiff of the perfume of a girl who waltzed pass me, something like burned cinnamon, and for the rest of the day I thought of the mother I never got to really know, sure that she'd worn a similar scent. But I was only trying to convince myself it was real. Earlier that week our English teacher had asked us to write a personal essay involving something to do with family, and while I thought I'd written a cohesive piece about my foster family, the Chandlers, my prick English teacher, this balding douchebag who had once been some kind of judge, asked me about my birth parents. That's the kind of place my high school was, an all-boys prep school that Mr. Chandler had gotten me into, since it was his alma mater and he was what you would call a legacy. I stammered out a half answer about how I never really knew my birth parents, before slinking away, and I tortured myself for days after about why I couldn't remember one thing about them. My only memory was of a little girl who'd lived next door. Maybe *she* was the one who'd smelled of burned cinnamon.

Once, when I was ten—this was when I was in Santa Fe with the McCallahans, my first official foster family after my grandparents briefly took me in—I remember waking one day near Christmas to find all the adults in a trance, shoulders stooped in sadness. I thought maybe the president had been shot, based on my learning about the Kennedy assassination earlier that year, but it was explained to me that John Lennon, one of the Beatles, had been murdered in New York City. I hardly knew who the Beatles were, but the effect of John Lennon's death on seemingly everyone everywhere in Santa Fe and beyond made an impression on me. I felt the pain the death was causing people, the anguish in their hearts. And I silently tracked the days and weeks and months before it appeared to lift, if not forever. When I hear about someone dying, I think of the cycle of denial and acceptance that I witnessed firsthand so long ago and understand that, for the loved ones of that someone, the early stages of the cycle are just beginning.

Why, if we can remember little else about someone, do we remember how he or she died? The last moment of a life is mostly irrelevant when applied against how that life was lived. Admit it: when you're watching an actor in a movie who you know has died in a peculiar way, you're thinking about that strange death. You're looking at the actor on the screen and thinking, *You have no idea how you'll die, or when, but I know.* Do we prefer to keep a catalog of endings as possibilities for our own final moments? Our obsession with the beginning, middle, and end lends unearned weight to endings, which are mostly elusive, except for death.

Every year you pass the anniversary of your death without even realizing it.

Our fascination with bizarre and even gruesome deaths is unfortunate, reducing the victim's life to the final act. You're thinking of one as you read this, and even if you can appreciate other facts about the person's life, or admit intellectually to his or her contributions to society, the paramount fact in your mind is the way that person died.

Know the painting on the cover of the Duran Duran album *Rio* by Patrick Nagel? Up to that point, paintings by Nagel were primarily found in *Playboy*. And before that, like Andy Warhol, he was an illustrator with corporate clients like Budweiser. He also designed Whitney Houston's mom's record album, among some others. Nagel also died young, of a heart attack, not yet forty , after participating in a celebrity aerobathon in Santa Monica, which, ironically, was to raise money for the American Heart Association. The aerobathon lasted fifteen minutes. Nagel made it as far as his car in the parking lot.

A lot of us in Arizona spent what little money we had on posters of Nagel prints at Spencer Gifts. Every mall had a Spencer's, and you could flip through the posters in the back, near the sex toys and other adult-themed merchandise. I once went to a house party that had a signed original Nagel hanging on the wall. Rumor was they were scarce, and I spent most of the party—a high school rager during my public school days at Leone Cooper High, before I transferred to private school—sipping watered-down beer from a red plastic cup and glancing at the original Nagel. Nagel painted beautiful women for *Playboy*; Thomas Kinkade painted cottages that glowed for Christians.

Another '80s icon, the author of the novel *The Hitchhiker's Guide to the Galaxy*, Douglas Adams, also died at forty-nine, and also after working out in California. Copies of the novel were as prevalent as Nagel posters. The zany adventures of Arthur Dent fit snugly into the Dungeons and Dragons culture that had gripped a lot of American youth. Whether or not you were in the know depended on your knowing the answer to the Ultimate Question. (Spoiler alert: it's 42 .)

Whose death sucked more: James Dean's or Jayne Mansfield's? Or Orville Redenbacher's, whose involved drowning in a Jacuzzi?

Those "Which Pop Culture Character Are You?" quizzes are about as accurate as fortune cookies, but absent any religious or political persuasion, both things you generally inherit from your parents, I can easily trace my personality through its pop culture influences. I realized it only recently, when Vanessa was out with her friends for going-away-but-not-really-leaving drinks at her favorite dive bar on the Lower East Side, and I happened across an old episode of the television show *M*A*S*H*. A long-buried memory surfaced, from my stay with the Alexander-Degners in Rapid City, about how much my foster parents loved the show. It always seemed to be on the console in their den, the old TV that weirdly also housed a record player under a wooden flap on top. The show was of no particular interest to me, but catching it again all these years later, I immediately recognized how much my personality aped that of chief surgeon Benjamin Franklin "Hawkeye" Pierce. The similarities were disturbing: the cynical but humorous deflection, the indignation that gives way to rage when finally pushed.

Then I thought: *Maybe I was born with a cynical, indignant personality, and so are a lot of other people, and Hawkeye Pierce is just a stereotype of people like me.*

But what children are born cynical and indignant? The *M*A*S*H* influence feels true, disturbing as it is, since it opens up the real possibility that our throwaway culture is actually having a formative effect on us. Did a child grow up to be a bit of an asswipe because he or she loved Calvin and Hobbes? Or did all those Garfield cartoon strips convince kids that it was okay to be a bully? Do Eminem's fans hear his multi-Grammy-winning music as satire and fantasy created by his alter ego, Slim Shady, or do they just hear anthem?

Was John Lennon murdered because of *The Catcher in the Rye*?

Is art responsible for its influence?

Is there a danger in making everything so egocentric?

Or is there no escaping egocentrism? And if so, does that prove second chances are a frivolous nicety more about the forgiver than the forgiven? How hard is it really not to say the thing you're not supposed to say, not to behave the way you're not supposed to? Do those who transgress reveal their true personality, letting the mask slip, or will they genuinely get it right the second time around? Can a life truly be corrected?

Is it okay to muddle through the long middle of our lives without considering these questions and others?

Is our upcoming move to the Hudson River valley more of the middle, or will it precipitate the end of our story together, or the actual end of one or both of us? As the apartment fills with boxes, the question remains unresolved. Our end could be in an as-yet-undetermined place, one familiar or unfamiliar to us, and our relationship to each other could be as strong or stronger than it is today, or it might be like those colored refractions you find in a kaleidoscope. Related, but without a clear bond. Will any of us be afforded the opportunity to ponder the end? Do we want that?

At least we can take pleasure in knowing our beginning. Not our birth, thankfully, or even the first however many number of years, when we practice living before generating our first memory. And not even our first memory. Our true beginning is that moment everyone can trace back to to mark the Before and After in their lives. For me, it was a moment in my teens, late in my high school life, when you could feel the pressure to become something not exactly bearing down, but beating its wings off in the distance. That time was infused with possibilities, and whether true or not, the pool of what you could do was a lot larger and deeper than anything you couldn't. But decisions would have to be made, which would or wouldn't come to bear on the outcome of how your life would turn out, and circumstances would inevitably prevail, which again might or might not dictate how things went. A neighbor had borrowed her parents' car, and the two of us plowed through the desert heat from Phoenix to Los Angeles to visit a friend of hers. I hadn't been back to California since I lived on Sterne Street in San Diego, and I'd forgotten more about Southern California than I remembered. We hit traffic as we entered the city and inched slowly toward her friend's house. Night began to fall. We rolled down the windows as we neared our destination, the lush greenery surrounding us like a hug as we breathed in the cool marine layer, a mist hovering in the air. You couldn't see the ocean, but you sensed its nearness. Our favorite song came over the radio just as a light up ahead cycled from yellow to red, and we slowed, stopped, and sat silently, listening, breathing, in no hurry for the light to change.